LIGHTBORNE

A NOVEL

HESSE PHILLIPS

PEGASUS BOOKS
NEW YORK LONDON

LIGHTBORNE

Pegasus Books, Ltd.
148 West 37th Street, 13th Floor
New York, NY 10018

First Pegasus Books cloth edition October 2024

ISBN: 978-1-63936-738-2

10 9 8 7 6 5 4 3 2 1

Printed in the United States of America
Distributed by Simon & Schuster
www.pegasusbooks.com

In memory of David G. Pierce and Paul D. Nelsen

PROLOGUE

6 JUNE 1588

Four years, eleven months, twenty-four days

❦

Marloe admir'd, whose honey-flowing vaine,
No English writer can as yet attaine.
Whose name in Fames immortall treasurie,
Truth shall record to endless memorie,
Marlo, late mortall, now fram'd all divine,
What soule more happy, than that soule of thine?

HENRY PETOWE, *THE SECOND PART OF HERO & LEANDER,*
CONTEYNING THEIR FURTHER FORTUNES, 1598

I

'KIT, ARE YOU ALIVE?'
The face of Tamburlaine appears through the upstage
curtains like a grotesque on a church door, oil-black rings of
kohl smudged around his eyes, revealing something of the
actor, Ned Alleyn, underneath.

'They are calling for the author – listen!'

Kit hears nothing but a dull, water-in-the-ears roar that
may be a thousand voices calling out or the thundering of
his own heart. His fingers make a clumsy gesture at the air
around his person, as if to say he has neither will nor strength
to step out of it.

'What, afraid, ye silly giant?' An arm wrapped in a silken
sleeve reaches through and cuffs him on the shoulder, pressing
him forward. 'Go now, go, and take your poison. Now, *now*!'

The curtains part, cutting a gash of daylight through the
backstage gloom. Beyond, the Rose Playhouse appears, a vortex
of timber and plaster and densely packed humanity that reels
upwards, three storeys, to a dilated eye of cloud-streaked sky.
Clad in Mongol furs and turbans, the players dodge aside for
Kit's entrance as if he were ten feet tall and equally wide. With
a grand flourish, Ned Alleyn draws his scimitar and waves Kit
downstage with the point, like the politest of threats.

Kit ventures a step into the light and sets off a surge of
cheers, then chants, one word hammered again and again:

Blood! Blood! Blood! Blood! But it cannot be. This is no execution, though Kit stands like a man at the gallows, hands behind his back, balls tucked tight with fear. As his eyes adjust so do his ears, and at last the word becomes clear:

'More! More! More! More!'

This is what 'tis like to be adored, he supposes, realizing in a panic that he knows not how to perform 'adored'. No one has yet written odes to his honey-flowing vaine, nor called him 'the Muses' darling', a distinction that shall come to him before the night is out. He is twenty-four years old, the eldest of four children, not counting the dead, and until this moment he has stepped but rarely into the light. Obscurity was safe, but that familiar house has, in one afternoon's course, burnt down around him. Here he stands in its ashes, exposed and soft and awkwardly tall. He has wanted this, has he not? He has pictured this. It means he has achieved worthiness. It means his old self is gone.

At last, he dips into an inelegant bow, rising with a grin. Adoration, in fact, feels slightly embarrassing, as if he had tripped on a stone and the whole city swarmed to steady him on his feet.

'Kit!' Hands clamber at his ankles. Down in the pit are several faces he recognizes, all poets like himself, some friends, others acquaintances at best: Thomas Kyd, Tom Nashe, Michael Drayton, Will Shakespeare. But no sign of Tom Watson.

Kit's grin falters. He scans the crowd for Tom's lean figure, his sly smile. He must be here, he must, waiting to clip Kit in his arms and tell him how proud he has made him today.

At Kit's feet, Thomas Kyd shouts, 'Jump!' as if for the fourth or fifth time. 'Jump down, we'll carry you out!'

Kit steps down into their waiting arms, on legs like stilts. The poets catch him at the thighs and backside and shuttle him across the pit like a beetle on its back. He twists his head left and right, tries to ask, 'Where's Tom Watson?' but no one hears him, they only deliver him to yet another frenzied hand-shake, another breathless laud: 'Seneca reborn – ay, England's very own Seneca! Shall we have more *Tamburlaine*?'

'I—well, if so—'

'What is your name?' demands another. And then another, and another.

Kit sputters, having temporarily forgotten it. By the time it comes to him, he is on the move again, and resorts to shouting his own name as if he were only the top half of a man in search of a rogue set of legs, as giddy as a boy riding on his father's shoulders. 'Marley! Marley!'

No – he is not even 'Marlowe', not yet.

Without warning, a hand grasps Kit's wrist and tugs him forward with such force that he stumbles onto one knee. 'Tis not unlike Tom to arrive like so, in a whirlwind, and thus, as the hand pulls him upright, Kit expects to come face-to-face with an ecstatic grin, to be wrapped in a jubilant embrace. But the face that finally appears before him is not Tom's. Not at all.

The man peels a crooked smile back over his half-empty mouth, teeth on the left side and exposed gullet on the right. As always, he looks as if he has lately crawled out of the earth, a fine layer of ash settled over his entire person, a scent of pitch and sparked flint clinging to his shaggy, grizzled hair. Kit has not seen him in months. He had prayed never to see him again.

Kit takes his embrace like a knife to the chest. 'Did ye burn a candle for me?' the man says, his mouth at Kit's heart.

Onstage, Ned has begun the compulsory prayer for victory against Spain. All around, at his cue, the groundlings take off their caps, bow their heads. 'God bless her Majesty's reign!' they chorus.

The embrace slackens. Like most, the man stands no higher than Kit's shoulder, and yet some part of him, his scent or shadow, looms high above his head. 'You have been avoiding me, my boy,' the man says. 'I've sent messages.'

'God protect her Majesty's kingdom!' the crowd intones.

Kit looks not at the pale eyes, only the lopsided mouth, one cheek sunken to the bone. He shrugs lamely at the whole of their surroundings, murmuring, 'I have been busy.'

'Of course you have,' the man says. 'And you should enjoy this day. 'Tis yours. But Sunday evening, you and I set sail for Dunkirk.'

Kit fears to turn his back on the man, though every nerve in his body aches to run. 'I have told you,' he says, too quietly. 'I do not do that any more—'

'What's that?' The man gestures at the crowd, who are now chanting for death to the Duke of Medina, death to the Catholic Armada, death to the Spanish king.

'Do ye not hear that?' the man says. 'Do ye not hear how sorely our country needs us just now?' He pauses, head cocked, a wounded sneer upon his lips. 'Someone has hold of your leash, do they? Who is he? Tom Watson?'

A wave of fear rushes to Kit's fingertips. He watches a crooked smile spread on the man's lips, cruelly amused, as if to see a child stumble in its first steps.

'Old Tom has himself a fine house now, is that right?' the man goes on. 'Up in Norton Folgate? And a pretty wife, too. A life like that is a delicate thing for a fellow like him. Very delicate creatures, your kind. A whisper can unravel you.' The man stands on his toes, leaning close to Kit's ear. Kit half-expects him to bite it off.

'I hope you are careful, lad,' the man says. 'I hope you know well enough to keep those who might whisper happy. The Council rewards those who whisper, after all. Even one like Tom, with his illustrious friends, even he could be ruined. But *you*? "Ruin" is too light a word for what they'd do to you.' He turns his head just enough that Kit's eye looks directly into his, so close that the pupil appears stretched, like the eye of a goat.

HESSE PHILLIPS

'Bull's House in Deptford, Sunday morning,' the man says. 'Come quietly; come by river. Who knows? Perhaps you and I will save the kingdom a second time.'

His shadow slips past Kit, behind him, and is gone.

Kit places a large hand over his stomach, disbelieving at first that he is whole, that 'tis not the dropping of his guts to the ground that he feels. He sucks in a breath. He is alive yet.

A celebratory mob of players and poets soon fills the Dancing Bears tavern on Bankside, just up the street from the Rose. Women run half-clothed through the crowd, shrieking like vixens; men pursue them in barking packs. 'To the Spaniards who'll fuck our corpses!' Ned Alleyn toasts, to grim laughter. Just days ago, the Spanish Armada set sail from Portugal, carrying twice the firepower of England's fleet. Soon, their hulks will be sighted from the southern shores, bursting with some fifty thousand battle-mad men. Victory shall require a miracle from God.

Kit has yet to find Tom Watson, though a host of new admirers have found Kit. After all, he cannot hide; he towers half a head higher than the second-tallest man in the room. Currently he stands pinned between the bar and a pack made up of Will Shakespeare and some of his Shoreditch friends, the former ranting excitedly about King Henry VI, oblivious to Kit's spiralling panic. 'To have your hand in it would be a boon to us all,' Will shouts over the roar of voices. 'Provided, of course, we all survive the summer. The English parts I shall write, and you, I thought, could write the French parts. For you have been to France, no? You've fought in the war, no?'

'No.' Something heavy and putrid floats to the surface in Kit's stomach. 'Fought, no, not exactly—'

'But you *do* speak French.'

'Ay, ay.'

'As I'd thought!' The little fellow looks overheated, wide eyed and red faced, like a hunter who, after a long chase, is poised for the kill. 'Did you know my father is a glover?'

'No.'

'And yours a shoemaker! We shall make perfect collaborators, you see? Or rather, I shall be your pupil, for my verses range wild at times, like fingers over a maiden's thigh, but *you*, you know a good *foot* when you see one—'

'I'll be sick.' Kit hands his cup to Will, shoves past sans apology. The same chaos of faces that had choked the pit at the Rose now form a wall between Kit and escape. After struggling through the crowd, he finally tumbles through a side door and into a low-ceilinged passageway, where he doubles over and vomits into an ash barrel.

The door to the passage opens and closes. Kit feels Tom Watson's familiar presence even before he sees him: a poet richer in laurels than Kit could ever hope to be, ten years Kit's senior, nearly as tall and every bit as thin. They look well stood beside one another, Kit has been told, like two portraits meant to hang on the same wall. Tom still wears his big-toothed, vulpine grin as if he's only just stepped away from his own circle of praise, but after one full look at Kit the grin sinks at the corners.

'Oh, come now, not this again! Kit, ye cannot do all your drinking ere the night has even begun—'

'Tom,' Kit pants, 'Richard Baines was there.'

Tom stammers, lips pursed as if about to ask, featherheadedly, *Who?*

'Richard Baines, Tom, *Richard Baines!*'

'Where?'

'At the Rose – in the pit—'

'Breathe, Kit.'

'He knows about *us*, Tom! I know not how, but he knows!'

At last, understanding dawns in Tom's gaze, followed by

dread. He starts to speak, but behind him the door bursts open, disgorging Kyd, Will, Drayton, Nashe, all in merry pursuit of 'Seneca reborn'. Deaf to Kit's protests, they drag him back into the breath-heated air of the Dancing Bears, and he can do naught but watch as the crowd sucks Tom away like a swell.

'What, long-faced?' the poets cry. 'We'll not allow it! Give us drink, here! Give us whisky! Give us a wench!' Kit accepts the whisky, declines the wench, and helplessly passes from one man to another like a bridal cup, though 'tis his own cup filled again and again along the way. Soon, a hush flutters over the room: all eyes turn to the stairs, where, one after another, the players climb up and offer toasts to Kit's health, declare their undying loyalty, and swear up and down that none had ever doubted him, which Kit roundly disbelieves. Before today, he'd barely had a name. Even among the players, he was only Tom Watson's 'squire', Tom Watson's 'boy'. Sometimes, Tom Watson's 'dog'.

After the supporting players have had their say, comes the great epilogue: Ned Alleyn, still in traces of Tamburlaine paint, minces down the stairs in a yellow wig and a toga, false bosoms swaying against his hairy chest. He introduces himself as Melpomene, the muse of tragedy, and launches into a rambling, falsetto panegyric in Kit's honour, riddled with tiresome innuendoes:

'... And to the gallish inkpot, I say this:
Rude vessel, thou art too base a well for dipping
The noble quill that composèd Tamburlaine!
O, that I were such a vessel, darling Kit,
So you would dip in me!...'

Here the clown Rowley puts his arse in the air and blows through his trumpet, lest there be any confusion about what vessel is meant.

Kit finishes his drink and sets off in search of Tom, refusing all further pleasantries along the way. He finds him in the snug, pontificating about Sophocles to an audience of lesser poets and bored-looking whores: Tom Watson, the reigning patriarch of English poets, arms wide open to his legion of clambering children. Many a time Kit has watched Tom hold court at his house north of the river, torrents of jealousy pumping through his heart. *But he is mine. They know, and of this they whisper. But 'tis enough that they know: he is mine.*

Kit takes a firm hold of Tom's shoulder and turns him around mid-sentence, very nearly kissing him on the mouth, right there, *publicaverunt.*

'Take me home,' Kit says.

They walk east along Bankside. Across the river, St Paul's gloomy tower juts out of a pile of gabled houses like a lone pillar out of rubble, its top lightning-struck decades ago, and to this day spireless. Half a mile ahead, a jagged spine of onion domes, parapets and chimney pots marches across the over-burdened neck of London Bridge, emitting trails of smoke that bow as one with the wind.

'They'll all bethink you terribly ungrateful,' Tom says.

'I care not what they think.' Kit rubs the cold tip of his nose. Even at a tipsy stumble he storms ahead faster than Tom can comfortably follow, weighted down as he is with his prized French rapier. With the curfew in place, Bankside is unusually quiet, and the clanking of Tom's scabbard resounds up and down the brick embankment as he jogs to keep up.

'You should,' Tom scolds. 'I'faith, you *must*. Men like us, we live by shows. Why, in a finer suit and with a courtlier air – a French bow, perhaps – you could do far better for yourself.'

'It matters not, Tom, none of it matters!'

'You have triumphed today! *How* can you be angry?'

Kit answers him not. Too frequently are such questions asked of him: *Why are you angry? Why are you sad? Why do you laugh? Why do you cry?* Other men are never so often called upon to explain their moods, a fact of which Kit has grown painfully aware with the onset of manhood. Howsoever he feels, it is either wrong or too much.

'Stop, stop.' Tom loops his arm through Kit's, dragging him to a halt, and for a moment they stand so close that Kit hangs his head for shame.

Tom embraces him, a gesture not without its dangers. Kit scans the empty street, the embankment walls above. For all these months he's thought himself safe, he never knew how relentlessly an unseen watcher has fondled him with his eyes.

'I cannot stay with you, Tom.'

'Hush.'

'I must go back to him. What else can I do?'

'I'll never let you do that.'

'Tom, he'll ruin you. One word from him to the Council, *one word—*'

'That man is a fly to me.' Tom steps back, holds Kit at arm's length. 'I know how to be rid of Baines.'

'How? Will you murder him?'

Tom takes this as a joke. 'If it should come to that...'

Kit turns a shoulder on him, walking on.

Tom follows. 'You are not a boy any more, Kit – 'tis high time you stopped seeing Richard Baines through a boy's eyes.'

Kit had just turned eighteen when he'd first met Baines – not quite a boy, but a man neither. A shoemaker's son from Canterbury in his second year at Cambridge; a scholarship boy, living on stale bread and beer. Baines was one of Sir Francis Walsingham's spies just returned from a long imprisonment in France, trolling the university's halls in search of a swift-footed lackey with a legible hand and a malleable mind. By the time Kit met Tom, which was two years later, in Paris, Kit had grown so accustomed to standing three feet behind

Baines that when he closed his eyes he could see the shape of him still, as if he'd stared at the sun.

'He's nothing, is he?' Tom goes on. 'Just another meddling spy scraping at the dirt. This country is teeming with villains willing to do the same filthy work for less than half his wage, and without the risks that ride upon his back.'

'The Spymaster cares nothing for those risks. Hell, there are some up at Seething Lane who credit him with saving the Queen's life!'

'Ay, none more than himself! Trust me, the Spymaster is but one voice in the Privy Council. And ever since the Archbishop of Canterbury joined, things are changing. Slowly, but they are changing. The days when a spy could disport himself however he pleased, with impunity, are coming to an end. One like Baines – his days are numbered as it is.' Tom falls silent, gnawing on his tongue. Then whispers, 'The rumours about yourself and him—'

'They are not true!' Kit says, too loud.

'Well, that is well.' Tom looks neither relieved nor credulous. Kit may deny the rumours a thousand times; no one will ever believe him. Certainly not Tom.

'But there were others before you,' Tom goes on. 'And there have been others since, though never for long. 'Tis a mainstay of gossip: "Baines and his boys". Some of them were young. Much younger than you were, at least when I met ye.'

Kit shivers, thinking of a particular room, a particular bed, as repeated across time; an endless succession of bodies in the same place where his own had lain. And yet he says, 'Does it matter? If it mattered to anyone, would it not be more than mere gossip?'

'Well,' Tom says, 'when gossip becomes troublesome...' He shrugs again meaningfully, showing a nervous grin.

Kit sighs. 'What would you have me do?'

'Tell the Council a beastly thing about Baines. Tell them a thing they are already likely to believe.'

'No!'

'Fear not,' Tom says, as if to soothe an overly imaginative child. 'Tomorrow I will take you to Seething Lane, to see Thomas Walsingham. He'll speak with his uncle for you.'

'That man makes my hair stand on end,' Kit says. Thomas Walsingham had been Tom's lover when Kit first met him: nephew to the Spymaster, Sir Francis Walsingham, and widely expected to take his uncle's place one day.

Tom laughs. 'Only because you do not know him. But I think he still loves me, the poor wretch! He'll believe you, for my sake.' He leans closer, reassuring. 'Of course, the matter will be kept quiet. Belike the Spymaster shall send Baines off to serve in some hellhole abroad, or at the furthest end of the kingdom. But the devil would be out of your life, forever.' He pauses. 'You do desire that, no?'

'I do,' Kit says, though it feels like stepping into blackness with his hands outstretched.

'And *if* – Tom steps forward, grasps Kit's hand – '*if*, Kit, Baines means what he says… You must speak with the Council before he does. It cannot come from me; it must come from you. You understand that? You understand why we must go tomorrow?'

Tom's grip is tight, his fingers threaded through Kit's. 'I do, Tom. I do.'

Tom lets out a breath. They walk on for a time in silence, heads bowed, hands clasped. But as the seconds pass and the light over London Bridge's southern gatehouse grows stronger, an invisible knife sticks between Kit's shoulders, sharper with every step, and does not let up till they let go.

Soon, the embankment sweeps upwards to meet the torch-studded hulk of Great Stone Gate, its crenellated ramparts busy with soldiers, as sheer and stern as a promontory on the threshold of the sea. From atop the towers and hanging over the portcullis, thirty human skulls roost in varying stages of preservation, slack-jawed like a row of mute choristers. One of the skulls had belonged to a man who would, perhaps, still be alive had it not been for Kit and Baines, for better or for worse. His skull takes pride of place on the gate, beetling over the archway on a long, horizontal stave, so that to enter or exit London is to pass beneath its eyeless stare. The jawbone swings wide, a scream frozen in time.

On the causeway, Tom pulls Kit behind a parapet, out of the guards' sight. 'I would kill Baines for you, if you were to ask it of me. 'Tis no less than he deserves.'

Kit shakes his head. Death is senseless, pointless. Many would say that the man whose skull now hangs above the arch had deserved to die. But his death was beyond death, beyond senselessness; Kit saw it with his own eyes. It was obliteration.

In any case, vengeance is of no use to the powerless. Kit's only aim is to survive.

Tom nods at Kit's silence, steps back. 'Exile it shall be, then.' He touches the tip of his tongue to the backs of his teeth, his habit when working over some delightful treachery. 'Where shall we send him? France? The Low Countries?'

'The Low Countries,' Kit blurts. Baines had always hated it there. It would be as good as sending him to hell.

'The Low Countries!' Tom laughs. 'You have a tint of spite in you.'

Kit shares not in his mirth.

Tom cuffs his arm gently, in that estranged manner he adopts whenever they are watched, or he presumes them to be watched. 'Come now, why so serious? What did he do to ye, to make ye so serious?'

Kit thinks, immediately, of Paris: candlelight on his desk in the underground cell. A man's scream, followed by a squelch, a crunch. Baines's face leaning into the light as he dropped an object onto Kit's desk which oozed darkly onto the blank papers: a finger, the nailbed black with filth.

'Put *that* up your arse,' Baines had quipped, and then returned to his work.

'Kit.' Tom touches his arm; the touch stings. His amber eyes look on Kit's startlement with kindness, but also urgency. 'Tell me what he did to you,' he says. 'Tell me as you will tell it to the Council.'

⋄⟨⋇⟩⋄

On a December night three years ago, in the cellar of a large house on the north side of Paris, Kit and Baines had climbed through a trapdoor, held open above their heads by a thin man with nervous eyes. Just before shutting the door, the thin man had handed Baines a lantern, in whose light Kit could see their own breaths. Underfoot, a creaking ladder plunged deep into the hollow-sounding earth.

'This is where God's work is done,' Baines had said, descending.

At the bottom, they'd found the first and largest of many pickaxe-scarred chambers. Candles flickered in niches in the chalk walls. Haggard, pallid faces greeted them, boys and men, their hands cupped around bowls of gruel. A boy was singing softly, *Glory to Her righteous name*, and it echoed like plainsong from the choir of Bell Harry.

They were soldiers, but they bore no weapons; they were at war, but the war had, in the fifteen years since its beginning, become a bloated, misshapen thing, defined not by borders but by faith. By Papal decree, certain salvation awaited any Catholic who could put Queen Elizabeth's papist cousin, Mary, Queen of Scots, on the English throne, a promise that no Catholic in England or without could take lightly. Some years earlier, Baines had infiltrated the infamous English seminary at Rheims, where exiled Catholics trained for holy war against their own homeland, but he had bungled the mission terribly: allowed himself to be caught, and lost half his teeth to the papists' torturers ere they let him go. This mission to Paris was a chance for Baines to redeem himself, for one of the seminary's men had been captured.

A superior led Kit and Baines to their charge, explaining on the way: the prisoner was known as 'Number 4', a follower of the fanatical Jesuit order – 'Cornelys' he called himself, though he was a Staffordshire man by birth – one in a vast web of couriers secreting messages from the imprisoned Queen of Scots to her followers abroad. Many believed 'Number 4' knew the name of Mary's contact in London, but all efforts to prise it out of him had thus far come to naught.

'Ha,' Baines said, 'give me an hour!'

They descended yet another ladder into a reeking pit, ten feet deep, equally as wide. The prisoner was chained to the wall by the wrists and eerily waifish in appearance, having only a few patchy wisps of beard, the berry-coloured lips of a boy, though it was said that he was older even than Kit is now. With a gesture of implied generosity Kit was shown his desk, a thing almost obscene in its Frankish elegance, a frost of white mould blooming from the narrow, turned legs. He'd nodded as if to say he found it acceptable.

Baines's instruments were somewhat different: tools of metalsmithing and surgery, awls, pliers, vices, shears.

So began the longest eight days Kit has ever lived. The Council had but one question that needed answering – the same question they always asked, in one form or another – and Baines never tired of asking it: 'What was his *name*?' From morning prayers till suppertime. 'What was his *name*? What was his *name*?' The prisoner would roll in his own shit to deter them from touching him. He would call the Queen a witch and a whore, call her ministers arse-licking pandars and her bishops a mob of sodomites. But he never uttered a name.

Nevertheless, every night Kit had to carry his interrogation notes, such as they were, to a victualling house owned by secret Huguenots on the far side of the Seine. There, Kit would go around the room with a pitcher, filling cups like any pot-boy, till he came upon a boisterous table occupied by seminary students, and among them, two of the Council's spies: Thomas Walsingham, nephew to the Spymaster himself, and Tom Watson, a poet whom Kit had long admired. It was there where, one night, after Kit had passed his notes to Walsingham under the table, that Tom had caught him by the wrist and dropped a little pie into his hand: buttery crust, rich beef filling, the most delicious thing Kit had ever tasted.

'If you ever need anything, lad,' Tom whispered. 'Anything at all.'

By then, Baines was growing impatient. During the next day's session, without warning, he picked up a set of tinker's shears and cut off the prisoner's index finger. Tossed it, still bleeding, onto Kit's desk. 'What was his name?' Baines repeated, over the howls of pain. 'What was his name?' and then another *crunch*.

Kit sat with his fingers over his eyes, the heat of his own whispers on his palms: "'The light of the body is the eye, therefore when thine eye is single, then thy whole body shall be light…'"

'What was his name?' Baines snarled.

"'… then all shall be light, even as when a candle doth light thee…'"

'What was his name?'

"'… be not afraid of them that kill the body, and after that are not able to kill the soul…'"

'What was his name?'

'Babington!' the prisoner screamed.

Baines paused, as if slapped. He squeezed the prisoner's pale face in one hand, and with the other snapped his fingers at Kit. 'What was that?'

'Babington! They told me his name was Babington!'

Kit put the quill to the paper and watched it quiver. The ink had dried. Out of reflex or madness, he dipped his quill in the blood that pooled from the prisoner's finger, and tried to scratch it down:

Babington.

The men who brought Anthony Babington down still make much of themselves, as if they'd dragged the fabled leviathan onto the beach by one of its several tails. In truth, Babington was merely a courier, a scribe, same as Kit. But the missives he'd delivered were between the Queen of Scots and a pack of her sympathizers based in London, lackbrains really, who were neither discreet in their schemes nor in those whom they invited into their confidence, Babington especially. Finally, after over a decade of looking for an excuse, the Council would have Mary's head, thus exterminating the last living hope of a Catholic England.

Within eight months of Kit scribbling the name Babington in blood, Mary, Queen of Scots was sentenced to death. Her seven conspirators were strapped naked to sledges and dragged through a stone-slinging mob that stretched three miles, from the Tower of London to the church of St Giles-in-the-Field. Babington arrived at the gallows with the tip of his nose and both earlobes sliced off, one eye-socket shattered, his hair matted in gore. When they pushed the sledge upright to display him to the crowd, he collapsed to his knees and made the sign of the cross with crabbed, black-fingered hands, ruined by the rack. He was twenty-four years old. Two years older than Kit had been then. The same age Kit is now.

Standing fifty yards from the stage, Kit had been able to smell him.

'You see that fellow, up there?' Baines had said, pressed close to Kit in the crowd. He was not pointing at Babington, but at a smallish man with a clean-shaven face who stood among the prisoners at the back of the stage and yet did not appear to belong to their number, his aspect subdued, his clothes tidy.

'He's one of ours,' Baines went on. 'Goes by Robin Poley, he does, but Babington called him "Sweet Robin", "Dear Robin", "Robin my love".' Baines grinned, exposing his half-set of teeth. 'Babington wrote him a love-letter, just last week!'

'Blood!' the crowd roared. 'Blood! Blood! Blood! Blood! Blood!'

Kit had seen executions before. This one dragged on far longer than most. The light changed, the shadows lengthened, the bells rang brickbats-and-tiles, and Babington's screams went on, as urgent as the gushing of an artery. He'd started out praying, but in time the only intelligible word left on his tongue was 'Mama'. He did not die. He unravelled, from a man to a boy, a boy to a child, a child to an infant, which little by little turned animal: a screeching, writhing, comfortless thing, a faithless thing, for whom the word 'God', as all words, meant nothing.

Through it all, Kit found himself watching the man with the clean-shaven face, who in turn watched Babington die, with a faint smile fixed at the corners of his mouth. Sometimes, Kit had thought the man's lips looked pale, and once or twice he'd noticed him swallow hard, but never once did the man glance away. When it was over, he'd sighed, as if having eaten his fill.

After a full seven such executions, lasting till sunset, a horde of blood-drunk spectators had repaired to the nearest row of taverns, filling every house with their jittery, overloud recapitulations of the spectacle just seen. Baines had dragged Kit from one tavern to the next, till midnight found them settled in over a full jug of brandy, celebrating their success.

At some point Kit had vomited all over the table and Baines and himself. Immediately afterwards, he'd begun to sob:

back-breaking, rib-bruising sobs that made him want to tear his own eyes out. *And I say unto you, my friends, be not afraid of them that kill the body, and after that are not able to kill the soul.* But Kit had seen it – he'd *seen* it – he'd seen the soul die. He knew now that it was possible.

Baines had flicked his gaze at his cup and tossed the contents to one side. He patted himself down with a handkerchief, which he then offered to Kit. 'There, there now,' he'd said, refilling his cup from the jug.

Kit had mopped the table first, then himself, before he'd gathered enough breath to say, 'I can no more of this, I can no more – I want to resign!' He took hold of Baines's wrist, splashing brandy. 'Please help me! Tell them I am unfit. Tell them I am a coward. Tell them anything, I care not what. Make them let me go!'

Baines had indulged him as he went on, for another minute or two. But then he'd begun to relate details of Babington's capture that Kit had known not of before, and of the man with the clean-shaven face, who some called a hero and others called, sneeringly, 'Babington's widow'. For not only had Babington written him love-letters and called him fond names: it was also said that Babington had given him a ring – a diamond ring, which he never took off. Not even now.

'I do not begrudge you your affliction,' Baines said, after a deliberate pause. 'Lads like yourself have ever been exceptionally useful to the Council. You do as you are told. You keep secrets well. That is why, for the time being, you are protected, your crimes indulged. But only if you remain useful.'

He knew everything, of course. Kit had never confided in him, but there was no need to do so, not in words. Kit had any number of words for the things he'd done with the other lads at university, and, before them, a neighbour boy from Canterbury, and before him, a seventeen-year-old apprentice with whom Kit had shared a bed when he was just thirteen;

who, one night, had taken Kit's hand and fitted it around something hard and warm under the covers, and said, 'I'll do you if you do me,' and whose face Kit's father had smashed into an eyeless wad of blood and teeth ere he'd hurled him into the street. What Kit lacked in words was in the scream that had stuck silently in his throat as he'd watched the apprentice's features dissolve into a scarlet smear and realized that such would be his fate too one day: to be obliterated.

'I understand,' Baines said. 'I know you cannot help it. Once that devil is in you, there's no getting it out. Most would say you are poison in the blood of Creation, a heresy made flesh, and that is why you must be purged. But I think your lot is sadder than that. Whatever part of you God made is gone now. That must be terrible, for if you are no longer of God's making, then neither are you of Creation. You are a bugbear. A trick of the light.'

Kit knew not whether that was true. What Baines said next, however, was no lie:

'Understand, a fellow like you has but two options. One you have just witnessed. The other is to serve.'

2

PAST MIDNIGHT, KIT AND Tom cross London Wall at Bishopsgate in the north, and soon after arrive at a gabled cottage on Hog Lane, Norton Folgate, commonly known as 'Little Bedlam'. Though the name was intended as a slur, Tom has embraced it, for after all the house is bedlam on the best of nights, with its ever-changing roster of players, poets and misfits. Six currently lodge in the attic, more than the law allows for a private house, but Tom need not fear the law; he still has powerful friends.

The nightly curfew shall detain Little Bedlam's other lodgers at the Dancing Bears in Bankside till morning. Inside, Kit and Tom find Anna Watson sitting alone upon the stairs in her nightgown, a single candle puddling at her feet, a gory clot of red yarn dripping between her fingers. She smiles her tipsy smile as she descends to meet them, stands on her toes and kisses Tom's mouth as if to bite into a ripe fig. 'The bed was cold without you.'

Tom and Anna stand with their hips almost touching while he untangles the knitting from her fingers, enquiring after her night, her supper, her prayers, looking as if at any moment he'll put her fingers in his mouth and suck them. Once freed from her handiwork, Anna turns her attention to Kit, stroking him beneath the chin like a favourite pet.

'Did they love you?' Her pupils gape at him, solid black, her breath sickly-sweet with the sleeping potion from which she takes sips all day, every day, whether she would sleep or no.

'I think they did,' Kit answers, trying to smile.

Behind her, Tom grips the banister, ready to ascend. His eyes hold fast to Kit's. *Tonight*, they say.

The waiting begins. Kit takes some water out to the privy and spends far more time than truly necessary washing up, and then creeps upstairs, past the closed door of Tom and Anna's bedchamber, the sound of her anxious murmurs and Tom's soothing replies. In the attic room, Kit huddles, shivering, beneath the blankets, ears attuned to every soft creak of the house's cooling timbers, waiting for a footfall on the stairs, for a shadow to rise through the trap in the floor. He half-expects to see Richard Baines appear. Indeed, to his shame, a part of him longs for it. Another chance to plead, to bargain, to fawn. To barter for liberty, with pieces of himself. Perhaps there's no remedy for one such as him, who had learned to love first by loving a father who had terrified him, second, by loving God, whose love can never be declined or refused. A child of God never truly owns his body. If God says, 'Give it to me,' it must be yielded.

By the time the trapdoor creaks open, Kit is near frantic. 'She was restless,' Tom whispers, kneeling upon the corner of Kit's bedroll, lined up in a row of other such bedrolls, all empty. He slides himself over Kit's body like the closing of a lid, and in the darkness kisses him, with urgency of purpose. 'Come now, the others shall not return for hours yet.' Through his nightshirt his body is hard and lithe and straight, a pine curtained in mist. Moonlight gleams in the whites of his eyes, silvers the small hairs of his beard.

'You belong to me,' Tom says. 'I will keep you in a golden collar.' He always says suchlike things, words of lordship and conquest, of benevolence and magnanimity. Facedown, with Tom's hot mouth on the nape of his neck, Kit could be a ruby, a crown, a kingdom, a spoil of war coveted and plundered. How he has yearned to be captured. To be possessed. Waiting has bred a kind of bedlam in him that gushes forth unabashed, raving of his desires with a voice made hoarse as if from screaming.

'Shh.' Tom covers Kit's mouth. 'Someone will hear.'

Let them hear, Kit thinks. *Let the world hear.* Eyes closed, his fingers squeezing the back of Tom's thigh. He lets his soft moan travel through Tom's fingerbones like a song through guitar strings, vibrating all the way to the heart.

Nay, *this* is what it is to be adored.

'Did you tell me the truth?' Tom says to him afterwards, when they lie facing each other, Kit almost asleep.

Kit knows what he means. On the way to Little Bedlam, he had told Tom a story he has told no one else: a bedroom in a house on Deptford Strand. Baines's hand burning like a firebrand on the back of his neck.

'I tried,' is the best Kit can answer.

'He is a monster.'

To this, Kit has nothing to say. Years, he has left these waters undisturbed, now doubt clouds his mind like silt. *He is not the only monster.*

'I am afraid,' Kit says at last. 'He can destroy me, Tom. And he will. One day, he will. He knows things about me, things I fear even to tell you... They would put my skull on the gate, if they knew!'

'Nonsense.' Tom strokes Kit's cheek with his thumb as if to wipe away a tear, though there are no tears. 'Your mind is prone to extremities. Know ye not how rare a thing it is to spend eternity on Great Stone Gate? You are as likely to be born with eleven fingers.' Kit smiles, but after a little silence Tom says, 'What things? What can you not tell me?'

Now there are tears.

'Listen to me.' Tom's hand sweeps over Kit's face, his hair, his shoulder. 'This man must go. Thomas Walsingham will help us. But understand, the story you have told me will not be enough. 'Tis dreadful, yes, but some may not see it as you and I see it. When we meet with Thomas tomorrow, you shall have to call that darling muse of yours into it, ay? I know you have a talent for that, for horrors.'

That word 'horrors' resounds, so limitless. 'I like it not, Tom. You know him not as I do—'

Tom lifts Kit's head by the chin. 'If you do this, you will never have to fear Richard Baines again. We will go on as we are, and in little time every Jack and Jill between Penzance and the River Tweed shall know the name Christopher Marlowe, and I shall grow jealous and resentful and fat.'

Kit laughs, for he loves this in Tom, the ease with which he assumes greatness, colours the world as he sees fit. He even loves the way Tom mispronounces his name, not shrinking 'Marley', but bold, round 'Marlowe'.

'I will love you,' Tom says. 'I will admire you, as I did today.'

'Tis rare that Tom says 'I love you'. Those words arise out of want, cousins of *I hunger, I thirst, I ache*, a reminder that joy is fleeting. But God above, how richly one may live within the stark circumference of an hour!

Nay, Kit shall not permit any man to threaten this life, such as it is, so beautiful and so cruel. He will defend it to the death.

❧❦❧

Two days later, as Sunday services end, crowds flow forth from every church in the city, converging on the eye of the Rose Playhouse. The pit fills in less than five minutes. Such a crush forms at the doors that the grooms cannot force them shut. The name flies through the crowd, from lips to lips, in doubt and wonder: *Tamburlaine*. No one has ever seen a play like it, splendid, ghoulish, perfumed in Orient spices and daubed in barbarian blood. Tamburlaine is a beautiful monster, a silver-tongued savage. Like spilled ink, he bleeds across the map of the world with his ever-growing army, neither conqueror nor king so much as Death itself:

> Now clear the triple region of the air
> And let the majesty of heaven behold
> Their scourge and terror tread on emperors!

In the same moment that Tamburlaine calls for his soldiers to slaughter the virgins of Damascus and hang their corpses on the city's walls, four miles downriver in the village of Deptford, a rabble of helmeted guards – mercenaries, really, like all the city's guards – break down the door of a house on the Strand. A woman screams, children cry. The master of the house, a stout, grey-haired man called Bull, blocks the foot of the stairs and demands a warrant. He is answered with a truncheon to the temple. His wife catches his body as it falls.

In a bedchamber upstairs, the guards find Richard Baines with one leg already out the window.

All hands wrest him backwards. They shove him facedown, manacle his wrists, pull a black hood over his head. 'I am here on the Queen's business!' he cries. 'Take me to Thomas Walsingham! Take me to Sir Francis! They'll have your heads for this, ye jades!'

A guard replies, 'Whom do ye think sent us?'

One man links an arm through each of Baines's arms and together they drag him downstairs, two more men in front and two at the rear. In the corridor below, Madam Bull sits on the floor with her husband's bloody head cradled in her lap, two boys and a girl clinging to her pooled skirts. One of the cutthroats drops a bag of coins on Master Bull's chest.

'Apologies from Master Walsingham.'

The rest haul Baines outside and bundle him into the back of a wagon. 'What did he say about me?' Baines asks. No one answers him. 'What did he tell you? The boy is a liar, I say!' They close the gate, make ready to go. Baines writhes about the wagon-bed, his hood pulsing in and out with his breaths. 'I tell ye he is the Devil! A traitor! An abomination! Take me to Sir Francis, let me tell him the truth about *Kit Marley*!'

On Bankside, *Tamburlaine* comes to an end – happily, by all accounts, with the conqueror's own wedding solemnized amidst the Damascene ashes – and applause erupts out of the Rose's open roof. When the cries for the author arise, Ned Alleyn announces him, 'Christopher Marlowe!' and at once a lean colossus strides out from behind the curtains, auburn hair swept back, a pearl in his ear, his humble russet suit concealed beneath a cut-silk half-cape that some in the pit recognize as belonging to Tom Watson. At the edge of the stage he swoops, elegantly, into the French bow that he's spent the past two days practising.

Kit stands upright, looks over the cheering mob. A single human face, a single human stare can often overwhelm his senses, and here they number two or three thousand. He cannot pick out any one face he recognizes, not Tom, nor the other poets. He searches for Richard Baines, despite knowing what had happened in Deptford just minutes ago. Already, a part of him suspects it was a mistake. He feels a clench behind the ribs, as if at the setting of a fateful clock.

From this moment forward, Kit has less than five years to live. Even now, there are three men within the audience who will be with him when he dies, all of whom are still strangers to him:

Seated up in the first gallery, a man with a clean-shaven face called Robin Poley climbs Kit's body with his eyes, smiling in satisfaction, as if after a rich and lovely meal. As he applauds, a ring flashes upon a finger of his right hand: a large diamond, shaped like a tear.

Ten feet below Poley, in the pit, a burly, long-haired ruffian of twenty-one named Nick Skeres wraps a meaty arm around the neck of his much smaller companion, pretending to strangle him. 'Look at you!' he teases. 'Lovestruck, you are!'

Wriggling free, Nick's friend – Ingram Frizer, also twenty, and as scrawny as the other is big – stands on his toes to see the stage. He trembles as if battle-giddy, his boyish, large-eyed face fixed in a mad-dog grin. For indeed, this is love that Frizer feels, for the very first time, love for a thing that cannot love him back, a thing he may only regard from afar, in wonderment. He is in love with *Tamburlaine*, in love with a play. Its words fill him, animate him, as a hand fills a glove: *Smile, stars that reigned at my nativity*—'*What is Beauty,*' *sayeth my sufferings, then?*—*I that am termed the scourge and wrath of God, the only terror of the world!*… Words like meat, to be chewed over and savoured; words that taste, deliciously, of blood.

That this man who now towers at the foot of the stage was *Tamburlaine*'s author, Frizer can readily believe. Just *look* at him! – he is the embodiment of those words. He is not so much a man as the fever-dream of a mad philosopher, a crazed poet, a deluded lover. *Magnificent*, Frizer thinks. *He is magnificent!*

Four years, eleven months, twenty-one days from now, Frizer's hands will be so caked in Kit Marlowe's dried blood that they'll crack like clay.

6 MAY 1593

Twenty-four days

❧

[Ingram Frizer] was something to Marlowe but we do not know what... The only link between them that we know for sure is that they shared the same 'master', Thomas Walsingham.

CHARLES NICHOLL, *THE RECKONING*, 1992

3

TOM WATSON IS DEAD.

And so, Kit's latest play is half an orphan, at least in his mind: *Edward II*, the child of Tom Watson, and grief. Now, it shall be the last play performed before the same plague that killed Tom shutters London's theatres for the foreseeable future.

Perhaps the looming catastrophe is a good omen. For the play, at least. Four years ago, when *Tamburlaine* had made the name Christopher Marlowe famous, the whole country had believed they would be either dead or bowing to the Spanish king within the month! Every rich merchant loses a ship sooner or later, but thus far Kit has never come close. *Tamburlaine*'s sequel was even more beloved than its predecessor, despite its eponymous hero coming to a bad end; the people marvelled at *Doctor Faustus*, though many called it blasphemous; they came in droves to see *The Jew of Malta*, *The Massacre at Paris*. Like Kit himself, *Edward II* was a difficult birth, but many difficult births thrive thereafter.

Fifteen minutes into the first act, the first of many cherry-stones is spat at the stage, landing almost unnoticed by the players' feet.

By the final act, the pit is on the verge of rioting. Much of the galleries have emptied. Those who remain have stayed only to see the highly anticipated climax: Edward II, the sodomite king, impaled through the anus with a red-hot spit. Two hours, they have waited to see the miserable bugger die, but the killer hired to do the deed draws the matter out past all endurance. Shouts of 'Get on with it!' and 'Go to!' well up, while onstage the murderer dallies with his wretched prey, a cat with a mouse. He even offers to go at one point; 'tis the king who begs him not to: 'for if thou mean'st to murder me thou wilt return again. And therefore stay.'

The ragged king then kneels, tugs a diamond ring from his finger – his last possession – and slides it onto the killer's hand. The killer smiles, just at the corners of his mouth.

At last, someone hurls a clod of dung at the stage, nearly missing the murderer's head. A bombardment follows: insults, refuse, stones. One by one, the besieged actors take flight, first the killer's two accomplices and then the killer himself, flinging down his unused roasting-spit with a *clang*.

Bravely – stupidly, perhaps – King Edward lingers, shielding his head with his arms. 'Good gentles – good gentles, I pray you, 'tis nearly over... Let us *finish!*'

He is struck square above the eye by a handful of horseshit. A voice in the mob cries, 'Hang them!' and soon the rest follow suit.

Through a crack in the upstage curtains, a dark eye watches it all unfold. Kit Marlowe lifts a silver flask to his lips and drinks.

Less than a week later, Kit is startled awake by a crash, the slamming of one heavy, solid object into another. He lifts his head from the pillow with a suck of air, still drunk from the night before. Downstairs, the crashes continue. Kit lies still, listening without comprehending, his gaze stumbling over the unkempt lodging-house room where he has lived the past several months: the unwashed bowls and cups, the laundry draped over every available surface.

The empty bed across from his own, where Thomas Kyd usually sleeps.

At last, he hears the front door give way with a crack of splintering wood. Boots tromp inside. A man's shout from the room below. The landlady's scream.

Kit reels to his feet but freezes in place. In the doorway of the bedroom, a bearded mongrel paces and whimpers, its wet brown eyes big with worry. The light is grey and rainy, just after dawn.

In the kitchen directly below, boots rumble back and forth, objects crash and shift. There comes another scream, a man's: Thomas Kyd, whose pleading Kit hears through the floor: 'What have I done wrong? What have I done?'

Kit snatches up a leather satchel from beside his bed, grabs some clothes off the floor and shoves them inside. He sprints into the room across the corridor and falls upon the cluttered table therein, scooping papers into his arms. Boots ascend the stairs; voices shout commands on the way up. Kit darts back into the bedchamber just as their shadows round the first landing, papers scattering behind him, the dog barking and dancing at his heels. He takes up his doublet and boots, throws the shutters wide open and hurls himself into thin air, plunging two floors down to the bare, black earth.

Hurt, though he knows not where, Kit scrambles to his hands and knees, lopes four-footedly to the fence and clambers over it like a cat. He can still hear the dog barking as he tumbles into the alley beyond. A second later, silence.

Kit runs barefoot into the next alley, sidles in with his back to the wall. As he puts on his boots he discovers a gash in his right knee, blood and dirt streaming down his shin. The lodging-house is just two doors behind him; he can still hear the shouts. Around the corner, a heavy object explodes against the ground and Kit needlessly shields his head.

He peers around the wall with one eye. A wooden casket lies in splinters in the street, weltering in old clothes and loose paper. The air is dense with the sweet, white smoke of a plague-fire, yet through it Kit makes out the shape of a wagon and two men, one holding the rearing horse by the bridle, the other bouncing on his heels, stretching his neck to see inside. He seems to make a joke to his companion, and then, turning his head in Kit's direction, the smoke parts just enough to reveal a hint of his unmistakable face: the sunken cheek. The crooked mouth.

Kit's legs become water. He shrivels into the alley, stifling his own shout behind a hand. For far too long he cowers, whispering curses and pleas up to the sky, but at last the front door of the lodging-house bursts open, unleashing Thomas Kyd's screams. Kit runs.

He pelts south through the empty streets, afraid to look back. Eventually the smoke in his lungs compels him to stop, doubled over and fighting for breath. His hands shake as they reach for his flask, in desperate need of a drink, one drink, to steady his nerves...

His flask, he realizes, he has forgotten his flask!

He could fall to his knees and weep. Tom Watson gave him that flask, not that it matters now. There is no time to mourn, not for a flask; not even for Thomas Kyd, nor the life Kit had valued but little till this very moment. Richard Baines is back.

Kit limps on towards London Bridge. Ten miles. That is how far he must run. Ten miles south, past Southwark, Deptford, Blackheath, Eltham, Chiselhurst, to Scadbury, and Tom's former lover, Thomas Walsingham.

❧❧❧

By midnight, rain pours over Scadbury Manor, a great half-timbered house built upon the bones of a Norman fortress, with a two-mile-wide bulwark of forest on every side. Up until three years ago, the house had rarely ever seen its master, who was formerly Sir Francis Walsingham, also known as her Majesty's Spymaster. Now, months have passed since Scadbury's new owner, the late Sir Francis's nephew Thomas, last left its sheltering walls. Even in darkness, he sits awake in his study, poring over the letters his eyes and ears in London have lately sent, many of which are concerned with the recent, abortive performance of a play in Shoreditch, of all things. Walsingham is no longer a spy; no longer anything at all, despite his storied lineage. Still, he knows already of Thomas Kyd's arrest this morning; moreover he knows, with the sick certainty of poison in the belly, that Kit Marlowe could arrive at Scadbury at any minute.

Inside a cramped stone sentry-box built into the house's western flank, Ingram Frizer huddles into a too-big coat, watching blades of rain streak through the light of his lantern like meteors, from blackness to blackness. He has been here since sundown. To pass the time, he spins a knife in his deft fingers and murmurs whole speeches from *Tamburlaine* to himself just above the rain, luxuriating in each sibilant: "'There sits Death, there sits imperious Death, keeping his circuit by the slicing edge...'" His little knife, just eight inches long, he imagines to be a scimitar. His tongue, he imagines, is made of steel.

A sound comes through the rain, silencing him. It might have been a shout, or only the creak of a window opening somewhere above. He holds his breath as he squints into the darkness, from whence it seems anything could be about to emerge.

Then it comes again: 'Help us! Damn it, someone help us!'

Frizer springs to his feet, sheathes the knife behind his back. He splashes down the gravel path and onto the sodden lawn, pausing at the foot of the wooden moat bridge. On the far side, a knot of limbs takes shape: three men, two dragging the third behind them.

Frizer rushes to meet them. The two men walking reach the middle of the bridge and there drop the other's arms to rest, wiping rain from their brows. They are porters from the gatehouse up the road, father and son. The body they have been dragging lies faceup to the rain, a great X sprawled across the wet boards, the arms nearly spanning the full width of the bridge. No coat, no hat, pale as a pearl beneath a mat of over-grown beard.

The porters take no notice of Frizer at first. One man flings his gun back on his shoulder, the other struggles likewise with a large satchel. They fumble for a grip on the arms.

'What can I do?' Frizer sputters.

The porters squint. In the half-second that passes ere they recognize him, hope flashes in their eyes, followed soon by disappointment, resignation. They pivot into place at either arm. The senior one mutters, 'Get his legs.'

They carry the big man between the three of them, Frizer at the legs, an arm to each porter. The body is more drunk-heavy than dead-heavy. Beggars come by sometimes in search of table-scraps, but this man seems too big to be a beggar. His body rambles, as vast as a Plantagenet elm, reminding Frizer of fallen Ajax rushed from the battlefield, of ailing Edward Longshanks in the arms of his grooms, of dying Tamburlaine borne aloft by his sons.

The three men burst into the kitchens with their load, start-ling the scullery maids from their beds. Frizer moves to kick the door shut but the porters speed on ahead, towards the kitchens' sweltering inner heat. Together, they shove through another door and into the glowing roast-room: a hellmouth hearth riddled with iron spits, stinking of carbonized flesh.

The head cook has followed them in, brandishing a large knife. 'I swear by heaven, if that creature touches a one of my girls, I'll strike its hand off!'

The porters back Frizer towards the hearth. 'Feet to the fire!' the older one says. 'Put his feet by the fire and get his boots off! Are ye deaf?'

Frizer kneels and tugs at the muddy boots, finding bare legs and feet underneath. One porter drops the satchel by the giant's head.

'Take him anywhere you like, but not here!' the cook says. 'We are not an almshouse, by God! And with the *plague*—'

'Know ye not who this man *is*, woman?' the older porter barks. 'He was a great help to us, back when the master was indisposed—'

'A great help, indeed! You know damned well what sort of "help" he was!'

The porter slaps her. Frizer drops his eyes. The giant's legs seem to stretch on forever, the feet nearly as long as Frizer's forearms. A wound in the right knee glows cherry-red within a cake of dirt, rivulets of dried blood running down to the ankle.

'We had better wake the master,' the older porter says to his son, at which the room gives out a collective, silent shudder.

The porter then snaps his fingers. 'You. You, errand-boy!'

Frizer looks up.

'Stay here.'

With the porters gone, the cook squats beside the door, her weapon at the ready, her horsey face clenched like a fist. At the far end of the corridor, female heads cluster around the entrance to the kitchens like cherubs at the door of a church, turning now and then to whisper at each other.

Frizer anchors his gaze to the man on the floor or to the bag beside him, for he feels the cook's glare directed more at him than at the sleeping giant, with a thin-lipped sneer that says, *I know of you. I know what you are.* Women unnerve him at the best of times, to speak true, all veiled and vizarded, bodies so deformed by their attire that, as a boy, he'd believed they had many legs under their skirts instead of just two. But he never had a mother. Women seem to hate him for this.

'What's that smell?' The giant's voice is surprisingly soft.

Frizer glances to the cook before answering, 'M-meat. The roast-room.'

The giant frowns without opening his eyes, as if he finds this dream very peculiar indeed. His nose has been broken before. A white scar shows through the hair on his chin. He looks familiar, but not as if Frizer has met him – as if he has imagined him, perhaps, as if he'd met him in a dream.

'Where's my bag?' the giant says, with a soft gasp as if just remembering it.

Frizer pushes it closer. 'Right here. Beside you.'

The giant reaches out and touches the bag with a big hand. No gloves either. An inch-long teardrop of scar glistens above the thumb, a long-healed burn. The hand trembles with palsy of a kind with which Frizer is all too familiar. He has seen it a thousand times before, in his own father, God rest his soul.

'Have you got any whisky?' the giant says, politely enough for one in his straits.

Frizer throws a pleading look to the cook, whose expression sours further still. 'Ay, certainly we have whisky,' Frizer says. 'Just a moment.' Reluctantly, he leaves the big man under the cook's guard and hurries to the far cooler ale-store, where the master keeps a full rack of Scotch whisky in glass bottles. Frizer takes the dustiest bottle, assuming it shall be least likely missed, and so returns to the roast-room, kneeling at the giant's side. The giant sits up unassisted, pulls the cork with his teeth. He sucks down gulp after gulp as if it were water, pauses for breath, drinks again.

Frizer watches the bone glide up and down in the long, white throat. It takes far too long for him to realize that the giant has paused again, looking at him with eyes that appear black in the firelight, as black as a horse's eyes.

'This is good whisky,' the giant says.

Frizer cannot speak. A memory stirs in his mind like a fish in murky water.

The giant starts to drink again, but stops to smile. 'Oh – your master will have you whipped!'

At once, Frizer remembers: the Rose Playhouse, the archangel towering at the foot of the stage, stark as a stake in the bonfire of applause.

Magnificent, he was. Magnificent.

Down the corridor, the maids' whispers turn sharp and short. Their heads peel away from the door, white bodies fluttering into the shadows like moths. Footsteps march in, and a moment later the steward, three chamber-grooms, and finally the master himself, Thomas Walsingham, round into the corridor one after another. A dressing gown of yellow silk billows behind the master, his long, dour face framed in prematurely silvered black hair. He cannot be more than ten years Frizer's senior, yet Frizer thinks of him as much older.

The cook and Frizer shoot upright and bow their heads. Only the giant abjures courtesy. In the six months that Frizer has been employed at Scadbury, the master has never said one word to him directly. Nor does he speak to him now. Like an owl, the master swoops down beside his prize, such as it is, takes the giant in his arms and says, 'God damn you, Kit! God damn you for coming here!'

Kit. Such a little name for such a big man.

The giant clings to the master's sleeves. The master strokes the giant's muddy hair. Frizer tries not to look at them, gripped by shame that seems to arise from nowhere and everywhere at once. It slithers behind his ribs like something undigested, fetid, lingering.

'Please,' Marlowe cries, 'hide me!'

4

THOMAS WALSINGHAM HAS NOT seen Kit in the flesh since well before Tom died last September, though Walsingham's informants in London have kept him apprised of Kit's condition. 'Tis still shocking to witness first-hand: so weak that the servants must help him upstairs, so bowse-sick that his hands tremble like an old man's. Years now, Walsingham has watched Kit move towards a precipice, sometimes at a stumble, sometimes at a sprint. Since Tom's death, Kit has been in freefall.

Upstairs, in a room Walsingham thinks of lately as 'the lady's chamber' (although he has no lady, as yet, to occupy it), a pair of maids come to help bathe and dress Kit's wounds, change him out of his clothes and put him to bed. When the servants have finally gone, Walsingham climbs into bed beside Kit and listens patiently while he rants and raves about his unfortunate friend Thomas Kyd, and about Richard Baines – that old bugbear! – whom Kit is convinced he saw among the men who had dragged his friend off in chains, plain as day. It would not be the first time that drink has fooled Kit's eyes. Need he be reminded, the breadth of the Narrow Sea now lies between himself and Richard Baines, as it has done, *almost* uninterrupted, for five years. And whom does he have to thank for that?

'I have not forgotten,' Kit says, lying back, rubbing one eye with the backs of his fingers, like a worn-out child. 'I have not forgotten what you've done for me...'

'Ay, but you would rather bend reality than blame yourself for your own misfortunes,' Walsingham says, propped on an elbow beside him. 'Do not feign surprise, Kit. I know what you've done. I've heard everything.'

Still, Kit has the audacity to frown. '*What* have I done?'

'You showed a man *kiss* another man,' Walsingham whispers, mindful of any ears at the door. 'You showed a king of England slaughter half the peerage and drag the kingdom into civil war, all to avenge the murder of his masculine strumpet! You showed a king of England *fucked* to death with a red-hot spit!'

Eyes closed, Kit bites his lip. As if he enjoys this!

'It would have been quicker to hang yourself. More dignified too.'

'Thomas, it does not matter about the play—'

Walsingham says, 'Of course it matters about the play! They could have you for sedition, if not worse. Sedition leads so easily to *treason*, these days... And one man, for that matter – one name – leads to another, and another. The Council burns through names like tinder; they are always hungry for more...' He cannot bear to go on, shaking his head. 'Marry, I know not why the guards took your friend Kyd, but any fool can guess why they came to your house. I only pray you do not bring ruin down upon mine as well!'

'Thomas—'

'*Why*, Kit? Why have you done this to yourself?'

'Because I cannot bear it any more.' At last, Kit opens his wet eyes. 'You may not believe me, you may not see it, but I have tried, I have. I am fed up.'

Walsingham looks away, lest he should start to feel guilty. Of course, this is all about Tom. Kit had not been at

St Bartholomew's Hospital to watch Tom die, and for that he surely resents Walsingham, who will carry the memory of that place to his grave. The crowded plague-ward. The moans of the dying. The putrefying stench. Kit will never appreciate Walsingham's kindness in sparing him the details. For he need know nothing of Tom's delirium and suffering, his racking cough, his incurable thirst. He need not know of the last words Tom spoke, before the blood had filled his lungs: *God forgive me, coward that I am!*

Anyway, even if Tom had wanted him there, Kit could not have come. He had been in Canterbury, in jail.

Quietly, Kit says, 'I wanted them to *feel* it, the vicious curs.'

Walsingham is startled. 'You wanted who to feel what?'

'The audience. I wanted them to feel what Edward feels, when the spit goes in. I wanted every one of them to feel their arse exposed, the man on their backs… I wanted the veins to burst in their eyes. I wanted them to taste their insides cooking on the back of the tongue.'

'What *for*, in God's name?'

'Vengeance,' Kit says. He then shrugs, diminishing the word. Still it lingers, a fly at Walsingham's ear. Sometimes Kit frightens him.

Walsingham shakes himself. 'That's enough now. You should sleep. *I* should sleep.'

Kit sighs at length, making room for Walsingham to lay his head upon his shoulder, his hand upon his chest. Gently, Kit fiddles with a large ring upon Walsingham's finger: a gold band set with amber, the stone inscribed with a hare in flight. A gift from Tom, given long ago.

Walsingham shuts his eyes, focusing on the thump of Kit's heart against his cheek, the rocking of his breaths, the scent of skin through his shirt. On the verge of sleep, he feels Kit's hand slide up the length of his arm, stopping upon his shoulder for the space of one breath. Two. The hand then moves down his flank, finding the curve of his hip, the outer part of his thigh, before at last the long fingers push their way into the opening of his dressing-gown, reaching deep.

Walsingham snatches hold of Kit's wrist. 'Stop that,' he hisses, as if to shove the words directly into Kit's wounded eyes. 'We do not do *that* any more.'

Two years ago, in March of 1591, Kit had turned up at Scadbury unannounced, in one of his rare spates of sobriety. Things had already gone wrong between Tom and Kit by then, though at the time Walsingham knew not how exactly. He only knew that Tom had spent much of the previous year in prison, for so had Walsingham himself, along with dozens of the late Spymaster's former men.

The mass arrests had come in the wake of Uncle Francis's death: in Walsingham's case, surprised by some of the Archbishop of Canterbury's mercenaries on his way home from the funeral, hauled off to the Marshalsea Prison with a bag over his head. Some of those who went in with him never came out again, though a handful were soon back at work at a reorganized Privy Court. Still others had, like Walsingham, only narrowly escaped the noose. His charge of treason could not be definitively proved, but as for the others – heresy and sodomy – the latter, being certain, was taken as proof of the former. For what is sodomy, if not a heresy of the flesh?

'We offer mercy – *this* time,' the archbishop had squawked, as Walsingham stood dazed and ragged in the Star Chamber before the full assembled Council. 'Next time, you'll receive none.'

When Kit had arrived at Scadbury, Walsingham had been a free man for a total of two weeks, and in that time had done little but lie in bed and pray for death. He'd thought of Kit then only as his former lover's much younger lover, and he'd hated that he was seeing him like so, a frail, rabbit-eyed starveling, who had to be carried up and down stairs in a chair and could barely hold a spoon for the weakness in his hands. Out of politeness, Walsingham had invited Kit to dine, and sat with him in tense silence for an hour or so, thinking only of his cell at the Marshalsea Prison, and of the voice of Dick Topcliffe, her Majesty's Master of Tortures, purring in his ear:

What was the name Tom Watson gave you, in the poem he wrote for you in Paris? 'Tityrus?' And you called him 'Virgil', did you? Did you call him that when he tied your hands to the bedposts and stuck his cock up your arse? Did your uncle know about that – about how Tom Watson made you his whore?

Of course not. Only Tom had known of those things. Only Tom could have spoken of them. But Tom had already been in prison, on a separate charge, when the mass arrests occurred. His release had, in fact, coincided remarkably with Walsingham's arrest, not to mention the arrests of all Uncle Francis's former men.

Over dinner, Walsingham wondered: did Kit know, or had he somehow guessed, as Walsingham had, that it was Tom who had first uttered Walsingham's name in the torture room? Was that why Kit had come – out of guilt? Or was it, perhaps, to see whether Walsingham would now hold his tongue?

Walsingham's suspicions made him the poorest sort of company, yet Kit was undaunted. He stayed the night, and the next, and the next. By then, Kit had become Walsingham's constant, thankless nurse, carrying him about in his arms, helping him wash and dress, urging him to eat and drink – soothing his nightmares, drying his tears, enduring his rages, mothering and making love to him with almost unbearable tenderness. As the weeks passed, Walsingham began to take it for granted that Kit would be by his side always, ready with whatever he required, smiling at him with a quiet ache in his eyes, the ache of distance. It maddened and unmanned Walsingham, this ache, it made him want to throw himself at Kit Marlowe's feet and wail like a girl.

For it was not Walsingham whom Kit loved, though he treated him with love: it was Tom Watson of course, who had also been imprisoned and tortured but would have nothing to do with Kit any more. Walsingham was only a surrogate. A ghost.

Once Walsingham's strength had returned, he'd begged Kit to leave.

Eventually, Kit's breaths lengthen with sleep. Walsingham slips free of him, lights a taper from the fire and quietly lets himself out. In the corridor, he finds the night-runner who had helped bring Kit inside lurking in the dark, the lad's startled blue eyes shrinking as the light hits them. 'You should not be here,' Walsingham says, and the runner sucks in a breath as if about to let out a stream of excuses, ultimately deflating in silence.

No matter. Walsingham has present use for him. He leads the little fellow down to his study, where he sets him by the door, too far away to see over his shoulder. Walsingham uncorks a bottle on his desk, pours himself a drink. 'What is your name?' he asks.

'Frizer, master.'

Walsingham empties the cup in one jerk of his head. 'You know my man Nick Skeres, do you?'

'Ay – yes, master. He recommended me to you.'

'I remember.' With his littlest finger, Walsingham flips open the amber jewel on Tom's ring and removes a key no longer than a tooth, with which he unlocks a drawer. Inside are dozens of letters: letters that speak of the riot at *Edward II*, of Kit's comings and goings from the taverns in Bishopsgate, of yesterday morning's raid and Kit's escape. All are written in a distinctive hand, needle-thin and arabesque. *You must understand*, the most recent letter says:

> *...the Devil never comes for just one man's soule. 'Tis not worth the trouble to him. No, he comes for that man, and all his friends to boot. Well, of course you understand this, perhaps better than anyone. So I sholde not neede to tell you that when the Devil comes for your friend – and God knowes he is coming right soon – you needes must looke first of all to your owne soule.*
>
> *I can helpe you to that ende.*

'Do you need me, master?' Frizer squeaks.

Walsingham shakes the inkwell, selects a sharp quill and blank paper from the box. With one half of his mind, he writes; with the other half, he speaks. 'I am writing two letters. One, you shall deliver to the Star Chamber at Westminster. The other is a message for Nick Skeres. Tell him to deliver it to his friend in St Helen's.'

> *Estimable Lords, with humilitie and reveraunce I bring you this news, that K Marloe may be found here at Scadbury should you seeke him, & so beg if I may such counsel as your Lo:ships see fitt regarding the question of his keeping. In any exigency I remain,*
>
> *Your faithful servaunt, Tho: Wals:*

He crosses out *with humilitie and reveraunce*, writes *in perfect obedience* instead.

The second letter, bound for St Helen's, Walsingham scratches down more hastily than the first. He slits the Star Chamber letter in several places and weaves a paper-bolt through the slits, as Uncle Francis had taught him. When all is done, he pours another cup of whisky and holds it below his nose without drinking, feeling anger where he ought to feel something else; thinking of Tom on his deathbed, a brittle, gasping husk: *God forgive me, coward that I am!*

When Frizer comes forward to collect the letters, Walsingham moves them out of his reach. 'How much do I pay you, Frizer?'

Silence. 'Tuppence a week, master.'

'And how much does a bottle of ten-year Scotch whisky cost?'

An even longer silence, a softer reply: 'I know not, master.'

'Perhaps you should consult with the steward on that matter, ere ye go raiding my stores again.' Walsingham lets him stew, and then, lesson imparted, offers the letters at last. 'God grant ye foresight hereafter.'

5

He is here. Confirm Baines, & charges if there be any. Kydd whereabouts.

FRIZER REFOLDS THE MESSAGE for Nick and then tucks it inside his coat, sprinting for the stables. The other letter, bound for the Privy Council's fabled inner sanctum, the Star Chamber, he dares not disturb. What could the Privy Council want with Marlowe?

Belike Nick will know what to make of all this. Nick Skeres always seems to know everything that goes on, a trick he must have learned from serving the master's uncle in his youth. Frizer has not the benefit of such an education, being nothing more special than Nick's childhood friend – and now, his kin, having married Nick's cousin Betsy last autumn, very much at Nick's tireless insistence that the match would be a good one. *For whom?* Frizer sometimes wonders. He is happy, at least, to live in the house that joins with Nick's on one side, so they live as something more intimate than neighbours; less pleased to share the house with his mother-in-law and Nick's three young sons, who have all their father's bombast but none of the charm.

With the sun just up, Frizer lets himself in at Nick's side of the house, where everyone will be gathered for breakfast. As predicted, he need not tell Nick anything. The moment Frizer steps into the kitchen, Nick heaves his great bulk up from the table, claps Frizer's face in his incurably damp hands and thunders, '"Was this the face that launched a thousand ships, / And burnt the untopp'd towers of Ilium?"'

'"Topless towers,"' Frizer corrects him, exasperated.

Nick's boys chase each other around the table in circles. At the sideboard, Frizer's mother-in-law stands hip-to-hip with Nick's perpetually flushed and harried wife, the feathers of a fresh-killed capon heaped about their feet. Frizer's wife Betsy – a pretty girl, as everyone says, despite her rabbity front teeth – bows into her sewing at the far end of the table, another tiny cap or smock or stocking balanced upon the teeming bulge of her belly.

Seated at Nick's elbow, Frizer leans close to whisper, 'Will I ever meet this "friend" of yours in St Helen's?' He catches Betsy glancing up at him, then down into her sewing again.

Nick chuckles, reaching for one of his aunt's caraway-seed cakes. 'Oh, I reckon you will someday.' It sounds almost ominous. 'Come, let me see the other one. You did not open it, did you? I know you cannot resist a paper-bolt!'

'No, by heaven!' Frizer says, handing over the Star Chamber letter. 'What do you suppose the master wants with the Privy Council?'

Nick holds the letter up to a candle, squints, and then hands it back. 'Knows how to keep his head, he does,' he says. 'More than I can say for his friends.'

Such enigmatic answers are all too common with Nick, who, from what Frizer can tell, also knows how to keep his head. Frizer shall have to ask the right questions. 'And what about Baines?' he says, after wracking his brain.

Nick frowns. Frizer opens the message for St Helen's again, pointing. 'See? It says Baines. "Confirm Baines."'

Nick is not looking, smearing butter on his cake. Vaguely, he mumbles, 'Just some devil or other, I imagine,' and takes a bite.

'You should have heard the talk at the well this morning,' Frizer's mother-in-law pipes up, without turning around. 'They say that man at Scadbury is the Devil himself!'

'Oh Mother, *please*,' Betsy mumbles, leaning deeper into her work.

'They say he had his feet in hot coals and the skin did not even singe.'

Nick smirks. 'That true, Ingram?'

'No' – a cough – 'no, ma'am. I was there. I put his feet *by* the coals, marry. To warm them.'

His mother-in-law turns, one hand upon her hip, a knot of entrails dangling from her wiry fist. 'You saw him close, I hope? Then you would have noticed if he had any horns under his hair or extra teeth. Markings upon the skin, perhaps…?'

Frizer and Betsy's stares meet, but neither speaks. There are things that only his wife knows. Things only she has seen.

Frizer grows achingly aware of every inch of exposed skin on his body: the barest sliver at the neck, for he wears his collars high; the glaring nakedness of his hands. He tucks his hands under the table, mutely shaking his head.

'Trust me, Auntie,' Nick says, dusting crumbs from his palms, 'if the Devil were come to Scadbury, I would be the first to tell you.'

One of Nick's sons starts to chant, 'Out, Devil, out, Devil, out out out!' and soon the rest join in, even Nick.

'Just the same,' Frizer's mother-in-law says, 'I've put a ring of salt around the house. If he wants inside, he'll have to tunnel his way in, like a mole!' She wraps her hand as she turns to the fire, taking the long iron spit off the hob. With one hand upon the bird's belly, she forces it up through the bottom.

With two of his mother-in-law's caraway cakes in his stomach, Frizer goes out to the barn, readying his and Nick's horses for the ride to London. As he tightens the saddle straps on his reddish gelding, he mutters, "'So burn the turrets of this cursèd town, / Flame to the highest region of the air—'" But a glance to the open doors stops him dead: there stands Betsy with the morning light haloed in her tousled hair, hands crossed over her belly.

Perhaps she thinks he was casting a spell. She could rid herself of him that way, if she wanted to. Tell the right people that her husband speaks with the Devil and he could be hanging from the village gallows ere the month is out.

But she says nothing of it. Only draws a nervous breath, and says, 'I have a favour to ask. I did not want to mention it at table...'

Frizer tries to say, 'Oh?' as if it were a challenge, yet no sound leaves his throat.

'It would please me, greatly, if you would allow Master Purcell to have a look at you. For the baby.'

'Master Purcell?'

'The astrologer.' Something must show in his looks, because her manner suddenly turns conciliatory. 'He comes highly recommended. Jane Riley says he predicted her boy's birth down to the very hour—'

'What has that to do with me?'

'The *marks*,' she whispers, as if to speak heresy.

Frizer bows his head. He is reminded of the wedding night, the first time she'd ever seen his body unclothed. *Please do not scream*, he'd said. But she'd screamed anyway.

Hastily, Betsy adds, 'Just to see whether there be anything questionable in them. Anything that may draw the Devil's eye, you know...' Frizer pulls the horses forward by the bridles, forcing her to step aside. Betsy follows him, hugging her belly. 'They say the sun will be in eclipse before the month is out... that it may even happen when I come to bear, or in the churching-time... Eclipses bring forth changelings, monsters!'

'Did you tell your mother about it?' Frizer says, halting.

Betsy stares, shakes her head. 'No. *No*. Have you *heard* her? I would not dare!'

''Tis no one's business but mine,' Frizer says.

'And mine.' She has overstepped, and seems to know it, reaching for his arm. 'If the baby comes out *wrong*—'

Frizer pulls away. 'You and your mother!' he growls. 'Astrologers and salt circles! By God, you are more likely to draw the Devil's eye with all your rubbish than I am just by wearing my damned *skin*!'

On the road north to London, as Chiselhurst vanishes behind them, Nick raises his eyebrows and says, 'So, did ye talk to him?'

Frizer is startled. For he had just been thinking about Marlowe: about how, the first time he ever saw him, he'd taken him for something supernatural – angel or devil; both, and neither – but now, he has felt the weight of Marlowe's bones, he has smelled the blood and sweat and whisky on him. 'Tis as if he has touched a wound, like when Tamburlaine cut his own arm and made his sons dip their fingers in it:

> *A wound is nothing, be it ne'er so deep,*
> *Blood is the God of War's rich livery.*

But hearing Nick's question, Frizer deflates, admitting, 'Ay, but he said nothing much. Only that the master would whip me for giving him that whisky.'

Nick grunts a dark laugh. He says, 'I know how you are, mind, with your Tamburlaine-this and Faustus-that, but he's best avoided, that one. Has a mark on him.'

Frizer's breath catches. 'A *mark*?'

'A bull's-eye,' Nick says, and mimes drawing an arrow, releasing it.

Frizer returns at dusk, exhausted and saddle-sore, stopping at the house only to deliver a reply to the master's letter before dragging himself up the path towards his sentry-box, for another long night's watch. But on the way, a figure on the lawn halts him in his tracks: Marlowe. How he towers against the white orchard at the base of the hill, the black band of forest, the scarlet sky.

> *Of stature tall and straightly-fashioned...*
> *Such breadth of shoulders...*
> *... amber hair wrapped in curls...*
> *... arms and fingers long and sinewy...*

Nay, not even Ned Alleyn so perfectly resembles his greatest part as does the creator of it. There he stands: conqueror of empires, slaughterer of millions, burner of holy books. Tamburlaine, and Marlowe. Both, and neither.

Frizer swallows. He stalks closer, heel-to-toe. Marlowe exhales a puff of smoke into the heady light. Frizer thinks he shall buy tobacco and a pipe first thing tomorrow.

What should he say? He could ask about Marlowe's newest play, about which he has heard many distressing, enticing rumours. He could ask Marlowe if he really knows how to conjure devils, like Doctor Faustus. He could ask why Tamburlaine had to die at the end of *Part Two*. He could say, *I have always admired the way you write about the stars* – for in Marlowe's words the stars are never still; they gallop and plunge, they cartwheel through the heavens. *Is that how the stars look to ye?* he would ask. To Frizer, the stars seem quite still.

A stone crunches beneath Frizer's boot. Startled, Marlowe reels about to face him. All at once, the words burst forth from Frizer's lips:

'"Smile, stars that reigned at my nativity,
And dim the brightness of your neighbour lamps;
Disdain to borrow light of Cynthia!
For I, chiefest lamp of all the earth,
First rising in the east with mild aspect,
But fixed now in the meridian line,
Will send fire up to your turning spheres,
And cause the stars to borrow light of you!"'

'What?' Marlowe sounds out of breath.

The bigness in Frizer's chest withers. '"Fire"... "turning spheres"... From *Tamburlaine*?'

Marlowe stares, blinking as if blinded by a sudden light. A frown forms between his brows. '"Cause the *sun* to borrow light of you." Not "stars". *Sun*.'

Frizer says nothing.

'Tamburlaine is *addressing* the stars. Cynthia is the moon.'

Frizer stammers, numb-tongued. 'Ay, "Cynthia". 'Tis what I said.'

Marlowe's lips crook into the cruellest of smiles. He takes the time to draw from his pipe before murmuring, 'Of course you did.'

Frizer's stomach lurches. He turns his back and starts to walk away as if the world had suddenly tipped sideways, past his sentry-box, out of the long reach of Marlowe's shadow.

He will never forget this.

❧❦❧

Nick Skeres stops up the doorway of Walsingham's study, all asweat and stinking from the long ride. His doughy face is caught in the same faint, elated smile he always wears whenever he returns from St Helen's, like a boy brimming with his father's praise.

At his desk, Walsingham unfolds a message written in that delicate, arabesque hand:

I can confirm Baynes. Youle find the services I offer convenient, I feare, in the dayes ahead. Shal we not speake of figures yet?

The reply from Westminster, which arrived minutes ago, was even briefer: *Keepe him there.*

Nick says, 'Baines has been at the Privy Court on Seething Lane. Twice now, that Master Poley's seen. Once on Monday, again on Friday.'

'Did he see who was with him?'

'That villain Phelippes, he said. Puckering's man.'

Walsingham shakes his head. If Baines has the ear of Puckering, the Lord Keeper – 'keeper', now, of the Council's spies – then God help Kit Marlowe.

'And the charges against Thomas Kyd?' Walsingham asks.

'No one will say. Master Poley reckons Archbishop Whitgift has got something to do with it, so heresy of some sort. They've got him in the Marshalsea, in any case—'

'*Marshalsea?*'

Nick nods, sheepishly. Perhaps he can see panic in Walsingham's eyes.

'Did *he* tell you this?'

'He suggested it.'

Walsingham falls silent again. If Thomas Kyd is in the Marshalsea, with Dick Topcliffe and his machines, his branding irons, his instruments, it shall be only a matter of time before the wolves come for Kit also, desiring what they always desire, *names* – and then God help Thomas Walsingham.

'How long do we have?' Walsingham asks.

'Master Poley says a week, at the most. All depends on Kyd. And Baines.'

Walsingham sends Nick on his way and begins searching the house and grounds for Kit, who is not mad after all, or not so mad as Walsingham had hoped. No, Kit is only mad in that he harbours that most dangerous of delusions, believing he knows precisely who the Devil is and what he looks like. But the truth is that Richard Baines is but a lesser fiend. The Devil is not just one man. He is a brotherhood.

A gardener directs Walsingham to the orchard. Even from afar, Kit's shape stands out in the white blooms, his back against a tree, head bowed over a book. 'You should not be out here,' Walsingham says, by way of a greeting.

Kit closes his thumb in the book, plucks up a bottle from the grass and drinks. 'You said I could go out at night. The sun's nearly down.'

'Apparently the village gossips have already found a new subject in you. I hear they accuse me of playing host to the Devil.'

Kit laughs. 'It would not be the first time for you, would it?' He offers Walsingham a drink, and its subsequent refusal seems to breed a touch of melancholy in him, his gaze drifting towards the dark woods. 'It matters not, anyway. They will find me eventually.'

Walsingham is exasperated by this, but there's no time to be angry. 'This Kyd fellow,' he asks, 'would you consider him a friend?'

Something tugs at Kit's lips. Remorse, perhaps. 'Of a kind.'

'*More* than a friend?'

'Only the once, and I assure you, he was very drunk.'

'Damn and blast ye, Kit!'

'He wanted to suck cock; thought he would be good at it. I tell ye – he was not.'

'How well does he know ye? Knows he about Tom, or about Baines, even? Kit,' Walsingham hesitates, suddenly short of breath, 'knows he about you and *I*?'

Kit's look darkens. 'Why?'

Walsingham can hardly utter the word aloud. '*Marshalsea*, Kit. They have him in the Marshalsea!'

Kit has nothing to say to this, though it seems he loses a drop of colour in contemplating it. He lifts the bottle and drinks again.

'I fear,' Walsingham says, but then stops, for he knows not how to ask what he would know, thinking aloud. 'This play of yours... 'tis a libellous thing indeed, but if the Council only wanted ye for libel, they would have arrested you days ago. They could allege buggery, I suppose, based on the play's contents, but to hang a man for buggery is to admit that buggery exists, and half the men on the Privy Council are as happy to fuck a boy as they are a girl, so long as he is nothing to anyone – the archbishop being no exception! To hang a man for buggery, they must charge him with something more: witchcraft, treason, heresy—'

'Thomas, you know my sins as well as anyone.'

'Do I indeed? Perhaps I know ye not so well after all, Kit. Surely you are no Puritan, or God forbid a papist, but are you even a Christian, in any sense? When was the last time you went to church? Christ, Kit, when was the last time you *prayed*?' Kit has no answer for this. Walsingham lowers his voice. 'You are so frightened of Richard Baines. Why? What does he know of ye?'

'You said Baines was in Flushing.'

'I have not said otherwise. Besides, you know well he is in Flushing, Kit. You saw him there yourself.'

'That was over a year ago!'

'And what of it? Why did you ask me to send him there in the first place? Was it Tom's idea?'

Kit scoffs at this, though he does so as if a nerve has been touched.

'Whatever Baines knows about you,' Walsingham says, 'did Tom know too? Is that why he brought you to see me?'

Kit says nothing to this either, his look of suspicion only deepening. He reaches up and takes a branch in his hand, pulling his back straight. 'Perhaps I should go home,' he says to the woods. 'To Canterbury.'

'No. You must stay here.'

'It would be safer for you, Thomas. They cannot fault my own mother and father for harbouring me, though God knows my father will take some convincing—'

'You cannot leave!'

'Why not?'

'Because they know you are here, Kit, and if they discover that I have let you go, it shall be my head along with yours!' Walsingham realizes he is shouting, but cannot stop. 'Know you not what a thankless chore it is to be your ally? We are all of us in pitch up to our necks, and you go about lighting fires left and right, as if 'tis your pleasure to see your friends burn!'

'I'm sorry, Thomas.'

'For *two years* I have kept my name out of their mouths! Two years! I flattered myself, I did, thinking I could know peace again!'

'Thomas—'

'Do not touch me. Drink my whisky, walk at night, walk in daylight, I care not. I will help you because I have no choice in it. Not for any other reason.'

This is the most hurtful thing Walsingham can think to say, and he feels nothing but shame to have uttered it. He turns at once to storm off so that Kit will only see the back of him climbing up the hill with long strides, not the anger in his face, nor the grief.

But Kit does not turn to watch him go. Instead, he gazes into the depths of the woods beyond the orchard with raw, rattled eyes, as if heeding a voice from within.

Now I've got you, you ungrateful little shit.

When the sky is nearly three quarters full of stars, Kit

picks up the bottle and walks into the meadow. The woods surround a circle of sky like the open roof of a playhouse. Kit turns, searching for 'North, north, north...' and finds what he seeks hanging high above the orchard: a jagged diamond snake, Cassiopeia.

He remembers a night in the garden at Little Bedlam, in the feverishly sweet summer that had followed *Tamburlaine*'s premiere and Baines's exile, easily the happiest months he has ever lived. He'd pulled Tom outside by the hand and pointed to a faint pinprick of light, just above the arch in the snake's back. 'The *nova stella*, they called it,' Kit had gushed tipsily, explaining all: a new star, birthed in the year 1572; it had appeared as a fireball, brighter than any planet, and has been fading ever since.

'It is the proof,' Kit said. 'You asked for proof, and there it is!'

Tom squinted. 'There's nothing there, Kit.'

'Oh, come now! You remember. I remember, when it appeared, the whole of Canterbury came out to look at the sky. People were praying; people were on their *knees*—'

'It was only a star.'

'Ay, Tom, a *star*!' Kit could not stop himself from shouting. 'A star that God did not create on the second day! A star that Adam never saw, if "Adam" existed at all—'

Tom grabbed hold of Kit's chin and twisted his head to face him, rougher than he had ever touched him before. 'Listen to me: *never* speak like that again. Not even to me. Do you understand?' Kit was too frightened to reply. Tom shook him, hard. 'Kit, they'll not just hang you for that. Do you want to end up on Great Stone Gate? Do you want to end up like *Babington*?'

The star is gone now. But the memory of it lives: a heresy in the heavens, defiantly outside of Creation. The deniers must contort themselves to explain it away, as a missive from God, an illusion of the Devil, an evil omen, when all it means is that the stars are alive in a way no man yet understands – they are not pinholes in the paper firmament, infinitely turning on a set dial; they live, they are born, and they die. Kit is watching a star die right now, though he does not know it.

And he too is watched, from atop the hill by the moat bridge, where Ingram Frizer stands spinning his knife in his fingers, practising his stab. Frizer tries not to look at the figure in the meadow, its long, still shadow cut across the grass like a gnomon. He tells himself he cannot bear the sight of Christopher Marlowe, but that is not true. He cannot bear to look away.

As he spins and stabs, spins and stabs, he whispers:
"'See where my slave, the ugly monster Death,
Shaking and quivering, pale and wan for fear,
Stands aiming at me with his murdering dart,
Who flies away at every glance I give,
And when I look away, comes stealing on.
Villain, away and hie thee to the field!
I and mine army come to load thy bark
With souls of thousand mangled carcasses—
Look where he goes! But see, he comes again
Because I stay.'"
He reels around and thrusts his blade at the darkness.
Death takes a step backwards.

18 MAY 1593

Twelve days

❧❀❧

Not inferior to any of the former in Atheisme
and impiety, and equall to all in manner of
punishment, was one of our owne nation,
of fresh and late memory, called *Marlin*, by
profession a scholler, brought up from his youth
in the University of Cambridge, but by practise
a Play-maker, and a Poet of scurrility ...

THOMAS BEARD, *THE THEATRE OF GOD'S JUDGMENTS*, 1597

6

ON THE 18TH OF May 1593, a clerk of the Star Chamber
draws up the order for Christopher Marlowe's arrest, on
suspicion of treason, suspicion of heresy, suspicion of sodomy,
and a host of other charges besides. The least comes with a
sentence of years in prison. The worst, with death.

Swiftly, this document travels east across the city, from
Westminster to the Privy Court on Seething Lane, where
it passes from the hand of another clerk to the office of Sir
John Puckering, the Lord Keeper, who peruses it disinterest-
edly, grunts his approval and then hands it back, for delivery
unto the arresting bailiff. But before the document can reach
its final destination, it is intercepted by a man with a clean-
shaven face who, every morning, brings the Lord Keeper's
clerk a pinch of tobacco and then sends him outside to
smoke it. The clerk thus occupied, the man then half-sits on
a corner of his desk and scans through the outgoing letters,
never regarding any long enough for an average reader to
glean anything. But Robin Poley remembers every word.

Later, from his home in St Helen's Bishopsgate, Poley dis-
patches a message bound for Scadbury, which is received that
same night by Ingram Frizer. Walsingham has the message in
hand by midnight:

You have two dayes to make ready, use them well. They
will demand a bail.

Walsingham spends the following day closeted in his study, sweating over his accounts. He will say nothing to Kit until the last possible minute. First, he must scrape together enough gold to pay Kit's bail, which he can only pray shall be within his means. Year after year, the little reserve left to him by Uncle Francis dwindles. Already he owes money to some of his informants in London, whose eyes he can ill afford to lose, especially Robin Poley, especially now. He must rekindle certain urgent negotiations which Kit's arrival at Scadbury had put to a halt – that is, the business of acquiring a dowry, a wife.

Walsingham therefore devotes two hours to the composition of a love-letter of the tawdriest sort, comparing eyes to the green of the sea and hair to the gold of autumn wheat, a thing which leaves him feeling sullied, and therefore satisfied that it shall be effective. Visions of a lavish wedding arise: himself hand-in-hand with Lady Audrey Shelton, the Queen's beloved handmaiden. With her by his side, he'll step back into the light of grace. There shall be a seat in Parliament for him, perhaps even a knighthood. A respectable, comfortable life, such as was once ripped from his grasp.

Stepping out of his study at last with the finished letter in hand, Walsingham stumbles into Kit in the corridor. 'Your staff seem preoccupied,' Kit says, darkly. They have spoken little since the other night in the orchard.

Walsingham decides upon a half-truth. 'As it happens, I must go to Greenwich soon. Next week, for Whitsuntide.'

'You never said so.'

'It was not necessary. You are not the sum of my concerns, you know. My life was flowing along freely before you stepped in it.'

This lands like a slap. Kit winces and storms away to his room like a churlish boy. But Walsingham lingers long after he has gone, the letter temporarily forgotten, a vice of fear squeezing his chest, tighter every second.

He instructs his steward to keep Kit under watch for the rest of the day, but this turns out to be an unnecessary precaution, as Kit hardly leaves his room. By nightfall, everything is ready for the guards' arrival in the morning, as ready as can be expected.

Still, Walsingham cannot sleep. Three or four in the morning finds him back in his study, brooding over a message from Robin Poley that he should have destroyed days ago:

Youle find the services I offer convenient, I feare, in the dayes ahead.
Shal we not speake of figures yet?

Walsingham knows precisely what 'services' Poley means. Not that he can bring himself to name them, even silently. He tries, instead, to pray. He tries to see his own future again, the same as before, except that Kit is there too in one way or another, that dissolute, baseborn friend whose company his wife begrudgingly tolerates. But there is no present that could engender such a future. The nerves that might have fed this limb are dying, one by one.

One hand upon his shuddering heart, Walsingham begins to compose a reply to Poley's letter – slowly, to disguise the weakness in his hand, which comes and goes ever since his year in the Marshalsea:

What figure... must one paye... to sleepe sound at night forever...?

A knock comes at the door, and Walsingham tears the paper to shreds. He finds Ingram Frizer in the corridor, white-faced with anxiety, saying, 'Nick – Master Skeres is back from Greenwich, master. He says the men are coming for Master Marlowe. They're on their way.'

❧❀☙

Kit awakens at the bang of the door, opening his eyes just long enough to see Walsingham barge into his room, a candle in hand, calling, 'Get up!'

Kit closes his eyes again and exhales. He knows already why Walsingham is here, he can feel it.

Walsingham throws the casement wide open and stands on his toes to lean over the window ledge, his head swinging left and right. 'They are coming. They would have left Greenwich an hour ago. We must be ready.'

Kit remains pinned flat to the bed.

'Kit, do you understand me? They have a warrant this time.' Walsingham lifts Kit's bag out of a corner and begins emptying it onto the desk, one handful of papers at a time. 'Have you sorted your papers like I asked?'

'What?'

'Your papers, Kit – have you *sorted* them?'

'I cannot. I could not.'

'You will do it now, or I will do it myself. I will burn every scrap!'

Two women come to light the fire. Kit drags a chair to the hearth and Walsingham dumps the papers at his feet. In ten years or more Kit has discarded next to nothing. Good paper is a luxury. Most of his manuscripts contain several works altogether, one written verso and another recto, yet another picking up where an earlier work had ended. On one side of a page, he may have a piece of *Doctor Faustus* and on the other, a note copied from a forbidden book – one of the many forbidden books that Master Kett, Kit's tutor in divinity at

Cambridge, would slip him after lectures: books by Bruno, Algazel, Averroes, Maimonides; heretics, Mohammedans, Jews. 'Do not copy from this now,' Master Kett would say, every time, and every time Kit would copy page after page anyway, knowing he would never see those books again.

The Jesuit Stephens writes of texts in India knowne as <u>pooranas</u>, which trayce the historie of Man from thousands of yeeres before Adam & Eve, and showe our Earth to be far moore ancient than Christian reckoning would—

Kit balls this up and throws it into the fire.

That the moiety of so-called prophets were but jugglers and conie-catchers was well-knowne to the moslem scholers of olde: Al-Razi, that we call Rhazes, who wrote <u>Of the prophets' fraudulent trickes</u>—

Into the flames with it. Just like Master Kett – stoop-shouldered, soft-voiced, grubby-bearded Master Kett – they'd executed him, for heresy, the year after Kit took his degree: doused him in hot tar, rolled him into a ditch and burnt him alive.

'You should burn every word of it,' Walsingham says, from the window. 'Leave nothing for the vultures to pick over.'

'I cannot burn every word.' Kit now holds a single page of *Doctor Faustus*, representing a whole day of his life, a day spent at the kitchen table in Little Bedlam with Tom seated across from him, smiling as he'd watched Kit work:

…now, body, turn to ayre…
O soule, be changed into littel waterdroppes,
And fall into the ocean!…

On the back of this same page, after half a second of scanning, Kit finds the words:

God is but the rod of powerfull men; with such they beate us into submition.

'May I have a drink?' Kit says.

Walsingham looks upon him pityingly, as if he knows something terrible will soon happen, as certain as if it has already happened. He goes to the door and calls to someone outside, 'Whisky.'

In this same moment, Ingram Frizer stands upon the ramparts of Scadbury's old Norman watchtower – a place where he has never had cause or permission to venture before – poised and waiting to ring the old alarm bell which has been up here rusting through untold decades. He can see for miles: far beyond the woods, where the needled spire of the church in Chiselhurst blazes yellow against the pink dawn. Due north, upon the horizon, a faint cap of smoke broods over distant London.

Yesterday, just as Frizer was sitting down to supper, Nick had turned up with something urgent in his looks, that childhood code. Frizer has, over the years, walked away from dozens of meals for the sake of that look. Out in the yard, Nick began to explain, but with such a roundabout manner that even after several minutes Frizer still had no idea what they were talking about.

'I mean *Marlowe*, man!' Nick said. 'Christ, I thought you'd shower me with a thousand thanks!'

'You want *me* to stay in London?' Frizer blithered. 'With *Marlowe*?'

'The master asked me to do it, but marry, I cannot sit nurse to the big bugger. I have other business in London, if you catch my meaning.' He'd looked sly, meaning that he had coney-catching business: selling some poor fool or other a false deed, or a phantom horse, or counterfeit silver. Nick always has a scheme in the works; his father was the same way.

'It should only be for a few days,' Nick went on. 'A week at the most.'

'But what will the master say? Will he not be angry?'

Nick smiled strangely, cagily. 'Man, you should worry less and less every day about what the master thinks!' Frizer had been afraid to ask what he'd meant.

Betsy – confined, these days, to her bed, looking every day a little more like a foot swollen with gout – had merely bowed her head at the news of Frizer's imminent leave-taking, fumbling with a talisman of pig-iron that her mother had tied around her neck. 'Iron keeps the Devil out,' she'd explained, when she saw Frizer staring at it. 'Or, it keeps him in.'

Frizer could not disguise a wince. 'Well, you'll not need it, I reckon. I'll be gone, and taking my accursed hide with me.'

He'd started to leave, but Betsy stopped him, blurting out, 'Master Purcell said… Master Purcell said, there's nothing to be feared of them, anyway. The marks.'

Frizer could only gape at her, betrayed. He had never so much as met this Purcell, let alone allowed the charlatan to examine him.

Betsy went on, 'He told me that you should pray for forgiveness.' Her eyes glanced off Frizer's body, as if it were too sad, too shameful to behold head-on.

On the watchtower, Frizer struggles to light his pipe from a wind-tossed lantern. He never should have agreed to this. He has no business going to London, not with a wife in such condition. What shall he do, alone with Marlowe for days on end? He has not even redeemed himself from their last meeting as yet, having avoided the poet entirely this past week, only watching his comings and goings from a corner of the sentry-box. A part of him hopes that everything will go wrong today, that Marlowe will not be bailed and the last he'll ever see of the man will be as he is dragged into the Privy Court, and oblivion.

From the distance comes a low, irregular drumming, a heart beating out of time. Gradually it grows louder, closer, and Frizer straightens up like a hare, watching the edge of the woods. A flock of starlings explode out of the trees like gunpowder. A moment later, four riders swing onto the orchard pass, a trail of dust at their heels. The horses move at a steady gallop, becoming nervous, jangling silhouettes where the road curves sharply towards the house, spreading ever longer, leggier shadows upon the earth.

Transfixed, Frizer watches them come: so unrelenting, so furious, like a personification of the Inevitable. He thinks of Faustus when the Devil comes to collect his due, begging earth, air and sea to hide him, crying out to the indifferent stars as the fateful hour draws near:

'*Lente currite, noctis equi!*' Run slowly, horses of the night!

At last, he remembers to ring the bell.

Still kneeling at the hearth, Kit lifts his head at the sound of the alarm. Across the room, Walsingham too freezes and looks up at the ceiling. Together they wait for silence, through twelve strikes, a quickfire midnight knell. When the bell stops, Walsingham finishes off his whisky, slams the cup on the desk and charges across the room. He snatches up a handful of Kit's papers from the floor. 'Enough!'

'No, Thomas, stop!' Kit grabs his wrist. He cannot bear it, foolish as it is; he cannot bear the thought of every word he's ever written turning to smoke. *He* might as well turn to smoke. 'Please, let me hide them!'

'There's no time!'

The papers scatter. Kit falls to the floor, scrambling them together again, but the sight of a drawing stops him, having landed inches away from Walsingham's foot: a crude sketch of two men, one arse-up before the other, rutting like goats – a thing Tom had pressed into Kit's hand one night, years ago, as both a proposition and a jest, never intended to be treasured, a thing he ought never to have kept.

Kit looks up, realizing from Walsingham's reddening face that he has seen it too.

Before either can speak, someone bursts through the door unannounced, releasing a gust of air that scatters the papers all over again. Kit gathers up an armful and recoils, his back to the wall, facing the intruder: that scrawny, boyish fellow, a watchman or something of the sort, the unreserved ardour of whose admiration Kit has felt like a spider on his back all week long.

'They are here!' the sentry proclaims with childish urgency, and then stands chastened in his master's silence. His big eyes dart first to Kit, and then to the papers. Lastly, to the fire.

'Get the horses,' Walsingham says, through his teeth. His man blushes and bows effusively as he retreats, taking care, after some brief consideration, to close the door behind him.

Kit hugs the papers, rocks on his heels. Through every nerve he feels a surge, teeming up to the throat, to the eyes, till it bursts out of him at last, a miserable, shameful sob.

Walsingham kneels and takes hold of Kit's sleeves. 'There, now, stop it. That's enough. Kit – we must go.'

'Please take them for me! Carry them with your things, they'll never look!'

Walsingham bites his lip, relenting. 'I will carry them for you, ay? But only for today. And if anything should happen – if the worst should happen – I will destroy them.'

'I should never have come here!' Kit says. 'I should have run for Scotland, or France—'

'It would have done you no good. Look at me: the time to

run may come, but not yet. Now, no more of this blubbering, do you hear? They delight in pulling a woman out of us. Do not let them. From now on, whatever happens, you must be strong: you must be a man.'

Kit looks away. He has been told this a thousand times, by Baines, by his father, even by Tom, and always in this same offhand way, as if he should know instantly what it means. *Be Tamburlaine*, they might as well say. *Pretend.* For he is not strong. If they start to break bones, chop off fingers, stop his breath, surely he will say whatever he has to say to make them stop. They'll ask for names, like they always do – and he'll give them.

But such would be a perilous thing to confess. Especially to one whose name he might easily speak.

'Do you think they will hang me, Thomas?' Kit rasps.

'You?' Walsingham smiles. 'You'd break the rope.'

Kit feels such gratitude for that smile that he can only laugh.

Frizer stands on the gravel path beside Nick, the ivy-covered portico behind him, the foot of the moat bridge some hundred feet away. He tries to look solid, square. A little nearer to the bridge the two porters stand guard, guns shouldered. On the far side of the moat, the four riders wait in a patient row, faceless under their brimmed helmets, horses flicking their tails. No one has moved for an eternity.

Nick offers a coin. 'A groat says he picks up his skirt and flies.'

Frizer shakes his head. He cannot find his voice; his heart hammers as if at the beginning of a bear-baiting, just before the dogs are loosed.

'They had better hurry,' Nick murmurs, with a glance to the house. 'These fellows'll not wait forever...'

'They're burning papers,' Frizer whispers, startled at himself.

'What?'

'They're upstairs, burning papers.'

Nick chuckles. 'Oh-ho! There goes your *Tamburlaine!*'

Frizer stares at him in horror. But finally the doors of the house open, emitting first the master, then the steward and chamber-grooms. Marlowe steps out of the shadows behind the rest, wearing the same old suit he'd arrived in, which may have once been black but rain and time have turned a shade of mottled grey, the breast studded in mismatched buttons and slashed with vivid wounds of amaranth-red. The servants all take a half-step back, as if to make room for him.

Hands raised, sword twisting slackly at his side, the master walks to the middle of the moat bridge before the lead rider commands him to halt. Inaudibly, they speak. Now and then the master gestures in Marlowe's direction; now and then the rider nods or broadly shakes his head. There is something reminiscent of a transaction about it, like horse-traders enumerating the qualities of their stock.

When at last the master turns to lead the riders on, Nick blows a fart through his lips, disappointed that it all fell out so peaceably. Marlowe stands in the lane, stone-still, even as the riders surround him and dismount. The man in the lead produces a paper, reading from it loud enough for a word to carry here and there: 'Accused... name of... Majesty... treason... heresy... sodomy—'

'There is our cue,' Nick says. They move forward. The steward and grooms jog past, arms laden with bags of what must be the master's effects, followed by stable-hands, with horses enough for all. Frizer stops short of the guards' circle of horses, not sure how to breach it. Inside, one of the Council's rogues lifts a black bag into which Marlowe, much too tall to reach, obligingly bows his head. The guard gathers the bag at Marlowe's throat with a string, saying, 'This one has a reputation, is't not so?'

'Meek as a kitten,' says another, watching.

'And to think they said we'd need more men!' says the leader.

Marlowe's wrists are shackled, his back ramrod-straight, his hoodwinked head twisted in Frizer's direction. At the lead rider's prodding, he swings his leg over the big gelding as if to hop a garden gate, and then paws for reins before realizing there are none. The bag pulses in and out over his open mouth, a hint of teeth sucking the fabric. Panic stirs from a hub near the base of Frizer's spine, near to where his knife rests in its scabbard, as though it were the knife and not his body that just remembered what it feels like to be bound and gagged, to know not where the next hurt will come from.

A memory hisses in his ear: *Is this what you want?*

'Here.' The master takes a large object from the steward and shoves it into Frizer's arms: the same shoe-leather bag that Marlowe had brought with him to Scadbury.

'Have a care with that,' the master says, with a worried glance to the Council's men.

Frizer hugs the bag tight. All that he might hold in his arms, in this very moment: *Tamburlaine, Doctor Faustus, The Jew of Malta, The Massacre at Paris,* and much else besides that a frightened man might burn. Something within seems to radiate its own living heat, as if the fire were not yet finished with its contents.

An hour later, somewhere in the sheep-dotted hills north of Eltham, the master slows his horse and waits for Frizer to catch up. Frizer slides Marlowe's bag behind his back.

'Master Skeres assures me you are a fellow with discretion,' the master says, quietly, as they ride on together.

'Yes, master.' Frizer tries to say it like a discreet fellow would.

'He shall require your full attention,' the master says, with a nod up ahead to where Marlowe rides at the centre of the guards, his head bowed so low he seems almost asleep. 'Often, he knows not what is best for him. You must keep two eyes on him at all times.'

'Yes, master.'

'And when I ask for your discretion, Master Frizer, I mean that you are not to speak of matters which you do not understand. He will ask, certainly, but you will deny him. You will plead ignorance. That is why I have agreed to let you fill this position, you see – because of your ignorance.'

Frizer nods, for 'tis true he feels hopelessly ignorant just now. He knows nothing; he understands nothing. Marlowe *is* the master's friend, and their purpose is to help him, is it not? That *is* why they are going with him to London – to help him?

'Well,' the master says, even softer, 'all of this may be moot. We shall see whether they set a bail. If not... I may have another use for you.'

But this other use, he does not explain. He spurs his horse, trotting up to ride alongside the Privy Council's men.

7

BLINDED, KIT ONLY KNOWS they have reached London by the savoury-sweet scent of burning rosemary, a safe-guard against plague-spreading miasmas; much good has it done. The deeper they move into the city, the heavier the smell becomes, overpowering even the usual scents of forge and charnel-house, muckheap and sump, stable and slaughterhouse. None of the familiar city noise can be heard over the chopping of hooves to Kit's left and right, only birdsong, as if the whole of London's population had been transformed into chittering starlings, cackling gulls.

But not long after they've crossed the bridge, a low roar rises in the distance: the sound of voices chanting in unison. For every turn of a corner it swells louder, until suddenly the noise is deafening and Kit realizes that the guards are leading him straight towards an angry mob, dozens strong.

'Hang him! Hang him! Hang him!'

The riders stop, dismount. From the left, a hand grasps at Kit's restraints and a man barks, 'Down, down!' to no avail. From the right, a fist grasps the tabs of Kit's doublet and pulls until he tips sideways, scrambling for balance, too late. The landing knocks the breath out of him.

'There's no need for that!' Walsingham says.

Kit is grabbed again, hoisted upright, given no time to find his own footing ere there are arms looped through his shackled arms, marching him into the rabble.

'Thomas!' His own voice sounds shrill. 'Thomas, what is happening?'

The buffeting begins: an elbow or a fist to his shoulder, his chest, his cheek. 'Traitor!' someone snarls, and spits. 'Atheist!' Legs try to trip him up but the crush around him prevents his falling. At last, a gate creaks and someone shoves Kit through, where he stands dazed and panting for half a second ere he is tugged forward again, into what must be the courtyard.

He knows the Privy Court well. First a stone gatehouse, through which they have just passed, and now the yard, a tight square of gravel and starveling weeds walled in on two sides by long, half-timber wings. At the back, the brick courthouse, crowned with gables as steep as fangs, its doors surmounted by a jawless stone skull: an effigy, or so 'tis said, of Wat Tyler, who spat in the face of Richard II. A Canterbury martyr; a London bogeyman.

'May I not speak with the Lord Keeper?' Walsingham whispers, as they enter the courthouse's echoing great hall. Invisible now are the chessboard floor of red and white tiles, the coloured-glass windows, the oak pillory, with chains bolted to the floor. Straight ahead spans the looming magistrates' dais; above that, an obligatory portrait of the Queen, attired in cloth of gold, strangling a serpent in her right fist.

Kit senses that the crowd inside is at least as large as the mob without, though more subdued. Their whispers rush like blood in the ears, becoming murmurs of alarm as Kit is thrust through their midst.

Someone says, 'Is that *him*?'

A gavel cracks three times. Perhaps they will put him to trial in this very moment, charge and sentence him within a single breath.

'The court calls John Penry.'

The murmurs swell up louder than before, and the gavel cracks again for order as Kit's captors rush him past the judge's voice, through another door and thence into silence, twenty feet, thirty feet. At last, he is jerked to a halt.

Still behind him, Walsingham's voice breaks above a whisper. 'Let me speak to the Lord Keeper. I *demand* to speak to the Lord Keeper!'

Old hinges creak. Kit is pushed forward; the hinges creak again, now behind him. They have breached the rust-coloured iron gate at the far end of the corridor that leads from the great hall to the courthouse's busy inner hive. Kit has been here a hundred times in his former service to the Council, but never once has he ventured beyond this gate.

'Who in hell is John Penry?' Kit whispers, without knowing whether Walsingham will hear him.

'A heretic,' Walsingham whispers back, from the other side of the gate. 'Puritan. Welsh.'

'I thought they were here for me. All those people.'

A grunt. 'Now you flatter yourself!'

Nearby, Kit's captors exchange words with some sort of gatekeeper. For the second time today, he hears his charges spoken aloud: 'Suspicion of buggery, suspicion of heresy, suspicion of treason. Suspicion of libel against her Majesty and the Church of England—'

'Kit,' Walsingham says, and Kit wonders if these shall be the last words he'll ever hear him say. 'You are a damned hero – let them not forget that. Remind them of Paris. Remind them of Babington!'

Upstairs, a hand grips the hood in a clump close to Kit's hair and pulls it backwards over his chin and lips. He must tug his head down to free himself. A camphor candle burns less than a foot away from his light-starved eyes, burning his nostrils. The room wherein he sits is only large enough to contain a table and two chairs. But upon second glance this is not a room at all, only a cell arranged out of heavy green curtains that skim the floor. Daylight seeps through just above the curtain rods, exposing a ceiling carved with birds and beasts, partly obscured by a thick layer of whitewash.

Outside there are footsteps, muffled voices. The curtains part behind Kit, cutting a wedge of light into the space. One man goes out as another comes in and stands close at Kit's back, like an axe over his neck.

Please God, not him. Anyone but him.

'Christopher Marlowe,' a man says, muffled. He takes the seat across the table, taking a moment to smooth out the wrinkles in his white linen plague-mask. A square forehead, sandy hair, small, squinting eyes – Kit knows him not.

The man sets down blank paper, a leather slipcase, a glass inkwell and a quill cut to a fine point. Only once these items are arranged to his liking does he look up, with an air of forced cordiality surely designed to disarm. 'Or Marley, is it? Morley?'

Kit coughs to find his voice. 'Marley, really. In London they call me Marlowe.'

The man pinches a set of thick spectacles to his nose, further obscuring his already half-hidden face, the lenses magnifying his narrow eyes. He stabs the inkwell with his quill. 'And Marlin? Merlin?'

'When I was in Paris,' Kit says, a subtle reminder of services rendered, not that anyone at Seething Lane should need any. There was a time when some would come out from behind the iron gate to greet him whenever he'd arrived at the Privy Court, sore-arsed and exhausted after the three days' journey from Cambridge. He would hand over Baines's letters and receive letters to deliver in return, and with them, sometimes, a slice of leftover Easter simnel or a half-dozen biscuits wrapped in paper, the work of this or that fellow's wife. Such kindness had seemed strange to him, coming from these men, but those who deal in cruelty also know how to use kindness, how to wield it like a weapon. Feed a stupid, hungry boy enough cake and he'll gobble up any poison put before him.

At last, the man begins to write, a task to which he commits himself entirely, head bent close to the page: 'Marlin... Merlin. Master Marley, are you acquainted with a Thomas Kyd of London, gentleman, son of John Kyd of London, gentleman?'

He has uttered this while still writing and without looking up. Kit trips over his own tongue, at last managing, 'Ay.'

'Do you, or do you not, reside in a lodging-house by the Leathersellers' Hall in St Helen's parish, Bishopsgate?'

'I did. For a short while.'

'You lived there with Thomas Kyd?'

'Yes.'

'For how long?'

'From October. But I left—weeks ago, I left—'

'You shared quarters with Thomas Kyd?'

'Yes.'

'Shared a bed with Thomas Kyd?'

'No, no. Separate beds.'

'Shared a workspace with Thomas Kyd? A desk, or a table?'

'Ay.'

'Would you recognize Thomas Kyd's handwriting if I showed you a sample now?'

'I suppose so.'

'Have you ever intentionally given Thomas Kyd papers of yours, or sent letters to him?'

'No.' Kit senses his left knee jittering under the table and forces it to stop. It starts again.

'Have you ever heard Thomas Kyd profess to deny the deity of Jesus Christ, and the Resurrection of His mortal flesh?'

Kit gasps out a laugh, unthinking. 'No!'

'Have you, yourself, ever given utterance to such a denial, in company where Thomas Kyd may have been present?'

HESSE PHILLIPS

Kit shakes his head. The Council's man continues filling up his notes with scribbled shorthand, or possibly code. Kit can make out almost nothing beyond the candleflame, which twists spindle-like in a draught. When Kit looks up again, he finds his interrogator's needling eyes fixed upon him in a wordless threat, a look that every child knows. 'Nay, never,' Kit says.

The Council's man stands his quill in the inkwell and folds his hands, passing his gaze over Kit's person as if to step over a carcass in the gutter. He says, 'Are you aware that Thomas Kyd is currently under the custody of the warden of the Marshalsea Prison?'

With only half a second to decide, Kit chooses to lie. 'No, I was not aware.'

'Why, Master Marley, do you imagine Master Kyd would be in prison at this time?'

'I have no idea.' At least this is no lie.

The man briefly lowers his gaze to the slipcase and then lifts it again, as if to offer Kit a final chance at some unspoken remedy. At last, he removes one item from the case: a worn and yellowed sheet of paper, covered in large, schoolboyish italic lettering that Kit does not, at first, recognize as his own:

We call God Everlasting, Invisible, Incommutable, Incomprehensible, Imortall, etc... But if Jesus Christ, even he, which was borne of Marie, was God, then so shall he be a visible God, comprehensible & mortall, which is not counted God with me.

The man taps the paper twice. 'This document was recovered from your former lodgings, Marley. Do you recognize it?'

Kit shakes his head.

'This is a passage copied from a book. An unusual book: *The Fall of the Late Arian*. These are, in fact, the words of that self-same Arian, spoken in defence of his own heresy. In vain, of course. If memory serves, the man was burnt at the stake.' He raises his eyebrows. 'I myself have seen but one copy of this book, in the private collection of the heretic Kett, late Master of Divinity at Cambridge.'

Kit realizes that he is chewing his lip. A pause descends, long enough that he feels pressured to speak, despite having nothing to say. 'I—I know not—'

'Do you know this book, Marley?'

'No.'

'But you were at Cambridge, Marley. You studied divinity there, with Kett.'

'I did, but—'

'How do you imagine Master Kyd, who has never left London in all his life, might have obtained a copy of this book? Because if this paper is not yours, Marley, then it must belong to him.'

'I would not say that.'

'That the paper is not yours?'

'That the paper is *his*.'

'Then whose could it be?'

'Other men have lived in that house. They – we – all of us – we come through there briefly, stay perhaps a few months at the most—'

'I'm afraid you will have to give us a *name*, Marley. A man who protects his friends as he protects himself is, under most circumstances, truly only protecting himself.' He leans closer, the shadow of his spectacles arching over his brows, and Kit clamps his jaws together. Already – they ask him for names already?

'Master Kyd did not hesitate to tell us that the paper is yours,' the man says. 'What can we do but take his word, in the absence of better intelligence?'

''Tis not mine,' Kit blurts out, 'nor is it Kyd's. I know not whose it might be, I know not the names of all the men that lived there before me; when I was there it was only Kyd and myself. But the paper is not mine, neither can it be Kyd's, because Kyd was trained as a scrivener and I know his hand – this is *not* his hand. If I knew more, I would tell you.'

Silence. The little eyes search Kit's; God knows what they find in them. Eventually the man drops his gaze, this time to his own notes. He writes something with great flourish, separating each stroke of the pen so that Kit may hear a word, or any one of several words, take shape out of the eight or nine distinct scratches. He cannot help but picture one word in particular blazing on the paper in block letters: *LIES*.

⋘❋⋙

Kit has been gone an hour. With his back to the wall and a sandalwood-scented pomander pressed to his face, Walsingham anxiously watches the trial of John Penry unfold: a chaotic affair, despite having a far smaller audience than is typical, made up mostly of clergymen and their bodyguards, who stamp and fume when cued. Bullish, shrill-voiced John Whitgift, Archbishop of Canterbury, presides as justice but might just as well be prosecutor. Penry – a much younger man than Walsingham had imagined, perhaps no older than Kit – stands with his wrists chained to the dock, attired in a filthy prison smock. For years, the Council has suspected Penry of distributing Puritanical pamphlets, but the archbishop makes no mention of these, only of a single, rambling, unfinished letter to her Majesty seized in a recent raid on Penry's home, from which Whitgift sneeringly reads aloud: "'… Your Majesty may well consider what good the Church of God hath gotten at your hands, otherwise as *great troubles* are likely to come as ever were in the days of your sister Mary…!'"

Hovering over it all, the Queen gazes haughtily out of her portrait, a gasping snake coiled helplessly about her tight, pale fist, the faintest trace of a smile upon her lips.

A man approaches and leans against the wall by Walsingham's shoulder with a sigh, as if to throw himself down in the grass on a lazy summer's day. For half a minute, Walsingham and he watch the trial, unspeaking. Then the man slides closer to murmur, with an air of schoolyard gossip, 'They wanted him for heresy, but the document amounts only to sedition. Under the Act of Uniformity, he should suffer no worse than lifelong imprisonment. Nevertheless, the Council seeks a penalty of death. Whitgift would slaughter three hundred virgins to see him noosed.'

Briefly, Walsingham slips into doubt. He lowers the pomander to say, '*Marlowe?*'

'Oh no.' The man smiles, a charming smile. He nods at the crowd. 'Penry.'

The man's face is clean-shaven. Walsingham has never seen Robin Poley with a beard. It affords him an illusion of youth, though he must be at least forty by now. Still slender, well-built yet slight, only a hint of silver in his golden hair. Handsome, and knows it too, with his dark blue, feline eyes, his strong, dimpled chin.

'I have something for you,' Poley says. 'For Master Marlowe, in fact.'

He unhooks an object from his belt and offers it with a hand of only four fingers, the ring finger amputated just below the first joint. Walsingham accepts: a round, silver flask with a copper cartouche on one side, inscribed with a familiar mark: Tom's mark, of the running hare.

'It was found at his quarters,' Poley says, 'but 'tis of no use to our intelligencers.'

The flask is still a quarter full. 'If I give him this, he will question how I came by it,' Walsingham says.

'Question he may. Let him take it as proof that no man on earth is more fit to help him than you. 'Tis better if he fears you a little, marry. He'll be more obedient that way.' Poley waits for silence as the mob across the room lets out a cry of outrage, and then: 'I assume he has made you promises already, has he not?'

Walsingham frowns. 'Promises? Of what?'

'His silence, of course. "If they take me, I swear never to breathe your name, no matter what beastly things they do to me—" Has he said that yet?'

Walsingham looks away, feeling a pinch somewhere, just behind his heart. 'No, he has not.'

'Well, perhaps he knows better than to make impossible vows,' Poley says. 'Or perhaps he is afraid to put the thought in your head...'

'Is there something else you want?'

'You have not told him that Baines is in London, I suppose,' Poley says, his expression that of one withholding a delightful secret. 'If he knew, I doubt he would have come so quietly as they say he did. Sooner or later, he will discover it on his own, and then you'll have some new trouble on your hands. I have not seen Baines about the court since last week, but they keep him close. You will find him in Newgate Without, at the Saracen's Head, dining on the Council's penny.'

'Whatever Baines has against Kit is but hearsay, hardly enough to convict.'

A chuckle. 'In your uncle's days, that would have been true.' Poley gestures broadly over the scene across the hall, rows of backs turned to the centre like greyhounds cornering a fox. 'This trial is part of a crusade, you see – Archbishop Whitgift's holy crusade, which shall not end until England is swept clean of all those who worship not at her Majesty's altar. Puritans, papists, atheists – Penry, Marlowe – to the Council, they are the same. And today's sentencing shall set a worrisome precedent. For, the law and the statutes be damned, John Penry shall swing ere the month is out, and on what evidence? – a single piece of paper, and hearsay.' He turns a malignant smile on Walsingham. 'But as for Penry's friends, they are luckier than you, you see, for they are already dead. Nothing he says in the torture room can harm them. They look down on us mortals from Great Stone Gate.'

'No doubt you imagine them to be in good company,' Walsingham scoffs, weakly. He has often wondered how Robin Poley must feel every time he crosses London Bridge, passing beneath the skull of Anthony Babington.

Poley's smile does not waver. He is made of water; every lance passes straight through those depthless eyes of his, leaving no wounds. 'We will speak again soon, I expect,' he says. About to leave, he stops, turning back to whisper, 'Best of luck to you at Greenwich. I hear Robert Cecil gifted Lady Audrey with a replica of his own cock, in goatskin, to keep her wet when he is away. But you know how gossip can be.'

He bares his white teeth, slithers away.

'They're not here for *him*, are they?' Frizer says, to Nick.

The crowd across the street has not let up for a minute. Spurred on by the earnest preaching of some firebrand curate (who had ranted on about predestination for a good ten minutes), the mob has found their voice again, still with nothing to say but, 'Hang him!'

Nick makes a doubtful noise, but then whistles, loud enough to draw the attention of one or two fellows on the fringes of the mob. He yells, 'Who're you here for?' and a woman lowers the cloth over her face to answer, 'John Penry, the Devil himself!' at which Frizer's heart enters a strange war of relief versus resentment, as if offended that Marlowe is not devil enough for them.

The master's other servants left their party near Greenwich. Now Frizer and Nick stand alone on Seething Lane, holding the four remaining horses by the reins and sweating in the sun. Tirelessly, Nick expounds upon a new scheme he has heard about somewhere, a method for fleecing well-moneyed gulls out of their inheritances. But Frizer only pretends to listen, his gaze buried in Marlowe's bag. If he could put his back to Nick for a minute or two, he could take a peek inside, perhaps scan a page…

Nick punches him in the arm. 'Just open it, man! What, are you afraid the master will put you over his knee?'

'Oh, leave it alone!' Frizer whines. 'You with your coney-catching! You care not for anything but knavery, do you?'

Nick takes no offence. 'Go on, I'll not tell. Probably the big bugger'll not come back for it anyway.'

'You cannot know that.'

Nick hooks a thumb at the gatehouse across the street, whispering, 'They would pay a *fortune* for that bag in there, I'll bet. If we brought it to the right men, by God…!'

Frizer squeezes in between the horses, too narrow a space for Nick. Nick makes no effort to chase him, leaning over the saddle of his horse to say, 'You know, I could *make* you give it to me, if I wanted to.'

Frizer feels a shiver, in spite of himself. Every now and then, Nick looks on him with these stranger's eyes, their stare as still as the centre of a wheel. It was with this same stare that Nick had told Frizer one night, after several drinks, that 'The quickest way to kill a man is to stick him in the eye. Not even a whimper. Like blowing out a candle.'

Frizer lifts the bag higher on his chest. 'I know,' he says, deepening his voice.

Nick takes a glance to the sky, seeming to consider well what he will say, then leans closer still. 'Listen, man – all *this*, this is nothing. I'm not even *here*. I've got two feet planted in the world as it will be a month from now, and you know what I see?' He grins. 'I see many changes, for you and for me.'

Either Nick has lost his mind or Frizer has. 'What do ye mean by that?' Frizer says.

Nick's grin wanes, turning cagey again. 'Ah, nothing!' He waves a hand. 'Nothing but: be patient, do your part, make me proud. But never doubt we'll *both* be coney-catching by June.'

Something about these words stands the hairs at Frizer's neck on end. He looks across the street, espying two men fighting their way through the crowd: one is the master, clutching his pomander to his face like a charm; the other towers over every head, conspicuously hatless in a world of identical brown Sunday caps, his mop of curly hair the same colour as dried blood. The master must have posted bail. Frizer had thought Marlowe and the master might look relieved, but neither one of them does.

They approach, Marlowe with his head slightly bowed, in the peculiar posture of one for whom the roof of the world hangs too low. Without so much as a glance to Frizer, he reaches for the bag and murmurs, 'I'll take that,' but the master very nearly slaps his hand.

'Not *here*, by God! You want to keep it or not?'

Marlowe crosses his arms, scolded. In daylight, and up close, 'tis clear that his eyes are not black as Frizer had originally thought. They are, in fact, the very deepest shade of brown, as deep as bog oak. There is something faintly animal about them all the same. They seem capable of seeing in the dark.

The master turns to Frizer and speaks quietly, firmly. 'From now on, every day, you shall bring Master Marlowe to this place. He will go inside, and may be gone several hours, but you shall wait for him here, as long as it takes. Afterwards, you shall see him back to your lodgings. You'll do nothing else. Go nowhere else. *Every day.* Until you hear from me.'

8

THE BAIL WAS AS high as Walsingham had feared. Worst of all was the moment he'd watched a spotty-faced clerk write his name in a ledger beside Kit's, as surety and bond: *Tho: Walsingehamm.* 'Tis on paper now, their entanglement, as binding as marriage.

He keeps the flask hidden from Kit as best he can, stuffed uncomfortably into his waistband as they ride north, through streets deserted of all but a few miserable-looking, masked creatures, scavenging the plague-fires for rosemary and kindling. On the way, Kit describes what little he'd seen of his interrogator's face: the yellow hair, the squinting eyes, the spectacles. It can only be Thomas Phelippes, who was one of Uncle Francis's best men back in the old days, a master of ciphers and codes, speaker of some fourteen languages. No ordinary spy. He was among a lucky few who had spent no time at all in prison after Uncle Francis died, but in fact found his fortunes much improved, as surely he hopes to see them improved again by delivering Kit. A sly fox, with the heart of a worm.

'Well,' Walsingham murmurs, mindful of his voice carrying, 'they have not held you. That is a piece of good news. Neither have they charged you with anything but suspicion.'

'But they knew the paper was *mine*, Thomas,' Kit says, his eyes narrow above the line of his plague-mask.

"Tis a piece copied from a book, as you say – the words are not your words. There's no proof of ill intent.'

Kit laughs bitterly at this. Ever since he'd emerged from behind the iron gate at the Privy Court, he has not met Walsingham's gaze for more than a second.

He says, 'There's one question that I cannot put out of mind: what brought them to the house in the first place? Whether they came looking for Kyd or for me, they had to have a reason for coming. Someone had to make a report, a complaint—'

'Anyone might have done that,' Walsingham snaps. 'Did you not, just two weeks ago, put living men on the public stage and rub them together like a wanton boy with his sister's dolls? Or do I misremember?'

Kit bows his head, stewing in silence. He growls, 'Do you think I am so stupid?' and heels his horse, trotting on ahead.

Walsingham rankles – whether at himself or at Kit, he could hardly say. He is deep in this lie now, about Baines. But sometimes, the best way to protect Kit Marlowe is to lie to him.

They arrive at Bishopsgate: an arched gateway set into London Wall like the façade of a derelict fortress, providing passage north to Shoreditch, Spitalfields, Norton Folgate. Even now, the gatehouse guards are inspecting a fly-buzzing cart bound for the grave pits outside the city, holding cloths to their faces as they peer beneath a stained, flesh-coloured tarpaulin. The braziers burning around the dry fountain in the square barely cover the stench, a putrid muddle of fetor and sweetness that Walsingham had come to know well, sitting by Tom's deathbed at St Bartholomew's Hospital.

Across the street stands the Inn-in-the-Wall, a five-storey stack of half-timber jetties, all bowed slightly with the settling of centuries. Inside a passage large enough to admit horse and rider into the inn-yard together, a doggish little man with a handkerchief wadded over his mouth awaits them. He must have received Walsingham's letter sent yesterday, though he is

HESSE PHILLIPS

discreet enough not to mention it. The landlord of the Inn-in-the-Wall is among the longest serving of Walsingham's many informants, inherited from Uncle Francis.

'From inside, I warrant you, there's hardly a trace of the smell,' the landlord says cheerily, leading them into the yard. 'And from your usual room, Master Walsingham, 'tis undetectable!'

Walsingham's usual room sits on the fifth and highest floor, well removed from prying neighbours, though not entirely, it must be said, from the whiff of death. 'Not one single case of contagion have we had!' the landlord boasts as he opens the shutters, throwing light upon the monkish little room's only form of adornment, above the desk: the same wall-painting one may find clumsily reproduced from a stencil in every public house in the kingdom, showing the Queen enthroned. In this case the face is subtly, alarmingly crooked, the image candle-stained at the base, as if she were rising out of black smoke. Many a night here, Walsingham has sat up in bed and stared at her white face like a child at a shadow, terrified to be caught thinking of ways to cover her up.

Just as the landlord is extolling the cleanliness of the sheets, an explosion sounds in the distance, causing Frizer to clasp Marlowe's bag to his chest like a shield. The landlord waves it off. 'Ah, 'tis only the gun foundry on Houndsditch, testing the wares! Happens no more than once, possibly twice a day...'

Kit moves to the window, his shoulders blocking out the daylight as solidly as a door.

'No bedmates, I presume?' the landlord asks, sweating at Walsingham's side.

'No, no bedmates – the same, friend, as if I occupied it myself.'

Kit remains at the window. Suppose he is taken in by the view, which spans clear beyond London Wall, over gabled rooftops and stony church towers, founts of black smoke and clumps of nodding trees. From here, it would be almost possible to spit on

Hog Lane, Norton Folgate, were doleful Bedlam Hospital not standing in the way. Perhaps Walsingham should have prepared Kit for this, though it had never occurred to him that Kit may find it strange, or even sinister, that Walsingham should have a 'usual' room practically overlooking Little Bedlam. Their every interaction is now tainted with a lie to which Walsingham cannot bring himself to admit. Poley is right, of course: Kit will learn the truth about Baines sooner or later, if he is not certain of it already, and from that point on he shall trust Walsingham less and less; he'll become reckless, frightened. Vengeful. Guilt is what Walsingham ought to feel, and yet all he feels is anger – anger that Kit should dare think him a liar, even though he is one. Is he not the same man who had pushed for Baines's arrest, and had fought to see him exiled? Is he not the one who protects Kit far better than Tom ever did, or ever could?

If, one day, Dick Topcliffe should wrap Kit Marlowe's head in a rag and pour water over his face, or bend his body backwards until the spine breaks, or hang him from the wrists until his lungs collapse and his hands turn grey and his fingernails flake off, what name will he cry out to save himself? What will he say? He could say anything. The truth matters not in the torture room. He could say, *It was* he *who led me astray, it was* he *who put the Devil in my heart, it was* he *who taught me to hate the Queen, to hate her church, to plot against her very life – it was Thomas Walsingham!*

When Kit turns around, Walsingham feels a look of guilt settle indelibly upon his face, as if caught in the act of a crime.

❧✳❧

The first trace of dusk finds Kit at the bar in the inn's low-ceilinged common room, drinking cup after cup of watered-down ale. A child's drink, but it keeps the sweats and tremors at bay. Kit can hardly think straight when sober; at least, he can hardly recognize the thoughts as his own. But he must not let Walsingham smell drink on him, not if he wants the truth.

Eventually, Walsingham enters from the yard as if he has been looking everywhere for Kit, announcing himself with one of his world-weary sighs. 'Come outside and talk with me.'

'You are leaving?'

''Tis late, Kit. The way to Greenwich is not safe at night.'

Kit could confront him now. Walsingham is all but begging to have it over with. But all Kit truly desires is for Walsingham to stay: tonight, and the next night, and the next. 'Did you stay here when Tom was at St Bartholomew's?' Kit asks.

Walsingham nods. 'Three nights.' Just this much is new information, never offered before: that Tom had taken three days to die.

'I keep things from you because it will do you no good to know them,' Walsingham murmurs. 'It will only bring you pain. If you had seen him, believe me, it would haunt you. 'Tis better that you move on—'

'You think *that* is what angers me? Because you lied about Tom?'

'I have not lied about that, Kit. I've only held my tongue.' In the sliver of space between their shoulders ice forms, unbearably, untouchably cold.

'To hell with you,' Kit says. He slams the cup down and storms out into the yard, under a lid of amber-tinted sky. The fat man waits upon his master at the inn's gate, holding two horses by the bridles. He nods at Kit. Kit does not nod back.

Walsingham comes up at Kit's heels. 'A fine trick this is, coming from you! You have lied to *me*, Kit, need I remind you! You keep such secrets from me that I might rightly say I hardly know ye!'

'Baines is back,' Kit snarls, but as soon as the words are out a measure of strength leaves him too, seeing guilt come over Walsingham's face, a silent confession.

Still, infuriatingly, he refuses to submit. 'Kit... how can you be so certain?'

'Because I have seen him with my own eyes, *my eyes*, which you made me doubt!'

'You, with more whisky in your brains than blood, you *should* doubt your damned eyes – you would be a fool not to!'

Kit raises his fists, wishing he could punch through a door, smash out a window, if only to prove the world exists exactly as he sees it. But Walsingham recoils in fright, and all at once Kit remembers himself: that wretched creature who, not so much as a month after Tom was taken to Newgate Prison, had slunk into the nearest tavern and effectively never came out again.

'Kit...' Walsingham speaks with his hand outstretched, as if to soothe a wild horse. 'This does ye no good. Now you are afraid, you are angry. Neither feeling shall be of any use to ye. You must carry on as if Baines were a thousand miles away, or else you will stumble, you will undo everything that I do for you.'

'Where is he?' Kit says. 'He must be somewhere in London. Where?'

'Ha! I have no inkling of where he is, and if I did, heaven knows I would not tell *you*.' Walsingham comes forward, bravely it seems, to set a hand on Kit's arm. 'Be patient. Let me work. I will not let you go to prison. I will get you out of the country first. Now, look, I hesitated to give this to ye' – he reaches for something tucked under his doublet – 'but, well, it belongs to you. I acquired this for ye today, at the Privy Court. Take it.'

Kit stares, disbelieving, at the silver flask. Liquid shifts inside as he takes it in his hand. Tom's sigil, the hare in flight, glows copper beneath his thumb.

'You must trust me,' Walsingham says. 'You must do as I say. Above all, you must obey the terms of your release. Remember, if they find you outside London Wall, or if you fail to make your daily appointment at the Privy Court, they shall mark ye a fugitive, and that will truly be the end of you.' His touch alights on

Kit's arm again, like the weight of a bird. Whatever they have been to one another until this day is slipping further away every second. Kit can smell the end coming like the scent of rain.

'If things go badly,' Kit says, without having planned to, 'if it happens, Thomas—'

'Do not even think of it.' Walsingham steps back and starts to fidget with his gloves, without putting them on. 'There's no need for you to think of that, because it will not happen, ay?'

Kit does not press him, glad to have been interrupted. He had been about to say, *If the worst happens, I will protect you, to my last breath.* But Walsingham would never trust such a promise from him anyway; it would only make him doubt him all the more.

'I really must go,' Walsingham says, putting on his gloves at last. 'At Greenwich, I will plead your case however I can. To the Queen herself, if I am lucky. The entire Council shall be there; I could speak with the Lord Keeper, or the archbishop, even—'

'The Council threw you in a damp cell!'

'Well, yes, but I remain civil with them. One must often be civil with one's enemies. You never did learn that, Kit; it would have served ye well.'

Kit lifts one hand from his side little more than an inch, finding Walsingham's gloved fingers. At first it seems they will shake hands as if at the end of a businesslike meeting, but neither man lets go; they stare at one another, Kit wondering what sort of heart Walsingham's breast contains, if it softens to look on him, if it holds him in any way when they are apart.

'We will see one another again,' Walsingham says, as if seeing doubt in Kit's looks. He turns to go, and despite everything Kit must cross his arms to keep from reaching out, wanting to grasp him by the collar, pull him close and offer him anything, anything he desires, so long as he does not leave.

Too loud, Kit says, '"Out of the country," you said. Where? How?'

'Let me worry for that.' Walsingham inclines his head towards the room at the top of the stairs. 'Go now and look to your papers. Frizer has them.'

From halfway up the stairs, Kit watches Walsingham and the fat man depart through the gate, a final flick of a horsetail ere they disappear from view. He lowers his gaze to the flask in his hand, which Tom had given him after the premiere of *Tamburlaine Part Two*: 'If y'are going to drink whisky all day long, at least do it in fashion.' Kit smiles – for one second, Tom is alive. But only a second.

He unplugs the cap. Warm, over-sweet whisky, the same rotgut he'd been drinking the night before the Council's rogues took Kyd, blazes down his throat like a purge. A spark of liveliness comes into his step as he climbs the stairs, and he must remind himself to approach the door to the room quietly, so as not to alert his strange companion. Ingram Frizer – what sort of name is that? And that stare of his, so unnerving, like the way a dog or a child stares. Kit never should have left him alone with his papers.

Kit presses his ear to the door. No sound at first. But after a moment of listening, the faintest patter of speech becomes audible. One voice, as in prayer.

Breath held, Kit turns the latch just enough to crack the door, squinting through the inch-wide gap. Frizer sits cross-legged on the floor beneath the window's fading light, his doublet removed, his shirtsleeves rolled up. Before him lie two neat, slender stacks of papers. He is whispering; Kit hears only consonants. When he finishes a page, he moves it to the stack on the right and straightens the corners with a proprietary sort of tenderness, like a woman finger-combing the hair of a child who is decidedly not her own.

Kit thrusts the door open. Frizer wheels about and freezes, his face whitening from crown to chin. Kit's bag lies open on the bed, papers spilling from its mouth, violated.

Frizer skitters backwards, scattering papers under his heels. 'No, I pray you—I was—I was only—'

Kit snatches him by a fistful of hair, readying his flask as a bludgeon. 'You busy little cunt! What were you looking for?'

'Nothing, I swear!'

'Who employs ye, the Council? Did Baines send you?'

'The Council? I am no spy, ye lunatic! I only wanted to see—I wanted to see—'

'See what?'

'*Tamburlaine*! I wanted to see *Tamburlaine*!'

Only now does Kit notice a strange mark in the side of Frizer's neck, at the sight of which some animal impulse in himself shrinks away, releasing him. Frizer seems to know precisely what Kit has seen, clutching at his neck as he clambers to his feet. It is a scar, a thin white line collaring the throat halfway, like a botched attempt at murder. And it is not the only scar. Frizer's arms, each exposed to the elbow, are tiger-striped, front and back, in scars: age-whitened, stretched thin and broad with his body's growing, like ice pulled apart in spring.

A child, Kit realizes. *He must have been a child.*

Frizer wets his lips. He draws a short knife from behind his back. It trembles in his hand, a bright blur of steel. '*Never* call me that again, do ye understand? Call me that again and I'll cut out your God-damned tongue!'

Kit cannot remember what he'd called Frizer just now. He cannot remember a single word spoken since he came into the room. But between Frizer's ears, the word pulses like blood from a wound: *cunt, cunt, cunt, cunt, cunt.*

9

MARLOWE SAYS, 'I'M VERY sorry.' Nothing else. And then, as if it were the most natural thing in the world, he kneels and begins gathering up his papers with solemn concentration, as if to gather leaves off a grave.

Several seconds pass ere Frizer realizes, with a start, that he still has the knife in hand. He backs away to sheathe it, that evil word still beating in the back of his head, but ever-fainter: *cunt, cunt, cunt, cunt, cunt.*

On the floor, Marlowe continues his work in deafening silence. Soon, Frizer grows so uncomfortable watching him that he too squats down and collects a few pages into an untidy heap.

'Let me help.'

'No, I have it.'

'I ought to help.'

'No, marry. No.'

Frizer hovers by the door in anguish, trying not to stare. Marlowe crawls about in the slanted light, taking all the time God allotted him to put everything back in order. After several minutes Frizer remembers that he is still half-undressed, takes his doublet from the rickety servant's cot in the corner and puts it on, fastening buttons all the way to his throat.

''Fore God, I only meant to read *Tamburlaine*, nothing else,' he says.

Marlowe clears his throat, bent over a semicircle of crumpled pages with footprints on them. 'I believe you.'

'I was afraid you'd burnt it, marry. This morning – I did not mean to see what I saw, but since I saw it, I feared it might be gone. Gone forever.'

'You are relieved, I hope.'

Frizer laughs shrilly. 'Oh, yes, by'r Lady! I would've grieved it like a Greek widow!'

Marlowe does not laugh. His body is so long that he need only kneel in one place and stretch himself left and right to reach under the bed, under the desk. Seconds grind past in silence.

'I've seen it more than a dozen times,' Frizer continues. 'Both parts. Anytime I hear about it playing, I go to see it.'

'Do you.'

'Ay. Mostly here in London, at the Rose, but I've seen it in Eltham too. I prefer the London stage, mind. When he comes out with the conquered kings pulling his chariot, no puny guildhall stage can do it justice: "Holla, ye pampered jades of Asia!"'

Marlowe lets out a soft, disinterested grunt. Frizer sinks down upon the cot, which leans and creaks at his inconsiderable weight. He picks through his mind in search of another way in, at last coming up with: 'Is it true that your new play brought men to riot at the Curtain?'

'Ha! I suppose one could generously call it a riot.'

'No more a riot than that time when the Devil himself appeared in the audience at *Faustus*, eh?'

Marlowe examines a page in the light: front and back, front and back.

'Well, I should like to see the new one. 'Tis a history, no? Like the kind the Queen's Men used to play: "London, awake, for fear the Lord do frown?"' Marlowe will not be baited into a reply, so Frizer asks, directly, 'What is it called?'

'*Edward II.*'

'Ah. Is that Longshanks?'

'No, his son.'

'I know not him.'

'Ay, you do.'

'I warrant ye, I do not.'

'He was the one buggered to death with a spit.' Marlowe shuffles his papers on the floor with a *bang* and then stands up.

Frizer knows not how to respond to a phrase like 'buggered to death' except to laugh. 'Holla, that *would* cause a riot! Now I must see it.'

'I doubt you will.'

'Why?'

'Because...' Marlowe pinches his brow as if stricken with headache. 'Because you will never see it, Master Frizer. Belike it shall never be staged again.'

'Because they have arrested ye? Why, that should make no difference. They say you know of necromancy, or some such, and that you can predict the future by reading the guts of dead men, and that you set a Bible on fire so that the Devil would teach you his language. People still come to *Faustus*. Marry, the more evil they speak of ye, the more eagerly they come!'

'Had I such powers at my disposal, methinks I would have put them to better use than writing plays.'

'Well, Faustus does little enough with his powers, no? Give a man the Horn of Gabriel and he'll trump jigs on it.'

Marlowe chuckles softly, delightedly, and Frizer wonders whether he might have stopped listening again. But then Marlowe looks at Frizer with unnerving frankness in his dark eyes, the first full look since his stare had roamed over the scars. The very air seems to stand at attention where his gaze penetrates it, like the hair on one's arms at a sudden chill.

'Shall we go down to supper?' Marlowe says. 'Try to meet one another over again?'

Frizer's mouth turns dry. Yet he smiles and nods, trying neither to smile too broadly nor nod too effusively. 'Yes,' he croaks. 'Yes.'

But at supper, an interrogation begins:

'What do you do for Thomas Walsingham, exactly?'

'How long have you been in his staff?'

'Have you always done this sort of work?'

'Where were you born?'

'How old are you?' This last asked in faint bewilderment, as if over the course of the interview Marlowe has felt some dearly held preconception slip away.

'I'm five-and-twenty, in God's name! What did you think?'

Marlowe seems abashed, stirring his porridge of peas and unidentified fish around in the bowl and then taking a bite to muffle his response: 'I thought you were somewhat younger.'

Everyone thinks so. 'Tis disappointing to find Marlowe in the same category. Frizer slumps in the bench and scowls at the other long table in the room, where a loud party of French folk appear far better provided for than themselves, sucking on bones and sopping up drippings with bread. Upstairs, Marlowe had seemed almost on the verge of taking a good impression of him, but now his only interest in Frizer extends no further than such tedious facts as a judge might demand at a hearing. There's certainly no talk of stars, no mention of fantastical gods or barbarous-sounding places, and Frizer cannot help but feel cheated, as if he had been promised a tiger but received a tomcat.

'You'll not eat?' Marlowe says, between hungry bites.

'*Fish*, they give us. Fish on a Sunday! How come those snail-eaters over there get meat and we do not?'

'You are accustomed to better fare?'

Frizer tries to stand his spoon upright in the bowl, feeling peevish. 'You want to know if I am rich, do you?'

Marlowe hesitates. '*Are* you?'

'What does any of this matter to ye?'

'Well, that we need not remain strangers.'

'I told ye, I am no spy!'

'And I told you, I believe you.'

'I am a runner, that's all I am; I serve Thomas Walsingham and no other; I know nothing about any papers, nor any Baines!'

Marlowe pauses. 'Baines?'

'Ay, when ye were poised to break my skull in, you mentioned a man called Baines.'

Marlowe shifts in his seat, hunches over his bowl. 'That is none of your concern.'

'Reckon he's some imp ye know how to summon, with one of your Faustus spells!'

Marlowe laughs bitterly. 'Yes, of course, he is but one of many imps I keep on retainer. Get me a quart of newborn baby's blood and I can send for him straight if ye like.'

This stuns Frizer into silence. Marlowe wipes the bowl clean with his bread, looking as if he would put his face in it and lap up the broth if they were in less formal surroundings. He eats as if in preparation for hardship. Perhaps he believes he shall go to prison anon. And, if he believes that, then perhaps he is guilty.

'You should not have said that,' Frizer says.

Marlowe shrugs.

'A man may take the wrong impression.'

'What man, Master Frizer? You?'

Frizer's face grows hot. He spends a second or two stirring at his uneaten porridge, and when next he looks up, finds Marlowe eyeing his bowl in sidelong glances, like a dog that thinks itself very sly. Frizer slides the bowl across the table, at which Marlowe barely smiles: a faint, upwards tick at the corners of his red, womanish mouth.

'Do you believe that I can summon devils?' Marlowe says, digging in.

Frizer inhales sharply. A fog of silence has swept over the room in the past minute; every clack of a spoon stands out. 'You ought to be charier with your tongue, man!'

'"As chary as with my life,"' Marlowe quotes himself, *Faustus* specifically, with a dry, sonorous tone of parody. Nay, the man is nothing like Frizer had expected, but of course he'd expected Tamburlaine, or Faustus, not a man at all, but a fiction. A man is a subtler creature. He may lie to his audience; he may lie to himself.

Another moment passes ere Frizer remembers the question Marlowe has asked, with a start. 'Nay,' he answers. 'If I were the Devil, and an Englishman summoned me, I should refuse him straight.'

'Well, they say I *am* the Devil,' Marlowe says, without looking up. 'They say that too.'

Frizer grunts. 'Y'are no devil. No devil would come all the way from hell to gobble up that pigshit so gladly.'

Marlowe's look brightens. His smile is generous, even warm. There's a subtle point to the canine on the right side, a hungry little fang, the sight of which makes Frizer's stomach churn. He wills the smile to linger until his eyes have drunk their fill of it.

'If I am a devil, I know it not,' Marlowe says, bowing over the bowl. 'My horns are so well hid, even I cannot find them.'

'Tis unclear from his tone whether he intends this as a jest. Such is his way of jesting, Frizer presumes. And yet, one ought to be wary with him. Marlowe may not be the Devil, but he could easily be a spy, who, like all spies, will have learned his trade from the Devil. He may only be sounding Frizer's faith in an underhand way, with jests and insincerity, probing for weakness. God knows he need not probe much. 'Tis painfully evident in the way Frizer courts favour with other men, like an overly admiring child, the way he so clumsily throws himself at their feet. The way he walks. The way he smiles.

He remembers his brother Elias saying, *Is this what you want, cunt?*

A wince follows like the snap of a whip.

Marlowe, thank God, does not see it.

After supper, Kit sits at the desk in his and Frizer's dimly lit room and hunts through the contents of his bag anew, fearing he might have missed something earlier. Walsingham was right: he should have burnt every page. But that would mean the death of himself, in a way; the death of months and years poured out in ink. Better to hide everything, one manuscript at a time, one under a loose floorboard, another behind a loose brick... But for whom? One must have hope to bury a message. One must believe that the right man will find it.

'Do you want a cake?' Frizer says, with his mouth full.

Kit glances at him: seated on the floor by the cot with his knees up, eating something out of his hands like a squirrel.

'No, I thank you.' Kit turns over a battered manuscript on the desk. At the top of the first page is a sketch of a dolphin, followed by the words *Hero & Leander*: tragic lovers divided by the surging Hellespont, the vestal virgin doomed to undo herself and the strong swimmer doomed to drown. Not a play, but a poem, begun years ago but never finished.

'I have enough for both of us,' Frizer says. 'Half a dozen.'

'No, thank you, no,' Kit murmurs, silently reading:

> *On Hellespont, guilty of true love's blood,*
> *In view and opposite two cities stood,*
> *Seaborderers, disjoined by Neptune's might:*
> *The one Abydos, the other Sestos hight...*

Frizer has begun to hum a repetitive tune, quietly but not quietly enough. Kit wonders whether he shall make a tolerable companion after all. As guileless as a child, this man, who wears such horrors on his skin. He has wit, though, like a boy, he is ashamed to vaunt it; he has a heart too, which he wears like a mark of disfigurement square on the face, so sore, so soft, so obvious. Perhaps what Kit feels for him is simply pity. Belike 'tis only because he pities himself far more than he should that he sees some ineffable spark of fellowship in Frizer, in his all-too evident wounds.

Besides, Frizer has yet to prove himself an ally in any regard. A wounded man is like a child, and children may be capable of monstrous things.

'Master Frizer,' Kit says.

Unnervingly, Frizer has that knife of his in hand again, though it seems he intends no violence with it. He holds it as casually as Kit might hold a pen. 'Yes?'

'When did your master tell you that you would be staying with me, here in London?'

Frizer's eyes dart back and forth. 'He never did.'

'Well, someone must have told you.'

'My friend Nick—' he starts, then starts again, 'It was supposed to be my friend Nick staying with ye, but he asked if I would do it instead.'

'When?'

'Yesterday afternoon. Evening.'

'Yesterday evening, your master knew they were coming to arrest me?'

'He has his ways.'

Kit remembers Walsingham storming into his room this morning with all haste, flinging open the shutters: *They're coming – we must hurry – we have only hours!*

'Your master put on a show for me this morning.'

Fear alights in Frizer's gaze. He seems tongue-tied.

'You knew nothing of this?'

'Why would I, man? I'm no one.' Frizer looks as if he believes this absolutely.

Kit turns away, his gaze settling upon the Queen's image above the desk, her right eye slightly off-centre to the left. If Walsingham cannot be trusted, then what must he do? What is the only sensible thing to do, save to run – tonight? Kit will wait until Frizer is asleep and then slip away, head for the river, follow the river to the coast... But then everyone will say he acted too rashly, that he made his confession in a cowardly escape. The sensible path seems quite mad, given its consequences. Exile is an unbroken sea. One becomes a ghost upon it. The last time Kit saw Baines – in Flushing, the winter before last – he'd looked like a memory of himself, like Agamemnon in hell.

Now I've got you, you ungrateful little shit.

The sinews in Kit's arms and legs tighten. He could crush that skull in his bare hands. He could rip out that throat with his teeth. Just to end it all, to make it stop.

In the corner of Kit's eye comes a flash, like distant lightning. Across the room, a bright vortex of brass and steel whirligigs in Frizer's hand, as if propelled by some otherworldly wind. For a moment the strange magic of this event is all Kit perceives. Then he realizes: 'tis the knife, dancing like a snared fish, as if at the command of Frizer's serious blue eyes.

Who *is* this man?

'Who taught you to do that?' Kit says, smiling.

Frizer does not smile. 'I did.'

IO

H<small>IS HEART BEATING HIGH</small> in his chest, Kit lies in bed and counts Frizer's slow snores. *Twenty-nine... thirty...* Across the room, the Queen's face glows out of the darkness, her lopsided, dollish eyes fixed upon him. He resists a child-ish impulse to pull the covers over his head.

Thirty-nine... forty. Surely he's waited long enough. Kit steps out of bed and lifts the neat pile of clothes he's left on the floor, dressing himself. Boots in hand, he tiptoes across the creaking floor, past Frizer's sprawled form in the cot: dead asleep, like a child at the end of a long day, arms over his face, legs over the sides. Kit cannot help but smile.

Perhaps he should leave a message for Frizer to find. Just in case. Apologies to Kit's mother, and to his sisters Mag, Anne and Dorothy, who had performed his first plays in their shared bedroom, by moonlight, in whispers. *They shall tell you things to make you hate me, but do not believe them...* How could he possibly ask that of them, when what he wants, and has always wanted, was for them to know him, fully, and love him regardless? But no man owns another's heart. Nay, not even his mother's. If Kit's father can hate him living, his mother and sisters can hate him dead.

Outside, at the top of the long stairs, a breath of clean night air steels him. He puts on his boots without looking and then ties his handkerchief around his face, eyes fixed on the light in the clouds where the moon should be.

If Baines is in London, Kit will find him.

And then what?

From a dark corner on Bishopsgate Street, a hidden watcher observes Kit's descent from the topmost floor of the Inn-in-the-Wall, and his eventual appearance at the inn's gate. The bells rang out for curfew some time ago. Even the lights on London Wall are out.

In such silence, Kit's watcher can hear him breathe at a distance. Without moving, it marks his long shadow's crossing of the damp street to the door of the Black Bull tavern, where Kit knocks, slips in through a lighted crack in the darkness, and is gone. Ten or fifteen minutes pass before Kit emerges and hurries on to the Green Dragon next door, where he remains hardly five minutes before rushing out, on to the next: the Four Swans, and then the Wrestlers, and then the Vine—

When finally Kit has exhausted the neighbourhood, he stands by the fountain and turns in a slow circle, as if lost, before suddenly darting west, in the direction of Threadneedle. His watcher follows.

No house in London is meant to be open at this hour, as if the plague should only travel by night. But there are plenty who welcome curfew-breakers, whether out of opportunity, necessity, or even disbelief that the plague exists at all. From tavern to tavern, Kit makes his way towards St Paul's, past the shuttered poultry market, onto broad, moonlit Cheapside, his search growing more scattered, more desperate, as the hours pass. Halfway to dawn, he despairs, standing in the middle of Cheapside with his head in his hands for minutes on end.

Reanimating at last, he makes his way to the Mermaid,

wherein he vanishes for an hour or more before stumbling out, still drinking.

Inside a crowded brothel north of St Paul's, among the narrow, knotty streets surrounding Newgate Prison – wherein Tom Watson had vanished for eight long months – Kit whispers a word through a slot in a door and then stumbles through onto a dark, narrow stairwell. The walls writhe with living frescoes, bobbing heads and twining limbs. Solemn eyes watch him shamble past, as if to mark a hawk in descent.

The cellar is larger than one would expect, loud with voices, fiddles, drums. A series of ancient-looking stone arches hold up the low ceiling over the many heads, illuminated in the fey glow of lanterns tinted amber, blue and green. Shadows jostle and leap within the light, the air thick with their sweat and breath, perfume and bowse. Many have their faces covered, though such is not unusual here even outside of plague-time: a simple cloth over the nose and chin, or a half-mask around the eyes; some even wear women's vizards: black, featureless masks which conceal the whole face but for the eyes, held in place by a button clenched between the teeth.

A series of hasty weddings is in progress between the stone arches. The guests stand crammed to either side of the aisle, loudly admiring the gown of a veiled bride as she glides up to meet her glowing groom, her skirts a heap of tailor's scraps, her bodice glittering with pins. At the beer-barrel altar, a portly, masked man in a cassock performs hasty rites, after which the groom lifts the veil, revealing his bride: a stage-woman's face, one may call it, that is, a face termed 'woman' by convention, in the plucking of her brows, the painting of her lips, the shaving of her beard.

The crowd approves of her – the groom less so, blushing with anxiety – and soon the happy couple bustle past Kit to the stairwell, to honour their vows, to consummate.

Kit is a fool if he hopes to find Baines in a place like this. But no, he is not here for Baines, if he is honest with himself. What he desires most of all now is to sink into the earth. To forget, and be forgotten.

A pot-boy dressed as a cherub comes to fill Kit's flask. Twice. When the last wedding is celebrated, the musicians strike up a dance. Kit presses his back to an arch as the clockwork of faces reels past, but can only keep to himself so long before someone takes him by the hand, dragging him into the fray. There is just room enough in that space for the dancers to circle one another, palm-to-palm, nose-to-nose, passing from one partner to the next, and the next. Men whisper things in Kit's ears that pull him further out of sense. He dances with Richard Baines. He dances with a tarred skull. He dances with Tom Watson.

Just before darkness consumes him, Kit tumbles into the chest of a man small enough to be Ingram Frizer, and is relieved to think he might have followed him here. Kit leans close, murmuring, 'Take me home.'

When at last he comes to he is outside in the alley, his hand against the cool bricks, dry heaving over a puddle of pungent puke. Above, the black curtain of Newgate Prison blots out the pre-dawn sky. Kit's breaths seem to redouble off the prison walls, like a name shouted into a cave:

Tom!

'You know,' a voice says to his left, as if from the midst of a conversation, 'I saw *Edward II*.'

Kit glances over his shoulder at his companion, a small-ish fellow, smoking a pipe. It could indeed be Frizer, but no: a stranger.

'Oh, did you now?' Kit says, almost laughing, as one is wont to laugh at anything that occurs in a dream. He rinses his mouth with the contents of his flask and lies back against the wall at the stranger's side, the world tipping around him like a raft upon a river.

The stranger says, "'You shall not need to give instructions;
'Tis not the first time that I have killed a man.
I learned in Naples how to poison flowers,
To strangle with a lawn thrust through the throat,
To pierce the windpipe with a needle's point,
Or, whilst one is asleep, to take a quill
And blow a little powder in his ears,
Or open his mouth and pour quicksilver down.
And yet I have a braver way than these.'"

Kit stares, astonished. 'Lightborne.'

The man snaps his fingers. 'Yes – that was his name! A good name for Edward's murderer. One would have to be a remarkable fellow indeed to come up with that "braver way".'

'Well, 'tis no ordinary way to kill a man,' Kit says, quite stupidly.

A chuckle. 'Indeed no. But what I found most remarkable was all that preceded the murder – the seduction, as it were. Your Lightborne might have slaughtered poor Edward the moment he entered his cell, but instead, he charmed him. Wooed him, as it were, to his death. For Edward did resist him, at first: "These looks of thine can harbour naught but death," he said, "I see my tragedy written in thy brows." Lightborne might well have killed him then. But still, he dallied. They even shared a bed, before it was over – a bed!' The man pauses, sucking his pipe. 'It seemed to me as though they were alone together, in that little room, for a time outside of time. Days, perhaps. Or even years.'

To think that Kit's unloved, orphan play should live so richly in another man's memory! He fights back a smile. 'You forget, there were four men in the room when the king was killed. Counting the dead.'

'Oh, but the others hardly matter! Only Lightborne matters. There was even a marriage…'

'Yes,' Kit says. 'Of a kind: Edward gives Lightborne a ring…'

'Yes: "One jewel have I left: receive thou this." And he twisted the last wretched ring off his wretched finger, and he knelt like any common groom…'

'"Still fear I,"' Kit says, '"and I know not what's the cause,
But every joint shakes as I give it thee.
O, if thou harbour'st murder in thy heart,
Let this gift change thy mind and save thy soul."'

The man whispers, breathlessly, 'Yes.' The coal in his pipe flares as he puffs, revealing a hungry, patient look in the eyes, like a dog waiting for the table to be cleared. His face is clean-shaven. Eerily familiar.

'Of course,' he adds, 'the consummation was somewhat unorthodox!' and snorts out a laugh that touches a trigger between Kit's spine and his heart, lifting the small hairs of his skin. He wonders what arrangements might have been made while he was in the dark place, what things he might have agreed to do. What things he might already have done.

'What are you after, man? A fuck?'

'Never you mind that.' The stranger offers his pipe. His hand is missing the ring finger. Strangely, it reminds Kit at once of Ingram Frizer's scars. So much pain hidden in plain sight.

'What happened there?' Kit says, drawing smoke.

The man glances at the gap in his own hand as if he'd quite forgotten about it, but then laughs again – a joke, one that Kit does not understand, but that he feels, suddenly, as if he will.

'You know,' the stranger says, 'you remind me of someone. You are much taller, of course, but 'tis more in the shape of the face. The mouth. 'Tis almost uncanny.'

The hairs on Kit's neck stand on end. Yet he senses, keenly, that he must not show this man his fear. He drinks from his flask, leans in to snarl, 'To hell with you,' and then swerves hastily onto empty Newgate Street. He strides east, feeling all the while as if someone were a step behind him, breathing into a spot between his shoulder-blades, until finally he can bear no more and turns on his heel. But the stranger stands just where Kit had left him, now far behind, watching as if to watch a player cross a stage, from entrance to exit.

Robin Poley puffs his pipe, and does not move to go until Kit Marlowe has vanished from sight.

21 MAY 1593

Nine days

❧❁❧

Robyn –

Sollicitae non possunt cure mutare aranei stamina fusi! I am ready to endure whatsoever shall be inflicted, *et facere et paci Romanorum est.*

What my course has been towards [Sir Francis] you can witness, what my love towards you, yourself best can tell. Proceedings at my lodgings have been very strange. I am the same as I always pretended. I pray God you be, and ever so remain towards me. Take heed of your own part, lest of these my misfortunes you bear the blame. *Est exilium inter malos vivere.*

Farewell, sweet Robyn, if as I take thee, true to me. If not, adieu, *omnium bipedum nequissimus.*

Return me thine answer for my satisfaction, and my diamond, and what else thou wilt. The furnace is prepared wherein our faith must be tried. Farewell till we meet, which God knows when.

Thine, how far thou knowest,

Anthony Babington

[LETTER TO ROBIN POLEY, 4TH? AUGUST 1586]

I I

ROBIN POLEY WALKS HIS horse through the arch of Great
Stone Gate, under another scarlet, smoke-choked dawn. As
the portcullis creaks closed behind him, he knows without
looking that the skull of Anthony Babington now hangs directly
overhead, the chin aligned with his right ear, as surely as if he
can feel breath upon his cheek. For one second, man and skull
look south together, in the direction of the Marshalsea Prison.

Wish me luck.

Three years ago, when Poley still had all ten fingers and
no limp at all in his walk, he had been borne through this
same gate in the bed of a rumbling wagon, chained up along
with several other men, all with bags over their heads. Quietly,
so their captors would not overhear, they'd passed murmurs
around the wagon-bed in a circle: 'Who's that?'

'Poley. Is that Young?'

'Yes. Young and Poley, here. You?'

'Drury. Drury, Young, Poley…' and so on. They were seven,
they'd determined. All had, at one time or another, been hired
as spies by Sir Francis Walsingham, then recently deceased.

'I heard they arrested Thomas Walsingham,' whispered
Poley's neighbour to the left.

'I heard they drove him to the heath and slit his throat!'
said the one to the right. 'Who's to say they'll not dispatch us
just the same?'

'Tush,' Poley said. ''Tis all a game.'

Eventually the wagon had stopped here: before the long, toothy colonnade of the Marshalsea Court. Poley and the others had rushed inside in a cluster, blind to the prodding of their captors' cudgels. Their arraignment, such as it was, had lasted all of five minutes: the bang of a gavel, a name read out and a charge of suspicion to commit treason, then another name followed by another, identical charge. Ambiguities and suppositions, but still enough to put all seven of them away for an equally ambiguous length of time. When the last charge was read, guards then herded them to the back of the court-room, and through the towering, oaken doors known as the Hellmouth, into the Marshalsea Prison.

Poley and the others marched double-quick past scores of jeering voices, clubs jabbing at their backsides. At the bottom of a flight of stairs, the procession paused just long enough for a hand to rip the bags from their heads and shove them, one at a time, through another door, into the Marshalsea's infamous Strong Room. It was originally meant to hold fifty men at a stretch, but had contained somewhere in the vicinity of two hundred, all standing shoulder-to-shoulder in at least three inches of grey water, whereon rafts of oily shit floated like seaweed. A chink in the stones high above emitted a coal of white light, a trace of breathable air. Ghastly creatures clambered over one another towards this source, or towards a hump of high ground in the centre of the room, shoving for the privilege of dry feet. Along the walls, in the corners, corpses lay in piles: laddered ribs, butterfly pelvises, long, smooth, knob-kneed bones.

All a game, Poley reminded himself – meaning, of course, that it may be played to win. Marshalsea, much like the world without, bends to the will of gold. He'd had a diamond ring concealed beneath the glove on his right hand that could have bought him the run of the place, but he would have sooner

HESSE PHILLIPS

starved than given it up. In his pocket, there were just enough coins for paper and ink and a courier's services, through which he'd sent a message to a friend – well, a woman, and something of a friend, who was more than happy to raid her husband's money-chest for him. She'd sent enough for a private cell upstairs, a feather bed, meals served at his own table. The diamond, Poley kept, and so spent the many long, dull days watching a greenish flame within its depths kindle and spark, like a soul sealed in amber.

After a month of monkish solitude, the warden himself paid Poley's cell a visit. All his life, Poley had been hearing stories about Dick Topcliffe, the Queen's own cousin, who might have chosen any office in the land but preferred to rule over the Marshalsea. Topcliffe arrived with a bottle of good French claret, a rarity since the war began, took a seat at Poley's table and poured two glasses. Poley found the company refreshing. The wine too. He imagined himself on the outside again, and soon, perhaps, regaling wide-eyed listeners with the tale of how he'd befriended the so-called Master of Tortures.

After they'd drunk the bottle dry, Topcliffe had suggested they retrieve another from his private chambers. Another floor up, at the end of an ever-narrowing corridor, Poley stepped through a humble door and immediately felt a club strike the backs of his knees, knocking him to the floor. Men descended out of the darkness, pinioned his arms.

'The right hand,' Topcliffe said, and wiggled his ring finger. The guards wrestled Poley's hand onto a block of wood. They folded down his fingers, exposing the one Topcliffe wanted. When the hatchet fell, Poley did not feel anything at first, he did not even hear the chop. He only saw the diamond flash like an eye just before death, then his own reflection in the hatchet-head: a gaping gullet in a hairy face, a wild, animal stare.

'Now,' Topcliffe said, 'we shall truly get to know one another.'

At the courthouse doors, Poley pauses to take a thoroughly unpleasant swig of home-brewed plague-water from the vial in his pocket. A masked guard then leads him through the currently empty Marshalsea Court into the Hellmouth. But rather than enter the prison proper, they turn upstairs and head straight for the little door at the end of the corridor, whose opening unleashes a gust of stench: piss, shit, blood, bile. Poley must pull a morbid grin to keep from retching.

How Topcliffe's thugs bear it, he will never understand. The Master of Tortures is never without his retinue of 'instruments', as he calls them: dead-eyed, stone-faced cretins who stand about and watch their master work with seemingly limitless patience. Today, the spectacle in the torture room is courtesy of Thomas Kyd, now in the grip of a machine of Topcliffe's own invention: a simple system of ropes and pulleys designed to fold the body in half, backwards, by gradually drawing the arms over the arse, the feet over the head. Thus hangs poor Master Kyd now, his wiry, naked body shiny with sweat and grime, bent back like a bow about to fire.

'I cannot breathe,' he sputters. 'Please, please, I cannot breathe!'

'My Robin-bird!' Topcliffe says, setting some notes down on his scribe's desk as he crosses the room, arms open. 'Back to the nest, eh? Did you miss it?' Topcliffe pounds Poley's back. He reeks of this room, distilled; his clothes soak it up like a sponge.

'You look well.' Poley tries to sound neutral.

'I *am* well. Why? Should I not be well?'

'Working hard?'

Topcliffe barks a laugh, takes Poley about the shoulders and turns him to face Kyd, from whose dangling cock piss dribbles onto the filthy table beneath him. 'You've never seen it from the outside, have you?' Topcliffe says, quietly. 'I've made some improvements. How is the old hip, by the way?'

Poley readies an indifferent response but cannot voice it. In the back of his head, he hears that terrible *pop* and pain shoots through his pelvis, though he is standing still.

Topcliffe plucks one of the ropes like a guitar string and Kyd lets out a shriek, followed by pleas. 'Peace, goat!' Topcliffe says, ruffling Kyd's hair. 'I call him my little goat. They tell me he's a poet, but I've never heard him utter even one pretty thing. He sounds like an ordinary goat to me, does he not to you?'

Poley squats down by the table, looking up into a prematurely wizened face, blood-vessels veining the skin like the surface of a leaf. The brow knits above the bulging eyes, in confusion and fear. *What new torments await?*

Softly, Poley says, '"When this eternal substance of my soul,
Did live imprisoned in my wanton flesh,
Each in their function serving other's need,
I was a courtier at the Spanish Court..."'

As he goes on, Kyd starts to sob. Occasionally, the young poet joins in, uttering a word here and there with a heavy tongue: 'perils', 'Acheron', 'soul', 'love'. But before Poley can reach the end of the speech, Kyd suddenly thrashes at his restraints, screams like a cat: 'Mama! Oh God, let me go home! *Mama!*'

Topcliffe's instruments subdue the prisoner. Their master helps Poley to his feet. 'What was all that about, you devil?'

'It was the prologue of his play, *The Spanish Tragedy.*'

Topcliffe shows Poley through another door and into his adjoining quarters, a six-sided chamber with panelled walls, a desk and – unsettlingly – a sumptuous, canopied bed, from which a young woman in a nightgown rises, sleepily, as they enter. She ambles to a sideboard racked with glasses, a long, heavy chain grinding across the floorboards behind her.

Topcliffe's desk, which sits near the room's only window, is at least half as big as a rubbish barge and piled high with papers, the record of hundreds of sessions in the black cells, with God knows how many victims. Above the desk hangs a youthful portrait of Topcliffe's beloved cuz, the Queen: a severe, red-haired girl with milk-white skin, a Bible clasped tight against her loins, a sweep of fierce scarlet falling from her nubile, small-breasted frame.

Topcliffe had used to talk often of those breasts. Soft as lambskin, he'd said they were, with nipples as pink and pert as rosebuds.

'Well, your letter intrigued me,' Topcliffe says, as his woman shakily offers him a goblet of that Bordeaux wine. 'You have stones the size of sinkers, my birdy, I'll give ye that. Now, lay it all out for me again, so I may hear this knavery in your own voice.'

Poley leaves his goblet untouched. 'You doubt my strategy?'

'I doubt your motives, man. A fellow like you sells me a boat, I expect a leak or two – not by oversight, but by design.' He toasts his cousin's portrait before lifting the glass to his lips, knuckles barnacled in gold and jewels. No sign of the diamond.

In the simplest of terms, Poley recapitulates his recent proposition, taking care not to admit that there are certain details of which he would prefer Topcliffe remained ignorant. Suffice to say, his intention is to take on the bulk of the work involved, leaving Topcliffe with the simple task of turning up when he is called for, to collect a prize Poley will have generously secured for him: the soon-to-be fugitive Christopher Marlowe.

'I'd say that's putting the cart before the horse, birdy,' Topcliffe says, when Poley is finished. 'The way I hear it, his Holiness is biding his time with this Marlowe villain. The old man thinks he's found himself one of the Devil's own foot-soldiers, you see. He'll not take him for some measly little charge of sedition or libel; he wants Marlowe on a platter, trussed and bled.'

'Oh, he'll be bled,' Poley says.

'And moreover there shall be nothing in it at all if Marlowe makes no attempt to 'scape justice, less than nothing should the Council then fail to set a bounty on his head. It shall have to be a substantial bounty, at that – to the degree of a Babington, shall we say – to make it worth my while.'

Poley smiles, undaunted. 'You know Richard Baines?'

'Why, who hath not heard of the great *Richard Baines*?'

Annoyed, Poley thoughtlessly takes a sip of wine and tries not to wince. 'Master Baines was once Marlowe's intimate associate, and has purportedly witnessed the full gamut of cardinal crimes on the poet's part: treason, heresy, buggery – more than enough to satisfy the archbishop, I should think, and to fetch a high price in the offing. Baines has promised to deliver a statement, detailing all, to Seething Lane—'

'Promised, has he? When shall we see this promise fulfilled?'

'Within the week, I should think. Alas, Baines is a man of many subtle designs. But once the statement is delivered, it should be no trouble at all to persuade Marlowe to take flight, especially with the promise of an escape, which I shall provide him withal: a counterfeit passport and passage to the Continent. All with the co-operation of Marlowe's trusted friend, no less.'

'And this "friend",' Topcliffe says. 'Is he in agreement with your end?'

Poley harrumphs. 'Agreement, yes – mind, he knows not what he agrees to, but that is neither here nor there. I have a little need of his purse, to pay my associate. To you, he shall be of negligible consequence.'

Topcliffe licks wine from the tips of his whiskers, sucks his teeth. 'I'll tell ye what I like: I like that I see small risk to myself should aught go awry, short of time and dignity. But I do not like hinging my hopes upon the actions of other men, with "designs", as you say, that I neither understand nor care to. Nor do I like the lingering mystery of your extraordinary generosity. Tell me, why do you offer me this fat pig, which you might just as easily enjoy at your own table, all to yourself?'

Poley falters, having glanced in the direction of Topcliffe's little slave, who stands by the sideboard with her head bowed, a curtain of dark hair over her face. In the silence, voices become faintly audible through the walls, even from behind the icy gaze of the young Princess Elizabeth herself, in her looming portrait: wordless groans, muffled screams.

'You want something from me, do ye not, birdy?' Topcliffe says.

'You know perfectly well what I want from you,' Poley answers, and coughs to find his voice. 'You have something that belongs to me, and I would like it back.'

Topcliffe fidgets with the largest of several rings upon his fingers, a pearl almost the size of a quail's egg. 'How do you reckon I have not sold it?'

'Because you do not need to.'

Topcliffe sniggers, raising his glass in approval. 'Well. We shall see. Perhaps this Marlowe will fetch a diamond's bounty.'

After less than a full second's thought, Poley blurts out, 'If I can bring you a copy of Baines's statement, for Kyd to memorize prior to testifying—'

'*Now,*' Topcliffe says, a finger aimed at Poley's breast, 'that would be useful. Corroboration, and all that. It shall go better if you can bring me that document ere the rest of your comrades at Seething Lane ever see it. Then, we need not wait upon this Baines, nor his designs.'

'But Marlowe must also be given opportunity to run,' Poley reminds him. 'That is essential.'

''Tis your worry, not mine.'

Poley stifles a sigh. 'Once the document is delivered to Seething Lane, I will have a copy made for you.'

'*Before.*'

'I know not whether that shall be possible.'

'Oh, but you *make* things happen, my birdy – that's what you do! You come in here, balls clanging like the bells of le-Bow, promise me a tidy fortune, stir my hopes up to a roaring fire, and then tell me some things are not possible?' He tucks his bottom lip over his teeth, showing a hint of slimy tongue, and in silence seems to consider several options, some of which bring him rich delight. 'Let's say this,' he begins at last. 'I require a week to think over your proposal. Within that week, you may hasten my decision, should you find yourself so disposed. Either way, in a week's time, we shall see whether this Marlowe fellow is the golden goose you suppose him to be.'

Poley stands, eager to be gone. 'I will talk with Baines.'

'Do that. And Robin – you have barely touched your wine.'

But Poley can smell it from here. Sometimes, he can smell it in his sleep. For in the seconds after Topcliffe had cut off his finger, Poley vomited up every drop of that red, rare vintage. Its stink had clung to him for the week or more that he'd spent with Topcliffe in the room behind the wall.

You took the Catholic Communion with him, did you? Got down on your knees and stuck out your tongue, did you? How does it taste, the Body of Christ, when a papist gives it to ye? All warm and salty, is it? Is it?

Indeed, no man on earth knows Poley so well as Dick Topcliffe, no man alive.

'Honestly, Dick,' Poley says, 'I have no head for wine.'

Poley takes his leave of the Marshalsea. His legs cannot return him to his horse swiftly enough; his horse cannot run hard enough. To make a deal with Dick Topcliffe is as good as to make one with the Devil, but there are times when one has no choice. Anyway, Poley had learned something of Topcliffe too during their time together: that he is as witless as he is soulless, and not at all unmalleable.

Soon, the Privy Court's staff will convene for morning prayers, and if Poley is not in the great hall with the rest, mumbling the daily oath of allegiance to her Majesty, suspicions will be raised. Not long afterwards, Marlowe will also arrive at the court, to make his daily report. Perhaps Poley would be better off keeping his distance from him, but truly he longs just to look at the poet again, in better light: the oval face, the red, epicene lips. How familiar they are!

Of course, the resemblance to Babington that Poley had noticed last night is by no means perfect. Near enough, however, to corrupt the memory slightly, as a counterfeit coin corrupts the gold it means to feign. Were Poley superstitious, he might wonder: what power may be gained over a man by writing his name in blood?

But the world has a way of making echoes, of repeating itself ad infinitum. Allow oneself to go a little mad and one begins to see oneself everywhere; all people look like the same two people, bound for the same two fates. Having lost a part of himself, Poley knows something of madness. Sometimes he feels a tingle upon the missing fingertip, or an urge to crack the knuckle no longer there, or the weight of the ring, as heavy as the day Babington had slipped it on:

One jewel have I left: receive thou this.

But he did not say that. Edward said that, to Lightborne.

At Great Stone Gate, Poley takes off his cap and waves it so that the gatekeepers can see him coming and open the portcullis for him, so that he need neither slow down nor stop within the lamplight of the skull's stare. Galloping through the arch at full bent, he feels the rupture of an invisible membrane, clinging to him like cobwebs that dissolve in the wind.

For bonny sweet Robin is all my joy.

I 2

FRIZER AWAKES FIRST TO the sound of the door bursting open, second to the collapse of the cot underneath him, leaving him sprawled and sore upon the floor of this strange, hot room. From high above, a face lowers into focus: Christopher Marlowe.

'Are you hurt? Can you get up? I have no time; we must be quick!'

Frizer sits up, rubs his head. 'Jesus, man! What?'

'I need you to do something for me,' Marlowe pants, sitting on his heels. He both looks and smells as if he's been pickling in bowse all night long. 'I only ask out of absolute necessity.'

'Blast ye, what?'

Marlowe sighs into his hands, as if what he has to say costs him dearly. 'You care for the contents of that bag, do you not?'

Frizer follows Marlowe's glance up to the desk, the bag of papers.

'If you care indeed,' Marlowe says, 'then you must stay here today. It must never leave your sight.'

'No, no, my master said—'

'I care not what your master said, ay?' Marlowe snaps, but then softens his tone. 'If the men at Seething Lane get their hands on that bag, they will destroy it. Do you understand? *Tamburlaine* – you like *Tamburlaine* best, yes? They would *burn* it, those men. Every page, straight to the fire! Guard it for me, please. I will try to think of something better for tomorrow, but for now...'

Marlowe trails off, his brown eyes pleading. Frizer must force himself to look away. At Scadbury, he has often heard the other servants say, over the minutest infractions, 'The master will have me killed!' Not, 'He will kill me,' which smacks of wilful exaggeration, but *have me killed*. Frizer has often wondered who might do the killing. Probably Nick. *Cannot be helped, Ingram. But fear not, I'll make it quick. Like blowing out a candle.*

'Well,' Frizer says, 'very well. But only for today, and my master must never hear of it.'

Marlowe exhales, taking hold of Frizer's shoulders as if about to clip him in a hearty embrace. 'Thank you! Thank you! Now I must go. I'll be late to the court. Do not leave this room, ay? Well, leave if you must, but take the bag with you. But not to the privy. 'Tis not for stool-reading.'

Already, Frizer suspects he'll come to regret this.

'Keep the pages in order. Clean fingers. Goodbye!'

Marlowe hurries for the door, but at last Frizer has found space enough in his thoughts to ask, 'Have you been out *all night*?'

This question stops Marlowe in his tracks. He holds the doorframe in both hands and presses his forehead against it, as if half-tempted to dash out his brains.

'Ye cannot go roaming about after dark, man,' Frizer says. 'That's what my master—'

'To hell with your damned master!' Again, Marlowe seems to check his temper, glancing up towards heaven. 'If I do not come back,' he starts. 'Well. I know not.'

And so, he is gone.

Frizer stares through the open door long after Marlowe's footsteps fade, fumbling over his memory of the past few minutes. This is a gift, is it not? Marlowe has seen how Frizer covets his papers and, generously, made him their keeper. He could not have given him a more precious gift! But probably 'tis not mere generosity that motivates him. For all Frizer knows, this is but a ploy to rid himself of Frizer's company, as men so often do, once they've caught a glimpse of his skin. From that moment on, he becomes an unpleasant presence in every room, which must not be spoken of and yet cannot be ignored, like a foul odour in a stranger's house. Every look at him births a thousand imagined tragedies: mysterious illnesses, capital punishments, horrific accidents. God only knows what sort of gruesome past Marlowe's mind might have invented for him, given the man's propensity for excess. Surely not even he could guess the sorrowful, miserable truth.

Like a trespasser, Frizer lowers himself into Marlowe's chair, mortified at every creak of the joints. The Queen herself seems to be admonishing him from above, one distorted pupil gaping in her crookedly rendered face. Below her, a stack of papers lies in the blazing sun, seeming to emit the light rather than reflect it, like an open door. 'Tis as if the devil has staged this just so, angled it within the light just so, presenting the pages like the rarest and richest of gifts. Like bait.

> His bodie was as straight as Circes wand,
> Jove might have sipt out Nectar from his hand.
> Even as delicious meat is to the taste,
> So was his necke in touching, and surpast
> The white of Pelops shoulder. I could tell ye,
> How smooth his brest was, and how white his bellie,
> And whose immortall fingars did imprint,
> That heavenly path, with many a curious dint,
> That runs along his backe...

Eyes wide, fingers to his lips, Frizer turns the page.

Kit stumbles into the Privy Court just in time to hear his name called by the magistrate, who sends him straightaway to the iron gate. There, the guards on duty summon a clerk, who leads Kit to a desk and writes his name in a book. When Kit glances to his left he finds a baby-faced guard clasping a black bag in both hands, looking at him like a mountain that must perforce be summitted.

Kit bows his head into the bag. Therefore, he sees nothing as the young guard receives a hastily palmed coin from Robin Poley, who then takes Kit by the crook of the elbow and guides him slowly, silently, up the well-worn stairs. In time, they arrive at a set of narrow doors, beyond which lies a long hall lined with windows on the left, the walls whitewashed into an eye-bruising void. In a row down the centre of the hall, seven cells fashioned of heavy, dark curtains appear to float between floor and ceiling. Outside each cell stands a desk, four of which are occupied by a harried scribe, each of whom has a minder bent over his shoulder, monitoring every move of his pen. A low babble of voices seeps through the curtains like water through rock: here, muffled weeping; there, rising terror.

A foreman in Puckering's livery marches up the hall, and Poley ducks behind a cell until he has passed by. In the innocent, trusting way of blind men, Poley's charge puts up no resistance.

When the hood comes off at last, Kit finds himself in what he can only assume to be the same curtained, camphor-reeking chamber as yesterday, seated at the same table. He turns in his seat to see the man who had brought him here, for he was not led to this place but pulled to it, as if by a confederate, not a captor. As the man sits, Kit recognizes him: firstly, as the stranger who had remembered *Edward II* so well earlier this morning, only secondly as the man who had watched, smiling, while Anthony Babington was butchered alive. *Omnium bipedum nequissimus*, Babington had supposedly called him at the end: the vilest of all two-legged creatures.

'Robin Poley,' Kit says.

The beardless face arranges itself into a blank smile, much like the one it had worn at the gallows. 'Master Marlowe. You have stamina, my lad, I'll give ye that. After last night's adventures, I confess I feel my age.'

Kit glances at the walls, such as they are. Poley has no papers with him, nothing to take notes. Still, 'tis safer to assume that they are not alone and that this is a trap, one set last night in Newgate, during the lost hours between midnight and twilight, now about to spring. Kit's mouth goes dry.

'You were looking for someone last night,' Poley says.

'How do you know?'

'Well, it began that way. By the end, I believe you were only in search of the best taplash in London. By the time I came upon you, you had certainly sampled enough.'

Kit digs through the dark part of his memory as if through sand.

'You remember nothing?' Poley is almost whispering. 'Then you shall have to trust my word that no liberties were taken. Not by me, at least.'

Kit looks askance, searching for a shadow, a movement at the curtains.

Poley says, 'No one is listening.' Perhaps he is lying, but in fact, the notion that they are now perfectly alone, in unsanctioned parley, explains too well Poley's haste in bringing him here, his whispering, the anxious *tap-tap-tapping* of a finger on his mutilated right hand.

'I can help you,' he says. 'Well, I can give you what you seek, but I would ask something of you in return.'

'It had better not be a fuck,' Kit sneers.

Poley laughs shrilly, looking down at his hands. ''Tis a delicate subject. But time is short. I would like to know whether the rumours are true.'

'What rumours?'

'The rumours about Richard Baines. The ones you yourself began.'

'I did not begin them,' Kit says. 'I ended them.'

Poley looks surprised. 'So, you mean to say they *are* true.'

Kit chews his lip. Only a fool would confide anything intimate in Robin Poley. And yet, somewhere in the Privy Court's archives there exists a document writ in Thomas Walsingham's hand that details all, quite intimately: the report that Kit made five years ago which had led to Baines's exile, a document which, Kit suspects, has plummeted in credibility of late. A part of him does long to be believed. Or simply, to be heard.

'Do you know what happened when Baines was in Rheims, in 1582?' Kit says. 'How the papists discovered him for a spy? There was a boy – a cook or a kitchen boy. With Baines, there is always a boy. Together, Baines and he had hatched a plan to poison the whole seminary, all at once. Ludicrous, mind you. Baines had scrounged up a vial of arsenic, which the boy was to add to the common soup. But the boy repented, you see. Or perhaps he was caught in the act. Either way, the Jesuits soon had the truth out of him. That was the end of it.'

Poley frowns. 'What on earth do you suppose inspired Master Baines to this knavery?'

'He wanted the boy to admire him.'

'*Admire* him? Is that what he told you?'

''Tis what I know.' Kit adds, 'Admire him, and fear him.'

Poley looks up at the ceiling, as if fondling over some novel object in his mind. But it seems he is brought back by a final, lingering doubt. 'Did Baines ever tell you what became of the boy?'

Kit shakes his head. 'No.' But he knows what becomes of boys once Baines is done with them.

A pause descends. Poley's stare feels over-familiar, even fond. 'It occurs to me that this story bears some resemblance to your *Jew of Malta*. When Barabas poisons the nunnery well...' He trails off. 'Is that something you poets do often? Cut scraps out of other men's coats, and patch together fictions?'

Kit scowls. 'When the man makes an impression.'

Poley exhales a chuckle through the nose, though he seems more agitated than bemused. Once more, his finger has resumed its tapping. He glances at it as if it were a clock, reminding him that time is short. 'Richard Baines may be found at the Saracen's Head, in Newgate Without.'

'Without?' Kit sputters. 'Outside the Wall?'

A shrug. 'Perhaps 'tis some imposition to you.'

'Imposition? To do what?'

'Only you know that. But you *know* it, let me assure you – you know already what you will do when you see him.' That smile returns, causing Kit's skin to bristle just as it did last night, as if at a gentle, undesired touch. A memory arises: of standing in among the crowd before the scaffold on St Giles' Field, watching Robin Poley as he'd watched Anthony Babington die, with this same expression on his face. That day, Kit now knows, a monster had begun to take shape in his mind, one that smiles the way Robin Poley smiles and kills the way Robin Poley kills, at the soul. In time, Kit would give it a name: 'Lightborne'.

Out of the silence, the curtains open. Poley shoots to his feet, a player falling expertly into the midst of a scene. 'Ah, Master Phelippes, speak of the Devil! In that case I shall be on my way.'

Phelippes – the yellow-haired, squinting fellow who had interrogated Kit yesterday – looks stunned, pinching his cloth mask tighter to his nose. 'What brings you here, Master Poley?'

'These *boys*, Master Phelippes! These boys whom we equip in the habit of guardsmen, having neither hair on their balls nor brains in their heads! This impressive creature I found on one such boy's arm, wandering up and down the gatehouse with not the slightest hope of finding his way here – the blind leading the blind indeed!'

All this, Poley has said as if perfectly happy to be caught in the most blatant of falsehoods, as if it brings him immense pleasure to lie with so little shame, so little care.

13

EVEN AFTER POLEY HAS gone, his presence seems to hover over the increasingly airless cell. Phelippes, not so much the cool, detached functionary of yesterday, squints at Kit through his spectacles like a drunkard who has forgotten the point of his own story, his enquiries about the matter at hand scattered, disinterested. Again and again, he returns to another subject: 'What did you discuss just now with Master Poley? Did he offer you something? Propose any deals? Has he spoken with you elsewhere – here at the court, or in another location?'

Kit denies all, though certainly not to protect Poley, only to take some small delight in frustrating this altogether disagreeable quidnunc, in whom 'tis all too easy to detect some bitter rivalry at play. Kit is like a rabbit pulled between two hounds, Phelippes at the forelegs and Poley at the back. If he is not careful, they will tear him in half.

Phelippes does not let up till afternoon, by which time Kit is ravenous, desperately thirsty, his flask still empty after last night. Outside, he finds London somewhat livelier than it had been yesterday, the unseasonable heat having driven listless, masked crowds into the streets, standing about in furtive clusters. Perhaps the sheer quantity of obscured faces begins to work upon his mind, for as he heads north, he grows more certain with every step that somewhere far behind him, too far for his waking self to see, a figure maintains its distance as if to march him forward with the tip of a spear.

'If you feel yourself followed,' Baines had told him once, 'do not look back until you're prepared to run.'

Which he is not. For perhaps he is only driving himself mad, or else being driven mad, purposefully, by an adversary whom he's faced twice today already, one better confronted than fled. By the time Kit reaches Leadenhall Market, he can no longer tolerate the thought of Robin Poley slithering after his heels and finally wheels about, nearly snarling aloud, 'What in hell do you want *now*?' But the words die on his tongue.

Just twenty feet behind him, two figures in the smoke, both nearly as tall as himself, jerk to a halt at his turning.

No one moves. Kit has never seen these men before – boys, rather, for even in the smoke he can see they are no more than twenty, pale-haired, pale-faced, unnervingly identical to one another. Twins.

At last, one boy takes a half-step forward, prompting Kit to stumble backwards. Kit takes a glance to the right, finding the entrance to Winding Lane through St Helen's, and so veers off at a sprint. He should not run. Running attracts suspicion, especially in plague-time. But safety is only a short distance away, and its promise drives him mindlessly on, shoving through the narrow alleys of his old neighbourhood until sheer luck lands him, panting, at the Inn-in-the-Wall.

In the yard, he hardly pauses for breath before charging up the five flights of stairs. The moment Kit bursts into the room, Frizer bolts up from the desk and shouts, 'What took you so long?' as if he's spent hours waiting upon this very cue.

Kit pushes past him to the window, looking out over spear-studded Bishopsgate and the street below, the Black Bull tavern across the way. No sign of any twins. Nor of Poley, for that matter.

'*Thank you*, Master Frizer!' Frizer sneers, at his back. '*Thank you* for giving up a whole day of your life for my sweet sake!'

Kit remembers his papers, turns to the desk. What if this was the twins' goal: to trick him into leading them straight to his lodgings, his papers—

'Nay, but you are *most* welcome, Master Marlowe!' Frizer goes on. 'Your *gratitude* is too much to bear!'

'What in hell do you want,' Kit snaps, 'a God-damned curtsey?'

Behind him, a sharp, wounded breath, followed by retreating footsteps, then the slam of the door. Frizer is gone.

Kit feels, keenly, that he has forgotten something. Of course: he should have asked Frizer whether he'd seen or heard anything odd today; perhaps he too had seen the twins skulking about, or even Poley! Kit moves to follow him, making it halfway across the room before he realizes that what he has in fact forgotten was only common decency.

Ashamed, he sinks into the room's only chair, spends several minutes staring blankly at the Queen, then several minutes more frowning at the slim manuscript on the desk: *Hero & Leander*. Kit had not intended to leave it lying out last night. Certainly, Frizer has read it, which would make him only the second man ever to do so.

The first had been Tom. 'A pretty thing,' he'd called it. 'But 'tis unfinished.' And so it remains, unfinished. *Hero & Leander* had died a sudden death, as had many things, in the wake of Tom's arrest. The poem should end in tragedy, but it stops just after Leander has completed his first great swim across the Hellespont to meet the vestal virgin, Hero, in her tower by the sea, where the doomed young lovers clumsily, tenderly deflower one another. Their inevitable deaths, Leander's by drowning and Hero's by suicide, never were of much interest to Kit anyway. All that mattered was the journey: the long, dark, foundering swim. There is no better metaphor for love.

Kit had often fancied himself the virgin locked in the tower, and Tom the amorous swimmer. But in the end, Kit was the swimmer, the prisoner was Tom.

Frizer has left the manuscript open. Not to the lovemaking scene, where one would expect most fellows' attentions to linger, but to the second page:

> And whose immortall fingars did imprint
> That heavenly path, with many a curious dint
> That runs along his backe...

Leander's hair, Leander's eyes, the smoothness of his body, the taste of his skin. This is what Frizer has been reading.

Kit touches two fingers to the words *that heavenly path* – the runnel that slopes from the nape of a man's neck to the top of the buttocks, that fingers, or tongue, or sweat may follow. A snap of arousal seems to leap off the page, like wool-lightning.

⊱❈⊰

Frizer dares not return to the Inn-in-the-Wall until a crier announces the start of curfew with, 'Bolts and locks! Bolts and locks!' leaving a wake of shuttered windows and snuffed lamps through the city. Soon, the only light in Bishopsgate shines from the Inn-in-the-Wall's common room, where guests gather to souse themselves before retiring. Marlowe is easily spotted from the window. With his elbows on the bar, he looks small among the other men – average-sized, rather – but when he rises to his full height and tips his head back to drink, his fellow patrons stop to gaze up at him, wonderingly, admiringly. *What a specimen!*

No more than a minute after Frizer has taken a seat halfway up the first flight of stairs, the door to the common room opens below, disgorging a long sheet of light wherein Marlowe's lean, equine shadow stands out like a stain.

Even as delicious meat is to the taste, so was his neck in touching.

Frizer shakes himself. That word, that wicked word: *Delicious!* 'Tis at the meeting of two sins, lust and gluttony. A slithering, needling, nibbling word; a serpent of a word, twisting down the trunk of his tongue. God damn Marlowe for putting that word in his head!

'Not hungry?' Marlowe says, not yet drunk but nearing it. Has he been here all this while, poised at the door, awaiting Frizer's return like an importunate suitor?

Frizer merely snorts. He'd dined elsewhere, he might say, on beef-collar braised in wine, but he prefers to let Marlowe suffer in silence. And indeed, it seems he suffers terribly, huffing and puffing at things unsaid a while before turning away as if to go inside, then turning back again. 'Listen, I... I have determined that I shall become better company to you. From now on.'

'*Determined* it, have you?'

'Ay.' Marlowe hunches his shoulders. From here, his head is level with Frizer's knees. 'I admit, I am sometimes... ill-mannered.'

'*Ill-mannered!*' Frizer echoes.

'I sorely regret my incivility.'

'*Incivility!*' Frizer would like to bite down on every word he speaks and shake it in his teeth.

'The truth is, I may need your help again, Master Frizer.' This Marlowe says while looking anywhere but at Frizer himself. 'I fear you will grow resentful of me, being so demanding of your time. But I am bound to the conditions of my bail, and you are not, and therefore are at liberty to do such things as are forbidden to me...'

Already Frizer has acquired a new knot in his stomach. 'What in hell would you have me do?'

'Deliver a message, that's all.'

Frizer laughs aloud, incredulous.

'There's no danger in it, I promise. No danger to *you*. 'Tis only that the message must go to Newgate Without, and as you know I am forbidden to cross the Wall.'

'And to what familiar of Satan shall I deliver this message, exactly? A cat, a toad, a salamander?'

Marlowe gnaws his tongue. 'Richard Baines.'

'Ha! The Devil himself, then, the way you talk of him!'

'A *man*, by category, and no threat whatsoever to you. I would go to see him myself if I could. You need only hand him my message and be on your way.'

'What message?'

Marlowe's answer is to throw a nervous look over one shoulder.

Frizer relents. 'Ay, indeed – not my business.' He realizes, upon these words, that he has already agreed in his heart. 'Tis an unexpected delight to be needed, not once, but twice now. Still, Frizer lets Marlowe wait upon an answer several seconds longer than necessary, at last saying, 'Very well. But there will come a day when I refuse ye, you hear? I have one master already, and Lord knows he'd have my head on a pike if he knew the things you have me up to.'

'He'll never hear of it, I swear.'

'Hell, I imagine you could get across the Wall yourself without much trouble if you only tried. The guards see you coming, a big brute like you, they'll run for the hills!'

Now Marlowe laughs. 'A big brute, am I?' That smile of his, which last night had seemed so warm, in fact has a vulgar edge to it: something slippery, effeminate.

Frizer says nothing, and in the silence Marlowe's grin diminishes. He spends an anxious moment pawing at the ground with the toe of his boot, and then, with an easy gesture borne out of much repetition, unclips his flask from his belt and holds it just below his lips. 'So,' he begins, breathing out with the word. 'What did you think?'

Frizer knows exactly what he means. His throat tightens; his gaze scatters over the quiet inn-yard. 'Think about what?'

Marlowe regards him with a rigid, retreating look, neither smiling nor frowning but something in between, something ready to go in either direction. 'Of the poem.'

'What poem?'

Marlowe pouts. 'Come now.'

'What does it matter what I think?'

'Well, of course it matters! I am a poet; I live always by the opinions of others. Indulge me. What did you think?' He seems to know that he has written a dangerous thing; he speaks of it like forbidden fruit.

Frizer cannot answer truthfully. That would be suicide. 'I think—' He hesitates. 'I think Leander should find himself a woman closer to home. No wench is worth the swim.'

Marlowe barks out a loud laugh that seems to surprise him, stifling the sound with a hand. Frizer wonders whether someone *is* watching them now – from a window? From the *moon*? Marlowe's bearing is like that of a captive, a man seated across a table from another man who could order his throat cut with a snap of the fingers. Or a woman, rather. He has that bargaining look in his eyes that women sometimes affect, the look that says, *I am all for your pleasure, so long as you are not for my pain.*

'I'll let you read the new play,' Marlowe says, 'if you care to.'

An hour or so after Frizer beds down on the floor by the cot, Marlowe comes blundering into the room like a blind man attempting a burglary, crashing shank-first into the bed-frame. At first he nearly slides down to the floor but manages to stop himself, perching at the edge of the bed, where he sways in place.

'Are you going to be sick?' Frizer says.

The spots of light on Marlowe's eyes blink out, reappear. 'You sleep on the floor now?'

Frizer starts to reply, but Marlowe tips sideways, slowly at first, then flops down hard, letting out a groan into the pillow. His breath lifts a lock of curls from his face.

'Say your prayers, man,' Frizer reminds him.

'Why, will you report me if I do not?'

Frizer knows not what to say. There's always a right and a wrong answer to such questions. 'No,' he admits, at last.

Marlowe seems to consider this response with great care. Eventually, he says, 'You can sleep here, you know. In the bed. Y'are not my servant.'

Frizer takes a corner of the bedroll and tucks it over his arm, shaking his head, though Marlowe cannot see him. 'I like to sleep on the floor,' he says. 'Anyway, that bed sleeps two average-sized men, and but one of you.'

Marlowe sniggers, twisting himself at the hips so that his torso faces the ceiling, knees drawn up, arms above his head. 'You are a discreet fellow, are ye not?' He sounds almost wistful.

Frizer's nerves bristle at the word 'discreet', the master's word. 'Why?'

'I can trust you?'

'With what now?'

'Oh, no more favours, I do not mean that. Other things. I know not what might come up.'

Frizer knows not what to say. 'As long as ye do me no injury, 'tis all one to me.'

Marlowe finds this amusing as well. 'Injury! What do you think I would do to ye, big brute that I am? You think I would pick you up and throw you?'

There's something sinister, serpentine, in the coiling of his body; belly exposed, like a dare and a threat all at once.

'Go to sleep, man,' Frizer snarls. 'Y'are drunk!'

Obediently, Marlowe closes his eyes. But neither of them sleeps. Even after several minutes, Frizer can hear wakefulness in Marlowe's breathing, an occasional soft catch as his thoughts stray where he would surely prefer they did not. *I should say something*, Frizer thinks. Always, there has been a void between himself and others, but with Marlowe the distance seems narrower than with most, as if they are each just on opposite sides of a door, shouting to be heard. He thinks of his brothers, Elias and Rafe, whose shared bed he'd slept beside as a child, on the floor. They would gab all night long, mostly about girls, wenches, lasses, whores, sluts, slits, cunts. 'Did ye turn her over?' Rafe might ask Elias, 'Did she spread?' Frizer would think of a woman in a full skirt, a handbell with arms. He'd imagine turning her on her head so that she became a cup, a sheath.

Even as delicious meat is to the taste, so was his neck in touching. Nay, he cannot get it out of his head. How does a touch have a taste, except with the tongue? He pictures the muscle that runs from behind the ear to the collarbone, the shallow depressions at the shoulder and the base of the throat. He imagines tracing every element of that anatomy with the tip of his tongue; he imagines it tastes rare. Salted. Bloody.

But now the Devil's in him, upright and restless, sharing his spine. He must not submit to it again. All day long he'd hung about this room, taking regular sucks from those pages as if from a pipe. He certainly cannot submit now, while Marlowe lies awake just steps away. If Frizer stretched out one leg he could touch the foot of the bed; that is how close they are. He can see moonlight whitening the hairs on Marlowe's forearm; that is how close they are. If he draws a sharp breath, Marlowe will hear it, he'll hear it and he'll know.

'Is this what you want?'

Elias – it was Elias who had asked him that. In his out-stretched hand, a jug, the kind with a bearded, grimacing face stamped into the neck, the very same jug their father usually kept hidden under his bed. Up until that moment, Frizer's brothers had never shared anything with him. He'd drunk greedily, nearly choked, swallowed with his eyes watering.

'You're a little man now, aren't ye?' said Rafe, slapping him between the shoulders, where he was sore. 'Time to drink like one.'

The three of them were alone in the stables, sitting on hay-bales, the only light a lantern. It was the night of Chestnut Sunday, the day when all the parish lads of a certain age were marched around the village border and whipped by their fathers at every boundary marker, so they would remember the shape of the map. When finally the limping procession had returned to the church, Papa had picked Frizer up from his armpits and swung him over the threshold three times, to make him a man. Frizer was the youngest in his family by nine years. The mother-killer. Elias and Rafe had been men for as long as he could remember.

Frizer's back stung from his ordeal, though the ritual at the church door had left him feeling unchanged. Now, as liquor seared down his virgin throat, he'd thought that *this* was the true moment of transformation, the burn branding him from the inside: a man. Now that he was a man, he would drink like Papa did, with his head tipped back. He would wear his drunkenness like a livery, taking swigs around the stable-yard as he'd often pretended to do when he was small. It was a game to him: *Be like Papa.*

The night turned hazy. For some time, the three brothers laughed and jested and swilled, as brothers do. They spoke mainly of women. Rather, Frizer listened as his brothers spoke of women, of the things one does with them and all the ways in which a woman might resist.

'Why?' Frizer said. 'Why do they resist?'

Elias and Rafe laughed in a way that indicated he'd made a

fool of himself. All he'd meant was that it seemed pointless to try. Elias and Rafe were big, strong men. Women were weak.

'You'd not resist, would you, Ingram?' Elias said. 'You'd lie facedown and bite the pillow.'

The floor seemed to sink several inches. Perhaps it had been sinking gradually, over the course of the night, and through all that time Frizer had been descending a slope all but imperceptible to him until he'd turned to look back and saw the way up impossibly distant, impossibly high.

'That's what a smart girl does,' Elias said. 'Are you a smart girl?'

He drew his knife from behind his back. That was where he'd always worn it, like a tail. Frizer had long admired it. How it followed him everywhere, a threat in the shape of a cross. *If I had a knife like that,* Frizer had often thought, *no one would ever harm me.*

'No,' Frizer answered.

Elias and Rafe cackled.

'He's a stupid girl,' Rafe sniggered.

'He's a cunt,' Elias said, and stood up. 'Time he learned what a cunt has coming to it.'

For a moment longer, Frizer felt as if he had a choice: to struggle or to submit. To be smart or stupid. To believe what was happening or to disbelieve it, disbelieve to the bitter end. He chose, perhaps, not to cry for help. He chose not to resist. He forced laughter, like a little dog with its throat in the jaws of a bigger one, belly-up, tail wagging: 'That's enough now – that's enough – that's enough!'

'Is this what you want?' Elias said, and cared not if the answer was no. 'Is this what you want?' as they wrestled off his clothes. 'Is this what you want?' as they shoved a dirty stocking into his mouth. 'Is this what you want?' as something cold and metal ran down the length of his spine.

''Tis what you'll get.'

From that point on all choices vanished. He could only fall, and scream.

But the knife is his now, given to him six years ago at Papa's graveside, like an apology, or a slap. *Here. That's for you.* It has not left his possession since. As he'd imagined, no one has harmed him since.

The scars, of course, are another story.

❧❀❧

In Richard Baines's luxurious private room at the Saracen's Head, which is exempt from the curfews within London's walls, Robin Poley stands close, but not too close, to the desk by the window. He strains his eyes to make out the papers under the candlelight: a list, that much he can see. A long list, of neatly inscribed, evenly spaced items, most two or three lines long. The pages, fanned out, appear identical from one to the next. Copies. At least a dozen copies.

Would anyone notice if just one went missing?

The trouble is the mutes: a pair of towheaded twins, tall, strapping lads who watch him from across the room, one with his elbow jabbed upon the mantel, the other straddling a hearth-stool. Not since their master left to fetch refreshments (an eternity ago) have they removed their colourless eyes from Poley's person.

If, for one instant, he could deflect the boys' attention elsewhere…

'Apologies for the delay,' Baines says, shoving a willowy serving-girl into the room. 'You will not believe the crush downstairs!'

'Indeed,' Poley says, 'you would hardly know there was a plague about.'

Baines tries to spit on the floor; it dribbles down the hollow side of his face. 'A plague upon the plague! Just you wait till the people grow weary of living like damned prisoners. The plague shall seem a trifle then!'

The years have not been kind to Baines. He is only a little older than Poley but already grizzled, one side of his face so withered that it looks as if the flesh beneath the cheekbone had been scooped out with a spoon. Still, he swaggers into the room as if he were Hannibal on a God-damned elephant, legions at his back, and not the sorry, shabby clown he is and always was, reeking of strife, of scrounging.

The boys, Poley notes, turn as bashful as maids upon their master's return, although Baines ignores them. He offers Poley a drink off the willowy girl's tray, an ale as thick and dark as swamp-water, which Baines declares, 'The sweet savour of home!'

'Those papers by the window,' Poley says, as soon as they settle in before the unlit hearth, 'I presume that is the document you have promised us?'

'"Us?"' Baines snorts. 'Did Puckering send you?'

'Not at all. But I must count myself among those eager to see the pages. Appetite increases, you see, at the promise of a feast.'

'You shall have to nibble elsewhere some while longer. From the moment the Council has their hands on those pages, Kit Marley will have one foot in either the Marshalsea or the grave. I care not which, s'blood, but the document shall remain with me until after I've finished my business with its subject – when I'm good and ready for it.'

'How long, do you reckon, till you will be good and ready?'

Baines blows air through his nose, a silent chuckle. 'You know, I spent *four years* planning what I would say, or do, if ever I saw Kit again. Then last year, out of the blue, the boy turns up at my doorstep! And what do I do? Four years of composing speeches in my head, plotting perfect revenges, all gone, in a flash! One look at those sad brown eyes and I crumbled.' He swirls the liquid in his cup. '*This* time… Well, if I have learned anything, 'tis that a man can never truly know what to expect of himself, till he is held to the fire. But if you think I have not made a plan, and secured whatever hatches I may, and plugged whatever holes need plugging, you would be wrong.'

When Baines falls silent, Poley can think only of what Marlowe had said to him earlier today: *With Baines, there is always a boy.* Those boys who used to trail Baines in and out of every room back in the old days – boys from the university, boys from the slums, wretched boys with bloody gums and shattered nerves, and rarely the same boy twice – somehow, Kit Marlowe had outlasted them all. There must be a reason.

'What?' Baines says, with a wrinkle of suspicion.

'Nothing. I only wonder whether Master Marlowe may once again turn up at your door, unannounced. I wonder if he would be so bold…'

Baines's left eyelid betrays an agitated twitch. 'What are you gibbering about?'

'I told him you were here. I saw him today, at the Privy Court.'

Baines seethes a moment, then scoffs. 'Well, he would be a fool to come here.'

Now, Poley is beginning to enjoy himself. 'I have known Master Marlowe only a short time, but if there is one thing of which I am assured, it is that he is prone to foolishness. Drunkenness, too. I imagine a drunk, foolish Kit Marlowe could leave quite the mark upon this room, ere the watch came to drag him away…'

'Now I wonder what your game is.'

'You are wasting time, old friend,' Poley says. 'I understand you've made certain commitments to yourself, but my superiors grow weary of waiting on you. Perhaps those sad brown eyes have seduced you yet again.'

Baines wags his finger. 'Do I look to you as if the Council's

HESSE PHILLIPS

impatience is of any concern to me? Do you know where I have lived these past five years? Do you know where I've slept? What I've eaten? The things I've done, simply to live another day? You should see the rags I came here in – hell, you should *smell* them! This room – those curtains on the bed, they are thicker by an inch than the coat I've worn these past four winters. Downstairs they serve us meat – not sinew, not the drippings, but flesh, flesh that oozes *scarlet* when you cut into it! For that the Council has but one use for me, I am in no hurry to spend it. And Kit – marry, I care not a fig for what the Council does with him. The archbishop can wipe his arse with those pages for all I care. You are welcome to them. But not until I'm finished with Kit, do you hear? Not until then!'

'What will be left of Master Marlowe when you are "finished" with him?'

'Enough, Robin,' Baines says, darkly. 'There will be *enough* left over for you.'

Poley gnaws his lip. He wonders if it shall have to come down to threats. 'I need him alive. Can you promise me that?'

Baines nods as if silently turning over that word 'alive'. 'Oh, he'll be alive.'

'And I need to see those papers. Tonight.'

Baines's scowl turns dubious. 'To what *end*, Robin?'

'That is my business. It shall not interfere with yours.' Poley detects a refusal on the way, and so speaks quickly. 'If you fear I shall hand your statement over to my superiors before your business with Marlowe is completed, then let me read it, here and now. Give me but thirty seconds. The gist is all I require.'

'A minute ago, you spoke on behalf of your superiors, or am I mistaken?'

Poley smiles, as if to forgive a fool. 'Much has changed since you were last on Albion's shore. The Council can go hang themselves. I am here on my own behalf.'

Baines thrusts out his chin in contemplation. He then utters something that Poley believes he mishears, until the larger of the towheaded twins stirs from his place at the mantel like a statue animated, shaking off the dust. Sullenly, the boy crosses the room and retrieves a sheaf of papers from the desk, handing it to his master. 'Dutch,' Baines says, to Poley's bewildered expression. 'I have tried to teach them English, but they are slow of study, the poor beasts. Somehow, they always find me – the simpletons, the orphans, the misfits. I think, when this is over, I will open a home for castoff boys, out in the country. That is what I'll do.'

He offers a page to Poley as casually as a penny in exchange for an apple or a peach.

'You have twenty seconds,' Baines says. 'I will count.'

As morning comes, Poley hovers red-eyed beside Dick Topcliffe's desk while the chortling imp reads a summary of the first page of Baines's statement, written from memory. From the bed, Topcliffe's little concubine watches them, her eyes gleaming gold in the reed-light. Now and then, Poley can hear her chains shifting, under the sheets.

Lord knows how much of Baines's note is true, not that truth is really the point of these things. At Seething Lane, Poley fields dozens of similar notes every month, the work of amateur spies looking to settle a score, or receive an informant's fee or some other favour: *Herein may you find the wicked and treasonous acts and words of my neighbour so-and-so, recorded with reverence and terror by your servant, etc.* Always the same tired accusations of witchcraft and sorcery, blood-pacts with the Devil, naked revels in the moonlight. This one is different, just strange and specific enough to be true, a neat list of such blasphemies of which only a man of Marlowe's particular ilk might be guilty: an educated man, a man who has had access to certain secrets, a man, surely, of promiscuous curiosity.

When Topcliffe is finished, he sits back and offers up one of his toasts to his eternally youthful, stern-faced cousin, the Queen, whose long, thin fingers seem to clutch the Bible over her nether parts a little tighter. 'My dear,' he says to her, 'this one we'll eat *alive*, you and I.'

22 MAY 1593

Eight days

❧

Pleaseth it your honorable Lordship, touching Marlowe's monstruous opinions: as I cannot but with an aggrieved conscience think on him, or them, so can I particularize few... Howbeit, in discharge of duty, both towards God, your Lordships & the world, thus much have I thought good briefly to discover, in all humbleness.

THOMAS KYD, LETTER TO THE LORD KEEPER
SIR JOHN PUCKERING, JUNE 1593

You are quoting from this Marlowe. Is he a communist?

CONGRESSMAN JOE STARNES, CROSS-EXAMINATION OF
HALLIE FLANAGAN OF THE FEDERAL THEATRE PROJECT, HOUSE
SPECIAL COMMITTEE ON UN-AMERICAN ACTIVITIES, 1938

14

I T TAKES THE LANDLORD and the chamberlain working in furious tandem to lug the Inn-in-the-Wall's only strongbox up to Frizer and Marlowe's room. At the door they drop their load and proceed to shove it across the floor to the window, a piece of metal screeching at the base all the way. At last, the box comes to rest: an iron-clad, age-blackened, toadish thing, armoured in the scraps of perhaps a dozen predecessors.

Panting, the landlord hands Marlowe a heavy-looking key. 'You lose it, you pay,' is all he manages to say.

As soon as they are gone, Marlowe begins emptying papers out of his bag and stacking them inside the box, taking his time as always, flipping through pages he has no doubt thumbed a thousand times before. Meanwhile, Frizer sits upon the sagging cot, holding a letter which Marlowe had dropped onto the floor beside his head first thing this morning. The paper-bolt with which it is sealed is heartbreakingly amateurish, as if Marlowe had grown bored or frustrated halfway through making it.

'This Baines fellow,' Frizer says. 'Will I have to talk to him?'

'No!' Marlowe says, barely glancing up from a bound manuscript. 'He may try to pull ye aside, but do not let him. Meet with him in a public place, hand him the message and be gone.'

'I thought you said there was no danger.'

'To you, no. Perfectly safe.'

Frizer opens his mouth to protest, but is interrupted as the manuscript in Marlowe's hands comes sailing at him, landing upon the cot. Frizer turns it right-side-up, squinting to read the title scribbled at the top of the first page: *The troublesome Reign & Cruell death of Edward II, unhappy Kinge of Engladne* – a mouthful, even without the misspelling.

''Tis not a good copy,' Marlowe says. 'If 'tis too much of a bother ye need not read it.' Practically blushing, he is. Frizer's heart swells just slightly with forgiveness, or something equally as generous.

They sit together on the steps above the inn-yard. Marlowe breaks the last caraway cake in two with his big hands and gives half to Frizer. A silence falls as the first bites are taken, then Marlowe probes, slyly, 'Did your wife make these?' Frizer has not yet mentioned anything of a wife.

'No,' Frizer says, and for a moment plans to leave it there. 'Her mother.'

'Ah.' Marlowe sounds pleased with himself. 'I knew it.'

'Knew what?'

'Any children?'

'Not yet.' A thought of Betsy comes to him – sprawled in bed, sweating, swollen, possibly labouring even as they speak – and Frizer adds, by rote, 'Any day now.'

Marlowe beams. Frizer can hardly bear the brightness of it. 'A father!' Marlowe says. 'How strange it must feel. *Does* it feel strange?'

Frizer scoffs, '"Strange?"' Ever since his wedding day, he has often felt as if a chasm had suddenly opened up before him, and that, when he looks out across the abyss, he can see himself, or a version thereof, standing on the other side – so distant, so unreachable.

'Ay,' he murmurs, bitterly. ''Reckon I'll have to call it "strange".'

HESSE PHILLIPS

Marlowe picks at his cake in silence, as if sensing an impasse. But then he smiles again, as if having thought of a good joke. 'My father is a cobbler, you know. His father too, and my mother's father – my father was his apprentice, in fact. A cruel old man he was, they say; I've never met him. But his daughter was beautiful, and as clever as her father was cruel.'

'Oh?' Frizer wonders where he means to go with this.

'One night, just after my father's apprenticeship had ended, he crept upstairs and met my mother in her bedchamber. Together, they proceeded to rob the old man blind. From room to room they crept, taking all that they could carry: his tools, his leathers, the spoons from the cupboard, the shoes from his bedside! But they'd been too greedy, you see, for as they made to leave the bedchamber, something fell from my mother's arms – a hammer or a block—'

'No!' Frizer gasps.

'The old man awoke, drew a cudgel from under his pillow and gave chase through the house, up the stairs. In the attic, my mother and father wrapped the leathers 'round their backs, embraced, and threw themselves out the window—'

'Full of fables, you are!'

'Ask my mother. You would not call my mother a liar, would you?'

'No doubt it runs in the blood.'

'So, by that logic, does thievery.'

They both laugh, Marlowe a tad shrill, a tad frenzied. He reminds Frizer of a hot horse: nose to the air, mane tossing, beating the dirt with its sharp hooves. Before Frizer realizes it, he is telling Marlowe about Papa – Papa before drink had become his only child – breaking the new foals in the paddock with such command, such ease. '"Begging for the whip," Papa would say. "A horse knows no god. He fears no god. He worships the whip."'

Marlowe's eyes grow wide, hearing this. 'Let me use that.'

Frizer's face blazes. 'No!'

'Yes, yes! I know not where, but I *must* use that!'

He is touching Frizer's knee with a hand that could wrap all the way around his leg. The hand is warm, a warmth that runs, via some channel of nerves, straight up Frizer's thigh.

'Well, I must go,' Marlowe says, turning away to drink. A second later he is on his feet, brushing the crumbs from his lap.

Frizer scrambles after him, down the stairs, across the yard. 'When will you come back? Where shall I find you? Should I come to Seething Lane after Newgate?' All goes unanswered.

With one foot already in Bishopsgate Street, Marlowe halts. 'I nearly forgot!' He reaches into a pocket and produces the same key which the landlord had given him not half an hour ago, offering it at arm's length, as if to offer a ring. 'This is for you.'

Frizer stammers. 'For *me*?'

'Of course. I cannot take it to the Privy Court. If anything should happen...'

'I understand.' Frizer holds the key close. It is as heavy as he'd expected. 'Wait, Marlowe? What should I do, if anything should happen?'

Marlowe walks backwards to say, 'Go to Greenwich. Take my papers with you!' The second command is of more importance than the first, it seems. Such is all the farewell that Frizer receives, for Marlowe turns again, his long strides speeding him across the street, towards many-gabled Crosby Place. He vanishes into the alleyway in a trice.

A knot of doom forms in Frizer's stomach. For a minute or so he waits for Marlowe to re-emerge through the smoke, rushing back with a final word, or something else forgotten. But as the seconds pass, he begins to feel foolish, and finally exchanges the key with the letter in his pocket.

The careless paper-bolt all but falls open for him, revealing handwriting so distinct from that of *Hero & Leander* that it could be another man's – scrawled, shaky; a howl, a whimper:

I begge you let us ende this. Commande me, I will do as you saye.

⬦⬦⬦

At the corner of Seething Lane, a man comes up at Kit's right shoulder and paces him, muttering as if to no one in particular, 'Today shall be difficult. Hold your tongue, no matter how hard you are pressed. Above all: trust me.'

This said, the man strides on towards the Privy Court as if nothing had occurred, a subtle, rolling limp in his step.

Kit enters, sceptical in mind but quivering with nerves. At the iron gate, a different guard from yesterday hoods him with a bag that stinks of some other man's breath, and then drags him upstairs by the elbow like a child to a caning. After several hard turns and a long corridor or two, the guard jerks him to a halt and knocks upon a door that sounds of metal. The throb of blood in Kit's neck grows suddenly loud, a lamblike bleating deep within his ears.

The door creaks open; he is shoved through. Several feet inside, a hand snatches his sleeve to halt him, swivels him about, presses him into a chair. Two men wrench Kit's arms behind him, one arm to each, binding his wrists to the backrest. No one says a word.

Some distance away, moans dribble from a man's throat.

At last, Kit's hood is removed. The light is dim, and yet he squints. This is a room he has never seen before, long and narrow, a window at one end showing a marble slab of sky. Several feet away sprawls a table that could easily seat ten, with one figure in the middle, like Christ at the Last Supper. At either end of the table, a scribe sits, each with an overseer hovering at his shoulder, devil- or angel-like: Phelippes on the right, masked as always; Robin Poley on the left.

The man in the middle hangs his head so low that Kit can only see the crown. A string of bloody drool dangles from the downcast face. The hair is grey with dust and filth, yet for all that, Kit recognizes something about its texture, the whorl of the cowlick, the shape of the shoulders.

'Kyd,' Kit gasps, and tries to stand. The rogues to his left and right press their hands down upon his shoulders, one gives his cheek a back-handed slap – not hard, merely spiteful. 'What is this?' Kit sputters, looking at Poley, who does not look back. 'What is happening?'

The scratching of pens on paper begins to whirl about the room like trapped wasps. Phelippes comes to the front of the table, hands behind his back, looking smug. Triumphant.

'Thomas Kyd of London, son of John Kyd of London, do you swear by Almighty God that the testimony you give today is the truth?'

A mumble: 'Yes.'

'Do you swear upon your faith in the Church of England, and your loyalty to Our Sovereign Lady Queen Elizabeth, and upon your own immortal soul?'

'Yes!'

Phelippes returns to his end of the table, takes up a paper and brings it to Kyd. He wipes the bloody tabletop with a handkerchief, sets the paper down beneath Kyd's nose. 'Be it written that Master Kyd has been presented with the heretical document recovered at his lodgings on the 12th day of May. Master Kyd, are you the author of this document?'

'No.'

'Can you name the author of this document?'

'Not positively, no,' Kyd says, with a mouthful of blood that obliges Phelippes to move the paper further off. 'I know not the author.'

Phelippes spiders his fingers upon the tabletop. 'Can you name the *owner* of this document?'

Kyd's head remains bowed. Slowly, he raises his manacled hands, lifting one arm with the other as if both are an all but impossible weight to bear. With one filthy finger, he points directly at Kit.

'Be it written that Master Kyd has pointed in the direction of Christopher Marley, alias Marlowe.'

''Tis not mine, I tell you!' Kit sputters, glancing again to Poley. 'I've never—'

'Master Kyd, have you ever heard Christopher Marley espouse heresies of the sort that are contained in this document?'

Kyd takes in a breath. He shoots a glance at Poley in the same childlike way that Kit feels himself looking at him, as if Poley were a cruel father, pitting his sons against each other.

'He said the prophets were jugglers,' Kyd says. 'He said Moses was a charlatan... He said there are Indians far older than Adam, or something like that—'

'Stop,' Kit rasps.

'And he said – he said that Christ and John the Baptist were... marry, I cannot say it.'

'Stop.'

'He said the Holy Ghost used the Virgin Mary like a whore—'

'Stop!' Kit cries. He has never said any such things to Thomas Kyd, not that he can remember. In this moment, his thoughts are all of Baines, straddling a stool in some grimy tavern, shaking with laughter as Kit tipsily improvised a dialogue between Mary and poor Joseph, surely the most gullible cuckold to have ever lived: '"A *dove*, you say? Came in through *this* window, you say? And y'are *dead certain* y'are still a virgin...?"'

In falsetto: '"Oh, yes, he assured me it counted for nothing, the way we done it!"'

'Stop, stop!' Baines had cried. 'Oh God, Kit, you must stop!'

"'Tis the truth,' Kyd says. 'I kept it secret. I took it for jesting.'

'You… kept it secret?' Poley says, the first time he has spoken. Kit stares at him like a drowning man at the shore.

'I mean,' Kyd stammers, 'I did not report it when I should have done.'

'Because you took these remarks for *jests*?' Poley leans forward archly, an irate schoolmaster. 'Master Kyd, did you *laugh* to hear such things?'

'What? No! No, I—'

'This business of the Holy Ghost and the Virgin, does that make you laugh?'

'No, I swear by God!'

'Master Poley,' Phelippes interjects. 'Master Kyd is not on trial.'

Poley bows his head, slipping on his customary, anodyne smile. 'I only wonder, Master Phelippes, whether we may not inadvertently expose ourselves to the Devil's meddling, should we leap upon this fellow's testimony. Must we not ask first of all whether one accused heretic is fit to testify against another? Especially one who, by his own admission, could *laugh* at remarks such as these?'

'I did *not*—'

Phelippes holds up a hand to silence Kyd, regarding Poley like a picture that simply will not stay upon its nail. 'That is a question for the philosophers, is it not, Master Poley?' he says. 'This is neither the time nor the place to eat of the lotus.'

'Oh, but 'tis our solemn duty to interrogate our methods, much as we do our subjects,' Poley parries. 'Two days ago, on this very ground, we condemned a man to hang for treason based on circumstantial evidence – nay, Master Phelippes, I would never decry the outcome; John Penry is a traitor, and shall die like one. 'Tis the path by which we *arrived* at justice which I fear was muddied by too much impatience, and God forbid we succumb to the same fallacy twice in one week.'

The scribes' stares bounce helplessly from one end of the table to the other. Phelippes pulls the mask down to his chin, revealing a ruddy-complexioned, toadish countenance, riddled with pockmarks. 'Master Poley, if anyone may be accused of muddying the waters just now, it is you!'

'Nay, but I suspect 'tis my clarity you find most inconvenient. And I do not speak solely of moral concerns. I ask you to consider: what sort of trial shall we mount if we move forward now? This – *this* is to be our witness?' He gestures to Kyd as if to a pile of dirty rags. 'Does this beseem the might of the Queen's Privy Council? This fellow who hath sworn upon his immortal soul, a thing in which, belike, he has no belief?'

Kyd starts, 'You *said—*'

But Poley shouts him down. "Faith, what a humiliating spectacle it shall be, to see the Star Chamber fall behind the word of an admitted atheist, who would make a laughing-stock of our God! What would his Holiness the Archbishop of Canterbury make of it? What would her Majesty make of it? What will the Lord Keeper say, when I—'

Phelippes slams his hand down upon the table, at which Poley finally falls silent – not, it seems to Kit, out of deference, but because there can be no clearer sign that he has won. For a second or two, the room holds its breath. And then, with a jolt, Phelippes comes alive again, storming down the length of the table towards Poley, as if intent on punching his teeth in. As Phelippes passes behind Kyd's chair, Kit meets Kyd's bloodshot eyes just long enough to see their terror dissolve into sorrow, regret.

Phelippes growls, 'Take them away. Put them in the cells.'

Kyd's face is the last thing Kit sees ere the black bag swallows him up.

Down a corridor and then a spiral stair, Kit stumbles on with a club jammed into his back. He hears the footsteps of several guards around him, plus the scuffle and scrape of

Thomas Kyd's blind footsteps. Somewhere below ground, where the air is chilled, Kit senses Kyd walking beside him – from the smell of him, perhaps, or simply the familiar feeling of his shoulder right up against Kit's shoulder, just as they'd used to sit at the table in Little Bedlam or at the lodging-house in Leathersellers', sharing the same inkpot – and come what may, life and limb be damned, Kit hurls himself at him. He feels the soft impact of a body between himself and a wall, his shoulder hard against a breastbone, a strangled cry in his ear. The guards shout, try to drag Kit back. For a moment they succeed and Kyd sputters, unpinned, 'Get him off me! He'll kill me!' at which Kit rams him again, with even less mercy than before.

His hooded head snarls to Kyd's hooded head, 'Crying home to mother – that's all you're ever good for!'

On the 18th of September 1589, the day that Tom was arrested, Kit and Kyd had been walking home together from the Curtain Playhouse in the afternoon: Kyd studiedly unkempt, ranting on about Bandello; Kit in his new suit, with fourteen pearl buttons gleaming all down the breast. They'd got as far as the corner of Hog Lane, where a man sprang out from behind a fence and shoved Kit clear off his feet.

The attacker lifted Kit's chin with the edge of a sword. His name was Bradley, an actor and inveterate gambler who had been banished from Little Bedlam after availing himself of Anna Watson's wedding jewels. To Kyd, Bradley snarled, 'Bring me Tom Watson!' and Kyd hopped to obey him, leaving Kit on his knees in the mud. When Tom appeared at last, his rapier drawn, Kyd upon his heels, Bradley had roared for the whole neighbourhood to hear of filthy buggerers and sodomites, half-women, suck-pricks, pimps and pederasts, and he offered to cut Kit's throat so deep his head would fall off.

Tom lunged. Kit dived out of the way. Bradley charged at Tom, windmilling his blade, and by sheer force drove him backwards up the street, all the way to the edge of the Finsbury ditch. Tom's heels slipped; he tumbled into the ditch. Bradley leapt in after him.

Kit had rushed forward, but it was already over: Bradley's body hung facedown over the ditch like a speared fish, Tom's rapier impaled clean through his chest and out the back.

So much ended in that moment: the halcyon days of Little Bedlam, the second adolescence of success and fame. Perhaps Tom's love for Kit also ended, or began to end, for afterwards he would ever blame Kit for what had happened – for making him lose himself, throw his life away so carelessly. Kit's trust in Thomas Kyd surely died that day as well, not because Kyd had brought Tom into the fray, but because of what he did next: turned tail and ran to fetch the constables who would, within the hour, haul Tom away to Newgate Prison.

'Coward!' Kit roars, as the guards chain his wrists to the wall. 'Milch-shitting coward! The Devil eat you, from the feet up!'

Nearby, Kyd snivels and begs forgiveness. It seems they are both restrained, each to the opposite wall of what must be an ample cell. Kit slides down until his arms are at full stretch, his head almost touching the floor, kicking like a cockerel without hitting anything. One of the guards suggests they stage a fight: 'Big blind bugger against little blind bugger – no hands, all else goes!' Eventually, Kit spasms and screams all the rage out of himself, till he lies panting upon the floor and the guards grow bored.

In the silence after the door closes, he can hear Kyd snuffling.

'Who told you what to say?' Kit snarls.

To this, Kyd merely whimpers.

Kit jangles his chains. 'Who told you what to say?'

'I know not what they'll do to me if I tell you.'

'Tell me or I swear by God I will do ye twice as worse!'

'It was *him*' – a whisper – 'it was Topcliffe. In the Marshalsea. He had a paper with him. He read from it. The man from upstairs was there too.'

'Which one?'

'I used to see him Sundays sometimes, at St Helen's. Has a limp. Topcliffe called him "birdy", "bird".'

Kit holds his breath. Somewhere high above his hood a chink of daylight glows, spinning a silvery web through the weave of cloth.

'He told me I would be released!' Kyd moans.

'Who? Poley?'

'Topcliffe.' Kyd shudders in despair. 'I knew he lied. I knew it. I wanted to believe—'

'What did Poley say? The man from upstairs? What did he do?'

'Nothing,' Kyd says. 'He *watched*.'

The floor seems to sway. So, this was what Poley had wanted with Baines: upstairs, Kyd had spoken of things only Baines could possibly know about. Kit feels a clench of betrayal, though there's no reason for it; Poley was never his ally. Kit has no allies. He imagines Thomas Walsingham sighing: *You see? This is what you do, Kit. This is why you cannot trust yourself.*

'He came before,' Kyd goes on. 'The man with no beard. A few days ago, I think, he came to the Marshalsea, and he spoke the prologue, from my *Spanish Tragedy*… He was looking into my eyes—' He breaks off, and gasps, 'I swear by Christ, Kit, I saw the Devil in that man. Or worse. I do not understand it. What does he want with me; what do any of them want with me? Why is this happening?'

'I wish I knew,' Kit lies.

'That paper Topcliffe had… what was it? Where did it come from?'

HESSE PHILLIPS

Kit shakes his head, thinking of poor Frizer, and of the message he carries: *Commande me, I will do as you saye.* Baines never could resist the abjection of a naked throat.

After several seconds of waiting on an answer, Kyd seems to give up. He snuffs, and murmurs, 'Everyone always said your mouth would be the death of ye.'

'You never heard me say such things.'

'That matters not. I believe you said them. I *know* you.' Kyd falls silent again, his mind grinding away so fiercely that it bestirs the air. 'I felt such a weight after what happened,' he begins again, 'with you, and Tom, and Bradley. I've played the scene at least a hundred ways, wondering if I might have been able to stop it. If I had tried... I know not. But I might have *tried.*'

All these years, they have never spoken of it. Surely Kyd dares to speak of it now only because he believes they will never see one another again. Kit remembers walking beside Kyd, in the moment before Bradley had attacked: the undiluted admiration in Kyd's shy glance, like a younger brother looking to his elder. Remorse pulls tight through Kit's chest like a rope.

'You know how they call me "Mad Hieronimo"?' Kyd says. 'Strangers, they say it as if it were a mark of distinction, but when you call me that, or Will, or Michael, 'tis a jest – a cruel jest, because I am nothing like Hieronimo, even though I created him. I'm not cunning. I'm not quick. I'm not brave. And you, they call you "Tamburlaine", or they call you "Faustus". As if either should be flattering!'

Kit laughs, glad of the hood for concealing his tears.

Kyd says, 'They think because God creates in His own image, that we do the same, but 'tis simply not true. We are not gods. We are just men.'

'I am sorry,' Kit says: sorry for all that he is and is not, for himself and for Kyd, for Tom Watson and Anna Watson and the prisoner in the cellar and Anthony Babington and even Baines. 'I am sorry.'

'You see?' Kyd murmurs, sadly. 'Tamburlaine would never say that.'

15

FRIZER PRESSES HIS HANDKERCHIEF to his face as he squeezes through the crowded common room of the Saracen's Head, envisioning a greenish vapour of pestilence radiating off the unwashed throng. He searches for a landlord, a chamberlain, a pot-boy, anyone who might direct him to Richard Baines, but encounters only soldiers with the winds of Hades at their backs and exhausted-looking whores at their fronts, singing, 'Men are fools who wish to die, hey nonny no!'

After doubling back to the entrance, Frizer finds a fellow who might be the chamberlain, to judge from his ring of keys, or possibly a jailer on repast from nearby Newgate Prison. 'I have a message for Richard Baines!' Frizer shouts at him.

The man with the keys cups his ear. 'Who?'

'Richard Baines! He's a guest here.'

'Richard who?'

Eventually this farce arrives at its obvious conclusion: the man has never heard of a Richard Baines, neither here nor anywhere. Perhaps Baines is here under an alias; perhaps Marlowe has sent Frizer to the wrong inn; perhaps this is a wild goose chase concocted by Marlowe for malicious purposes, intended to keep Frizer busy, and far away... Any rogue in this crowd might be Richard Baines. The man with the keys might have been Richard Baines!

Frizer squeezes his way to the bar, where a malnourished wench ignores him a while, scurrying back and forth at others' beck. He leans over the plank to shout his enquiry as she passes by, to which he receives a blank look that might just as easily be panic as ignorance. 'Sorry, master.'

Baines *is* here, Frizer is sure of it now. Armed with conviction, he pushes his way back onto Newgate Street and turns to look up at the inn's timber-clad, gabled façade, a sign above the door displaying its gruesome namesake in profile. He expects to see a figure appear in one of the glazed windows, watching him, but the Saracen's Head is enigmatic, fittingly enough, the glass showing nothing but a reflection of the darkening sky.

Raindrops begin to fall. Frizer finds a dry spot beneath the awning of a derelict building across the street, where in little time he is joined by several stinking beggars, who look so puzzled at his presence that he suspects himself an intruder in their customary squat. What an ass he is indeed – and Marlowe too, for that matter! How had it never occurred to either of them that a description of the devil's person might be *useful*?

One of the beggars approaches Frizer and stands uncomfortably close, open-handed.

Frizer presses the handkerchief tighter to his face. 'I carry no coin,' he says, the same lie he always tells.

The beggar goes nowhere. He shifts gently from one foot to the other, like a small child with a terrible urgency which he is either too polite or too abashed to name.

'I said I carry no coin!' Frizer dares to glance in the beggar's direction and finds, to his astonishment, that the dirty hand is not empty. It already contains a coin. Silver, by the look of it, but like no English coin that Frizer has ever seen; no image of the Queen's hatchet-headed profile, no 'ELIZA-REGINA'.

The beggar looks down to the coin and up again with wide, innocent eyes. Somewhere behind the mat of grizzled beard a lopsided mouth grinds away speechlessly, lips tucked together.

Frizer holds out his hand. Smiling, the beggar tips the coin into his palm.

Hunger eventually drives Frizer back to Bishopsgate, under a tepid drizzle. He examines the coin as he walks, the beggar's swift disappearance having denied him any hope of an explanation. The coin neither feels nor smells like silver, but is not heavy enough to be lead. Tin, perhaps, or pewter. One side shows a faint impression of a crest with an animal, possibly a lion; the other side, a bust of a man with a sword.

He has seen a counterfeit coin before. Nick had showed him an example once, some years ago, having taken a brief interest in the art of forgery. 'Let no one see it,' Nick had said, cupping his hands around Frizer's hand. 'They catch you with one of those and—' the finger across the throat. As always, Nick had seemed extraordinarily proud to have something so deadly in his possession.

But Nick's coin had been far more convincing. Frizer cannot even say what currency this one is meant to feign, not that he's an expert in foreign coin. Marlowe might know it; he seems to know many odds and ends of things. Oh yes, he'll say, that's an Egyptian guilder, or a Roman ducat, or a Spanish shekel, and Frizer shall have to take his word for it.

Frizer gobbles down his dinner at the Inn-in-the-Wall and then heads south for Seething Lane, arriving just as the clouds open. The closest shelter is the lychgate of St Olave's Church, where he squeezes himself into a corner, too squeamish to sit upon the coffin-rest. Within minutes, the world outside turns slanted and grey. Thunder dances across the sky, like cart-wheels over a rutted road. Across the street, the gates of the Privy Court open sporadically, releasing figures who scatter in every direction, arms and cloaks over their heads. But no sign of Marlowe.

Perhaps he is gone, truly gone. And then Frizer shall have to ride for Greenwich in the rain, to tell his master – but first, of course, back to Bishopsgate, to collect the papers. Marlowe never did specify what Frizer ought to do with the papers. Perhaps he would not mind if Frizer kept them, so long as he kept them safe. He could do that. Hide manuscripts in the barn back home, in the loft or in the walls. Read them at luxury, when no one is around to hear him, playing all the parts.

"'I that am termed the scourge and wrath of God, the only terror of the world!'"

The next time Frizer glances at the lion-fronted gatehouse, a great hop-stalk of a man stands in a puddle upon the sunken stoop: dripping wet, his posture a question mark.

Frizer sheathes his knife, steps into the downpour and waves his arm high above his head. No response. Both arms. Marlowe looks in his direction and still seems not to see him.

'Hallelujah,' Frizer cries, 'he is God damn risen!'

Sheets of rain vibrate off the muck on Bishopsgate Street as first Marlowe, then Frizer sprints under the shelter of the Inn-in-the-Wall's gate. Frizer doubles over and gasps for breath, worn out from trying to keep up. Marlowe rakes the wet hair back from his eyes and immediately grows still, hands at his temples, a look on his face as if he were plotting out the finer details of an especially gruesome murder. He has not said a word since he emerged from the Privy Court.

'Ho,' Frizer pants, and prods Marlowe's arm with two fingers, 'shall we go in and have a drink?'

Marlowe throws that same fearsome look in Frizer's direction, silent far too long.

Then, 'Ay,' he says, letting down his hands. 'Ay, a drink.'

They splash across the muddy inn-yard, arriving at the

door soaked all over again. The rain has driven a small crowd into the common room, which reeks both of mildewed wool and frying oysters. Marlowe wedges himself between two damp merrymakers and sets his flask on the plank. Frizer burrows in beside him, wondering how long he should wait to be asked about Newgate. Marlowe could not have forgotten about it, could he?

'By the way,' Frizer begins at last, 'I went to the Saracen's Head and asked for Baines, but no one would confess to knowing him. I waited most of the day, but well, I knew not who to look for, so I gave it up. But I can try again tomorrow. 'Tis better than waiting around on you. What kept ye so long, anyway?'

Still Marlowe says nothing, fumbling with a pearl button on his doublet, the only button of its kind, like a blind man trying to tell a sixpence from a groat.

Frizer empties his purse into his hand, picking through coins in search of one of the Inn-in-the-Wall's tokens. 'I shall have to find a way of passing the time while you are inside.' A thought occurs to him. 'The playhouses are still closed, no? For the plague?'

'Ay,' Marlowe grunts.

Frizer stares at him, startled to hear his voice at last, then looks down at his hand again. 'That's a shame. I could see a play while you are inside. Or we could go together, afterwards.' Frizer's face feels hot, having said this. We. Together.

'But we could not,' Marlowe says. 'Not even if the play-houses were open.'

'Why not?'

'I'm not allowed outside the Wall. All the playhouses are beyond the Wall.'

'Ay, right.' The beggar's coin appears in Frizer's hand, so bright that it takes him by surprise. Perhaps now is not the time to bring it up. In retrospect, the incident is so strange that Frizer would not believe it himself had he not the evidence at hand. Perhaps the only proper time to have mentioned it would have been immediately upon Marlowe's release, and having delayed, he can do naught but delay indefinitely. 'Tis clear, from the pinch of fear in his guts, that 'twere best to say nothing now.

He pockets the coin, places a token on the bar. 'Small ale with water, is it?'

'Whisky,' Marlowe says. 'No water.'

Night falls and the rain moves on, but the crowd at the Inn-in-the-Wall only grows larger and louder as curfew draws near, as if intent on drinking the plague away. Having reached his limit some time ago, Frizer now feigns every sip from his cup, for he would not have Marlowe think him less a man than himself. Marlowe's capacity is tremendous, as if he can fill himself like a bottle, from the feet upwards. Emboldened by drunkenness, Frizer thinks, *Now is the time to mention the stars*, and blithers, 'The stars... the way you write of them... I have always admired it.'

Marlowe puts down his cup just to grin at him, with an expression somehow vain and hungry and fragile all at once, as if he needs, and expects, more. Frizer's mind goes blank.

'You are interested in the stars?' Marlowe says. It comes off almost like a threat.

'Well. I reckon so. The way you write about them.'

Marlowe responds not with a discussion of the poet's craft, but with a rambling lecture on astronomy, delivered with exponential imperiousness and replete with obscure references, each one like another barb in Frizer's ear: Aristotle, Copernicus, Maimonides, Thomas Harriot, Tycho Brahe; cosmos, metaphysical, parallax, *nova stella*. After close to half an hour, he regrets having brought up the damned stars at all.

'...Faustus ought not to have asked a devil, you see,' Marlowe is saying. 'Of *course* the heavens are not as Mephistopheles describes them! Ptolemy, the old fool, he knew no better which way the heavens turned than he knew the colour of his own arsehole. *Per inaequalem motum respectu totius* – 'tis a convenient deflection, nothing more, and Faustus – having reached the limit of his understanding, and too ashamed to admit it – lets it go, sans argument! *O crassa ingenia, O caecos coeli spectatores!*'

Frizer has no idea what any of the Latin means, nor much of an idea who Ptolemy ever was, nor how this somewhat tedious subject could make anyone so enraged and enrapt all at once. 'Man, if astrologers are all charlatans, then the heavens matter nothing anyway.' (Marlowe has also just declared all astrologers to be charlatans, an opinion with which Frizer half-agrees.)

'But there you are wrong! The heavens matter, not because they are understood but because they are utterly *mis*understood. Look, when a man gives the lie to your face you may tell from his eyes that he is lying. When the world lies to your face, where do you look for reproof?'

Frizer shrugs.

'*In the eye!*' Marlowe intones, as if he finds his audience hopelessly stupid.

'You say… that the heavens *lie* to us?'

'No! Great God, how many ways must I say it? *We* lie, Master Frizer, *Man* lies! Nature cannot lie – the stars cannot lie!'

Frizer holds his head and whispers, 'Blind me.'

'You see, you see, *this* is how our childish nature overmasters our reason, that we may be shown a painted cloth and take it for the doors to Paradise! On the better stages, they fly gods and angels in on ropes – every man in the playhouse sees the ropes, and yet they all gasp like credulous infants—'

'I'm going upstairs,' Frizer announces.

'And you should know better, Master Frizer,' Marlowe rants on, unstoppable, 'for you have seen both the play and the playmaker, and know well enough how one has no magic in't in the slightest.'

'What has that to do with anything? What does it even mean?'

Marlowe's smirk has a terrible mischief in it. As if he is angling for a fight. 'If I put before you a stripling boy with scruff on his chin and rouge on his lips and tell you, "Lo, this is fair Helen of Troy", you'll believe me, no?'

Frizer squares up to him. 'Oh, I see, I see: a coney-catcher, are you, playing us all for fools? Ay, how clever you are, how stupid the rest of us!'

'Nay, I am no cozener, Master Frizer, only a juggler. Like you.'

'Now, what is the meaning of that?'

'Just as it seems. You do your tricks, I do mine. But let me tell ye, in confidence: 'tis no magic to conceal a cock beneath a petticoat.'

Frizer considers striking him on the chin. Instead, he downs his drink all at once, slams the cup on the bar, and storms out wishing he had struck him indeed, wishing he were man enough to drop him to the ground.

Upstairs he summons the chamberlain, orders the candles lit, and then sprawls on the cot, waiting for his dizziness to pass. The manuscript of *Edward II* lies on the floor, within reach, bound at one corner with a ratty knot of green thread. He pictures Marlowe leaning down, breaking the thread with his teeth.

With the candles melting into their stands and still no sign of Marlowe, Frizer takes up the manuscript and sits at the desk, his heavy head propped just inches above the paper. The quill with which Marlowe wrote *Edward II* must have been drunk, taking winding loops that give rise to phantom letters, transpositions. Patiently, Frizer untangles it. In time, a stage appears before him, and from behind the curtains a pompous, surely overdressed fellow called Gaveston struts. He clutches a letter to his breast, and sighs:

'"Sweet prince, I come! These, thy amorous lines
Might have enforced me to have swum from France
And, like Leander, gasped upon the sand,
So thou wouldst smile and take me in thine arms—"'

A knock at the door. 'Tis the chamberlain again, looking nervous. 'Good sir, I beg your forgiveness that I must beseech you look to your companion. I have tried, but...' He hesitates, casts a glance down the stairs. 'He's too heavy.'

Frizer suppresses a groan. He throws a longing glance to the desk, the state of which might suggest to any stranger that *he* is, in fact, the poet, and the big, blundering sot downstairs merely his useless bodyguard. *He* is Christopher Marlowe, that is *his* candle burning in the stand, those are *his* papers upon the desk, *his* handwriting upon them, *his* words.

'Where is he?' Frizer growls. He follows the chamberlain's gesture over the railing and spots Marlowe lying just above the bottom of the stairs, as if flung there at the head of a wave.

Frizer thumps down, heavy-footed, unpitying. The chamberlain claims that Marlowe would not rouse for him, but he does so for Frizer soon enough, clambering upright as clumsily as a new foal. 'Do not touch me,' he snarls, and immediately trips over his own feet.

Marlowe climbs the five flights of stairs on all fours. At the top, he staggers through the door and collapses on the edge of the bed, both hands over his face, looking as if he might weep. Perhaps he is past the mad-dog stage of drunkenness and nearing the point where one could sit and howl all night long.

'Can ye get your own boots?' Frizer says, exasperated.

Marlowe says nothing, and so Frizer kneels, tugging the old boots off one at a time. He thinks of the kitchens at Scadbury, the livid red and white of those blistered feet. What kind of cobbler's son has a hole in the sole almost big enough to put your finger through?

''Faith, I am sorry,' Marlowe says.

'Lie down now,' Frizer says, pushing his shoulder. 'There you go.'

Marlowe sinks into the pillow, curling up on his side like an exhausted child. Frizer feels sorry for him. Disgusted too. There's a smell about him, not merely the stink of drink but something sick, something terminal. Papa had smelled that way, even on his bier.

'I am so sorry,' Marlowe says again, sounding practised in such apologies, quite weary of making them.

As if by suggestion, or out of sympathy, Frizer feels a resurgence of his own drunkenness. He can only laugh, and forgive. 'Marry, y'are insufferable!'

Marlowe laughs also, his eyes closed, and then lies still for so long that Frizer wonders if he's fallen asleep. His face turns smooth, ageless, restful. The broken nose, the scarred chin, they are of one face, and the lips, so full and red, are of another, a vestige of some gentler, untarnished creature. But suppose all men look innocent in sleep. Papa had. Elias and Rafe had.

But Marlowe is not asleep. His long fingers fiddle with that single pearl button on his breast, twisting it on its threads. 'My father was apprenticed to my mother's father,' he says. 'That much is true. She was sixteen. He was eighteen. He did steal into the house one night... into her room... and left her with child.'

Frizer smiles, happy to have earned the truth. 'Let me guess, that child was you?'

'No. My elder brother. He died before I was born. And the next boy after him. I was only a baby. My elder sister, Mary, died when I was four. She was six. And my little brother, he died while I was away at Cambridge. He was ten.' He is quiet for a moment. 'I am the only son now, and the eldest. Four sisters. I mean, three. Jane, she died while I was in Paris. Fourteen... Fourteen is too young to bear a child.'

Frizer knows not how to respond to such sad, intimate revelations. 'I have two brothers,' he says, but of course neither one is tragically dead, a terrible inadequacy on his part. And then he remembers. 'My father is dead. My mother too. She died when I was born.' He sometimes forgets he ever had a mother at all.

Marlowe chuckles darkly. 'Are we not a pair?'

Frizer's smile broadens. *We.*

'My father, he was a sot too,' Marlowe says. 'I always swore up and down I would never be like him. Choirboy. Pious little shit! But… after Jane… I came back from France, and my sister was dead, and I could not tell them where I had been, why I had not come home. It began, then. Grew worse later, after…' He stops. A pinch of discomfort tugs at the space between his eyes, as if with pain or dizziness. 'Take my hand.'

'Why?'

'Because I think I am dying.'

Frizer sniggers, sits on the floor by the bed. He stares at Marlowe's hand a while, wondering if he might have been serious – about taking his hand, not about dying. Perhaps he could touch Marlowe now, without it being strange. After all they are both drunk, both in a companionable mood. Rafe and Elias used to hug one another when they were drunk asleep. Sometimes Frizer would find Rafe snuggled against Elias's back with his arm around him. Which was quite strange, come to think of it. Strange what sorts of things drunkenness and darkness and the privacy of a bed may permit.

Frizer had tried it once, with Nick, when they were both young: they'd lain down in the deep summer rye, side by side, and Frizer said, *now you turn that way*, and Nick did as he was told; and then Frizer said, *now I hug you, like this.* Frizer must have clung to him for twenty minutes before Nick had stood up and said, 'I'm tired of this game,' and pushed Frizer down and ran off for home. Frizer feels that old slithering in his stomach to think of it. That sense of something lingering.

Marlowe's long fingers flex gently, as if with anticipation, the droplet of pink scar on his hand shining in the dim light.

The gesture reminds Frizer of the coin in his purse. Having guarded this secret so long, it startles him how immense it has grown while his watch was elsewhere. It seems to fill the room, to darken the candles like a draught. 'Marlowe,' he whispers, with nothing planned to say. 'Listen: something strange happened today, in Newgate...'

Marlowe breathes almost as if asleep. He murmurs something, a half-finished thought: 'They want me to— What?'

Frizer takes Marlowe's hand, but only to peel his fingers apart and press the coin into his palm. 'I should have told you before, I know. Look, a beggar gave it to me. It could be nothing. But I think... I think it may be counterfeit.'

Marlowe opens his eyes. 'Counterfeit?'

'Why would a beggar give me a counterfeit coin?'

Marlowe's eyes close again, again with a look of pain, sharper than before. He rubs the coin in his fist. 'That was no beggar. That was the Devil.'

16

To explain the coin, Kit must also explain what happened in the Low Countries early last year, with Baines. But he must be careful with his words. He omits entirely the circumstances that had led to his going abroad, which had really begun in the spring of 1590, with Tom's release from Newgate: rushing to Little Bedlam, only to find the doors bolted against him. Returning day after day for a fortnight, knocking on every shuttered window, pleading with a locked door, knowing, all the while, that he was being watched from within. The last time Kit ever saw Tom was another whole year after that: not Tom exactly, but one eye peering through the upstairs shutters while the parish watch wrestled Kit from the doorstep below, a scratch from Anna Watson's fingernails bleeding fresh upon his chin. 'What did I do?' Kit had screamed, drunkenly. 'Tell me! What did I do?' But all this, Kit omits from his story.

Instead, he begins in January of 1592: with the letter he'd written to the Lord Keeper requesting employment in the Low Countries, because there was nothing left for him in England.

Kit had been given letters to deliver, which he'd thrown overboard halfway across the Narrow Sea. After arriving at last upon the fortressed, island city of Flushing, Kit had spent his first few nights at a tavern by the English barracks, until a soldier recognized Baines's name and told Kit his whereabouts – in exchange for a cocksucking, of which Kit makes no mention to Frizer either. The soldier directed him to a pedlars' camp by a gull-infested dump, where Kit found Baines living in a scrap-wood hovel with a tarp for a door. Strangely, Baines had not seemed surprised to see Kit. There was but a blinking of the pale eyes in a haggard, soot-blackened face, after which Baines stepped aside, a wordless invitation. Also wordlessly, Kit stooped in.

They'd sat on the dirt floor, on opposite sides of a sputtering firepit. Kit drank some acrid, vagabond fermentation out of a Bellarmine jug that grinned at him with a ghost of Baines's old, crooked grin. Little was said by either man, at first. Baines bowed into the work which Kit had evidently interrupted, tending to some object which a second glance revealed to be a miniature forge or kiln, assembled out of singed bricks. Baines pumped a bellows, sent sparks dancing about the dark room. From inside the kiln a light flared, lemon yellow to pith white.

Kit soon realized that the hovel's walls gleamed with all manner of metal objects: dented pots and plates and pitchers, bent spoons and knives, spade-heads, axe-heads, hammer-heads, all of which reflected the fire's soft surges like hundreds of watchful eyes.

'This here,' Baines had said, holding up a rectangular object, 'is a coin mould. It may look solid, but 'tis a fine sand mixed with a little gun-oil. The oil keeps it pliant, you see. And this – here, inside the crucible – this took me months to perfect. 'Tis three parts pewter, one part lead, for the weight.' Thus, he'd lectured, as if Kit had happened in upon a demonstration in progress. Baines withdrew a coin from his pocket, a genuine Dutch dollar, and let Kit hold it with greatest pride but also greatest reluctance, as if to let a child handle glass. 'From that coin,' he explained, 'was birthed a score of bastards. I do not use them myself. Only a fool would try to spend his own mint. No, the goal is to sell them on for some other wight to try his chance. Gamblers like them. We have many gamblers here;

soldiers love to gamble. At table, in poor light, with all present in their cups – many times, even a lacklustre impression will pass unnoted. Eventually, I'll have made enough to buy my way off this accursed island. At a few pence per coin, it shall take time, but if I am rich in anything these days, 'tis time.'

Silently, Kit watched him work, the way he'd used to watch his father work as a boy, when even the trade of shoemaking had seemed to him a marvellous alchemy. A memory came to him from years earlier, when he had just returned to Cambridge after a few weeks back home, in Canterbury. Baines had no sooner looked at him but he'd swept a lock of Kit's hair aside, exposing a bruise that Kit had tried to hide. *If he ever touches you like that again*, Baines had said, *I'll kill him.* When a man says that about one's father, he becomes another father, the true father's shadow: kind where the other is cruel; cruel where the other is kind. When a boy finds his father's shadow, he tends to live in it. He loves it as he cannot love the man who casts it.

Soon, half an hour had passed, and still, Baines had not asked Kit why he'd come to Flushing. Yet Kit felt the need to explain – to confess.

'I fear,' he rasped, 'I fear I may be… evil.'

What he'd meant was that he feared they might belong together.

Baines had looked up from his work, the flame catching something like sadness in his gaze. 'It does not matter what you are,' he said, in a paper-thin voice. He then picked up a set of tinker's shears – a tool Kit had seen him use in Paris, for other purposes – and offered them across the fire. 'Would you like to help me?' He almost sounded ashamed.

Kit set the bottle aside. He crawled towards him.

But Kit cannot tell Frizer this story, which he never has and never will tell anyone, because no one could ever understand.

It is like the sand in Baines's coin mould, so seeming-solid, so quick to dissolve. He can only tell Frizer the barest facts: that he became a willing accessory in Baines's counterfeiting scheme, a part which he'd played for nearly two weeks, earning the scar upon his hand in the process: a burn from molten metal, soothed in snow. One night, while Kit slept, Baines had gone to the governor's office and reported him as a coiner, a betrayal which Kit admittedly did not comprehend until the morning after his arrest, when he'd awakened in his cell to Baines flinging nutshells at his head through the bars: 'Now I've got you, you ungrateful little shit.'

Frizer remains silent for a long time after Kit has finished his story, his head bowed over the coin. He runs a fingertip around the edge that Kit had once so carefully filed smooth. 'I thought the Council was after ye for... other reasons.'

Kit, seated now upon the windowsill, frowns in confusion but dares not speak.

Frizer goes on: 'So you're a coiner? That's the worst of it?'

Kit can hardly bear the hope in his eyes. The man must be someone's little brother to be so practised in this look that begs never to be let down.

Kit tries to laugh. 'The worst of it? According to whom?'

Frizer lowers his head. Kit is grateful for his silence. He turns to the window, scanning the empty street. At so late an hour, none but two or three sleepy guards roost upon the ramparts at Bishopsgate, chins upon their chests. Now would be a perfect opportunity to run. But to run is not so simple. 'Tis a thing that, once done, cannot be undone, not the petulant running away of an angry child but the becoming of something precarious and truant, a paper escaped from a bonfire, burning as it flies.

'Why,' Frizer murmurs, but then hesitates. 'Why does this Baines fellow hate ye so much? And why do you do what he says? I'm sorry – I did not mean to – I saw the message. You said he should "command" you. Why would you let a man like that command you?'

Kit will step outside; say he needs the privy. He'll simply walk away, and be halfway across the city before anyone, even Frizer, knows he's gone.

'Marlowe?'

Something moves on the far side of Bishopsgate. In the corner where a tower meets the Wall, two figures lean close together, as if to shelter some delicate object from the wind. Two men. At first only one of them notices Kit in the window, nudging the other, as if caught. Both stand upright, facing him. They are both tall, rangy creatures like himself. A matched pair.

They speak not, but their bodies say it: *Now I've got you.*

'Marlowe?' Frizer says again. 'What is't?'

Kit commands himself, in Baines's voice, to *Move, breathe, do something*; in his father's voice, he admonishes himself that he is a man: *Act like one.* What did Frizer call him yesterday? A big brute? And yet how small he feels, like a hare in the grass – a tiny gyre of terror spinning in place.

Poley arrives on Deptford Strand just after midnight. A mist rises off the Thames that smells not unlike unclean skin, unwashed sheets. Upon the high bank, houses stand in a gabled row running towards the somnolent village green, as dark as racked skulls and each as similar to the next.

Poley's destination lies on the riverside extreme of this row, the only house with a lit lantern above the door and a sign at the front, of a bull. Two horses are already tethered to the fenceposts, pawing at the squelching earth. After securing his own horse, Poley knocks at the door, which is answered by a woman in mourning attire, her white face floating upon the blackness like a moon. She and Poley share the same strong jawline, the same dimpled chin. The same father.

'God by'ye, Eleanor,' Poley says.

Eleanor instructs Poley to step back, takes a bottle of vinegar from a table by the door and pours a little over his hands, leaving them stinking straight up to his nostrils. *'He's at my table,'* she mutters, as he steps inside at last. 'I would have spiced his wine with quicksilver, but alas for me, the devil will not deign to drink.'

'Arsenic, sister,' Poley whispers, handing over his hat and half-cape. 'Quicksilver is far too fickle for table use. Now be a good hostess. Your guest will hear you.'

Eleanor throws Poley's things over the stair-rail. 'I care not if he hears me!'

Into the dark she leads him, down the narrow corridor that runs like a vein through her over-large, lifeless house. To the right is the staircase where Poley's niece and nephews had used to put their heads through the railings and bay like goats, and to the left lies the stain where, five years ago, Eleanor's poor husband Master Bull had bled out on the floor, his cracked skull cradled in her lap, on the day that Richard Baines was dragged away to exile.

Eleanor has been in mourning ever since. But the children are gone now too, the eldest to crack skulls himself out on the Irish moors, and the others to stay with their late father's family in Lincoln. In their absence Eleanor has taken on that humiliation most commonly reserved for childless widows, to operate as a sometime victualler for travellers and other single gentlemen, who may be found guzzling ale at her table or stinking up the beds with their post-prandial farts two or three nights out of every week. A sad burlesque of the old days, when it was Privy Council spies who had lodged here, on their way to and from the Continent.

Tonight, Eleanor has but two guests at her dining table, one

Nick Skeres, munching on roasted almonds, the other Thomas Walsingham, begirt in so many layers of courtly damask and fustian that he sits as straight as a spit, emanating a fug of rose and almond-oil from his gleaming, silvery-black locks.

'How goes the courting, Jack Robin?' Poley says, just to see him turn red.

At once, Nick puts down his cup and rises to pull out a chair for 'Good Master Poley'. The big ape had taken an inexplicable liking to Poley back when he was only a spotty-chinned little pudding of a lad, one of Sir Francis's personal runners, and has remained steadfastly loyal ever since. Boys raised by the rod are always looking for a man to follow. And Nick has proved himself useful over the years.

'I'll begin with the good news,' Poley says, lifting his cup of brandy as soon as Eleanor has filled it. 'Despite Master Phelippes putting up a terrible fight – one in which I daresay my time at Gray's Inn did me yeoman's service – I have persuaded him not to act upon Thomas Kyd's testimony against Marlowe. For now.'

Walsingham does not look especially relieved. 'And what of this testimony? I assume you heard it yourself.'

'Oh yes, I was in the room. That, too, took some persuasion. As to the veracity of Kyd's accusations, I have no comment. I did observe, however, that his statement seemed well rehearsed. No doubt he'd received instruction from our dear Dicky Topcliffe.'

Walsingham baulks. 'You would accuse Dick Topcliffe of *falsifying* Kyd's testimony? To what end?'

'Falsifying, no! I would not credit the warden with the necessary powers of invention. But if I may offer another theory?'

Walsingham gives his hair an insouciant flick, as if drawing deep from the well of indulgence. 'Go on.'

Roundly, Poley regales him with his 'theory': that Dick Topcliffe has – somehow – made contact with Richard Baines, through whom he'd acquired unique knowledge of Marlowe, knowledge which Topcliffe had, in turn, passed on to Kyd. The Council, for their part, might well have arranged the whole scheme, and rewarded Topcliffe for his part in it – whyever not? Inconveniently for them, their case against Marlowe is currently founded on the word of Thomas Kyd, accused heretic, and of Richard Baines, late exile, long-suspected deviant – two witnesses of dubious character, whose separate testimonies may be easily coloured as the desperate or vindictive ravings of old friends scorned and creditors unrepaid. 'Yet,' Poley concludes, 'as your uncle used to say: "two doubts, when they agree, equal a certainty".'

Walsingham looks as if his stomach has turned several times since Poley began speaking. His hand makes a nervous gesture at the tabletop, as if to pluck furiously at a phantom loose thread. 'And, Kyd's accusations?' he says at last, voicelessly, and takes a drink before saying more. 'What leads you to believe that they come from Baines, and not Kyd himself?'

Poley bows his head. 'Let me put it this way, Master Walsingham – if there's more than one man on earth who knows your friend's sins as intimately as that, then you have troubles beyond my skill to solve.'

Walsingham laughs once, strangely. He rubs at his chin as if to rub the hair right off.

'Tell me,' he says.

Poley takes in a breath, rolls his eyes up to heaven, and paraphrases three or four examples from Baines's letter, his favourites: the charlatan Moses, the hypocritical Protestants, the whorish Virgin Mary, the sodomite Christ and his Ganymede St John—

'For God's sake, Kit,' Walsingham whispers, ashen-faced. 'For *God's* sake!'

Poley bows, as if ashamed to have sullied his tongue. In truth he crawls from head to toe, as if with fleas. He is so near now. Walsingham needs only a little push.

For a few moments Walsingham only clutches his head in his hands, looking as if he might either be sick or start to weep. Then at last he draws himself up, saying, 'If we take this theory of yours as truth, then who else besides Topcliffe might have seen Baines's statement?'

'There's no knowing, really,' Poley says. 'At the very least, it has not yet been officially received at Seething Lane.'

'And no word on when that should occur?'

'None. I have spoken with Baines myself, or tried to. He will show his cards only when "good and ready", so he says.'

Walsingham sinks once more into his thoughts, no doubt scrabbling around the cluttered attic of his brain in search of any shred, any glimmer, of hope.

'Perhaps there is a way,' he says at last. 'Perhaps Baines will have a price—'

'Look now,' Poley says, bemused, and growing annoyed that he need say this at all. 'One way or another, the Council will make a meal of your friend. Baines's delay may be up to them, or up to Baines himself. Either way, 'tis revenge that motivates him, and revenge may wait, but not forever. You, Master Walsingham, should count yourself lucky. After all, it was *you* who convinced your uncle to order Baines's arrest, *you* who sent a gang of bumbling cutthroats here, to this very house, to collect him. Yet you are not the target of his ire, but only likely to be a collateral victim of it.' This, Poley has said with a glance to Eleanor, who has been staring at the back of Walsingham's head incandescently all this while, as if dreaming of putting a bullet through it.

'We may sit here night after night hammering away at increasingly absurd schemes and counter-schemes,' Poley goes on, 'but the fact of the matter is that Kit Marlowe is a liability to you, Master Walsingham, as surely as Tom Watson once was. I need not remind you how *that* ended. Not that Master Watson should be held at fault for what happened to you, of course.

Or to any of us. We cannot be blamed, can we, for the pain we inadvertently cause in the torture room. A name – 'tis but a word, on the rack. Such a little word, with which, so we are promised, we might buy our wretched selves one moment of mercy... A man in pain has no loyalty. A man in pain knows no love.'

Walsingham speaks not, his dark eyes – his uncle's eyes – fixed upon his own nervous hand as he, no doubt, ruminates upon the torments of the Marshalsea. 'Tis an intimate thing they share, Walsingham and Poley, for they share Topcliffe. Almost as intimate as if to have shared a lover.

'When Marlowe's turn comes,' Poley says, growing restless, 'I warrant you, it will be the same—'

'It shall *not* be dealt with your way,' Walsingham snarls.

'We would not be here now, were there another way. You know this—'

'If you persist in telling me what I know or what I think, by God, I will terminate our business. Ay, though it would inconvenience me greatly, I will!' Walsingham strikes the table, causing every object upon it to jump.

Nick catches Poley's eye with a worried, doggish look, poised over his decimated bowl of almonds as if interrupted mid-coitus. Poley offers him the slightest of nods in reassurance, and to Walsingham, says, 'Stewards solve inconveniences, Master Walsingham. I forestall catastrophes.' To this, Walsingham merely grunts. So, Poley tries again. 'I assure you, in my trade, far more suffering is avoided than dealt. I am familiar with methods both swift and painless: "mercies", some call them—'

'We are finished here,' Walsingham says, standing up. 'Nick, come!'

He storms out. Nick hesitates upon his orders, staring helplessly at Poley, to whom Eleanor looks also, with betrayal in her glare. To both, Poley says, 'He's no fool. Give me time.'

Nick moves to follow his master. Seconds later, the front door slams. Poley puffs out his cheeks, rising to go also, but Eleanor catches him by the sleeve. 'You promised me Walsingham would suffer!' she hisses. 'You said he would be back in the Marshalsea by summer's end!'

Poley feels a headache coming on all of a sudden. 'Always so quick to doubt me,' he says. 'I do wonder whereof it comes, this lack of faith.'

Her eyes dart. 'He's not taking to it, Robin. Perhaps 'tis time you tried it another way...'

'What way might that be, sister?'

'Give the snake what he wants. Tell him you'll help Marlowe escape!'

Poley but raises his hand, and Eleanor skids backwards into the wall as if he had grabbed her by the throat. Gently, he cups the hand beneath her chin, she looking proud and stoic all the while, too good to meet eyes with him.

He leans close to say, 'Silly girl! Master Walsingham would never trust me to do that – but he *will* trust me to kill him.'

Outside, Poley finds Nick hovering anxiously by the front door while, some distance away, Walsingham paces the yard in all his glittering frippery, a peculiar sight against Deptford's effluvial muck. Some hundred yards beyond him, on the grassy lawn facing Eleanor's house, lurks one of London's most peculiar monuments: a hulking, hundred-foot galleon, buried up to its cannon-ports in the muddy earth. In another life, she was the *Golden Hind*, Sir Francis Drake's celebrated flagship, but clearly her days of capturing Spanish gold are long behind her. Beached and listing, she seems to have erupted out of the ground, her three naked masts, denuded of sails, reaching towards the sky like bony fingers. Walsingham stops to gaze upwards as if the skeletal hand were about to close around him.

Perhaps he is in love with Kit Marlowe. How tragic!

When Poley is just steps away, Walsingham says, without turning around, 'You would have me take the coward's course.'

'The coward's course?' Poley says. 'Nay – the wise man's.'

Walsingham scoffs. 'Perhaps it is so. In this world, only the wicked are wise. Or long-lived.' He pinches his brow, momentarily still. Then says, 'You are a poisoner, I hear. A woman's weapon.'

Poley feels the fist around his heart ease its grip slightly, just slightly. 'Those who say so misunderstand how poisoning works,' he counters. ''Tis an intellectual endeavour, a game of wits and patience. But I am loath to extol the virtues of an unvirtuous profession. Suffice to say, it keeps the tailor and the grocer happy, when other sources run dry.'

'I have no doubts as to your "expertise",' Walsingham says. 'But if it must be done, I trust you not to do it as I would have it done: kindly, quickly.'

Poley pities him that he should think either kindness or quickness were feasible, under the circumstances. 'If you agree to my terms, then my hand is yours. And, in my own defence, let me say that I do not delight in suffering. No, not even in death, despite what you may think. I believe that death should be expedient. Quiet. 'Tis a private matter between the dying man and God, or it ought to be.'

Walsingham laughs, bitterly. 'A repentant assassin, are you?'

'Yes. Profoundly so. But I am defiant too. I repent not my actions, I repent only such times as I failed to act. I repent not that our Queen lives. I repent not that Anthony Babington is dead. I repent that I did not kill him myself – kindly, quickly – in some opportune moment, ere the headsmen had at him.'

'Babington was a traitor.'

'So is Christopher Marlowe. Just look at this Penry fellow: heretics are traitors now, and suffer traitors' deaths. I suppose not to burn alive is a kind of mercy. But believe me when I say that you do not want to see your friend butchered upon the gallows. You do not want to see them pull the heart out of him, still beating.'

Walsingham gazes up at the stars, saying nothing for long enough that Poley begins to doubt himself, to feel the squeeze around his heart once more. He must not grow desperate. But he regrets not having put a gun to Baines's head and forced him to hand over his blasted statement; he wishes that this, now, were a simple matter of putting a gun to Walsingham's head, and forcing him to buy his friend's death. He has come so close; he is so close – close enough that he cannot so much as blink without seeing the diamond's flash, as it had passed from Babington's fingertips to his own—

Walsingham says, 'Why were you there?'

Poley shakes himself. 'I beg your pardon?'

'If you delight not in suffering,' Walsingham says, looking at the ground, 'then why were you there that day, at St Giles' Field? Why did you watch?'

Poley had not expected this. Least of all did he expect the sudden vertigo that overtakes him in hearing these words, remembering the night before Babington died. Sir Francis had come to Poley's room at the Tower to inform him that he would witness the following day's executions: that he would stand at the back of the stage among the prisoners, and watch it happen as they did. 'I hope,' the Spymaster had said, before leaving, 'that the next time you do either myself or her Majesty service, you will conduct yourself with restraint.'

Restraint – Poley knows it well now. A closed fist, a locked jaw. A tooth-breaking grin.

'Because I hated him,' Poley says, as if uttering it unburdened him, though he has given this answer before, word for word. 'With all my heart, I hated him. It did haunt me so, that hatred, that even food did taste of it, my sleep did churn with it! I imagined it would give me some relief to see him torn apart, as if by wolves… but imagination is a weak substance. Blood, and pain, run thick. Marry, I am fed up with them.' His voice has dropped to only a whisper; the world tips slightly underfoot.

Walsingham lets out a long breath. 'What are your terms?' he says.

Just like that, it happens: we think the unthinkable. From then on, the rest comes easily.

23 MAY 1593

Seven days

❧

I have read – or rather re-read – *Edward II*...
There is nothing in it, no possibility of success;
and the infernal tradition that Marlowe was a
great dramatic poet... throws all the blame of his
wretched half-achievement on the actor. Marlowe
had words & a turn for their music, but nothing
to say – a barren amateur with a great air.

GEORGE BERNARD SHAW, LETTER TO HARLEY
GRANVILLE-BARKER, 1903

... that fine madnes still he did retaine,
Which rightly should possesse a Poets braine.

MICHAEL DRAYTON, *OF POETS AND POESIE*, 1627

17

FRIZER SPENDS THE MORNING of Wednesday the 23rd reading *Edward II*, even to the expense of breakfast. But by the time Marlowe and he must set out for Seething Lane, he contemplates swearing off the play altogether. He must never say so much to Marlowe, the man being of so volatile a disposition, but the thing is a rudderless mess. Not one person in all the play has an ounce of worth in him; all are weak, corrupt, despicable creatures, right down to the king and his beloved minion Gaveston, an insufferable upstart, with queer, unsettling appetites. There's not a single Tamburlaine, nor even a Faustus among them, certainly not the king, who spends every minute on stage either pining after his Gaveston or swearing revenge on those who would keep them apart. 'Tis disgraceful indeed for Marlowe to write of a king who desires no more lands, nor wealth, nor maidens than he already has. All Edward desires in all the world, and therefore all he speaks of, is some odious, mincing mollis whom the whole of Creation detests.

At one point, some minor player asks the king, *Why do you love him whom the world hates so?*

The answer: *Because he loves me, more than all the world!*

Hours later, Frizer's face is still hot from having read these words. As he paces up and down Seething Lane, waiting for Marlowe to either come out of the Privy Court or vanish forever, his chief thought is for the manuscript he'd locked up in the strongbox this morning and the taste of anger it had left in his mouth.

How powerfully he yearns to taste it again!

In this same moment, inside the Privy Court, Phelippes throws back the curtains on Kit's stifling little cell, startling the flame of the candle, which has burnt halfway down in the time Kit has spent waiting on him. A vein of rage already throbs at Phelippes's temple. 'I suppose after yesterday you think yourself to have ducked the noose,' he hisses. 'Is that what you think, Marley? Did you sleep sound last night?'

Kit had not slept at all last night. From the window of his and Frizer's room, he'd watched the twin shadows by the gate, watched them watching him, until the first light of dawn had appeared beneath the dun clouds. At that point, the two lads had looked at one another and started to walk away, headed west. One of them had turned, and winked.

They are even younger than Kit had first assumed. Eighteen, nineteen. The same age Kit was when Baines first found him in the buttery at Cambridge, soaking his ration of stale bread in beer. He wonders where Baines had found them, what unwholesome and desperate place he'd reached into and drawn them out of, what kind words he'd said.

Phelippes slaps a sheaf of papers onto the table. 'This is you,' he says. 'This is every record from our archives that you have touched, or that contains some version of your name. You recognize this one? Signed by Thomas Walsingham: "... that Richard Baines did on several occasions enforce himself bodily upon the aforesaid Christopher by use of violence, against the conventions of Nature and the Laws of her Majesty, her Church and Realm..." How old were you when these alleged violations took place – nineteen? Twenty? A big lad, were you? And Richard Baines, he is of average height, would you not say? He must have used a weapon, no? Or drugged you? Tricked you? The word used here is *contrectus*, which would imply something stolen. Was it your manhood, Marley? Did he make off with it?'

The following afternoon, after Phelippes has finished with him, Kit blindly estimates that he is just steps away from the staircase to the great hall when a four-fingered hand reaches out of the void, grasps his arm and pulls him sideways, out of his guard's grip. Behind him, a door closes; that same hand touches Kit's chest, presses him backwards until his spine meets with a wall, and then finally pulls the bag from his head.

Robin Poley looks relieved to see him. "Tis harder every day to have your ear for a moment!' he says, overly friendly. The room is crammed to the ceiling with dusty boxes. Poley stands so close that Kit must look down his chin at him. 'How is it with Master Phelippes these past two days? He's making you pay for that humiliation with Kyd, I trust?'

Kit answers him not. These past several hours, he has barely kept the impulse to drive his fist into Phelippes's face at bay. Just now, any face will do. 'What do you want?'

'Well, no pleasantries, then: were you able to find Master Baines?'

'I'll no longer discuss such things with you.'

A pout. 'May I ask why?'

'Ask Thomas Kyd. Now put the damned bag on and lead me out.'

Poley exhales a nervous chuckle, somehow manages to inch even closer. 'Listen now, for I must say this quickly: whatever Master Kyd may have told you, make no conclusions out of it. You know not my mind, Master Marlowe. I do not move in straight lines.'

This begs several retorts, all too cheap to dignify. Kit can but laugh, and say, 'Ay, marry, I know your mind, Poley. All the world knows your mind. That is what happens when you build your reputation on deceit. Now let me go.'

Poley's jaw tightens. 'You would be in jail now, were it not for me.'

For one blazing instant Kit believes he will punch his perfect teeth in after all, if not do far worse. But all he can think of is what little good it would do him – what a poor substitute Poley would make for the one Kit most desires to destroy.

Before the tears can reach his eyes, Kit shoves past Poley, making for the door. But of course, there is no escape.

'Tell me of your session with Phelippes today,' Poley says. 'The questions asked, and your answers.'

Kit does not turn around. 'He asked me no questions today. He read to me. He read the interrogation notes, from Newgate. From Tom Watson!' Kit falls silent, and for a long moment neither speaks; the silence grows so deep that Kit believes he can hear, somewhere inside himself, the sound of the rack: the strain of a rope, or a ligament, pulled tight enough to break.

'He toys with me,' Kit goes on. 'That's all. He knows he has me. You have bought me nothing but the walk to and from this hell every day!'

'Spoilt little boy,' Poley says. 'I have bought you an inestimably precious thing. I have bought you time.'

Kit cannot deny this. Thoughtlessly, he has looked back, allowing Poley to see his face, the ugly, weeping wound of it. Something shifts in Poley's gaze at the sight of him, as if to blink a third eyelid, so strange and startling that Kit prays to see it again, uncertain of what he's seen exactly.

Poley lays a hand over his own heart. 'I am not your enemy,' he says, softly. 'Your enemy resides in Newgate Without, and has already trained his cannons on ye. You felt the wind of them with Thomas Kyd, but I tell ye, the fire will be much worse.'

'What do you *want* of me?'

'Master Phelippes read Tom Watson's interrogation notes

to you, you say?' Poley nods to himself. "'Tis true: he toys with you. I suppose he hopes you will crack in the tempering, and undo yourself in some tawdry outburst. You do realize, that is the strategy of a man rich in appetite but poor in resources.'

'So?'

"'So?'" he laughs. 'Master Marlowe, you have a lovely mind, on paper. This is an opportunity, you see, if you are willing to take it. Clearly, these fellows have nothing, if they have not Richard Baines's testimony against you, which is as good as to say *they have nothing*. If you are quick enough, you may yet catch the devil by his tongue.'

At supper that night, after having left Frizer to stew in the heaviest of silences all afternoon, Marlowe shoots up from the table and bolts for the door, a hand clasped over his mouth.

Frizer pauses to take a final gulp of ale before following. Outside, he finds Marlowe on his hands and knees under the stairs in the inn-yard, puking his guts out and making sounds like a dying dog. Frizer crouches beside him, close but not too close. He watches his own hand reach towards Marlowe's heaving back, slowly, as if to reach inside an animal's den, anticipating a snarl, a snap of teeth. But it never comes. Only the soft shock of contact, followed by dizzying awareness of the body beneath his hand, as if to realize that there is a whole globe turning underneath him: a body not unlike that of a large animal, whose lungs swell with breath like a cathedral with song, whose bones are as timbers, whose heart is a forge.

Kit crumbles at Frizer's touch. He would like to smash open his own skull, if only to pull Phelippes's voice out of it, droning away over page after page of yellowed paper: the record of Tom's many hours spent racked, or with his head held underwater, or hanging by the wrists, and all the many secrets he'd screamed out in hope of relief, from the fond names that Walsingham and he had once called one another to the intimate details of their lovemaking – and, within this record, exacting lists of what methods had proved most effective with him, and to what degree they were applied, how long he'd held out before fainting or falling into incoherent screams, claiming, at one point, to have done 'unnatural acts' with the Devil himself, whom he kept in the attic of his house, in a golden collar—

'Make it stop,' Kit whispers into his hands. 'Make it stop, make it stop!' This agony has but one source, and it is not Phelippes. It is not Poley. Take the Devil's head, and hell shall empty itself.

How many times has Kit sat by Baines's side and imagined it?

How many times and in how many ways has he already killed him in his heart?

On the following afternoon, when Kit staggers out of the Privy Court at five o'clock with naught but a long, flat note of pain inside his skull, Frizer meets him in the street and wordlessly hands him his flask, seeming to understand – despite all his usual tics of sighing and grumbling and singing under his breath – that now is a time for silence. He lets Kit drink, lets him stand for a moment within his own subterranean darkness, within the smells of earth and blood… and then he cuffs Kit's arm gently, the way Tom used to do whenever they were in company, as a way of reminding him *I love you*.

Frizer says, 'Look up, man.'

How lovely he is, Kit realizes. How astonishingly beautiful! A little brown wren of a fellow, slow to smile, as if to do so exposed some tender spot to injury; his serious blue eyes a site of confluence between light and flesh, like mirrors turned to the sky.

⁂

Marlowe's miserable silence persists long after they have left the Privy Court. For three days, Frizer has practised a saintly forbearance with him, but now, over supper, the last thread of his patience breaks. He sets his spoon down, with a clatter that startles himself far more than his drooping companion, and then asks, in an accusatory tone that he had not intended, 'Is Gaveston the villain?'

Marlowe keeps his gaze trained upon the window at his right shoulder, with its view of the crowd outside the Black Bull tavern across the street. 'The villain?' he says, distantly.

'Ay, the villain, Gaveston, is it he?'

Marlowe shakes his head. 'There is no villain.'

'No *villain*?'

'No, no villain.' Then Marlowe shifts his shoulders gently, as if feeling an itch, and adds, 'I suppose Lightborne is a villain.'

'Lightborne!' Frizer is relieved. 'What does he do?'

'He kills the king.'

'Thank God! When does he come in?'

'Not till the very end.'

'The *end*?' This is too much to ask. 'I must wait till the *end*?'

''Tis when the most important ones ought to come in, no? At the end.' This said, Marlowe drinks with his head tipped back, the way Papa used to do.

Lightborne, Frizer puzzles, silently. Something in the name stands his hairs on end. It calls to mind Lucifer, 'Light-Bringer'. But it is the opposite of that, is it not – not to bring, but to be borne?

A name in reverse is like a key. Frizer had learned that from *Doctor Faustus*. It can be heard through the veil that separates worlds. It summons, it invokes.

He tries to disguise a shiver by shaking his head, muttering, 'I confess I understand it not one whit.'

Marlowe sighs down at the table, faintly combative. 'What do you not understand?'

'Nor do you understand it yourself, by God. 'Tis not that this play is without villains, 'tis that every wight in it is a villain, every single one, on all sides! There's not even a fair speech in it, as far as I can see. 'Tis all in verse, ay, but it sounds of ordinary talk.'

'Ordinary enough.'

'No man goes to the playhouse to hear ordinary talk! Whatever became of your whirling stars and blazing swords and fireballs out of hell? "What is Beauty, sayeth my sufferings, then?"'

Marlowe smirks. Frizer recognizes this look in him by now, itching for trouble. 'I wonder how you enjoyed *Tamburlaine* so much, understanding it so little.'

'What?'

'Tamburlaine is a clown – know ye not that? Tamburlaine, Faustus, even Edward, they are all clowns. They see themselves not, that is the jest. They see not how small they are, how weak, until 'tis too late.' Briefly, he studies Frizer's expression, and then laughs. 'You think Tamburlaine is the *hero*, is that it?'

Frizer is too furious to speak.

'Tamburlaine is no hero, by God! *Tamburlaine* is not a play of heroes and villains, only buffoons and philosophers – Tamburlaine bethinks himself one while in truth being the other. Which do you suppose it is?'

'Eat your damned bread, Marlowe,' Frizer snarls.

Marlowe gives the hunk of maslin a childish flick. ''Tis mouldy.' His eyes drift again to the window at his right, blowflies dancing in and out of the candlelight like dandelion fluff. He drinks and then swats a fly at his neck, leaving a drop of blood behind, and Frizer cannot help but feel infinitely superior to him, if only for a moment: this shabby, gloomy fellow, to whom life has clearly been unkind. Night could borrow darkness of him!

'"What is Beauty,"' Frizer blurts out, '"sayeth my
    sufferings, then?
If all the pens that ever poets held

Had fed the feeling of their master's thoughts,
And every sweetness that inspired their hearts,
Their minds, and muses on admired themes;
If all the heavenly quintessence they still
From their immortal flowers of poesy—
Wherein, as in a mirror, we perceive
The highest reaches of a human wit—
If these had made in one poem's period,
And all combined in beauty's worthiness,
Yet should there hover in their restless heads
One thought, one grace, one wonder at the least,
Which into words no virtue can digest."'

Marlowe sits in silence. Stunned, perhaps. Hopefully not because he's noticed the tremor in Frizer's voice, the brightness in his eyes. Frizer clears his throat, but still can only whisper, 'Now *that's* a speech. *There's* your blustering Tamburlaine!'

Marlowe's smile returns, somewhat sadder. 'You remember when he says that, no? While his men are busy slaughtering all the virgins of Damascus, and hanging their corpses on the city's walls.' He downs a gulp of whisky, looks again to the window. '*There's* your Tamburlaine, indeed.'

Frizer seethes. There must be something he could say to break this man's heart, if only he could think of it – a word or two that would strip him to the very bones! – yet the best that he can muster is a mewlish growl: 'Why do ye have to be so God-damned *cruel*?'

Marlowe shoots to his feet. Frizer nearly dives under the table for cover, but Marlowe's bloody gaze is fixed not on him but the window, and so remains until he turns and marches for the door, an army of one.

Frizer shouts his name and gives pursuit, across the yard, into the street. He calls out again, but Marlowe continues his charge, aimed straight for the crowd outside the Black Bull. A tall man awaits him, grinning wickedly at his approach, and keeps on grinning right up to the instant that Marlowe punches him in the teeth.

Frizer halts and curses. The jeering crowd makes way for the brawl, such as it is, with Marlowe holding the tall fellow off the ground with one fist and pummelling him like a billet with the other. A second man struggles in vain to pry Marlowe off. At last, Frizer finds courage enough to move, rushing forward and wrapping both arms around Marlowe's neck, pulling with every ounce of weight. He might as well try to uproot an oak.

Somehow, the beaten man scurries free into the arms of his friend. Together they retreat several yards backwards towards the Wall's torchlights, then stop. They could be the same man in two different stages of injury, Frizer realizes: both young, hair and skin and eyes all one pale colour, both nearly the same height as Marlowe. The battered one spits out a tooth and runs his tongue over his bloody maw. He almost looks as if he's enjoyed it, something in his gaze beseeching, *More*.

'You tell him to come find me!' Marlowe roars, with Frizer's arms around his waist. 'Tell him to come himself! Let him bring what fire he will bring – *I am ready for him!*'

26 MAY 1593

Four days

❧

I endeavoured to persuade my superiors [at the English seminary] that I was embarked upon the study of sacred literature, while in fact I was much more attracted to profane authors of the worst sort...

So far was I advanced in self-love and personal pleasure that... I found a way of pleasing myself and gaining greater familiarity with certain younger students. These I sought to lead astray...

This, then, was my course: the scandal and ruin of many young men.

RICHARD BAINES, FROM 'A RECANTATION', GIVEN TO THE CATHOLICS FOLLOWING HIS CAPTURE AS A PRIVY COUNCIL SPY, 13 MAY 1583

I 8

O N SATURDAY MORNING KIT awakes dry-mouthed and sweating, sunlight searing his face, his insides begging for a drink as if for breath. He reaches for his flask on the floor and hears it clunk onto its side, empty. Such is enough to bring childish despair crashing down upon him, helpless to do anything save lie with his eyes closed, cradling himself.

'Are you sick?'

Kit rolls onto his back. Frizer has been awake for some time already, it seems, for he is nearly finished with plucking out the slashing on his sleeves, a tedious process in which he is surprisingly fastidious. 'Well, be sick or get up. 'Tis late.' He turns up his collar, rounds his arms. A blaze of red runs down either side of his face in some secret shame.

Perhaps something inadvisable had transpired between them last night. Kit would not be surprised if it had. He searches his memory, coming up far short of a full evening: in one minute, he had been standing in the middle of Bishopsgate Street with sore knuckles and spots in his eyes, his very bones crying out for violence, and from that moment on all he can recall is a fearsome desire to fuck, and to be fucked – to let Ingram Frizer throw him down and split him in half like a top-sawyer, to make him climb the walls like a bell-ringer, to be *broken, shattered, ruined*, to be left so spent he is but half-alive—

One could believe that Kit has said all this aloud for how suddenly Frizer's blush deepens. He retreats across the room, shooting a tyrannical look from the doorway. 'Five minutes. I will be counting!' And then he is gone.

Kit looks down, unable to miss the tenting of the sheet between his legs, as surely Frizer could not have missed it either. He lies back with a whispered curse, fists balled at his sides, waiting himself out.

Perhaps he has misjudged Frizer entirely. Perhaps Ingram Frizer is cut from the same cloth as most men: lusting after the neighbours' daughters, sating his unspeakable urges on the bodies of sad-eyed whores, and on the hide of a long-suffering wife. Perhaps – as with most men – it would take no more than an immodest look, a whispered suggestion, for Frizer to draw that knife of his from behind his back and bury it in Kit's neck, right up to the hilt.

Downstairs, Kit's parched brain soaks up his first drink of the day like a sponge. He then follows Frizer south, keeping a few paces between them so that he may scout for any sign of Baines's wheyfaced henchmen. For the first time in days, they are nowhere to be found. So preoccupied is Kit with his search for them that he only realizes he has arrived at the Privy Court when he nearly stumbles into Frizer's chest, meeting a familiar look in his blue eyes. 'Tis a look Kit has often seen in his father's and mother's eyes; in his sisters', Tom's and Walsingham's eyes. Frizer has joined them, it seems, the ranks of all those whom Kit has profoundly disappointed.

'Your flask,' Frizer says, impatient.

'Ay, ay.' Kit takes a final drink. Frizer accepts the flask as if 'tis the most despicable of gifts, and then seems to wriggle upon the hook of something perhaps better left unsaid. He blurts it out just as Kit decides to leave. 'You should not drink so much, marry. It will be the death of you, this wicked thing!'

Kit takes a measured breath, weary of hearing this, wearier still at how the world always expects him to respond with gratitude, humility and promises to reform himself, to turn to God and sober prayer. As if anyone would ever believe him if he did!

'I'll take it under advisement,' Kit mutters.

'I mean it, Marlowe. Last night, you might have killed that fellow. Hell, what if the constables had come? What if you'd been arrested!'

Kit sighs, confessing, 'I did not think of that.'

'You would be in jail now. And then where would I be? My master would have my throat cut!'

'He would not!'

'Look, all that matters is you keep your damned head!' Frizer pauses as if to collect himself, then lowers his voice, ready to forgive. 'Think no more about this Baines devil. 'Tis draining you of your wits. What can he do to ye anyway? Y'are an innocent man!'

Kit feels a pinch, echoing, 'Innocent?'

'Well, innocent of *treason*, and all the rest. I reckon they cannot hang a man for being an ill-tempered sot, though you make me wonder sometimes whether they should!' He is grasping for levity now, his eyes a silent plea.

Kit would like to blurt a secret out of spite, slap the faith clean off his face. This is a game, this withholding, played until he is sick up to the back-teeth and desires only to break the silence over his knee.

'I have to go,' Kit says.

As he passes through the gatehouse, Kit senses two or more men falling into step behind him. They touch him not, speak not, yet their nearness strikes his back like a wave, the sound of their footsteps bowling him helplessly on towards the court's skull-topped doors, in futile search of escape or shelter.

In the narrow, crowded vestibule, a murmur just behind his right shoulder stops him in his tracks, the voice filling out the familiar shape of its speaker from the inside, as smoke fills a burning house. 'Kit.'

Kit sucks a breath into his lungs, high and sharp.

Baines has heard him. 'Did you burn a candle for me?'

⊗

When at last Marlowe reappears at the gate – long after the court has closed – Frizer nearly runs to embrace him, having spent the past several hours envisioning one catastrophe after another, reliving their final exchange with regret so sharp he can feel it between his ribs. But Marlowe is not alone: the two tall fellows from last night walk with him, one at either shoulder. They are twins, Frizer realizes, now that he can see them in the light, one still bruised and bloodied, with a fearsome, wounded look in his eye, the other skittish, apprehensive. Together with Marlowe, all three resemble one another faintly, like dogs of the same breed.

There is a fourth man too, following behind the rest. Middle-aged, grizzled, the right cheek hollower than the left. As they approach, Frizer recognizes him, and almost laughs aloud.

'You're the devil with the coin,' he says, at which the older man cracks a cockeyed smile, the right side of the mouth being entirely denuded of teeth.

Marlowe paws the earth like a nervous horse, casting a look to the older man without lifting his gaze. 'Frizer,' he says, quietly, 'this is Richard Baines – Baines, Ingram Frizer.'

Baines offers his hand. His eyes no longer bear a simpleton's innocence, which was obviously feigned; today they are wreathed in deep lines of hardship, as wary as the stare of a mastiff on the verge of biting. His handshake is a touch too firm.

'Did it take a quart of baby's blood?' Frizer says, to Marlowe.

Marlowe does not laugh. Nor does he offer an alternative explanation for Baines's presence. He seems unwilling to explain his acquaintance with this man altogether, though the question hovers over them, gathering ice. He only says, 'Master Baines and I must speak privately. We will be at the Black Bull.'

Frizer stands firm. 'Well, I have often thought of going to the Black Bull. 'Tis infamous in Chiselhurst. They say the Devil himself could find sport enough for a thousand years in there.'

Marlowe and Baines glance towards, though not directly at, one another. 'Lusty fellow, no?' Baines remarks.

Frizer adds, 'And I am to be repaid – handsomely, I hope – for keeping two eyes on him at all times. Take it up with my master: Thomas *Walsingham*.'

Baines smirks with just one half of his mouth. 'I know who your master is.'

No one speaks. Marlowe is about to protest, but Baines interrupts. 'Well, I see no hurt in it. May you find the Devil's sport!' He places a hand to the chest of the boy with the mangled face, pushing him aside like a door. His pale attendants smile blankly, like deaf men at a feast.

Marlowe slips himself between Baines and Frizer, quick as a cat.

As they walk north, Frizer asks twice, in different words, how Marlowe and Baines know each other, and neither time does anyone answer. The third time he asks, Marlowe turns to face him, and suddenly it seems their eyes are but an inch apart. So much blood, so much breath do they share in this instant that Frizer believes he hears quite plainly Marlowe's voice in his head, imploring, *Silence!*

19

O N THE WAY NORTH, Baines confers with his boys in
their native language, a harsh tongue, like a kind of pri-
mordial English. Kit can only decipher a phrase or two, but
they discourse in code anyway. Something about horses,
about riding a wild mare.

'Your Dutch has improved, I see,' Kit says.

'It had no choice but to improve,' comes the reply.

The streets are emptier today. The smoke of plague-fires
hangs like curtains in the still air. But a sound carries from
the distance, growing gradually louder the nearer they come
to Bishopsgate. By the time they turn the corner at St Helen's,
Kit has long since identified the sound as the clamour of a
large crowd, hundreds at least, who sometimes bark and howl
like dogs, other times chant a word or a phrase as one. From
outside the Black Bull, where activity teems in the otherwise
vacant street, Kit can hear them railing:

'Blood! Blood! Blood! Blood!'

The crowd around the Black Bull has all the makings of
a mob. A few men are exchanging insults with the guards
perched along Bishopsgate's ramparts, while nearby, another
bellows away like a street-preacher about how there is no
plague at all, only a conspiracy to lock up London's Christian
population so that foreigners and Jews may take over: 'They'll
shut the churches next, mark my words!'

Kit and the others must push their way into the tavern's gaudy, roisterous common room, a space that reeks of spilled bowse and something heady, masculine, like the aftermath of a brawl. Baines leads them through the room, up a leaning staircase. Above, they emerge onto a gallery so crowded with bodies that the daylight hardly penetrates. Baines turns towards an inner corridor, shouting, 'This way!' but either Frizer hears him not or cannot contain his curiosity, for he shoves into the throng at once.

Kit follows, squeezing through sideways to the gallery's edge. He finds Frizer perched above the churning inn-yard, where men clamber and moil over every inch of space, bursting from the sagging galleries, hanging over the stair-rails, clinging onto the posts. Myriad voices bay as one, for blood, blood, blood.

Below, within a circle of roaring spectators, several creatures are locked in ferocious combat: four dogs piled atop one writhing, reeling creature, slightly larger than they. Each dog is chained about the neck, the chains held by men who stand at the edge of the circle with their heels dug into the dirt. The whole picture resembles a cartwheel, the dogs' chains radiating like spokes out of an axle of fur and fangs.

'I thought all the bear gardens were closed by the plague!' Frizer says.

Kit is startled by Baines's voice at his shoulder: 'Does this look like a bear garden to you?'

Strings of bloody foam fly from the dogs' chops as their keepers drag them back for a rest. At the centre of the circle, a little bear is revealed: standing on its hind legs, hugging the stake to which it is chained through a ring in its nose. Its frightened wailing is uncannily human, the cry of a small child in pain.

''Tis not a fair fight,' Kit says, quietly.

Frizer shouts, 'What?' but somehow Baines has heard Kit, clapping his shoulder, at which Kit tries not to flinch.

'Still a Puritan at heart, I see!' Baines remarks. 'Fear not, I have a room reserved for us inside.' He turns to Frizer. 'You – with that appetite for sport – I trust you'll want to take in the game.' He bows slightly, glancing again at Kit before slipping away. Frizer follows him with narrowed eyes, like a watchdog.

'Frizer,' Kit says, leaning close to be heard, 'remain out here awhile, ay?'

'You want to be *alone* with that fellow?'

Kit grunts bitterly. Indeed no, he wants none of this. He glances over the crowd, to the doorway where Baines stands between his boys, one of whom is speaking into his ear. But Baines has no eyes for the boy, only for Kit, his glare steady and cold, as if he knows, somehow, what Kit intends to do.

'I like not those Dutch fellows,' Frizer says. 'They have dead eyes, marry. Like fish!'

Kit laughs, surprising himself. Frizer too looks surprised, but then the blare of a trumpet pulls his attention below, where a clown dressed as an ape has started to do somersaults about the yard. The turning of Frizer's head reveals a scar where someone must have burnt him with a round object: the tip of a poker, perhaps, or the heated pommel-cap of a knife. Kit imagines running his thumb over the mark.

Kit takes a steeling breath. And then, as if someone had shoved him from behind, he stumbles hard into Frizer's back, mumbles an apology. In that same instant, Kit grips the handle of Frizer's knife and pulls. He had feared a struggle, but the blade slips free of its scabbard easily, and the crowd is so tightly packed that he need only tuck the knife against his forearm to conceal it.

He touches Frizer's shoulder. 'Come and find me when the bout is over, if I do not find you first.'

A few feet into the crowd, Kit stoops to slip Frizer's knife into his right boot – hardly an ideal hiding place, but the best he has – and then sidles his way to the door off the stairs, where

Baines takes him by the arm. 'I hope to God you do not trust that creature over there,' Baines says, aiming a scowl in Frizer's direction. 'A man like that will betray ye for a slice of cake.'

Baines knocks upon a door in the adjoining corridor. A child of about fourteen with drugged eyes and bare breasts limply shows them into the room beyond, where an older woman, also bare-breasted, welcomes them in effusively. Baines ignores the woman; gives the child a coin and says, 'Get out.'

The hostess says, 'If she displease you, master, I'll fetch another.'

'Fetch yourself the plague, crone.' Baines moves directly for the carver chair at the candlelit dining table, like the lord of the manor. One of the Dutch lads has already taken on the host-ess's duties, filling a cup from a stoneware pitcher. The other boy, the one with the bruised face, receives some barely verbal command from his master and comes barrelling across the room, shoves both girl and woman outside and slams the door.

Kit scans the room: walls lined in skins the colour of fresh liver, which glisten and breathe in the candlelight. No other doors; no windows. One way in or out.

'When I heard you were at Scadbury, I thought such would be the very last I'd ever hear of ye,' Baines says. 'That you would be found tragically drowned in a washbasin, or taken fatally sick after a surfeit of pickled eel, that sort of thing.'

Behind Kit's back, the boy with the battered face snuffs truculently, as if to snuff back blood. When Kit turns to look, the boy wriggles the tip of his tongue at him, through the still-fresh gap in his teeth.

Kit shifts inside his boot, the knife hard against his ankle-bone. 'If Walsingham wanted me dead, it would have happened years ago.'

'I never said Walsingham *wanted* ye dead. Wanting has little to do with it. Considering how well he fared the last time the Council had their way with one of his friends, he would be a fool to let them take ye still breathing.'

Kit tries to look unmoved. 'You've come here to sow doubts, I take it?'

Baines offers an empty chair. 'Sit down, have a drink with me.'

The Dutch boys have not moved to sit. 'May we not talk alone?' Kit says.

'These fellows cannot comprehend a word of English! Surely their presence is of no concern. *Hier, kom hier!*' Again, Baines snaps his fingers. The battered one leaves the door and takes a place at his brother's shoulder, glowering across the table at Kit.

Kit takes the seat to Baines's right, facing the two boys, as Baines leans over the table to fill Kit's cup. A wave of muffled cheers rises and falls from the gallery, several walls away, a reminder that Frizer is not far.

'Not the sort you usually go for, is he?' Baines says, with a cock of his head in the direction of the noise. 'Could pick your teeth with him!'

Kit takes a drink. He must be calm, above all else. He must be made of stone.

'I want to know how all this began,' he says. 'Did the Council come to you or did you go to them?'

Baines tugs at the hairs beneath his chin, as if arranging pieces in his mind. 'They came to *me*. The first time was late last spring, early last summer. The archbishop's men, they were.'

'The archbishop?' Kit rasps.

'Oh, yes. They visited me several times. Even came on Christmas, brought me a slice of cold ham, and firewood. They gave me this suit, these gloves, this handkerchief. They paid passage for my boys. Courted me like a rich man's ugly daughter, they have.'

In the pause that falls, Kit tries to decide whether all this might be a lie calculated to terrify him, but, lie or not, it has worked; he is too frightened to speak.

'You understand,' Baines goes on, 'this goes well beyond you. There's that Penry fellow caught up in it, and his Brownist friends. There's your friend Thomas Kyd. And, once they have you in their clutches, well – these things spread like wildfire, my boy. They keep going till there's nothing left to burn.'

He folds his hands upon the table, fingers interlaced, like a physician delivering a poor prognosis. 'What I mean to say is, there's no stopping this, certainly not on my end. Even if I wanted to, I could not put a stop to it.'

'But you could,' Kit says, too quietly. 'You know right well you could.'

Baines looks amused. 'Is that why you think we are here now, Kit? To negotiate? You think you have something I want, something that would appease me?'

Kit finishes his drink, pours another. He has never killed a man before, though suppose he has come close. It had taken rage and drunkenness and perhaps something more than both, like madness, to bring him to violent extremes, yearning not so much for another man's pain as for the relief of his own. Try as he might, he cannot summon that madness now. All feels eerily, menacingly calm, like sitting on his father's knee.

'What do you want to do, Kit?' Baines asks, his voice low, ashen.

'Did you hope that they would hang me,' Kit asks, 'when you turned me in, in Flushing?'

'Marry, I know not what I'd hoped for!' Baines admits. 'To *hang* ye – well, I knew it would be unlikely. I thought they might brand ye, perhaps, or flog ye. Cut off some fingers, or a hand. I wanted you to suffer, that much I know. I wanted you to feel some of the pain I felt, when you and Tom Watson sent me off to die—'

'Do not say his name,' Kit interrupts.

'I have turned my every other thought upon that name and yours for *five years*, so indulge me while I give it breath, for once!'

This outburst has split the air like lightning. The Dutch lads stare on Baines with mounting anxiety, the timid one murmuring something to the other who says nothing in reply, merely watches with his head inclined slightly forward, as if in readiness to spring.

But then, 'God damn it all!' Baines sighs. He refills his cup, leaning over to refill Kit's as well. 'You know, we were both of us heroes once. *We* gave the Council Babington. Certain others may take all the credit, but without us, without the work we did, God knows if they ever would have caught the traitorous buggerer. *We* saved her Majesty's life, you and I. *We* made safe the crown upon her head. And look at us now! Just look at the miserable, bedevilled creatures we are now.' He offers a mirthless toast that Kit declines to join. 'The damage you do. Does it not haunt you?'

Kit is startled by the lack of air in his chest, whispering, 'Of course.'

'I mean, to *me* – the damage you have done to *me*.'

Kit's blood runs thick for a beat, an impulse to flee. Yet he cannot move.

Baines settles, briefly, into melancholy, emerging again with a twinkle of suppressed pleasure in his eyes. A savoured secret. When he speaks, he addresses his boys, muttering a word or two: '*Zut ryden.*' One of the boys murmurs something in protest but Baines says it again, a snarl: '*Zut ryden!*'

Baines is breathing hard, sweat upon his forehead. He dabs it on his sleeve. 'I will admit,' he says, 'I am sometimes weak. I *was* sometimes weak, with you. But you boys – all you boys, with the Devil in your hearts! – you cannot blame me that the Devil is a powerful foe. And anyway, I never, ever hurt you,

HESSE PHILLIPS

God knows I never hurt you! You hurt yourselves, by letting the Devil inside you in the first place.'

A scream presses at Kit's throat like wind at a windowpane, pressing till the glass cracks. He knows what will come next: Baines will say, 'I love you,' or some version of it. Kit dares him to say it, say it, say it—

'I cared for you,' Baines says, 'and the ones before you.' He indicates the Dutch lads with a thumb. 'I care for *them*, though they understand but half of what I say! I reckon they'll turn on me too one day, like you all do – like you sit there planning to do, yet again.' His face falls into a look of grim anticipation, a twitch in his neck as if readying to take a punch. 'What are you going to do, Kit? Go on, time's a-wasting. What are you going to do?'

For an instant, Kit knows not the answer himself. Then, like the hammer on a pistol, he is sprung, reaching to draw the knife from his boot. But as he dives, Baines shouts a word in Dutch, '*Mes, mes!*' and across the room the bruised boy pulls something metal from inside his doublet and throws.

Kit lunges at Baines in time to dodge the boy's dagger. Baines's chair topples backwards; his head strikes the floor. Kit straddles his chest, blind with tears, having but one aim: to let all the myriad deaths Baines might have died at his hands be realized now, all at once. Certainly, he too will die here. Both Baines and he will die here; he embraces it. A scream escapes him as he rears up, the knife above his head, but before he can stab, light and liquid explode in his right eye. A hard, heavy object shatters; it might be his own skull.

The world veers sideways. Kit lands on his chest, one eye watching a curved shard of the stoneware pitcher rock back and forth upon the floorboards near his head, settling to still-ness. A single sharp note stretches out in both ears, reedy and stomach-turning.

His body has gone mad. His arms seem to be jointed in a hundred places, far too many to control; his lungs flatten and stay flat. Above, a blurry shadow grows tall, looks down on him as if upon a rat in a trap. To the right, the brass acorn at the cap of Frizer's knife gleams. Kit reaches for it. Baines puts his foot over the blade and slides it away.

One of the boys utters something, like a voice from another room. Baines growls a response. A tearful protest follows from the other lad: the word 'nay' is the same in both languages, and the word for 'please' is one with which Kit is already familiar: *'Bitte, bitte!'* But Baines insists. Kit knows not the precise words, although he's heard many such commands from Baines in the past: *Wretched coward, do as I say!*

Kit props himself up on his wobbling forearms, for which he receives a kick to the ribs. Arms scoop him up and he melts right through them, soft as an egg.

For some length of time Kit is nowhere and nothing. He awakens on a staircase, steps birling under his feet like barrels through a chute. At the top of the stairs the boys drop him, facedown, and start to argue. Short, snarled phrases. One sounds reluctant to continue, trying to bargain his way out of it – an ally, thank God, an ally!

'Bitte,' Kit says, or tries to say, his jaw sideways, his tongue limp. He finds the ankle of the lad he presumes to be of better nature and lays his aching head upon his foot.

A hand lifts him up by his hair and drags him backwards, flinging him to the floor in the dark room beyond. One boy sits astride his hips as the other pins his arms above his head. A knife flashes and Kit shuts his eyes and cries out because he is about to die, but then he feels his doublet cut open instead, hears buttons rattle across the floor. Above, the boy with the battered face holds a button up to the light that rises through the floorboards, the pearl glinting like an eye rolled back. The boy grins, puts the button in his pocket.

Suddenly 'tis clear what they mean to do.

Kit tries to scream, 'No,' but it comes out in a whisper, a

moan. Within seconds he is facedown again, hands behind his back, a loose nail digging into his cheek. They wrestle off his clothes. One ear is pressed to the noise of men laughing and shouting in the room below; with the other, Kit hears a rattle of metal behind him – a belt unbuckled – followed by a strange, high-pitched grunt. All at once, he starts to cry.

"'The light of the body is the eye—'"

Silence is shoved clear through his body, to the back of the tongue.

Across the room, the open door shows him the top of the stairs. If he could but scream, someone would hear him. Any second, footsteps will ascend. A man will appear at the door. He will draw a knife; he will draw a sword. He will look ten feet tall; he will look like an archangel. Any second now, someone will come. Someone will save him.

20

SOME OF FRIZER'S EARLIEST, happiest memories are of afternoons spent at the bear garden with his brothers, when he was still small enough to sit on their shoulders. As the bout goes on, he all but forgets Marlowe for some little while, clinging white-knuckled to the railing as a cur snatches the bear by its lower lip and tugs, a high-scoring hit, leaving the other dogs to nip at the beast's hindquarters or snap at its mutilated ears. One dog hangs back, yelping womanishly, dancing on its forepaws. As if to say, *Stop, what are you doing, have you all gone mad?*

Frizer imagines the dogs are devils, and the bear Faustus. The circle is the clock. The spectators are the angels of the firmament, placing bets.

But then some knave spills ale down Frizer's back, prompting him to reach for his knife – not to attack, of course, simply to reassure himself that 'tis there, should he care to attack. He grasps thin air. Slowly, like a vein opened in the heat of combat, its absence becomes real.

'No!' Frizer whispers.

He drops to the floor, clambering through the forest of legs. No, no, no – nothing.

But the knife would not *leave* him, he thinks, half-deranged. Someone has stolen it! A thousand times, he has been warned not to wear the knife at the back. Papa always said, even back when Elias had worn it like so, that he would lose it that way one day. But soon another thought grows heavy in his mind, remembering how strange Marlowe's manner had been before they'd parted – the way he'd looked at him, as if for the last time. And Marlowe has been gone far too long, for that matter. The sky, bold blue when they'd arrived, is now a tawny shade, like the stains at the bottom of a pipe-bowl.

Baines is easy to find, once Frizer sets his mind to it. Through the doorway at the back of the gallery he finds a corridor lined in doors, one door ajar to the left. It opens on a dim dining room where Baines sits alone at the table, drinking. The fingers of his right hand are bound in a handkerchief. One chair is on its back, and at Baines's feet lie the remains of a smashed jug or pitcher, little left intact but for the handle.

'What happened?' Frizer sputters.

Baines turns and blinks. A gash on the side of his head oozes dark blood.

'Jesus!'

The old fellow's eyes brighten with tears – for truly, he seems much older than before, his gaze lost, in the way that Papa had often seemed lost towards the end. Baines touches his wound and examines the blood on his fingertips with a start, as if noticing it for the first time. 'Oh, Kit!' he says, fondly, but not without great pain. 'He has a temper, does he not?' He sways to his feet, reaching for the overturned chair. 'Let me make you a seat.'

'No, no, by'r Lady!' Frizer swoops in, righting the chair himself. He fumbles his handkerchief out of a pocket and reaches in to staunch the blood.

Baines takes the handkerchief from him. 'My thanks, young fellow. 'Twas not the reunion I'd anticipated, i'faith. Troublesome lad. No longer a lad, of course, but he'll always be a lad to me.'

Frizer sits, for his legs are useless to hold him upright. There is blood on the floor by the chair. And something else too, darker, thinner, floating with gobs of white foam. Vomit.

'This belongs to you, I take it?' Baines is gesturing to an object on the table: the knife, so alien in the aftermath of another man's use that Frizer barely recognizes it.

'God, yes!' Frizer gives the knife a brief examination before sheathing it, relieved to find no trace of blood. 'Where did he go? And those fellows that were with you, did they go with him?'

'Ay.' Baines's tone is weary, deep. 'To entreat him to return, though I doubt they shall find success. I would have gone myself, but alas, I cannot take a knock as I used to.' He seems to have something to say in confidence, though they are alone, looking this way and that before murmuring, 'He's never done ye violence, has he? Always goes for the head, he does.'

Frizer swallows. 'Not exactly.' In the corridor, men whoop and bellow as they thump downstairs. The bout must have finished. Someone in the crowd outside has begun to sing and bang a tabor: the ballad of the *Golden Vanity* – *as she sailed by the Lowlands-low.*

Baines leans to one side, reaching into the breast of his doublet. He withdraws a damp letter, folded in three and sealed with a paper-bolt daubed in red wax, like a bloody blade. He slaps it wetly against the table. 'I have something for your master. Tomorrow is already Sunday, no? I recommend you be sure it finds him before then. I take it he is still at Greenwich, angling for a wife?'

'A wife?'

'A woman.' As if this clarifies the matter.

That shall have to wait. Frizer blots the letter on his sleeve. It contains probably two or three pages. He stuffs it into the breast of his doublet, the paper unnervingly warm.

Baines looks him up and down. He laughs. 'Take my advice and go to Greenwich, lad. You'll bring worse upon him if ye stay. Such is how it always falls out with Kit and his – well, I would say "friends", but 'tis not the word for it, is it?'

'The word for what?'

'Come now, I am not green. I can see it in the way he looks at you. All babes-in-eyes.'

Everything stops. Even Frizer's heart, for just a moment, seems to stop.

Baines chuckles again. 'Nay, look not so on me, lad. I mean no judgement! I pity you lot, I do. How strange it must be, to live without a soul – to be more beast than man – but then, you've never known another way, have you? Gets you young, the Devil does.'

He grins, the tongue a wet flash in the empty side of his mouth.

The bubble of fear behind Frizer's ribs bursts. He shoots upright, overturning the chair behind him, and runs to the corridor. To the left he finds no exit, only a staircase leading upwards into blackness, into nowhere, so he pivots instead to the right, which will eventually take him across the street, to the Inn-in-the-Wall. Where else would Marlowe go?

Footsteps drum hard upon the stairs to the left, in swift descent. Frizer turns in time to see the Dutch lad with the mangled face spring over the final step, wearing a sickled grin that fades as he meets Frizer's eyes. The other brother follows soft-footedly, and together they stand at the bottom of the stairs, their foreheads bright, their clothes dishevelled. For three seconds they stare at Frizer, and he at them, before the bruised boy erupts into crazed, piercing cackles, knees buckling, eyes yellow in his scarlet face.

They let Frizer charge past. Upstairs, he finds a little landing followed by a door through which he must duck, ramming his head on a beam on the other side. Pigeons scatter into flight somewhere above. One step forward and he trips on something soft: Marlowe's doublet. A grid of light stands out between the floorboards, rising from below.

A few feet away a body lies with its hands bound behind its back, near naked, knotted up like a bloody skin. One dark eye rolls upwards to see him and then closes, the face around it a livid scarlet smear.

'Frizer,' Marlowe whispers. 'You came. You came.'

Whatever Frizer does, he must not cry. He must carry this numbness with him like a coal in his bare hands, however much it burns.

Of Marlowe's clothes, he is able to salvage only the tattered doublet and breeches; the rest are ruined with blood and filth. Frizer dresses him with care, slings Marlowe's long, heavy arm over his back and drags him to the door on all fours. Downstairs, they find chaos. In the street outside, a skirmish has broken out between the Black Bull's mob and the local constabulary, the latter of whom are desperately outnumbered. Those same men who'd lately howled for blood in the inn-yard now swarm the plague-fires in search of weapons, hurling stones, burning sticks, horseshit. Some are shouting, 'Open the gates!' Others are chanting, 'Liberty!'

Someone barges into Marlowe's side and he sinks like a stone, taking Frizer down with him. Frizer strains to lift him again. The moment he stands upright, a burning log sails overhead, forcing him to cover Marlowe's head and duck.

'Tom,' Marlowe murmurs into his shoulder. 'Leave me, Tom, I am dead...'

'Almost there,' Frizer pants. 'Almost there.' Across the street, the Inn-in-the-Wall's windows glow, full of gawking shadows. He charges towards it with no more awareness of his surroundings than of the earth's turning, dodging swinging clubs and whirling flames by sheer luck. Beneath the inn-yard gate, he stumbles headlong into a man on his way out, the night porter.

'Help me!' Frizer pleads.

Together Frizer and the porter struggle up the long stairs, Marlowe braced between them. Frizer clings to his numbness, tries to float above his body like an ember above a flame. At the door of the room, the porter fumbles through his ring of keys, sputtering questions: 'What is happening out there? Is it rebellion?'

'I have no idea, man,' Frizer pants. 'We need a doctor.'

'*Tonight?* With all that going on?'

The door opens and Frizer bursts through, letting Marlowe slide off his back at the edge of the bed. He lifts Marlowe's head, tries to examine his eyes. To the porter, Frizer shouts, 'Bring water!' but the man is already gone, having left the door wide open on a sky of still, watchful stars. A gun fires in the street, and people scream. Three more reports follow.

Marlowe has started to sob. Frizer wraps him in both arms and Marlowe does the same. He screams into Frizer's stomach, a burst of hot breath through his clothes.

Frizer strokes his hair and whispers, 'You'll be well.' Such was said to him once, and he can think of nothing better. 'You'll be well, you'll be well, you'll be well, you'll be well...' The words strike like a chisel at his numbness, exposing the soft yolk of himself. It seems that Marlowe's embrace is all that keeps him from sinking to the floor.

'Please tell no one of this,' Marlowe says.

⊱✤⊰

... it shal happen Wednesday next, Poley writes, to Topcliffe. *My syster hath graciously offerred the use of her home for the transaction—*

And then: gunshots.

Poley lifts his head from his cluttered desk, looking into his own warped, candlelit reflection in the window, through which he can see nothing. Outside, in the distance, more shots follow – four altogether – and voices call out in the street, 'Did you hear that?' 'Is it fire?' 'Nay, do not go out – you'll be killed!'

Poley stabs the quill into the inkwell and stands, putting on his doublet. In the listing stair-shaft of his old, narrow, stork's nest of a house, he stumbles into his manservant, who had been on his way up: a tall blackamoor of twenty-odd years called Ignacio, one of several hundred who, some years ago, were heroically liberated from a captured Spanish slave-ship and then dumped, penniless, on the dock at Rotherhithe. He has another name, but Poley cannot pronounce it.

'Men at the door,' Ignacio says, looking stricken, one hand upon the handle of his knife.

Poley draws back slightly. 'What men?'

'I know not them.' He hesitates, as if unsure of how to say it in either of the two languages they have in common. '*Mucha sangre, señor, mucha.*' Blood.

Warily, Poley follows him down to the little-used front room. Torchlights flash past the windows, headed north. The passing glow illuminates three shadows, which is all Poley has time to take in ere Richard Baines steps forth and clasps him in a stinking, bowse-soaked embrace.

'Robin, you villain! Still have the old house, eh? And your famous poison garden too? I remember this room – this was the room where we captured Babington's comrades, was it not? Lured 'em in like fish in a trap!'

Another flurry of torchlights passes outside, revealing a gash on the side of Baines's head, blood dribbling down to the collar. 'Master Baines,' Poley says. 'You seem far merrier than a man with your aspect has any right to be.'

Baines laughs. 'Yes, I *am* merry, by God!' He snaps his fingers at the other side of the room, at which his two Low Country wags step into the meagre light. One wears an unnerving, wild-eyed smirk, despite having a face still more abused than his master's; the other looks startled. 'The lads and I are here with good news,' Baines says. 'That statement of mine, which you'd so longed to see delivered, shall be submitted tomorrow.

I've made enough copies to paper the Star Chamber's ceiling with it!'

Poley glances to the open front door, through which Baines must have barged in. In the street another group of men rush past, armed with shovels and clubs. 'Master Baines, have you lately escaped some unrest? Perhaps in the vicinity of Bishopsgate?'

Baines's only response to this is a cold grin, waxing impatient. 'I came here to thank you, you know,' he says, and reaches into a pocket, offering a sodden sheaf of paper. ''Twas you, you old adder, who pushed me to my purpose. I want you to have the first copy of my statement, as a gift...'

'You've had your "reunion" with Master Marlowe, I take it?' Poley asks, quite honestly no longer interested in the damned statement.

'"Reunion", ay! My boys did me proud tonight. That was all I needed – to see the ungrateful bitch put in his place. Never was a man more richly served, I tell ye, except perhaps for his own King of the Buggerers!'

Poley need hear no more. He flies back upstairs to fetch his pistol, which must be assembled, loaded and charged, delicate work with only nine fingers, all of which are trembling. Setting Marlowe upon Baines was risky, but at the time it had seemed necessary – Baines had appeared content to dally about forever, for which Topcliffe will not wait. But if Marlowe is dead, what then? All will be lost.

Sprinting downstairs again, Poley shouts to Baines, 'Stay, stay here until I come back!' and so rushes into the street, the pistol in his belt ready to fire its single shot.

Outside, the commotion sounds quite near indeed. A bright light emanates from beyond the long, peaked rooftop of nearby Crosby Place, throwing the spire of St Helen's into shadow. Just as Poley turns the corner onto Bishopsgate Street, a rank of mercenaries in the Mayor of London's livery march past, spears at their shoulders, headed for the Black Bull tavern with the unhurried menace of those who come not to start a fight, but to end one. Where the street ends at the gate, the last traces of an angry mob dance towards retreat, flinging flaming logs and sticks behind them. The remains of pillaged plague-fires lie strewn about the cross-topped fountain, sputtering at the smoky air.

Poley waits until the mercenaries have passed to limp across the street, planting himself in a spot where he has already spent a collective hour on several mornings and several nights – for from here he can see the topmost gallery of the Inn-in-the-Wall, and the door to Marlowe's room. Many times over the past week, he has watched the poet's tall frame uncurl itself from behind that little door, stand upon the stairs and take a drink. Now, Poley finds no sign of Marlowe. Instead, a slight, large-eyed creature straddles the stairs, motioning for someone below to hurry up.

Ingram Frizer. Nick's dear, boyhood friend, on whose behalf Poley has heard scores of promises. He has spent this past week observing Frizer too, often from the window of his office at Seething Lane: watching Frizer and Marlowe's daily farewells, a silent, stilted handshake one day, a friendly exchange of waves on the next. He has seen Frizer wait hours on end for Marlowe, drifting up and down the street in circles like a seed on the wind; and he has seen Frizer greet Marlowe again at the end of the day, the spine springing erect, the ears practically pricking upright. So much to be gleaned from watching one man wait for another.

At last, two men ascend into view on the stairs, one with a bucket, the other with a satchel. A physician, it seems. Frizer herds them into the room, lets the door swing shut and then stares at it, unmoving. Such pain in that face, gold with firelit tears. A cherubic face, one might call it. It reminds Poley of his eldest son, who lives with his mother out in the country. Which is to say, it reminds Poley of himself.

For a minute or more, Frizer moves not. Poley has seen young fathers look so, anticipating bad news from the birthing-bed. But what is this agony in his gaze? Is it grief? Is it fear? Is it something else? Behind that door, is Kit Marlowe alive or dead?

'Look at me,' Poley whispers. 'Look at me. Look at me. Look at me.'

Frizer's shoulders lift and fall with breath. He opens the door, and seems to push himself into the room as if to dive into icy water, braced for shock.

❧❀☙

Silence. Kit sleeps like the skulls at the bottom of the river, with darkness reeving through his eyeholes, between his teeth. When he wakes, 'tis to the sound of his own whimpering, to the sensation of a man hammering away at his soft insides, where a sinew is breaking, thread by thread: *The light—of the body—is the eye—therefore—when thine eye—is single—then is—thy whole body—light—*

A hand fumbles for a grip on his hand, squeezing. 'Stay awake, man. I told ye to stay awake!'

Frizer's wide eyes draw him up. They lie across the bed width-wise, Frizer at the foot and Kit at the head, as if swept here by either wind or tide. A bandage squeezes Kit's throbbing ribs, but otherwise he is naked beneath the bedsheet. Something slimy and foreign seeps from his insides, pools in the sheets; the sweat upon his neck cools like fresh spit. He could rend every inch of his own defiled and unfamiliar skin with his fingernails.

Frizer nods at the open window full of dizzy stars, looking at Kit to be sure he looks too. 'Up there, see? Cassiopeia. You were telling me all about the "stella novi", remember? The new star?'

'*Nova stella*,' Kit corrects him.

'Ay, that one. So keep talking. Stay awake, that's what the doctor said.'

'There was a doctor?'

'Yes. He was just here.'

'I told you, Frizer, I *told* you—'

'He had to look at your head. Just your head. I promise. I was afraid you would die.'

Kit smirks, or thinks about smirking. 'And your master would kill you for sure!'

'Well.' Frizer hesitates. 'I know not. If you died, *I* might well kill me too!' He laughs a threadbare laugh, as if immediately abashed at his own words, and to reassure him Kit tries to laugh also. But simply to smile disturbs some tenuous balance in the tender part of his skull, just above the eye, a soft bubble-burst at which his head begins to fill with silent, empty ocean.

Frizer pulses his grip on Kit's hand. 'Who is Tom?' He sounds afraid to ask.

To hear Tom's name is another shock, plucking him back from the edge. 'No one.'

'Must be someone,' Frizer says. 'You've been saying his name all night. So who is he?'

The last person to ask Kit this question had been his father. When Tom fell ill, Kit had been staying with his family in Canterbury. One day, a letter had arrived from Walsingham: *Tom is dying. But come not to London, Kit – it will only bring him pain to see you.* Kit remembers nothing more of that day. Only waking up in Westgate jail the following morning with a splitting headache and a broken nose, and a charge of assault and battery on his head.

His father was straddling a stool on the opposite side of the bars, Walsingham's letter rolled into a pipe in his thick-knuckled hands. 'Who is Tom?' he'd asked, as if a part of him already knew.

Kit said, 'The man who used to fuck me.'

To Frizer, Kit answers, 'He's dead.'

'I'm sorry,' Frizer says, and then falls silent for several seconds, as if from those two words he has gleaned volumes. 'You know so many dead people.'

'Ay,' Kit agrees. He'll know many more, he suspects, before his own time comes, lest it come soon. Anxiously, he adds, 'It makes me feel old,' as if to make a dark jest of it. Such only drives the blade a little deeper.

'You *are* old,' Frizer says, turning faceup, a smile in his voice. 'You are an old man, given to rambling about nothing, and to chastising youths for their fancies. You tell fables. You put on a sour face at other men's good humour, and you laugh out of season—'

'I do not!'

'But you do. I wish you could see yourself, marry, I wish you could know how it feels – be me, for a moment, looking at you.'

Kit turns to see him. Frizer stares at the ceiling as if he can see clear through it, the long stare of the drowned. Something stirs just beneath his fine, boyish features, like the dawn.

Kit lets an impulse move down his arm, slipping his fingers between Frizer's fingers. Frizer's eyes close. His breath swells, ebbs. His grasp tightens, his thumb strokes the side of Kit's hand as if they have touched in this way a thousand times before, as if, indeed, there were no other way to touch one another but this. But it is simply too much to bear: the weight of Frizer's grip on Kit's hand, the ghost-weight of a man upon his back, the weight of Kit's own profaned and desecrated hide. He cannot bear so much, and still try to imagine a future when he will hold every ounce of another man's weight against his body and not merely bear it but desire it, with every ounce of his own.

'Not now,' Kit rasps. 'Please, not now.'

Frizer eases his grasp. He clears his throat, turns onto

his side. A tear rolls over the bridge of his nose and makes a dot upon the sheet. 'We must keep you talking,' he says, as if nothing at all has happened between them. 'Till morning, that's what he said. Tell me a story... Tell me how *Hero & Leander* ends.'

27 MAY 1593

Three days

❧❀❧

We return to a prime consideration. Who
and what was Ingram Frizer?... Was Frizer a
servant? If he was, whom did he serve, and in
what capacity?

LESLIE HOTSON, *THE DEATH OF*
CHRISTOPHER MARLOWE, 1925

2 1

I N THE MORNING FRIZER wakes to the familiar weight of
Betsy's body beside his own, her belly teeming-hot, like an
egg about to burst.

But then a fly swings past his ear like a scythe, startling him
bolt-upright into the room at the Inn-in-the-Wall: silent but for
his own breathing, the birds in the street, the murmur of distant
church bells. The weight beside him in the bed is Marlowe,
naked in a blaze of sunlight. He looks as if his body had crashed
down from the clouds, blood and dirt scattered around him in
the sheets like feathers. Half his face is a black fist.

Elias and Rafe's faces come to mind, a flash like the firing
of a pistol.

Marlowe betrays no sign of life. 'We fell asleep,' Frizer realizes. He shakes Marlowe's shoulder, gently, then harder. 'No.
No. We fell asleep!'

Suddenly, the bells at nearby St Ethelburga start to clang –
not to toll the hour, but to announce with almost unbearable
urgency the start of Sunday services.

At last, Marlowe draws in a sharp breath and stirs, alive.
'Thank God,' Frizer gasps, his forehead on Marlowe's arm.
'Thank God.' He jumps out of bed, hopping clumsily into
his boots. 'Get up, man. 'Tis Sunday – the Privy Court will
close early.'

Marlowe moves not. Now that Frizer looks on him again, the strip of bloody bandage around his ribs seems only to throw his nakedness into high relief, to lend his abused body an air of perversity: so much skin, so scantly interrupted; the sex lying soft against his thigh, like a lost glove.

Frizer draws the sheet up to Marlowe's waist. He leans in close, one knee upon the bed, shouting over the ongoing bells, 'Listen! I'll be gone a few minutes! When I come back, you must be out of bed!'

One eye flickers partway open, wet and dark in the bruised, misshapen face.

Frizer stops short of touching him. Last night, he would have done it. The urge to be close remains, strange as it may seem: to hold Marlowe the way he'd once held Nick in the grass, only face-to-face; to whisper, *hush, hush – I am here*. But these things are impossible now. Last night was another world.

Frizer merely whines, lamely, 'We have to hurry!'

'I cannot,' Marlowe murmurs.

'You must!'

'I cannot.'

Nay, there's no time for this. Frizer must hasten downstairs before the whole inn clears out, order food and drink, water for washing, the services of a laundress for Marlowe's clothes... Frizer is still buttoning his doublet when, at the door of the common room, he nearly collides with the landlord, who has exchanged his customary stained apron for a gaudily pinked doublet and Sunday cap. One look at Frizer and the landlord's merry expression crumples. 'Is he dead?' he says, shouting to be heard, for the church bells have yet to cease.

Frizer was unprepared for this question, and so says nothing. Suppose the night porter must have blabbed, or the doctor, a stringy-haired, odd-smelling creature whose face Frizer had never seen, it being concealed beneath a muzzled mask like the snout of a pig.

The landlord clarifies, 'Your master's man – has he come up dead or what?'

Frizer has no right to lie, nor is the truth for him to speak. He only holds out Marlowe's flask and says, 'I need brandy, and something to eat.'

'For yourself?'

'For the present moment!'

The landlord rumbles back to his post behind the bar. But on the point of returning the flask he withholds it, leaning in to growl, 'Your master and I have an understanding, you know. But if you fellows make trouble for me, you make trouble for him. He knows that.'

Frizer takes three long, greedy gulps from the flask, scorching his empty insides. Having drained it partway, he hands it back. 'Water this time.'

Halfway upstairs, the brandy works its way to Frizer's brain. He must catch himself on the railing to stop a swoon, nearly dropping the slice of stale bread-pudding wrapped in paper with which the landlord has also begrudgingly provided him. The nearest bells have faded to silence, but in the next neighbourhood over, and in the parishes beyond the Wall, down by the river or even across it, they peal on like lambs lost in the smoke, calling every man, woman and child to their places.

Frizer puts a hand over his pounding heart and feels paper crackle inside his doublet, reminding him: Baines's letter.

In all the chaos, he had completely forgotten it. Now he knows not what he is to learn and yet fears to learn it, like a guilty child upon the doorstep of a church. He sets his things down on the stairs, lowers himself to sit. The letter is still damp from last night, or perhaps from his own sweat – warm and damp, the way it had felt when Baines first handed it to him. The paper-bolt is skilfully made and takes some time to puzzle out, time Frizer does not have. He rips through it, sucking in a breath as the pages unfold:

A copy of this letter wasse delivered to Sir John Puckeringe Lord Keeper of the Prevy Council on xxvi May & other copies hath bin furnisht to his holinesse Whitgift & Lo: Cecil Treasurer & divers others. For courtesies sake, I give ye the same, to plot whatsoever exit you will. Lest ye be slowe to act upon this message I advise ye read the sequel, for in cauda venenum.

There's venom in the tail.

Frizer reads on.

Even the most distant bells have gone silent by the time Frizer shoulders into the room with his hands full, announcing, darkly, 'I'm back.'

No response. Marlowe has squeezed himself into a corner of the bed, out of the light. At the sight of him Frizer feels the fist around his heart unclench itself, just briefly, then tighten again.

'Marlowe!' He slams the door, steps around the traces of last night's disarray – the scattered clothes, the bucket of water, the bloody rags – and sets his offerings on the floor by the bed, his head spinning when he rises again. Marlowe's face is turned to show only the damaged side. It hardly resembles him. The right eye is too swollen to open, the gash above the eyebrow pulling at its stitches like a mouth sewn shut.

Something heavy unlatches itself from the bed of Frizer's chest, rising perilously upwards:

Christ was a bastard and his mother dishonest.

The first beginning of religion was only to keep men in awe.

St John was bedfellow to Christ, and he used him as the sinners of Sodoma.

All they that love not tobacco and boys are fools.

He can see it – he can see Marlowe saying it and then

curling his mouth into its vulgar smile, eager to see what harm his words have caused.

Frizer shakes him, roughly. 'Get up. Now.'

'Frizer,' Marlowe gasps, cringing.

'I'll hear no more of it, man! You moved yourself this far, you can get up!'

'I cannot,' Marlowe says, 'I cannot.'

Frizer tugs his arm, at which Marlowe fights back at last, albeit weakly, crying out in pain. 'Please stop, Frizer, stop!'

'God-damned fainting woman! A whimpering boy, you are, ye milksop!' Frizer turns and gives the strongbox a kick that he regrets instantly, leaving him temporarily lame. He limps to the wall beside the bed, leans his back against it and slides down to the floor. Across the room, the Queen's image descants upon him haughtily, pitilessly. He imagines standing before a judge sometime in the future, being commanded to explain himself: *How could you not know what he was?* – or stood before God, rather, to whom there shall be little point in lying. And Frizer can imagine damnation of course, all his life he has been imagining it. But there is a chance, just a chance, that this is all but a test of his faith against the Devil's lies (for what is Richard Baines if not the Devil himself?) and if he should pass this trial, he will be shown mercy, he will be redeemed.

His very existence might have led him to this moment. Indeed, how could it be any other way? He was hewn and honed to be at Marlowe's side – in *this* moment, no other – to be comforter, guardian and guide. God saw what was done to him in the stables, even if no one else did. God saw everything, and He did not put a stop to it because God had plans. God forgive him that he ever questioned or lamented it. He must love himself, or try to love himself, because he was made by God, for Marlowe, and surely that is a beautiful thing.

If ever he sees Richard Baines again, he'll kill him. He'll stab him in the neck with his knife until the bones give up their mutual grip and the skull rolls harmlessly away.

'I'm sorry,' Frizer says. 'I did not mean it.'

A large hand reaches out, squeezes his shoulder and then settles upon his chest, gently gathering up a heart-sized wad of cloth. Frizer's breath rushes out and in, as if it were his heart indeed that Marlowe held, as if he could but squeeze a little tighter, and stop it at will.

Frizer puts his hand over Marlowe's hand. 'I'll go to Seething Lane,' he says. 'You stay here and rest.'

'I'm sorry I brought you into this, Frizer,' Marlowe says.

'No need, ay? Just stay alive while I'm gone.'

'You must be careful.'

'I will.' Frizer has yet to fully recover his breath. He aches in a place he dares not name, an ache connected, somehow, to his heart and lungs, to Marlowe's grip upon his chest.

'Frizer.' Marlowe lifts his hand to touch Frizer's cheek, turns his face towards him. He looks like a wax figure, halfway melted. Yet the stare of his single open eye is as straight as a bolt. 'Be careful at Seething Lane. There are worse men than Baines. And cleverer.'

In this moment, Robin Poley sits in his usual pew at St Helen's Church, hunched over a Book of Common Prayer with Baines's letter tucked in between its pages. Sleepily, he mumbles the Confession from behind a perfumed cloth, in chorus with the rest of the masked congregants. Last night, he'd watched the Inn-in-the-Wall till his eyes had dried out in their sockets, from darkest night to the first light of dawn. In all that time, Frizer had never left the room again, and neither had Marlowe, alive or dead. By the time Poley had returned home, Baines was gone, and his child-brides with him. Thankfully, however, he'd left the letter behind.

'... Almighty God, our heavenly Father, I confess and acknowledge that I am a most miserable and wretched sinner, and have in manifold ways most grievously transgressed Thy most godly *Christ was a bastard and his mother dishonest—*'

Poley bites his careless tongue. He glances left and right at his neighbours – row after row of half-concealed faces, as similar to one another as they are to his own – then peers over his shoulder towards the church doors. There are guards on every corner in Bishopsgate today, even here, in God's own house: two of them hovering like shades, faces covered, halberds gleaming at their shoulders. London has crossed some deadly threshold overnight; one can feel the hairs of the city standing on end.

After the service, Poley finds Nick Skeres at St Helen's lych-gate, trembling with news. 'Good Master Poley!' Nick bows and doffs his Sunday cap, revealing a crown of sweat-plastered hair.

'Good Master Nick,' Poley mutters, and keeps walking.

'Good sermon?'

Poley takes a sip from his vial of plague-water, tries not to wince. 'A predictable sermon, I would call it, given last night's events: Homilies 2:21, "servants, obey your masters", et cetera. I suppose you have heard?'

'Heard what?'

'Well, I imagine a letter must have arrived for Master Walsingham this morning, from Richard Baines. Or am I mistaken?'

'For Master *Walsingham*? No.' Nick says this despite already having a letter in hand, a copy of the copy which Poley carries in his prayerbook. 'I caught this on its way to Master Caesar's office at Greenwich. There was nothing for Master Walsingham, not that I saw, and trust me, I was looking.'

'Hah!' Poley grunts, limping along somewhat too swiftly for his companion.

'Well,' Nick fumbles, his jubilant mood in retreat, 'so I need tell *you* nothing, do I? He's finally gone and done it, the devil! Now we can get on with the rest.' This receiving not the desired reaction, Nick pouts. 'I thought you would be happy.'

Poley slows his pace – for ay, he should be happy. If all is well and the wind looks favourable, then this is indeed good news, the news they have been waiting for. 'Ah, never mind me, my boy. Sleepless night. Let me see it.' Nick hands the letter over and Poley pretends to read as they walk, so weary-eyed that he stares at the last page two or three times longer than necessary, lingering on the postscript: *I, Richard Baines.* Like the signature of a monarch!

'So,' Nick says, 'you think Walsingham's got one coming to him?'

'And half the men in London, if Baines is to be believed. Either way, be you sure that your master sees this. I'll come to him in Greenwich this time, I think, spare my poor sister the torment of his company.'

'What will you tell Marlowe?'

'Tell Marlowe?'

'When he comes in today, at the Privy Court?'

Poley is incredulous at himself, then furious. How could he have failed to consider this? If Marlowe is severely wounded, dead or dying, he shall certainly miss his appointment with Phelippes today, and that in turn will ignite a series of fuses, all of which shall inevitably lead to the dreadfully ill-timed explosion of the Council's wrath: a hunt, a chase, and that with the prey lying helpless at the Inn-in-the-Wall, waiting to be scooped up!

'This is—' Poley starts to say 'a disaster' but holds his tongue, answering Nick instead. 'I will say nothing to Marlowe until I've confirmed a date with Master Topcliffe. Wednesday shall suit our purposes best, I believe – the Council will meet in Westminster that day, for the Whitsuntide sessions. Marlowe may try to take flight before then, but he must be dissuaded.

I suppose your friend could be of some use to that end...' He pretends to forget the name.

'Ingram. Frizer.'

'Master Frizer, yes.'

Nick looks faintly troubled. 'You want to bring Ingram in on it?'

'No! No, by no means. Not yet anyway. Let me meet him first.'

'Ay, of course.' Still that soft frown tugs at Nick's face, as if at a fleabite. 'He's a good fellow, you'll see. Like a little brother to me. He'll do whatever I say.'

Poley says nothing, for none of it matters if Marlowe is either dead or in the Council's custody by nightfall. What they need is a reprieve – time enough to cobble together some other use for Marlowe's body, if necessary; some other solution that will pay a 'diamond's bounty'...

'You sure y'are well, Master Poley?' Nick says. 'You seem angry.'

Poley laughs, perhaps a touch too immodestly. 'Why, I am *anything* but angry, Master Nick! Everything is going *precisely* according to plan, at the *most* convenient pace, and with the full complement of my confidence behind it!'

Poley sends Nick back to Greenwich. He must think; the plague-water is addling his brains. First, to deal with Marlowe's appointment at the Privy Court. It would be easy enough to offer the clerks a pinch of tobacco in exchange for five minutes alone with the Book of Rolls, wherein he may forge Marlowe's name under today's attendance. But come midday, Phelippes shall expect Marlowe in the questioning chamber. There's no forging one's way out of that. The only expedient remedy that comes to Poley's mind is to make use of the vial of tincture of aconitum he keeps hidden in his desk – to somehow intercept the small ale that Phelippes habitually takes before interrogations ere it reaches him in his office, and slip a drop or two into the cup. They'll find the meddling rat dead at his desk, facedown in his crypto-logy books…!

Even as Poley begins to smirk at the very idea, he stumbles into the man himself, on the spiral stairs of the Privy Court's gatehouse. 'Tis so narrow a space that for two men to pass in opposite directions, they must crabwalk around one another. But neither budges, long enough for Poley to observe Phelippes's person, albeit from the level of his loins: dressed if not for church then for some other appointment requiring zealous ablution, his whole homely face exposed, a thick sheaf of papers tucked under one arm.

'Are you leaving us, Master Phelippes?' Poley says, hopefully.

Phelippes rubs the space between his eyes. 'You did not receive the Lord Keeper's message? It was sent last night.'

Of course, Poley did not, for reasons he leaves unsaid.

Begrudgingly, Phelippes explains. 'The execution of John Penry is to be expedited. Tuesday afternoon at the latest. Until the deed is done, all other business is suspended.'

Poley tries not to sound breathless. 'And… interviews as well?'

'*All.* It seems you failed to notice that the moiety of our guards have been sent out to keep the peace. Need I inform you of the incident that occurred in your very own neighbour-hood last night? Are you so sound a sleeper?'

Poley says nothing. He could kiss every pox scar on the ugly bastard's cheeks, by God!

Phelippes seems to notice a change in Poley's looks, a touch of scarlet creeping into his face. He sidles down another step, the buttons at his shoulder scraping the stone wall. 'I will find it out, Robin,' he says.

'Find what out?' Poley pouts innocently.

Phelippes responds by lowering himself another step, so Poley's chin is now aligned with his chest. Poley moves not, braced, eagerly, for whatever challenge may come, but at last Phelippes merely says, 'Go *home*, Master Poley. Take a bath.

Methinks I have never seen your face with quite so much beard upon it.'

He sidles past, the buttons on his sleeve leaving long, white claw-marks upon the wall.

As soon as Phelippes is gone, Poley rushes back downstairs and across the yard, to the unnervingly empty courthouse. Just two guards at the door, clearly spares by the measure of them, and only a pair of clerks on duty to take names, both of whom Poley knows to be cheaply bought, one a little cheaper than the other. 'Anyone comes in by the name of Marlowe,' he says, having paid a few pennies to each, 'find me.'

Poley then makes his way to his low-ceilinged, Spartan office in the gatehouse – a room utterly unrepresentative of his domestic habits – and sits with his elbows on the window-dowsill, biting the inside of his cheek to keep his eyes open. Weariness overcomes him insidiously, first with an impulse to rest the eyes, just a moment or two, thereafter by darkness, grave-deep.

A knock comes at the door, starting him awake. Poley picks himself up, turns his chair to the desk. He poses himself over some papers as if deep in toil, and shouts after the second round of knocks, 'What is't?'

The cheaper of the two clerks sidles into the room and closes the door at his back, uninvited. 'He's here,' the minion blurts, seemingly having sat upon this information, incomplete as it is, for some time already. 'Christopher Marlowe.'

Poley takes a glance around the room, observing the light, the shadows. How long was he asleep?

'We put him in a box, in the east wing. Turner's watching him, but I doubt he'll sit still much longer. He is most belligerent.'

Belligerent – that sounds like Marlowe, indeed!

Poley follows the clerk into the hall of curtained cells. Today there are no scribes at the desks, no foremen pacing the gleaming floors. Outside the fourth box a single guard, barely more than a child, watches Poley's approach as nervously as if he came with his sword drawn.

Poley sweeps through the curtains, trying not to sound breathless as he chimes, 'Good afternoon!'

At the table, a runtish fellow with a gaze like a fish on a hook turns sideways in his chair, craning his neck in hope of catching a glimpse of the world outside: Ingram Frizer. 'What in hell, man? "*Good afternoon?*" Have I been arrested? Where am I?'

Poley rounds the desk. Frizer spins on his backside to follow him with his eyes, which are quite large, quite blue, even in the candlelight. 'You,' Poley says, almost laughing, 'are not Christopher Marlowe.'

The lad looks as if he has spent the entire day in conversation with madmen and seems to be losing faith that such shall change any time soon. 'No, I am not!'

Poley perches atop the desk on one thigh, moulding his expression into a generous smile, one that assures a return of courtesy. Frizer's eyes are ill-slept, his face long unshaven, his clothes dirty, dishevelled. His doublet bears a stain just below the breast on one side, a worrisome, rust-coloured smudge.

'I understand you have come under somewhat unusual circumstances,' Poley says. 'How may I be of aid?'

Frizer bobs his head, as if he believes himself worthy of better service than he has received thus far. 'Well, you can have it set down that Christopher Marlowe gives his attendance, but through me. He's ill today. Bed-sick, marry. It could be the plague, for all I know!'

His gloveless hands fidget upon the tabletop, the bitten-down nails ringed in dirt. Nay, blood. Frizer notices Poley's look, and, too late, slips his hands under the table.

Poley keeps his face arranged just so. Perhaps Frizer had been caught up in the fray between Marlowe and Baines last night. Perhaps he came by his bloody aspect innocently, in the aftermath. Or perhaps nothing Poley has assumed thus far is true and this unbeseeming lad, not Baines, has killed Kit Marlowe for one reason or another, and is so foolhardy as to come here in search of an alibi, red-handed, as 'twere.

And yet, be any of this true, or none of it, the lie must stand, uncontested. Below the hem of the curtains, Poley can see the shadows of Puckering's minions lingering, one shifting uneasily from one foot to the other.

Poley sits, shuffles his papers, prepares his quill. 'Well enough. But I should think it only prudent that we establish your knowledge of Master Marlowe's condition and whereabouts, do you not agree?'

Frizer shrugs, his knee jittering.

'What is your name?' Poley asks. When Frizer answers, he writes it down. 'And your county of residence? Your status? Your master?' Frizer makes much of the fact that he is a gentleman and that he serves Thomas Walsingham, as if anyone at Seething Lane should be either impressed or intimidated by this. 'And where did you last see him?'

'Who?' Frizer says.

'Master Marlowe, of course.'

Once again, Frizer's face empties of all but quiet panic. 'The, the, the Black Bull. In Bishopsgate.'

Poley gives him a confidential look. 'Master Frizer, if I were to send a man now to the Black Bull, would he find Master Marlowe there, indisposed, as you have described?'

Frizer nods, wall-eyed. And then, 'No,' he says abruptly, starting forward in his seat. 'Nay, I misspoke – the Inn-in-the-Wall. 'Tis *near* the Black Bull, marry. I was confused.'

Poley nods and smiles, writing a line or two of nonsense in shorthand. Glancing up, he finds Frizer's stare locked upon his four-fingered hand as if upon the barrel of a gun.

With the same amiable air as before, Poley asks, 'How well do you know Christopher Marlowe?'

A wince. 'How do you mean?'

'Are you passing acquaintances? Familiar associates? Friends? *Intimate* friends?'

Frizer's cheeks flush. 'I… I do not understand.'

'Come now, 'tis not so difficult. You know Master Marlowe in some regard or other. Categorize it for me: half-strangers? Cohorts? Bosom companions?'

'Friends,' Frizer says, quickly, and seems to regret it at once. 'Ordinary friends. 'Faith, I hardly know him.' His colour whitens now, surely wondering whether he might have just betrayed himself. A lad like him will wonder so much even of his own walk, his voice, the way he draws breath. 'Tis like a grindstone, this wondering. It never ceases.

Poley says, 'Master Frizer, to your knowledge, has Master Marlowe ever been given to blaspheme, denigrate the Holy Sacraments or utter false heresies?'

For a second or two Frizer appears not to breathe. The poor beast, he has a face like the aftermath of a slap. 'Nay. Not in my hearing.'

'Have you ever overheard or heard report of Master Marlowe denying the Trinity or the incommutability of Christ?'

'No!'

Poley hesitates, thinking of Baines's letter. He drops his voice to just above a whisper: '"The Virgin Mary was bawd to the Holy Ghost." Does that sound to you like something Master Marlowe might say?'

'Nay.'

'"Christ was a bastard." Have you heard him say that?'

Frizer shakes his head. Poley elects not to speak again for some time, to see what else silence may bestir. Sweat brightens on Frizer's pallid brow; the lump bobs in his throat.

Frizer has read the letter. He must have had it from Baines.

'You know,' Poley says, 'to give insult to Christ, to deny his very divinity, these things are assaults upon the Church of England, of which her Majesty, our Queen, is sovereign. They are, therefore, assaults against her Majesty, which as you know is high treason – the very highest form of treason, second only to regicide.'

Frizer blinks hard, tongue-tied.

'When a man is found guilty of treason, often those who have been known to indulge him or to harbour him may be treated as accessory to his crimes.'

No response at all this time.

'You *do* know the penalty for treason?'

'Ay.' The word escapes as mere air.

Poley squints. 'And you *know* yourself, do you not? You trust yourself to confront the Devil head-on? You trust yourself to know his lies from God's own truth?'

In the silence, Frizer's eyes almost seem to change their colour, to go from sky blue to livid green, a bright filament of unshed tears appearing along the eyelids. Angel-faced, dim-witted, weak-willed – this lad is so perfectly suited to Poley's purposes that he might well be a gift from God. Better yet, Poley may now rest easier with the knowledge that Marlowe is still alive. For clearly, Frizer is protecting him.

Poley laughs, startling himself and Frizer both. He could kiss him too, the poor, spineless pullet; he could unhinge his jaw like a serpent and swallow him whole!

❧❀❧

Downstairs, a rough hand snatches the hood from Frizer's head and thrusts him backwards through a door, leaving him pinwheeling his arms for balance. His effects come sailing out after him, clanging on the floor at his feet: his knife, his purse, the key to the strongbox. The letter, which they had not found, remains tucked inside his doublet.

'Ye cannot knock me about, ye stew-house whelps!' he shouts, gathering up his things. 'My Master is *Thomas Walsingham*!' In response he receives only a bolted door and a silent, hateful look from behind the iron lattice, as if he were an insect too small and far away to bother swatting.

He skulks down the corridor into the empty courtroom, pursued by his own echoing footsteps. A sea of red and white chequered tiles sprawls emptily through the unlit hall, rippled with the wear of many centuries. The court has been closed for some time; Lord knows how long. And all the while, Marlowe has been alone.

'Tis not yet safe to run. Outside in the yard, Frizer turns in place, scanning the surrounding windows. Finding no sign of watchers, he begins to jog and, once through the gate, tarries only three or four paces before breaking into a dead sprint.

They have seen Baines's letter at Seething Lane. The man with the clean-shaven face had made that abundantly clear. And if the letter has reached the Privy Court, then surely the Lord Keeper and the Archbishop of Canterbury and all the 'diverse others' mentioned in the preface have seen it too. It shall be Marlowe's death warrant. It matters not whether there's a shred of truth in any of it. The man with the clean-shaven face was clear about that too: heresy is treason, treason is heresy.

Frizer races north, smoke burning in his lungs. A new phrase has replaced the meat of Leander's neck in his thoughts:

I, Richard Baines, will Justify & approve, by mine oath and testimony, how all men in Christianity ought to indevor that the mouth of so dangerous a member may be stopped.

22

'WAKE UP, WAKE UP!'
The voice comes through bottle-glass, or snow, or earth. Kit would reply, but his body is only meat on a butcher's slab, his tongue a lump of bloody gristle. His skull echoes, emptied of all but a single impulse, lower than thought: *Run, run, run, run, run!*

'Come on, man, wake up!'

Kit sucks spit and sets his jaw straight. For a moment he feels nothing but the first rush of air in his lungs, like the first drink after an unbearable abstinence. But then pain follows, a web of cracked bones and burst vessels that stretches into every extremity, even his gums, his eyelids, his fingernails. No matter how many times he has started awake this day, 'tis always as if from one nightmare into another. But this time is different. This time Frizer is here.

'Man, I thought you were dead!' Frizer says. He is out of breath. He shudders, leans his head against the edge of the bed. 'Christ, you gave me a fright!'

The sheet sticks fast to the wound above Kit's eyebrow. With a wince he peels himself free, feels fresh blood seep from the gash. His heart throbs in the bleeding, rapid, drumming footfalls: *Run, run, run, run, run!*

'Jesus, man,' Frizer says, squinting at the sheets. 'Did you piss yourself?'

Kit knows not what to do with this information besides laugh. 'But you're well, are you?' His eyes are still frightened. 'You're not dying?'

Kit reaches out and finds Frizer's sleeve, trying to hold the world still, or to hold himself still. All day, he has been steeling himself to say something urgent. Now his mind is blank. 'Frizer,' he says, 'Frizer,' hoping the rest will come to him.

Frizer collects the untouched food and drink from the floor and stands up, fluttering around the room. He speaks all the while, almost as if to himself but clearly for Kit's benefit. 'I'll have them make you a bath... Clean the room... Get ye some new clothes... I hope you have clothes in here, man, otherwise I know not where I'll find any to fit ye!' He hunts through Kit's bag, turning up the rust-coloured, quilted doublet and long, Venetian-style breeches of a winter suit that Kit had taken with him when he'd fled Leathersellers'. 'I'll take the sleeves off,' Frizer decides, turning the doublet in the light. 'You'll look like a sailor but at least you'll suffer less for the heat. The air is more like a soup every day!'

Something about his fussing makes Kit smile. 'Tis oddly maternal – a word he had never expected to associate with Ingram Frizer – the anxious busywork of a mother who knows not how to show love except through her labours. But 'tis also terribly sad to watch Frizer plan out a future for him, even if only an immediate future. In his nervous hands there's a hope of hours yet to come, days even. Kit can see him anticipating the day when yesterday's wounds have become scars, as if they shall be together when that day comes.

Run, run, run, run, run, run.

'Frizer,' Kit whispers.

'I'll go downstairs to order your bath. Stay still, ay? Just a little longer and I'll have ye out of that filth.'

He is gone. The room hums in his absence, as if all his hurry has produced a little whirlwind, gusting with hope. To that ghost Kit manages to say, at last, 'I have to run, Frizer. I have to get out of England.' But to say it even to an empty room is a knife in the heart.

Frizer is gone long enough that Kit slips into half-sleep. When he returns, 'tis with even more noise and haste than before. 'They're coming,' he says, and Kit's heart leaps in his chest before he adds, 'Coming to clean the room.' Frizer hooks his arms beneath Kit's, pulling gently. 'Come on, now. They made you a bath in the laundry. 'Tis too heavy to bring upstairs.'

With a roar of pain, Kit labours to his feet. Air from the open window runs down the backs of his legs like a tongue, trailing filth, blood, piss. Another man's scad. Every breath is a reminder of the snap of that sinew inside him, the blinding shock of its recoil. The door to the stairs, with no one outside it.

The light of the body is the eye—

'Shh,' Frizer says, holding him.

Kit cannot stop crying. How can he live, if only sleep will cure him of crying?

'There, now,' Frizer says. 'There, now. A bath, ay? A bath will help.' He steps back, looks down and blushes, seeming to have only just realized that he has been embracing a naked man. He hurries to the cot and searches inside his own bag, retrieving an extra shirt. 'Put this on. It'll be short on ye but better than nothing.'

Through this, Kit somehow stands unassisted, propped up on his legs like a scarecrow on its stake. Frizer helps him lift his arms through the shirt, helps him slide on some used underclothes, as there's no sense in wasting clean ones, followed by his winter breeches. There's devotion in Frizer's gaze, or else Kit imagines it. Suppose 'tis only kindness, though kindness alone is a rare and precious thing. Kit feels abashed, as if undeserving, looking at the floor.

'You should have been a doctor,' Kit says.

Frizer laughs. 'With my piss-poor Latin?' For a moment they are still, Frizer with his hands upon Kit's arms, Kit ashamed to look him in the eye.

'Frizer,' Kit says, in disbelief that he has the will to say it, 'if I stay in England, they will kill me...'

'I know. I know.' Frizer's eyes are as clear and melancholy as sapphires. Kit parses every flicker of his expression, reading into even the way he clears his throat ere he speaks again. 'Just come with me. Can ye walk?'

Kit nods. 'Ay.' Indeed, he can run. Broken as he is, he could take Ingram Frizer by the hand and drag him all the way to the sea.

⊸❦⊷

Frizer settles Marlowe in the bath and then rushes back upstairs to retrieve all the things he's neglected to bring: Marlowe's boots and stockings, fresh underclothes, a tooth-scrub, a washcloth, a satchel of rosemary ash for the underarms, the little ball of almond-scented soap that Betsy had given him at Easter. In the room, he finds three chamber-maids gathered around the bloody bed like mourners around a coffin. All at once, they turn to him with stifled gasps, as if fearing that the savage beast that lately fed here might have returned to feed again.

'I will pay for everything,' Frizer says, fumbling in his purse. 'Your silence on this matter too, ay?'

They take the coins but go on staring at him, their expressions unchanged.

''Tis not his fault. He was attacked. They almost killed him!'

But of course, he need not explain himself to a pack of scullery wenches. This shall be practice, he decides, for when he must lie to the master later.

Downstairs in the yard, Frizer hesitates at the door to the laundry, his arms laden with clothes. Something watchful seems to prowl about the redolent, smoky interior. Clearly, the space was once a stable. Rows of hanging sheets recede into the dark, strung between posts, vestiges of former stalls. Even with a fire smouldering just inside the doorway the place reeks of mould and lye, and of the slough of innumerable bodies, and the musk of long-departed animals, thick as a lungful of dust.

In a far corner, behind a half-wall, Marlowe sits crammed into a linen-lined washtub with his long arms hung over the sides, fingertips touching the sawdust floor. The bandage is gone, exposing his bruise-blackened ribs, his sinewy, undernourished nakedness. Frizer feels an impulse to pull a clean sheet from one of the laundry lines and wrap him in it.

Instead, he hands him the soap and a washcloth and says, 'Scrub yourself. I intend no insult, marry, but you need it.'

Marlowe stares at him. 'What happened at Seething Lane?'

'What do you mean?'

'You were there, no?'

'Ay.' Frizer's face feels hot. He sets most of Marlowe's things by the tub, then pulls a low stool into a shaft of daylight and arranges the woollen doublet in his lap, unknotting the laces that hold the sleeves in place, delaying answer until he can bear the silence no longer. 'Nothing happened, marry. They asked some hundred and sixty questions of me, and then they let me go.'

'What questions?'

'Just... my name, and whom I serve, and how well I know ye—'

'Anything about Baines?'

Frizer grows suddenly aware of the paper folded against his chest. 'Had they made any mention of *him*, I damn well would have said so!'

Silently, Marlowe takes this in, and then shifts onto his knees, bending forward to palm water over the back of his head. The row of dints in his spine stand out like pearls.

'Can you look after yourself tonight?' Frizer says.

'Look after myself? Where will you be?'

Frizer hesitates, knowing this next shall be ill received. 'At Greenwich, with my master.'

'Your master,' Marlowe scoffs. 'And what will you tell him?'

'The very least that he need know.'

'Have you heard one word from him this week? Has he sent a single message?'

'No, by'r Lady, he has not.'

The water becalms. Frizer senses Marlowe's eyes on him. 'Frizer,' Marlowe says, and then seems to wait. The word unspoken: *Come.*

Frizer makes no move. He knows what Marlowe will say, for he has said it already. Why say it again, except out of cruelty? But this is no time for hand-wringing. Marlowe is helpless. Frizer must lead. And here he is with a man's doublet in his lap, altering sleeves, like a damned housemaid!

Finally, Marlowe says, 'I have no choice, Frizer. I have to run.'

Frizer bites his lip, silent.

''Tis not what I want.'

'I know,' Frizer says.

'I cannot wait for Walsingham.'

'But *look* at ye, man! Ye would not get as far as Bishopsgate!'

'Then help me.'

''Tis my master's help you need.'

'Your master has left me to rot!'

Frizer stands, flinging the doublet down. 'And what am I to do for ye? What more can I possibly do? You want me to carry you to the mountains on my back?'

Marlowe hangs his head as if ashamed.

'Ay, I thought so!' Frizer starts to pace but after only a

stride or two sinks onto his haunches, trying to think. He can produce no sensible argument against flight, for indeed there is none. If Marlowe knew of Baines's letter, there would be no stopping him, not even his injuries would stop him. He would be gone before sunset and he would be right not to delay.

'I can help ye but one way,' Frizer says. 'I can go to my master and beg his help. That is all I can do. Do ye understand?'

Marlowe nods at the floor between them.

'You'll need money, for one thing. You'll get nowhere without money.'

At last, Marlowe sighs in surrender, with a wince that makes Frizer wince also. 'Whatever he says, you'll return by morning?'

Frizer nods.

'Promise me.'

'I promise, man. I promise.' If all else fails, he shall find a hole somewhere, an unsuspecting, inconspicuous place, like a hermit's cave, and hide Marlowe there. Hide himself too perhaps. They shall live together, unmolested and unmissed, like men on the moon. Frizer will read *Tamburlaine* to his heart's content, and Marlowe will write new plays, and Frizer will read those too, one player playing every part, one specta-tor to watch him.

'Tis all so ridiculous that Frizer laughs aloud, his head in his hands. Marlowe says, 'Are you well?' and it occurs to him to answer, *No, marry, I have never been well.*

But instead he stands up, makes a henpecking gesture at the tub. 'Stay not so long in there or you'll catch your death.'

'Ay, Mother.' Marlowe smiles, warmly. They are friends. But there's danger in friendship, especially in the beginning, before it becomes worn-in and comfortable, maintained by habit, like the shape of one's boots. Perhaps it always begins like this, with the pinch of wanting more than any man could reasonably give to another. Perhaps 'tis the wanting by which friendship endures. Perhaps that is love.

Nay, he is too much a coward, too stupid, too wicked to be touched by a thing like love, which was, after all, invented by God! How dare he aspire to love, a loveless thing like him? This very place is an admonishment. Everything herein exists to remind him of what he is: the hooks, the ropes, the skeletons of old stalls, the faint musk of beasts and hay. The air reeks of pain ere it comes, as with a storm.

With his eyes on the floor, Frizer hears Marlowe take in a sharp breath, and then the suck and swell of the water as he pulls himself upright, the silence as he stands still, his body dripping. Seconds pass. Frizer cannot look up; must not look up.

'Frizer.' Again, unspoken: *Come.*

Frizer lifts his eyes. He has seen Marlowe naked before, but not like this. His body is pale and bright like a tallow candle, long-necked, broad-shouldered, narrow-hipped. Knife-shaped. His sex could be either weapon or wound – like a wound, Frizer feels a throb of sympathy in himself at the sight of it, how sorely it begs for soothing; like a weapon he longs, strangely, to find its slicing edge, to prove its sharpness by touch. To draw a drop of blood, and suck it from his fingertip.

Marlowe appears poised on the edge of speech, his breath pitched high and cold. Perhaps he has no words to say. His desire is simply to be seen. And then what?

Frizer steps backwards. He turns, facing into the maze of laundry lines, and so retreats, pushing through blankets and bedsheets, towards light.

23

A COLUMN OF CARRIAGES AND riders stretches the full length of Placentia Palace at Greenwich, awaiting entry under a froth of white garlands. Along the wayside, drummers thunder away at their tabors; pipers squeal over one another. Far ahead, the column vanishes into the dark mouth of a barbican, footed in the Thames, from whose windows maids in white gowns scatter handfuls of rosemary, to be crushed underfoot below. In London, Frizer has seen women fight like cats over a single sprig of charred rosemary, scrounged from a plague-fire.

He has never been to Greenwich before and spends a great deal of time wandering about the palace's perimeter, lost. Eventually, he happens upon a dirt lane crammed with wagons, each one bearing grotesque quantities of meat and fish, the stench of which hangs ripely in the humid air. Following this train leads him to the riverside kitchens, a village in their own right and one that might as well be under attack, for all the chaos therein. Haplessly, Frizer dismounts and leads his horse around the courtyard, seeking help from the several liveried men he encounters, none of whom have a moment to spare for him. One after another, exasperated servants of apparently middling authority listen to his demands and respond in kind: 'Your master is *who*?' No one has heard of Thomas Walsingham.

A bright explosion thunders somewhere beyond the high palace walls, at which Frizer alone ducks for cover. The echo resounds for three seconds, followed by an upswell of applause and cheers, hundreds or even thousands strong.

The Queen must be somewhere just beyond the walls, so near, yet out of sight. Frizer feels a potent mixture of fear and awe at the thought, as if she were herself the source of the flash, the boom. A fickle goddess throwing thunderbolts from her fingers. A puff of smoke where lately stood a man.

Presently, Robin Poley stands atop an eighty-foot-high viewing tower, perched above the very tiltyard where Henry VIII famously tumbled from his horse some fifty-odd years ago. Just a few layers of red-coated bodyguards now lie between himself and the Queen. She sits high upon a brightly painted throne dead-centre of the platform, her body, if indeed she has such a thing, entombed in pearl-studded billows of gold silk jacquard, her head framed in a rebato as broad as a battle-map, the diadem set far back on her head, elongating the skull in a way that reminds Poley of some strange, frilled eel. Altogether, a vision of such monstrous, incandescent might that one may only behold her indirectly, like the sun, or the Gorgon.

Upon her periphery, ladies-in-waiting, courtiers and privy councillors sit by order of rank, those of greatest value practically hanging upon her hem, those currently out of favour seated further back, like Robert Devereaux, the Earl of Essex, looking sullen in a hat like a plumed chamber-pot. To her Majesty's right sits white-bearded William Cecil, the Lord Treasurer, and at Cecil's feet, his dwarfish, hunchbacked youngest son Robert leeringly returns the moon-eyed gaze of Audrey Shelton, handmaiden to the Queen, who droops unhappily beside her royal mistress, limply holding up a silver spittoon. Poor girl, today her Majesty has sentenced her to death – to die, that is, in Scadbury, as Madam Thomas Walsingham.

The other half of the happy couple stands at Poley's side upon the rampart, well outside the sphere of glory. In the tiltyard below, men take cover as a rocket shunts off into the air, screams and bursts, showering the turf with yellow sparks. Applause and cheers.

'I have not the luxury to deliberate,' Walsingham says, without looking at Poley. 'This business must be done with before Baines's letter makes its way to her Majesty.'

'Would that I could see it done with all haste!' Poley says, only slightly bemused at how swiftly a man may change his tune. 'But you know well what would happen if Master Marlowe were to die tonight or tomorrow: an inquiry, a trial. If Marlowe dies in London, he dies on your bond; if he dies in Deptford on Wednesday, he dies while in violation of that bond – a transgression on his part for which you need not be held accountable, being a victim of his treachery yourself.'

Walsingham's eyes dart towards the royal dais. 'Her Majesty may not see it that way.'

'I imagine her Majesty will be satisfied to have yet another tongue that has wagged against her silenced, and leave it at that.' Poley hesitates to say more. There's a secret, or else an unspoken suspicion behind Walsingham's looks.

'Baines's letter changes nothing, you know,' Poley adds. 'We anticipated it. Our actions thus far have been contingent upon its delivery—'

'Do not use that word with me.'

'What word might that be?'

'"We".'

Walsingham brushes past him to the furthest corner of the platform, where sparks leap and dive like dolphins just below. There he remains for a moment, quietly seething, before turning to say, 'What do you intend to do with his body?'

Poley laughs. 'I have no place for it at home, if that is what you mean.'

'You mean to collect a bounty on him, is that not so – to draw him to Deptford, have him declared a fugitive?'

Poley opens his mouth but no words come. What should he feign – indignation? Ignorance? Both?

'How much will they pay you for his corpse?' Walsingham says. But these very words prove that he knows nothing of Topcliffe, and so Poley may rest. For now.

'Not so much as they would pay for the living man,' Poley answers, truthfully, then quickly adds, 'Let it be a balm to your conscience that my intentions for Master Marlowe's remains are every whit as practical for you as they are profitable for me. By this way there shall be no lingering questions for the Council to pursue.'

Walsingham grunts. '"Profitable", you say? Yes, I wonder about that. I wonder why one such as you would take less when you could easily have more. I wonder why you should be so solicitous with me, for a partial reward.'

A wave gathers behind Poley's ribs: the fright, the thrill of being caught. 'Oh, one such as *me*? I beg your pardon, but is it not hypocrisy of the highest order for the judge to hate the executioner? Were I not at your service, you would find another to do that which you have not the stomach to do yourself, some back-alley cutthroat no doubt, who should do away with your dear friend as lovingly as he would quit the life of a saucy whore. I wonder, would you despise that fellow as you do me?'

'Perhaps a little less,' Walsingham admits.

Poley takes this confession as a victory. Down in the yard another rocket bursts, a misfire, sending the brave pyromancer, such as he is, diving into the grass for cover as the fiery petard corkscrews over his head, drives itself into a pyramid of sandbags and flatulently explodes. The whole bejewelled audience roars with laughter, even the Queen: a full-throated, masculine guffaw at which Poley cannot help but glance her way, glimpsing her against the setting sun. Her toothless gullet. The wattle of her neck. Never has he stood so near to this woman whose life he'd evidently saved, this dazzling, world-cleansing flame whom Babington had sworn upon his soul to extinguish. Look at her, just look at her: a painted hag munching sweetmeats, puffed up in bombast like a bustard in rut!

If I had a crossbow right now, Poley thinks, *I would put a bolt straight through her eye.*

As he had anticipated, one of the palace's nimble, scarlet-coated runners soon arrives to inform Walsingham that his servant, Frizer, is here looking for him. Walsingham sends the lad away, saying nothing else until Poley and he are alone again. 'A plague upon him! Go, have Master Skeres take him somewhere outside the palace. Somewhere remote. I must stay till the dancing's done with.' Poley bows, about to depart, but Walsingham says, 'I shall send him back to Scadbury. Nick shall stay with Kit from now on. A damned fool I was, leaving Kit in the care of some lackwit boy!'

Poley knits his hands behind his back. There is much he has withheld from Walsingham tonight. 'Be not so quick to dismiss Master Frizer,' he says. 'That lackwit boy is utterly essential to my plans.'

❧❀❧

'*Nick?*' Frizer sputters. He could hug him!

Nick, having just stepped forth from a high gate across the kitchen-yard, beams and flaps his arms like a goose, sweeping the muzzle of the nag at his left. Naturally Frizer is full of questions about where he's been and what he's been doing all this time, but Nick will disclose nothing, his cagey smirk implying his silence to be for Frizer's own good. As they mount their horses and ride inland, past the palace's high walls, Nick unburdens himself of all the gossip he's stored up about the master's bride-to-be and her legendarily questionable virtue, her shameless carrying-on with the Lord Treasurer's crook-back son, which apparently shows no signs of abating. Frizer can only think of what Baines had said, at the Black Bull: 'Angling for a wife. A *woman*.' What other sort of wife is there?

'And,' Frizer ventures, anxiously, 'anything from home? From your aunt, maybe?'

Nick is silent a fraction of a second too long. 'Are ye *mad*, man? My auntie cannot even write her name! She thinks that every time a woman picks up a pen, the Devil writes a letter!'

Frizer lets out a breath, attempting to dispel all thoughts of home with it. Half a mile ahead, the dome of Greenwich Hill flashes with reflected light just before the boom of another explosion tears the sky, a punch of sound Frizer can feel in his chest. Turning about in the saddle, he sees smoke hovering over the palace walls in still, star-shaped clouds. 'Where are we going?'

'Just up the hill a jaunt.'

''You going to slit my throat?' Frizer asks, half-certain the answer will be yes.

Nick laughs, but then falls silent again. 'The master prefers that we meet privily, you know,' he explains.

'You mean... with me?'

'Well, things are out of sorts now. Marriage has got his head turned around. All he talks of is Lady Audrey this, Lady Audrey that...'

'But what about Marlowe?'

'Marlowe?' Nick laughs again, more spitefully. 'Reckon he'll be one lady too many for him now!' A snigger comes, and then a jab to Frizer's ribs, conspiratorial, clannish. All the blood in Frizer's body seems to pool in his stomach.

At last, they come upon a crumbling gate surmounted by a weathered royal crest of the old style, on one side a dragon and on the other a dog. The hunting lodge beyond is likewise in ruins, a grid of carbonized beams protruding from the roof, wet with moonlight. 'Go on,' Nick says, an order to dismount, though he makes no move to do so himself. 'Might as well settle in.'

Frizer obeys, huddling close to his horse. 'What am I to do here, man?'

'Wait.'

'How long?'

'There's naught here'll bite ye,' Nick laughs at him. 'I'll be back with the master anon. Spin your knife, do a speech. You know how to stand and wait.'

Frizer takes his advice with the knife-spinning, if only to keep a weapon in hand. The woods crackle with unseen creatures. Now and then a rocket screams and bursts in the distance, though from here nothing shows except a flicker of light at the rim of exposed sky. Lightning on a cloudless night. He wonders if Marlowe can hear it all the way from Bishopsgate, if he is asleep or awake, if he is thinking of him or only of escape.

The knife spins and stops, spins and stops. Often, it stops with the blade aimed at Frizer's chest, making him wonder, also, what it might feel like to stab himself in the heart. Suppose it would require a good, sharp effort to break the breastbone. One would have to be determined. Or reckless. It could be done in a flash of rage, like punching a wall: *My heart is the wall. The blade is my fist.* To punch a wall is to quench thirst with vinegar; to imagine relief where there is only regret: that hateful grin wiped off that hateful face, that hateful tongue struck silent.

Is this what you want?

He must not think of what he wants. For what he wants is to be back in the laundry with Marlowe, as if he'd never left. To go to him, to step into the water... And then what? Nothing perhaps. Just to feel that moment of transformation. That baptism. To touch Marlowe's body with his hands, not even lustfully, but with curiosity and care; nay, but with healing, to hold Marlowe's body against his own and draw the wounds out of his skin like a poison, draw what was done to him out of his soul like a poison. *Give it to me, I will bear it for you.*

Is this what you want?

He wants the fear to stop. That small, panicked creature that kicks within his chest, that, though snared, tries to run, though limed, tries to fly – he wants it stopped. Forever stopped.

With a roar, Frizer launches his knife at the lodge. The blade strikes the wooden door, sinks like a fang into some hidden heart.

The release is there, though 'tis not what he'd imagined. Knock-kneed, he staggers forth to retrieve his knife, taking with it a large, bright splinter of wood that hangs in place. The object in his hand has never felt deadlier. It remembers the taste of blood, and perhaps quietly thirsts for it.

A light comes swaying through the trees behind him, and with it the sound of voices, feet hitting the dirt as men dismount. At the gate across the overgrown yard, Nick holds his lantern aloft. 'Ingram, did I hear ye shout?'

'Ay,' Frizer admits, and then pulls together a hasty excuse, putting the knife away. 'For despair of waiting!'

'I have the master here,' Nick says, a sharp reminder.

The blood rushes to Frizer's face. He bows at once. The master strides into the yard ahead of Nick, attired in his finest suit of coral-coloured silk, paired incongruously with knee-high buskins. 'You have something for me from Richard Baines, I take it?' He stops close enough that Frizer can see how he suffers in his finery, face aglow with the heat.

Frizer opens his mouth to reply but falls silent as a third man enters the yard: the man with the clean-shaven face who had interviewed him at the Privy Court this afternoon.

'Well?' the master says, startling Frizer out of his trance. He holds out a hand, some sort of musky perfume rising off the kidskin glove.

Frizer hands over Baines's letter, his eyes lingering over the paper-bolt. Earlier, he'd tried to replace it, but the letter has come out looking dishevelled, like a strumpet who had dressed herself in a great hurry.

'You have read this,' the master says. 'Do not deny it.'

Frizer's frightened glance meets a look of warning in Nick's eyes.

The master sighs, tearing through the bolt. 'I suppose it matters not. There are so many copies flying about that all London will know of it by tomorrow afternoon.' He scans the first page, uninterested in the rest, and then looks Frizer in the eye. 'Has he seen this yet?'

Frizer shakes his head. His gaze sticks fast to the third man, who has broken away to inspect the ruined lodge, hands behind his back.

The master folds the letter and returns it to Frizer, still at arm's length. 'Give it to him.'

'What shall I say, master?'

'Nothing, by God's bloody wounds! Let him read it! That does not require you to speak, does it?'

Frizer shrinks. At the lodge door, the man with the clean-shaven face bows close to the bright scar left by Frizer's knife. He removes his right glove, one finger at a time, four fingers altogether, and then probes the fresh fissure with a bare fingertip. Frizer feels a phantom prodding against the base of his spine.

'How is Master Marlowe?' the master says. 'How is his mind?'

'He's been hurt, master,' Frizer admits. 'He wants to flee the country. He's been harping on it all night.'

'For God's sake! Hurt, how? Brawling, was it?'

Frizer shakes his head.

'An incident with Richard Baines, last night,' says the third man, still lingering by the door. 'It happened during the riot in Bishopsgate. You helped Marlowe to the Inn-in-the-Wall. A doctor was summoned.'

Frizer realizes that the third man is speaking to him.

'You said nothing of this before!' the master snarls, to the third man.

'I would not trouble you with but half a story,' comes the reply. 'Only Master Frizer can divulge the rest.' He turns his gaze on Frizer, who hears an echo of Marlowe's plea between his ears: *Please tell no one of this.*

'It—it was those Low Country rogues,' Frizer stammers. 'Baines's men. They attacked him. Beat him almost flat. At Baines's instruction, I warrant you.'

'Can he travel?'

'Marry, I know not. He seems eager to try.'

'That shall have to be enough.'

Frizer starts to speak but bites his tongue. *Enough for what?*

The master glances from Frizer to the third man. For a moment he seems uncertain of how to continue, at last making an exasperated gesture in the stranger's direction. 'I know not what to call you at the moment.'

'Call me Robin,' the stranger says, to Frizer's open-mouthed stare.

The master bites his lip, his gaze penetrating, wary. He speaks slowly, as if out of fear of tripping upon his words. 'Master Frizer, Robin is going to secure passage to the Continent for Master Marlowe. He must be ready to move by Wednesday morning.'

Frizer stammers. To the Continent? The Continent means nothing to him. 'Tis but a shape on a map, one that could contain a hundred Englands, one that stretches into a vast unknowable east, beyond the edge of the paper.

'Where?' Frizer says.

'That remains to be seen. But in three days' time, the papers will be ready. Will they not, Robin?'

Robin merely nods, with a flicker of a downward smirk as if 'twere a burden on his honour to provide assurances. His lips appear to be forever frozen in the faintest of smiles. Frizer has seen a few men go to the gallows with such a look of smug salvation, as if they cannot wait for the Rapture to come and prove them right.

Seeing an opportunity, Frizer turns to whisper in the master's ear. 'Master, I've met this man before—'

'Yes, we met at the Privy Court,' Robin says, approaching at last. It seems his habit to speak gently, as if to a starting horse. 'You came to report on Master Marlowe's behalf. I questioned you. You claimed he was sick. Now you say that he was beaten.'

Frizer looks to the master for help, receiving none. 'Ay.'

Robin has kept walking, forcing the rest to follow. 'You lied to me today, at the Privy Court. You do realize that is rather dangerous, do you not?'

Frizer looks up in panic, first to the master, then to Nick. 'I—I thought I had to.'

'Think nothing of it, lad! I lied at the Privy Court a dozen times just this morning. Fortunately, you had only lied to me. But no, you were under no obligation to speak falsehoods. Do you believe that Master Marlowe is guilty? Do you wish to protect him?'

'Guilty of what?'

Robin's smile twinges. 'You have read Baines's letter, Master Frizer.'

'Ay, but surely they are lies.'

'Lies? How do you know?'

Frizer sputters: 'Baines, he *hates* Marlowe, and seems to me the sort to lie. The words – the things he says Marlowe has said – they sound not like Marlowe to me.'

'And you would know, would you not, being Master Marlowe's "friend"?'

Frizer turns another frightened glance on the master but catches Nick's gaze instead, the eyes narrowing in a kind of threat, one that he has seen often before, in the eyes of other men. Are they truly friends, Nick Skeres and he? Is any man truly his friend?

Robin stops at the edge of the road and Frizer must jerk backwards to avoid stumbling into him. Robin catches him at either shoulder, his smile pinched, yet not unfriendly. Intimate. He says, 'I shall have to ask you not to inform Master Marlowe of my involvement in his affairs. If you truly desire to help him, you will not give him the opportunity to decline my assistance.'

'Why would he decline it?'

'Between fame and infamy is a thing called repute.' Robin leans closer. 'I am a man of some repute.'

He continues up the slope for several minutes, his stride slightly hipshot. Once they've cleared the trees by about a hundred yards, Robin stops again in the middle of the lane and begins to speak, gesturing at the view. Frizer follows his hand with his eyes, but does not listen. The Thames bends as if it would break just here, with the Isle of Dogs protruding out of the north like a swollen black tongue. To the west, a rat's nest of shipyards and piers look on from the bend in the river. On the shore below, a great courtyard glows by the silver water, a perfect box wherein some loud, garish ceremony swirls, its pipes and drums ebbing on the wind like the innermost throbbings of the body, a heart beating much too fast, a branch of nerves thrumming down to the tips.

Is this what you want?

He wants to take Marlowe's face in his hands and hold it to his own as if it were a mask he could put on. He wants to stitch every fibre of his body to its counterpart in Marlowe, vessel to vessel, vein to vein, ache to ache. He wants to fill him with himself until he bursts.

Could other men know his wants just by his looks, they would cut out his heart. But he has always known this of himself. The Devil has had one hand upon him ever since the day the midwife wrestled him out of his mother's corpse. Such was his brothers' admonishment, beaten into him like the parish borders so that whenever he treads close to the boundary, he will know. One toe over the line and his skin lifts, as if at a sudden chill.

Robin is looking at him. Watching him, rather. His eyes are never passive. He indicates a wharf just upriver to the west, facing Greenwich across the bend in the Thames. 'That's Deptford over there,' he says. 'You know it?'

Frizer coughs. 'More or less. From the road.'

Robin nods, smiles. 'When the time comes, you'll bring him by river.'

They descend the hill again. The master and Robin speak quietly together on the way, walking too far ahead for Frizer to overhear. As they come upon the horses, the master says something about seeing to his 'lady', and Nick gives Frizer that old knowing smirk and taps his nose, which is as good as to say, *If ever I was to learn the truth about you, I'd kill you.*

Frizer stands paralysed by the lodge gate, watching Nick's lantern bob away through the trees. All feels precipitous, as if the ground has vanished beneath his feet, a drop so sudden he knows not that he is falling; he cannot comprehend it.

Behind him Robin comes closer, gravel crunching underfoot. 'Shall I ride with you to Bishopsgate? I live close by.'

The plunge accelerates. There's no going back.

24

POLEY DIVERGES FROM THE path back to London to lead Frizer through slumbering Deptford, pointing out the relevant landmarks, so that he'll remember them on the day: Eleanor's house in the seeping mist. The tide-slapped water-gate. The ghost-ship on the green. All the while, Frizer barely utters a word, communicating in grunts and nods, his gaze darting about as if a flood had started to rise all around him.

'Tis not until they are nearly to Southwark that he cracks his lips and bravely squeaks, 'You say y'are a man of some repute, but *I've* never heard of ye.'

'Really?' Poley grins. 'How many Robins do you know of?'

This shuts the boy's mouth for a good five minutes.

And then: 'Does Marlowe know ye?'

'Not on *intimate* terms.'

'So why keep it secret, then?'

Poley gives no answer.

They make slow progress. The Council's hired rogues, some in Puckering's livery, some in the archbishop's, some in the Lord Treasurer's, have the run of every bridge and gate between Deptford and Southwark, putting all travellers to lengthy questioning. The sky is just turning pink as London Bridge finally appears in the distance, floating above the water like some maledicted barque, its many arches swirling with bats. Soon enough, St Mary Overy's pitchfork spire juts above the rooftops, guiding them to Great Stone Gate, with its crown of thirty-six skulls. One still bristles with sun-bleached hair, a single, shrivelled ear clings to another like an oyster to a rock, another admits daylight through a vacant eye-socket.

Here, too, they find more guards than usual. As they wait in line to cross, Frizer cranes his neck, gaping childishly at the mounted skulls. Perhaps he does not even know the story of the one set above the portcullis, on which Poley himself declines to look directly. Frizer would have been hardly more than a child at the time. He will not turn and say to Poley now, as men often do in this place, *There's your lover, Sweet Robin!* Or, *Your husband looks unwell! Do ye never feed him?* To Frizer, the skulls are merely warnings, relics of a strong and well-defended state. To him they have no names.

'You see that fellow up there?' Poley says.

Frizer squints upwards again, with a start as he realizes where Poley is pointing. 'Ay?'

'Master Marlowe and myself both had some hand in his capture, though in quite different capacities.'

Frizer glances aside, astonished, perhaps, to learn this portion of his new friend's history, endeavouring not to show it. 'Who was he? What did he do?'

'He plotted to murder her Majesty.'

'And... *Marlowe* caught him? And you?'

'I can only speak for my part,' Poley says, modestly. 'Circumstances were dire, and therefore I took certain measures which proved controversial. I found it necessary to befriend him, you see, which required me to adopt a pretence of treachery. In my defence, I had only a minimum of support from the Council, for at the time I was no agent, merely an informant – a concerned citizen, if you will. That man up there came to *me* in the beginning. I did not have to go to him.'

'Came to you? For what?'

'A passport.'

The line moves, and they walk their horses a few paces closer.

'Well, as you see, the plot was foiled,' Poley says. 'I consider myself a private man. I never looked to receive any lauds, nor public honours. I saw an opportunity to avert calamity and duly took it, as any honest fellow would have done. But the Council, for whatever cause, saw fit to reward me for my pains with a year's repose in the Tower. For my safety, they said.' Poley lifts his right hand, spreading the fingers so that the gap is clearly visible. 'Now, does that look like safety to you?'

All lies, of course. Not long before Babington's skull found its way here, Poley had entered the Tower for a stay of three gloriously debauched months – for his safety, yes, but also as a reward for services rendered. Wine. Women. Boys. Such a reckoning did he run up with all the pimps and wine merchants in the Liberty that, in the end, Sir Francis had ordered him forcibly removed.

But Frizer stares with horror upon Poley's missing finger, perfectly credulous. He must shake himself to say, 'But why? Why did they disapprove?'

'I reckon that, between a deceiver and the deceived, the latter always wins the sympathy of the mob. Deception is the Devil's sidearm, after all. But at times one must wield the Devil's own weapons against him – an invidious position for a Christian fellow to find himself in, but it could not be helped, and I begrudge it not now. Nor do I begrudge men like Master Marlowe, who never did me any harm, their opinion of me. I know well to whom I owe my resentment.' He smiles at Frizer shyly, concluding, 'This world hath such double-dealing in it that we often find ourselves with common enemies among uncommon friends.'

Frizer nods, as if accustomed to feigning understanding of that which is above his intelligence. 'And that is why you mean to help him?'

Poley's smile widens. 'Ay, to make a fine point on it, 'tis so.'

HESSE PHILLIPS

Frizer seems about to speak, but then glances straight up and tugs at his collar, as if afraid that a tooth or a piece of flesh will drop down the back of his neck. Unthinkingly, Poley too looks up, meeting the stare of those empty sockets and tumbling headlong into their depths: a midnight room in Holborn. An evening by a lake. *For bonny sweet Robin is all my joy.*

'What if he distrusts me?' Frizer says, dragging Poley back into the world. 'He's grown suspicious of everything – rightly so. What's to say he'll not take me for an enemy too?'

But his eager gaze holds another question, another demand, unspoken: *Tell me, tell me I am not his enemy.*

Poley pities him terribly, for all that is about to come. Perhaps he pities Frizer even more than Marlowe.

He reaches out, touches Frizer's arm. 'You'll see.'

❧❀❦

This is the truth about Anthony Babington: when, in April of 1586, he came to Poley's then rather derelict house seeking a forged passport, it had not been out of any desire to join the seminarians' little army in Rheims, nor the Catholic League in Paris. Babington's only desire had been to get out, anywhere, so long as his companion, some drooping, yellow-haired Welshman, could accompany him. France, Italy, Spain, it mattered not. 'Anywhere,' he'd said, quite boldly, 'that a Catholic may live free.'

His gaze had been a dare, a boyish masquerade of bravery. He had grey-green eyes, Poley had noticed, neither fully one shade or another, as lonely and unknowable as the sea. What a thing to notice about a man he'd only just met!

Poley was no spy in those days – that too was true – but his work had given him contacts at the Privy Court, through whom he'd learned that Babington had recently been named as the Queen of Scots' courier by a Jesuit prisoner in Paris.

In his youth, Babington had served as page to the Earl of Shrewsbury, Mary's long-time custodian, during which time the lad had fallen under her papist spell. Poley also knew that Sir Francis Walsingham had had his spies sifting through Mary's supposedly secret correspondence for months already, in hope of unearthing due cause to wield the axe. And so, the day after Babington's visit, Poley had met with the Spymaster in his office, and promised to soon deliver what Sir Francis sorely lacked, but dearly wanted: proof positive that Mary and her minions were plotting regicide.

The only trouble was, Poley had no such proof. Nor was there any forthcoming. Sir Francis knew not of this, of course. Poley could see the old man pretending to consider his offer well ere he licked his lips in none-too-subtle hunger, and shook his hand. 'Proof first, then payment,' the Spymaster said. 'If you fail, it shall be *your* head.'

When next Babington had visited Poley's house, the yellow-haired Welshman was nowhere to be seen, and the requested passport was now for one man only. Heartbreak had dulled Babington's eyes, made his speech heavy and slow. Poley made an excuse for the passport's delay and offered the lad a drink, which was heartily accepted. After the fourth glass of wine, Poley put his hand on Babington's arm and said, 'Listen to me: you must not leave England. Our cause needs you here. You know what I mean. Our queen loves you well – I do not mean that *usurper* in Whitehall, I mean the queen who loved you when you served her jailer, when you were only a boy. She loved you then, and loves you still, and laments that you have abandoned her.'

Poley had not needed to go on so for much longer before poor Babington was blubbering like a baby. He did love Queen Mary, he said. Twice as much as he loved his own mother, who was ever cold to him. He had not abandoned her in his heart; he prayed day and night for her restitution. He simply doubted he was the man to see it done.

'Why?'

'Because I am a coward!'

'No,' Poley assured him. 'I see no cowardice in you. I see strength, immense strength. The strength that bore the cross to Golgotha hill!' He touched Babington's tearstained cheek, a liberty, at the taking of which the lad offered no resistance. Poley said, 'Blessed boy, you are the only one who can save England's soul. This is your Gethsemane. Come out of the garden. Be what God intended you to be.'

Lo and behold, the next letter Babington had received from France – which was, like the last several preceding it, crafted by the Spymaster's men – was soon in the hands of Mary, and her coded reply soon in the hands of Phelippes, Sir Francis's best codebreaker. No express plans to kill her Majesty, not yet. Mary had simply seemed glad for the illusion of friendly company.

Babington too seemed to crave companionship. Over the next few weeks, wherever Babington went, Poley went too: to visit Babington's complotters at their various hideaways around London, to meet with Jesuit priests from the Continent, to stay at Babington's house in the city, to go fishing and hunting at his house in the country. Clearly, Babington had no one to talk to openly. He had a wife he was intent on leaving, and young children whom he barely saw. He had many friends, who demanded much of him and gave little in return. 'All great men are alone,' Poley had said to him, as they'd sat by the lake near Babington's country house, fresh from a swim. 'That is your burden. Even to you, God's love comes not on bended knee to your door. You must *believe* in His love. You must fight, you must strive, you must suffer to believe in it.'

Babington lay beside him in the grass, worryingly silent, as if he'd heard the rote insincerity in these words.

'*Am* I,' he'd whispered, 'alone?'

Such terror in his eyes, the terror of reaching into the unknown. Such suffering too, the suffering of one who desires, desperately, to believe. In one look, Poley realized that he'd been going about everything the wrong way, all that time. He saw, plainly, what he must do. And he did it.

Was that really any different from love unfeigned – to look into a man's eyes, and know what must be done? What was feigned in that first kiss, if a kiss can be feigned at all? It had begun like any other first kiss, a fragile proposition, and then came a slip from one state to another, a sudden reeling of the world at which Poley had heard himself murmur, into Babington's mouth, 'Oh.' That was not feigned. If he told his hand what to touch and when, did that make it feigned? If he told himself to look into Babington's eyes, did that make the act of looking less real? If he willed even what came upon him involuntarily – willed it by wanting it, by thinking, or saying, *Yes* – was he, for a moment, unreal?

In the evening's hum, Babington walked his fingertips up Poley's chest and sang softly, shyly, 'For bonny sweet Robin is all my joy…' and Poley had laughed like a reflex, like the jolt one feels on the edge of sleep. Surely that was real.

A few days later, Sir Francis summoned Poley to Seething Lane, a meeting which he'd fully expected to leave in a bloodstained sack. But the Spymaster greeted him with a generous hand-shake, congratulations, and a bagful of money. The last letter Babington had sent to the Queen of Scots was in his own hand, stating, unambiguously, his intent to 'undertake the delivery of your Royal Person from the hands of your enemies' – more-over, his intent to 'dispatch' the so-called 'usurper'. How he hoped to achieve this exactly, he did not say. Mary, to her credit, was cagey in her reply, but hardly dismissive. Phelippes had grown so jubilant upon the decoding of her letter that he'd sketched a gallows-tree in one corner of the transcript.

'Now what?' Poley had asked Sir Francis, feeling a peculiar emptiness, with his thirty pieces of silver.

'What do you mean, "now what"?' rumbled the Spymaster. 'Go home, spend your money. After tomorrow, your part in this is finished.'

The next evening, Babington turned up at Poley's door and told him to gather whatever was most precious to him. 'Your pistol too.'

Numbly, Poley packed a random assortment of objects: a change of underclothes, a favourite cap, his father's Bible, one half of his best pair of gloves. Babington and he rode off together, breaching London Wall just before the gates closed. Well after dark, they arrived at an inn up in Holborn, out past the fields, where Babington gave a false name to the landlord and treated Poley as if he were his manservant, for which he apologized as soon as they were alone. 'We shall use false names from now on,' he said, circling the room and pausing to listen at every wall. 'Tomorrow, we ride for St John's Wood. My friends will meet us in Harrow. We shall ride all day and night, if the horses can bear it. North – we must go north.'

Poley sat upon the bed, the pistol in his lap. Babington's friends had already been arrested that very morning, at Poley's own house no less; there was no one waiting for him in Harrow. Poley wondered how much further he could go along with this. If he stayed the night, did that make him an accessory? If he followed Babington to Harrow, would that make him a fugitive? And when the end finally came, as inevitably it would, would it come peaceably? Would there be a standoff? Would he have to fire that gun?

'I cannot do this.' Poley laughed, grimly. 'I cannot do this!'

He moved for the door. Babington caught him by the arm, but Poley shoved him away. Again, Poley reached for the door, but this time Babington threw his back against it and embraced Poley, his arms like strangling vines. 'I did all of this for *you!*' Babington cried. 'You said I was strong, you said I was a soldier of God, you said I was beloved, you said you would be by my side, to Calvary Mount! You said it, you said it!'

'But *I* am not strong,' Poley said. There was no feigning there. 'In myself, I have ever been mistaken. In you, never. My part in this is finished – but my love for you, that is unending.'

Even so, he anticipated having to fight his way out, the pistol ready in his hand. But to his surprise, Babington grew pale and silent, not with rage, but grief. He nodded, understanding. 'It is too much to ask,' Babington said. 'I am sorry I asked it of you. I am sorry I gave you no choice...'

Poley put the gun away, folded both hands around Babington's hand. '*Never* say you are sorry to me. Listen, you know I have ears at the Privy Court. I will be vigilant of any action against you. Tell me what way you'll take to Scotland, and if I hear anything, I'll send a warning.'

Babington mulled this over in silence, long enough that Poley feared a return of his suspicions. But then he twisted a ring from his finger – a diamond left to him by his father, who had died when he was but nine years old – and said, 'Do not send messages. They will be intercepted. Send this ring. If I receive it, I'll know they are coming for me. If not, well, keep it. Remember me by it.'

Gently, Poley plucked the ring from his hand, turning it in the light. Some facet of green flashed in its depths – as if the colour were caught from Babington's eyes – and then fell dark.

A few days later, still less than twenty miles north of London, Babington had sent Poley a final, panicked letter: *I am the same as I always pretended. I pray God you be, and ever so remain with me.* He'd begged for a reply, for the diamond, for any shout from the wilderness, but Poley sent none. This last letter from Babington, he never received. It would be a full year before he read it, in the dusty archives at Seething Lane.

This was the truth about Anthony Babington: it took him an hour to die. A quarter-hour was spent on his hanging, for after the cart drove away, they let him swing several times, with breaks to catch his breath. After they sawed off his private parts, they tormented him with them in unspeakable ways. This was before they gutted him, and hacked off his limbs, joint by joint, a butchery which they forced him to watch, dousing him with water if he fainted. Eventually, it had seemed that he could no longer feel what they were doing to him, he'd just lain there, watching them take him apart, empty him out, as if incredulous that this meat and offal and bone were all that had ever stood between himself and Death.

Some days later, Sir Francis called an urgent meeting at the Tower, where Poley was already ensconced. The Spymaster had apparently received a letter from the Queen, who was horrified to learn of what atrocities had been committed in her name. So the story went. But the truth, which Poley had heard from Nick Skeres, was that her Majesty was well pleased with the events on St Giles' Field. In fact, she had written to Sir Francis the day before Babington died, filled with anxiety at the thought that the would-be regicides might not suffer *enough* – let their suffering be prolonged, she'd said, 'for more terror'.

Nevertheless, Sir Francis made a grand show of it. 'We are men of God,' he'd said, pacing the length of the room, past Phelippes, past Thomas Walsingham, past Poley. 'We are the agents of her Majesty's will. We act by her grace, by her leave, by her *conscience!*'

He stopped behind the bailiff, whom Poley had last seen with Babington's severed head swinging from his fist, and the two executioners – boys, they were, boys with long, smooth, simpleton's faces – who had laughed as they'd shoved

Babington's severed cock into his mouth. All three flinched when Sir Francis raised his voice:

'An *hour*. By God, an *hour*! May God forgive us all for that wicked hour!'

Poley pressed the pad of his thumb against the diamond on his finger, rubbing at the setting's sharp edges. No matter how hard he pressed, he could never draw blood. His skin had already developed a rough, whitish bulge, numb at the surface, though he sensed that the flesh beneath it was tenderer than anywhere else on his body. He tried to breathe without thinking about it. If he thought about breathing before he drew his next breath, did that make the breath a lie? If he thought about this thought before he thought it, did he feign to think? If it was easier to feel nothing, think nothing, be nothing, did that mean he only feigned to exist?

This is the truth about Robin Poley: he does not exist. He is a mask with no face behind it; he is a cloak with no one inside it. And the gullibility of other men never ceases to astonish him – how he has fooled the whole world into seeing him, when in fact there is nothing there at all.

28 MAY 1593

Two days

❧❀❧

I have a great respect for Marlow as an ingenious poet, but I have a much higher regard for truth and justice; and will therefore take the liberty to produce the strongest (if not the whole) proof that now remains of his diabolical tenets, and debauched morals... The [attached] paper is transcribed from an old [manuscript] in the Harleian library... and was never before printed.

JOSEPH RITSON, 'OBSERVATIONS ON THE THREE FIRST VOLUMES OF *THE HISTORY OF ENGLISH POETRY*' (FIRST PUBLICATION OF 'THE BAINES NOTE'), 1782

25

... These thinges with many other shall by good & honest witnes be aproved to be his opinions and commen speeches and that this Marlow doth not only hould them himself but almost into every company he cometh he perswades men to Atheism, utterly scorning God and His ministers, as I, Richard Baines, will Justify & approve, by mine oath and testimony...

A WAVE OF SICKNESS COMES, and Kit turns the pages facedown upon the bed. Even with his eyes closed, he can still see the shapes of the words, a palimpsest of Baines's spiny, spidery handwriting. Letters crawl about beneath his eyelids like fleas.

A shadow shunts across the window's light, in the corner of Kit's bad eye: Frizer, pacing the room with his hands yoked around the back of his neck, his eyes fevered and slick, a bright veil of sweat on his brow. He only returned from Greenwich some five or ten minutes ago and seems to have gone all night without sleep.

'Ay, me!' he groans. 'Ay, me!'

'Frizer, be still.'

Frizer sits atop the strongbox but continues to twitch and mutter, mouthing silent denials to himself.

A sound like the hiss of something boiling rises in pitch between Kit's ears. None of this comes unexpectedly. He has been preparing himself for weeks. The indignity of it is what takes him by surprise, to be assassinated in ink, all the most shameful, hateful parts of himself splayed out for the world to sneer and poke at. *All Protestantes are hypocriticall asses... All they that love not tobacco & boyes are fooles!* He cannot help but laugh. Suppose he must have thought that very clever, when he was himself a boy.

Frizer sits upright and tries to laugh also, unconvincingly. ''Tis a pot of lies indeed, no? Why, a man would have to be half an idiot—'

'Frizer, let it be.'

Frizer seems to bite his tongue. And then: 'Marlowe, this is serious. My master knew of the letter even before I gave it to him. Look, it says a copy was sent to the archbishop, and the Lord Keeper!'

''Tis my privilege to be the last to see it.'

'There's not a single phrase in this note that will not send a man straight to the gallows. Or worse!'

Kit laughs again. The man must have been raised among lunatics, to so frequently state the obvious as if it were in doubt! But to die at the gallows means that one shall be seen in death, and heard too. The gallows are a stage. Each condemned man is granted the opportunity to speak his own epilogue before a captive audience, which runs contrary to Baines's intentions, for so he has plainly stated them, here, in the postscript: to see Kit silenced forever. To stop the mouth.

'Look at me,' Frizer says.

Kit shuts his eyes. He fumbles with the lace at the edge of his cuff – Frizer's cuff, for 'tis Frizer's shirt that he wears, too short in the sleeves, smelling faintly, sweetly, of his almond soap.

'Look at me!' Frizer repeats, and this time Kit obeys.

Frizer's eyes are silvered with unshed tears. 'Will you not deny what it says?'

'What does it matter if I deny it?'

HESSE PHILLIPS

'It matters to me! I have defended ye. I have risked much for ye. I have been seen with ye everywhere – I, I stood for ye, at the Privy Court! They know my name there; they know who I am!'

Kit looks away. To apologize is to confess, which he is too cowardly to do. To lie would be more cowardly still. He can say nothing at all.

'I did not agree to this!' Frizer says. 'Christ, what in hell was I thinking?'

'Frizer, just breathe a while. Tell me what your master said.'

'Well, you should be happy – he agrees with you. He says you'll have to flee the country, and is making plans to that end.'

'Thank God.'

'Oh, is *that* who ye would thank?' The hurt in Frizer's face has soured into something darker.

'What do you want me to say, Frizer?'

'Nothing. It matters not, does it? You'll be on a boat in three days' time, anyway.'

'Three days?' Kit sputters. 'I cannot wait three days! With this letter they may come today or tomorrow—'

'Wait three days or wait forever. I care not either way.'

'Frizer—'

'Stop saying my name!' He rises in a jolt from the window-sill and falls to pacing again; rubs his nose on the back of his hand. 'Ay, he tried to warn me, he did. Baines. Said you were like a *son* to him! I should have known then. You're both the same. You with your tricks! How proud of yourself you must be, laughing at me behind my back!'

'I've never lied to you.'

'You made me think you were innocent!'

'Innocent of *what*, by God?'

'You read the God-damned letter!' Frizer's tears have escaped at last. He smears his face in shame, storms across the room and snatches up his doublet from the cot, pausing to spit, 'Godless cocksucker!'

He runs for the door. Same as last night. Though truly, what in hell had Kit expected? What an ass he'd felt, standing there in the bath naked and rejected, like an abandoned bride! He would like to let Frizer go without resistance, feign indifference, but in the last moment Kit rises from the bed and hurls his flask at the closing door with such force that the wood cracks, the stopper bursts. A gout of whisky splatters like the trace of an exploded skull, Frizer already vanished behind it.

'Coward!'

⁂

Muck leaps after Frizer's heels as he stumbles, panting, into Bishopsgate Street. Where will he go? To church? To claim sanctuary, asylum? He is in flight, after all. He could run all the way home, if home would take him back. He could run to Greenwich, to the master, and say, 'I have failed.' For he has failed, is failing, as they say the wall of an old house fails when water gets beneath it and the plaster cracks up to the roof – he has failed, he is cracking, he will collapse.

A warm, dreary rain sweats out of the clouds. He keeps walking. South. Everything he knows is south of the river. Marlowe, it seems, is the only northern point on the map, the polestar, glowing watchfully over his shoulder. Why does he feel as if Marlowe can see his every move, hear his every thought? He'd felt that way about Papa once, just after he'd died, as if the house his ghost had haunted was Frizer's own mind, drifting up and down its corridors, peering into its rooms, even the locked ones. So often had Frizer found himself thinking in apologies in those days that they'd cut short his own thoughts: *I'm sorry, Papa; forgive me, Papa...* And, in time: *Now you know, if you did not know before. How could you not know?* Indeed, how can a man fail to see it when his son is a monster, not the fearsome kind, but the sad kind

HESSE PHILLIPS

born of dead wombs, often born dead themselves; the kind that, if it survives, shall be pecked and clawed to death by its own siblings, for shame that it exists?

But Marlowe's haunting is not so passive as Papa's had been. He stalks the halls of Frizer's mind as if he's considering buying the old place; he picks up objects and blows the dust off them, he lies down in the beds. And Marlowe is no quiet ghost, either. All those words – those marvellous, tongue-tying, spittle-shot words – words that hammer at the ceiling, that defy, threaten and denounce – they follow Marlowe's spectre like bees on a beekeeper's cloak. *Even as delicious meat is to the taste... My slave, my ugly monster Death... 'What is Beauty?' sayeth my sufferings, then...*

Without realizing it, Frizer arrives at Great Stone Gate's northern counterpart, Bridge Gate. Every platform and parapet bristles with guards, more guards than he has ever seen on the bridge at one time. Halberds ready, faces masked. For a moment Frizer stares, frozen, and then backs himself into an abutment overhanging the river, out of sight. The guards could easily be here for Marlowe, to snatch him up should he try to escape. To them, Marlowe is the fearsome kind of monster: the kind that honours nothing, having no god; that feels nothing, having no soul. But Marlowe has a soul, he must have a soul, even if he does not believe in it. Could a man without a soul write *Faustus*, of the pain and terror of losing one's soul? Could a man without a soul suffer to ask, 'What is Beauty?'

Marlowe, Frizer answers silently, looking out across the river towards the distant white playhouses, the Swan, the Bear Garden, the Rose: *Marlowe is Beauty.* He has the arrogance and cruelty of beautiful things. He scorns, he needs; his desires are vast, and voracious. But Beauty is but a small part of what Marlowe is. Perhaps the word is wrong, there should be a better word, a word for this monstrousness they share, Frizer and he, this commonality exceeding blood. Perhaps

Frizer is too cowardly to lock it up inside a single word. The truth terrifies him so much he would rather die than speak it. Even think it.

"'One thought, one grace, one wonder, at the least,
Which into words no virtue can digest.'"

Love. The better word is Love.

⁂

Frizer has been gone several hours. Over a neglected midday meal, Kit peers through the common room's windows, trying to count the guards on Bishopsgate: forty, fifty? He lingers long after the tables are cleared, and in all that time sees but one or two furtive souls scurry past outside. No washerwomen at the fountain, no beggars at the wayside. Even the smoke from the bonfires feels tenuous, fugitive, as if begging the slow breeze to carry it away.

The day darkens rapidly. Kit can wait no longer. But the moment he steps onto Bishopsgate Street, a dozen stares lance his body, pinning him in place. They are quiet, the guards. As if they are looking for someone, and wonder if they might have just found him.

Kit backs into the wall and turns south, keeping one shoulder close to the bricks, a glove pressed to his face, not that there's any hope of disguising himself. He would run, even though he could not possibly do worse, but the ache in his side holds him to a halting limp. All through St Helen's and Lime Street Ward he sees hardly a soul, up until he turns the corner at the northern end of Seething Lane and a whole pack of heavily armed men, ten at least, stumble drunkenly into his path.

'Could never miss *you* in a crowd, eh? Can you see Greenwich from up there? Why, put him atop Muswell Hill and fly a flag from him!' The usual. Kit dares not defend himself. He recognizes the livery badge stitched onto their sleeves: a white bishop's mitre on a crest of blue. Seven years ago, when Anthony Babington had gone missing, London had been crawling with the Archbishop of Canterbury's blackguards, charged with keeping the peace but far better at doing the opposite, starting brawls in taverns, raping women in alleyways, slaughtering any who crossed them. Kit can see well over their heads, to where a crowd of them stand guard outside the Privy Court, two tussling in the street like dogs while the others goad them and laugh.

As soon as he sees an opportunity to retreat, Kit turns and heads for Bishopsgate. Every so many paces he looks over his shoulder, questioning his every step. Phelippes is surely waiting for him at the Privy Court. Before the day is out, he'll be declared missing. A fugitive. It had taken them a week or two to hunt Babington down, if memory serves, but they'd found him eventually, his hair shorn, his skin dyed dark as a Moor, hidden among itinerant farmhands up north. Kit would not make it out of London. *Could never miss you in a crowd!*

The drizzle is turning to rain as at last the Inn-in-the-Wall comes into view. Kit finds Bishopsgate still practically deserted but for the guards on the gate, and for a figure seated under the singed stone cross at the fountain, something bright flashing in his hands: Frizer.

Kit could either laugh or cry. He nearly breaks into a sprint but then remembers the guards, all perched high enough to see but not hear. A few have their eyes on Frizer already, watching him with arms folded over the butts of their weapons, nodding as if to murmur to one another, *Here comes another one.*

Kit says, 'You should not sit here like this, with the guards watching.'

'You were not there. In the room.'

'I was looking for you.'

To this, Frizer says nothing. He strums the edge of his knife with his thumb several times, a faint, icy note.

'Where were you?' Kit says.

'Around. I was thinking.'

'About what?'

Frizer takes in a long breath, lets it out slowly. He looks everywhere but at Kit, glancing up at the cross behind him ere he says, 'What do you have, if you have no God?'

What do you have? Kit's mind reels at the question. The truth is that he did have God, once. Failing that, he'd had his father, his mother, his sisters, his friends, Walsingham, Tom, even Baines. Taken altogether, they were a kind of God, one whose love he'd craved, whom he'd often sinned against but worshipped just the same. *What do you have?*

You, he could answer. *I have you.* But that would be mad.

Kit sits beside him. 'I do not know.'

Frizer grunts as if sensing a lie or a half-truth. A drop of rain has formed at the tip of his nose. 'You do not seem like a monster,' he says.

'I am not a monster. I am a fool, and a drunkard, but not a monster. Were I a monster, I suspect I would not be the other two things. I would be sober and shrewd – a lawyer or a deacon. My father would be well pleased with me.' Frizer grunts again. Kit feels a chill run up his back as a thought of Babington's screams surfaces, lightning-sharp. 'Such things as I have seen... I often wonder whether it takes some measure of inhumanity to believe in God. I've never met a monster but he believed that God smiled on him.'

'God does not smile,' Frizer says, and then half-smiles himself, though the expression soon fades from his lips. 'That's where they're wrong. God watches. He feels no pleasure. He watches, and lets things happen.'

He gives his knife another spin but his hands tremble, halting the blade. A sliver of pink scar appears at his wrist, running diagonally across the veins. Kit glances up at the gate, not certain what he will do, or can do, under such scrutiny. So little does he know this man, and yet so much would he like to give him, more than what seems either possible or sane.

'What are you going to do?' Frizer asks.

'I am going to leave,' Kit answers. 'Tonight after dark, or tomorrow before sunrise...'

'Where will you go?'

'I have no idea. None. I doubt I will make it to safety. I doubt... I doubt there is any safety, for me.' Kit draws a sharp breath, though it hurts to breathe. 'But I must try. What am I, if I do not try?'

Frizer's hand slides into Kit's hand, fingers interlaced, holding tightly. His eyes are closed, his head bowed.

'I have never done this,' he says.

At once, Kit feels the certainty of what is about to happen drop through his chest: a thrill, an ache. Arousal. Terror. God knows why he should be afraid. What is this hunger that has gnawed at him all his life, if not to be touched, to be loved? But he is not himself; he is not his own. Even now, at the apex of a stiff breath, he feels the boot of another master in his side, hounding him back to the place where his body was taken from him: just there at the Black Bull, across the rainswept street.

'I am so afraid,' Frizer says.

The light in the empty doorway, Kit remembers. Frizer's shadow, where the emptiness had been.

'So am I,' Kit admits, shivering.

❧❀❧

Marlowe shuts the door on the rain, panting after the climb upstairs. He starts to take off his soaked doublet as if merely flustered and abashed at the state of himself, his gaze fixed on his own hands, though he must know that Frizer is watching him: every twitch of his nervous fingers at the bone buttons, every drop of rain that gathers at the ends of his curls.

Frizer watches himself also, from the ceiling. He is in two places at once: he is one of two men in a room, watching the other undress, but he is also a child sitting in a stable at night, fresh whip-scars on his back, drinking his first whisky. *Is this what you want?*

'Let me,' Frizer says, or tries to say, the words a click in his throat. Marlowe's hands grow still on the buttons, and Frizer's replace them. Marlowe looks about the room, checking every shadow, every corner. His stare settles on the bed, as if it holds a new kind of peril for him.

'Shall I stop?' Frizer asks.

'No.'

Truly, Frizer had half-hoped he might say yes. 'Tis peril enough to touch the buttons on his clothes, to breathe in a different, more intimate heat as they open, one by one. When finished, he slides his hands inside Marlowe's doublet at the shoulders, easing it back till it falls away. He pulls a lace just beneath Marlowe's throat, exposing a strip of bare skin that runs halfway down the chest, yet dares do no more than stroke the edge of the shirt between his fingers, fearing what his own body might do. Frizer closes his eyes. He feels his jaw settle into the cup of Marlowe's hand, the thumb grazing his lip. His mouth is open; he had not known.

Marlowe brings their foreheads together, a touch, and then removes his shirt himself, with a murmur of pain, or something like it. He returns his hand to Frizer's face, exactly as before. There comes a faint sting of salt upon the inside of Frizer's lip, followed by the taste of skin upon his tongue, and just as suddenly comes the impulse to close his lips around the bone, to draw back, to suck. As he breathes out, another mouth, inches from his own, breathes in.

Frizer realizes, halfway into a kiss, that he has never kissed anyone before, not really. He cannot count the chaste, ritual kiss given to seal his marriage. But Marlowe is patient with him: a soft, untoothed bite, long in the unfolding. A mutual shudder at the first press of their tongues. A pause, eyes meeting, before they press in again, gradually deeper.

Frizer stands on his toes. He has his hands in Marlowe's damp hair; he is biting his lip, the tip of his chin; the side of his neck. His mind seems emptied of all but a bruising, erubescent light, like closing his eyes against the sun; his body moves in arcs, in jolts, in waves. He feels a big hand cup him between the legs and thrusts into it until he shudders as if with sobs. He feels another hand slide into the opening of his shirt, the fingertips becoming blades of sharp, cold metal the very moment that they touch his skin—

Frizer grabs hold of Marlowe's wrists. 'Stop! Stop!'

'I'm sorry,' Marlowe pants. 'I'm sorry.' They both bow their heads. For a long moment neither moves.

Frizer breathes into the coal of his own courage. It brightens and dims. Upon opening his eyes, he finds his own hands still wrapped around Marlowe's wrists. A mark shows near the heel of the left hand: a raised droplet of scar-tissue, like wax.

Frizer tries to look Marlowe in the eyes. To prepare him without saying a word. He then steps back to remove his doublet. Unpins his collar. Strips off his shirt. The humid air is an ice-bath upon his nakedness. Again, he is in two places at once: watching these men as one reveals his ruined body to the other; watching also the boy in the stables, who has stolen his sleeping brother's knife from under his pillow – stolen it for purposes that feel, to him, absolutely necessary, though God knows there's no explaining it to another. Madmen cut themselves. Lost souls desecrate the house that God gave them; they are buried facedown, with stakes through their hearts. But there is sanity in this act of opening himself, in every cut and slice. His body is a vein fat with poison, and if he does not bleed it, he will die.

Rain dances upon the windowsill, rattles in the street, thumps the thatch on the roof.

Marlowe is biting his lip. His eyes have stars upon them, moving as they move. 'May I?' he whispers.

Frizer can only nod.

Marlowe steps forward. He touches two fingertips to a spot between Frizer's collarbones which is permanently numb, and then traces down the breastbone in a thin, straight line – a line that Frizer knows broadens towards his belly, ending above the navel in a delta of shiny, blush-pink tissue. Dots line the edge on either side, like a seam in a glove. Suture-marks.

Marlowe's fingers travel half the length of the scar before Frizer can bear no more and pulls back.

'Who did this to you?' Marlowe asks.

Frizer answers, 'I did. I did.'

Marlowe exhales, slowly. He is trying not to cry. Frizer can sense him thinking, *What should I say? What can I say?* And this, he finds so endearing that he could smile, in spite of everything: that Marlowe cares enough to search for the right words, for his sake.

'Are you afraid of me?' Frizer says.

'No.' If Marlowe speaks true, there's no way of knowing by the look of him. To Frizer's eyes, he looks terrified.

'Am I a monster?'

'No. God, no. You are beautiful.'

These words sink into Frizer gradually. He winces at first, but then sneers, disbelievingly, at the thought of 'beauty', and then of 'grace', letting out a bitter laugh at the last, 'wonder'. This man, this man of all men, says he is beautiful! And he says it again and again, between kisses to Frizer's hair, his temple, the side of his neck. He says it as Frizer sobs into his chest, his arms around him, his voice a hum against his skull: 'You are beautiful. You are beautiful. You are beautiful.'

26

FIVE O'CLOCK COMES TO the Privy Court with a toll of the bell at St Olave's, followed soon after by All Hallows Staining, then All Hallows Barking, a riot of competing hours. Robin Poley, his elbows on the windowsill, his head in his hands, surrenders to the wave of dread that he has held behind his heart all afternoon. Marlowe never came today, and Frizer neither. The bond is broken; now the hammer will fall – too soon, much too soon!

And too late to circumvent any consequences. Twice already, Phelippes has knocked on Poley's door, tearing him away from his red-eyed watch for an interminable minute or two to mention some tedious business for which neither man cares a jot, their respective minds being all on Marlowe. Duly, just as the last, leaden *bong* fades to silence, Poley's door opens again, this time sans any courtesy. 'His lordship has called a meeting,' Phelippes rumbles gravely, meaning, of course, the Lord Keeper, Sir John Puckering. 'You and I are to find him at the Marshalsea tonight.'

'*Marshalsea?*' Poley blurts out.

'Yes – Marshalsea.' Perhaps the molelike eyes narrow even further; 'tis difficult to tell. 'Penry's been moved there. 'Tis nearer to the gallows at Thomas-a-Watering. His lordship means to stay close till the hanging. All of this was discussed at morning prayers.'

Poley had been half-asleep at morning prayers. God knows his stamina is not what it used to be, and with this, his third day without sleep, he hovers somewhere between exhaustion and madness.

'Are you quite well, Master Poley?' Phelippes says, head cocked.

Poley lets forth an unconvincing titter of laughter. 'What,' he sputters, on the verge of asking after Topcliffe's place in all this, which would only prick the cipher's ears to some mischief at hand. 'What is the *purpose* of this meeting, I pray?'

Phelippes harrumphs softly, declining to answer. He scans the bare walls of the little room, as if in search of something incriminating. 'You have shown great interest in Master Marlowe's case this past week.'

'I find the case very interesting, ay.'

'Marlowe did not come yesterday either, did he?' Phelippes checks a paper in his hand. 'According to our records, another reported on his behalf... Frasier, was it? – no, Frizer.'

Poley shrugs innocently. How should he know?

Phelippes says, 'I suppose we shall be searching for *two* men, in that case.'

'A search? Is that not premature?'

''Tis the Lord Keeper's prerogative. Given the... revelations of these past two days, I assume there shall be a proportionate reckoning.' He hesitates, for perhaps he can see Poley sweating. 'You, being so familiar with this case, and evidently with its subject, perhaps you might know something which could be of use to us in our efforts to locate him, something you'd rather impart to me now, and not later?'

Poley fidgets with a wick-trimmer, opening and closing the blades. 'I can resolutely say I know no more than you. Master Marlowe *did* register his lodgings here in London when he posted bond, did he not?'

Phelippes deigns not to answer this either, glancing at his paper again. 'Thomas Walsingham stood surety for Master Marlowe. I suppose we shall have to call him in—'

'Oh, no,' Poley blurts thoughtlessly. 'No, I would not think...' He trails off, suddenly aware of the wick-trimmer's chittering in his hand, absurdly, piercingly loud.

Phelippes takes Poley apart with his gaze. At last, 'Seven o'clock,' he growls, and so departs.

Two hours. Before heading home, Poley writes a frantic letter to Nick Skeres: *Keepe your master in ignoraunce, but get ye to Dettford. Make my sister ready.* Once this message is on its way, Poley is left with just enough time to drag his bad leg up to St Helen's, retrieve his horse and, just in case, his gun, before setting out for the Marshalsea. He would stop at the Inn-in-the-Wall, just to have a look, but there's no time. He must have Puckering's ear ahead of the rest. Belike with all the trouble about the city, the Lord Keeper will prefer to keep Marlowe's case quiet. Somehow, Poley must convince him to raise a bounty – a 'diamond's bounty', no less – despite the obvious need for discretion. God knows how he'll manage it. He can only hope Topcliffe's presence at the meeting shall be a boon, but when has it ever been?

With a low, carmine sun sneering below the clouds, Poley finds the Marshalsea surrounded by two layers of mercenaries in concentric rings, spears at their shoulders, rain rattling upon their helmets. At the courthouse doors, a stoic boy of some sixteen years mutters, 'This way,' and leads him into the unquiet darkness. Upstairs, even before he reaches the door of Topcliffe's office, Poley overhears Puckering's booming voice bark, as if at a bad taste in the mouth, 'Marlowe!'

'Am I early?' Poley says, letting himself in, and then promptly freezes. Twelve pairs of eyes glower at him, including those of the young Queen, in her portrait. In the corner, Topcliffe's slave-girl – a ghastly spectre in a dark prisoner's smock – keeps her head bowed.

Topcliffe, no doubt annoyed at the Lord Keeper's intrusion on his evening, seems content to treat this gathering as if it were his own personal Privy Council, being the only one seated. The rest of the men in attendance are either of Puckering's private retinue or spies like Poley himself, Phelippes among them. In the terrible pause that descends, Puckering picks up a goblet from Topcliffe's desk, fills his mouth with wine and swallows. He then crosses the room to regard Poley up close, a faint, apoplectic twitch in his small-eyed, high-coloured face.

It takes Poley several seconds to realize that Puckering is waiting on a bow.

'You were meant to be here at half-past six,' Puckering says – quietly, which is unusual for him, therefore all the more unnerving.

Poley darts a scowl at Phelippes, who is gazing at the wall to his left. 'I beg your pardon, Lord Keeper. Delayed due to the rain.' He bows a second time, just to be sure.

In his previous office as Lord Speaker, Puckering once had a man thrown in the Tower for turning up late to a session of Parliament. But for now, Poley is only made to suffer through the coldest of stares ere the Lord Keeper turns his back on him, addressing his grim little assembly in a typically stentorian tone. 'A team will be dispatched to Bishopsgate early tomorrow. His Holiness the archbishop has generously lent us two of his men, the rest shall be drawn from among our ranks. Master Maunder, since you executed the arrest in Scadbury, I believe you shall be up to the task a second time. And your two deputies of course, which makes five altogether. *Five* should be sufficient.'

'I took the big bugger with three, in Scadbury,' Maunder boasts, chuckling.

'And if Marlowe is not to be found in Bishopsgate?' Phelippes asks.

Puckering seems impatient with him; no doubt Phelippes has spent the past half-hour earning it. 'Our *singular* aim tomorrow is that John Penry should have an altogether ordinary hanging. If Marlowe has taken flight, a writ of capias shall be issued in due time. I understand he is quite conspicuous, no doubt he shall not go far.'

'You would not set a bounty?' Poley blurts out, at which all heads turn to him again. Topcliffe sits up, licks his lips.

Puckering harrumphs. 'If I were to put a price on the head of every scoundrel to shirk his bond, men would be hunted throughout the land like pheasants and the Council's coffers would soon be empty!'

Polite laughter follows, which Poley feels obliged to join, half-heartedly. 'And yet, my lord,' he says, taking a step forward, 'if a bounty is set, may we not then leave the business of bringing Marlowe to justice to the public, thereby keeping our ranks at full strength? May we not, in that case, better attend to tomorrow's hanging?'

A silence falls, through which Puckering rubs at his chin, regarding Poley with grinding intensity. Ultimately, Phelippes is the first to speak, shaking his head as if in disbelief of his own words. 'My lord, I must say I find myself in agreement with Master Poley. On *this* point. I've no doubt his Holiness would also—'

'I will not publicly set a bounty on a man who can in no sense be termed a fugitive,' Puckering interrupts. 'Do you know something, Master Poley? Something you'd like to share with us?' All eyes turn to Poley, Phelippes's glittering with predatory intent.

Poley draws himself up. 'Why, I know *Marlowe*, my lord. I should think that anyone who had spent but five minutes in the man's company could see that he is liable to take flight!'

Puckering pauses briefly, and then says, 'We shall see, will we not? If, tomorrow morning, Master Maunder should have no luck retrieving Marlowe from his lodgings, then perhaps we may find room in the treasury for a small reward, should he be returned discreetly.'

'*Small*, my lord?' Poley says.

'This is not a negotiation, Master Poley. I have read this note from Master Baines, and I see nothing in it but that Marlowe, like most playmakers, hath both a loud mouth and a bent cock. Now, his Holiness may disagree, but to my mind, Marlowe is neither a violent nor imminent threat, and we've had enough trouble from the rabble as it is!'

Puckering's little pack all chuckle, save Phelippes, in whom Poley now sees a potential, if merely temporary, ally. 'A play-maker he may be, my lord,' Poley says, 'but that is no trivial thing. When Nero suspected Seneca of treason, did he hesitate to punish him? Certainly not, for even Nero, for all his faults, understood the power of a poet's influence. A poet is not just one voice. His words travel about with the wind; they hop from one mind to another, indiscriminate of pedigree. Men commit his speeches to memory, they murmur them aloud in private moments, as one does in prayer. I ask you, is there any man better positioned to topple an empire by stealth, soul by soul? Were I the Devil, I would prize such a vessel as Christopher Marlowe!'

'You'll speak for the Devil, now, will you, Poley?' Puckering mutters. His minions snigger again, this time uncomfortably.

Poley tries not to smile with obvious spite. 'Why, I speak for the *kingdom*, my lord. I speak of the nightmares that plague her, nightmares we all have suffered: Jesuits in attics, black-caped Brownists and Marprelates storming our cities, poisoners in her Majesty's larders! And, for all that, nothing is so fearful to our dear country as a man of Marlowe's ilk: a man with no sworn cohorts, no organized doctrine, no obvious stratagems in store. But is a man with no God truly a man? Imagine if a beast could walk among us undetected, a beast that in every way resembles the divine form of Adam, that

HESSE PHILLIPS

mimics our customs, our speech! What harm might that beast do? What if he be a rat, a swine, a fox? What if he be a wolf?'

The eleven pairs of eyes follow him now, every gesture, every step, and Poley plays to them like Ned Alleyn to the lords' box: 'Gentlemen, we are accustomed to battling with those who seek a new order, or a return to the ancient one, but in any case, *order*, under God, or a misguided notion of Him. A godless man, what use has he for order, for the divisions of light and darkness, heaven and hell? I tell ye, he has none. 'Tis chaos he craves, and I would, truly I would fain my imagination could describe that to ye, but when I look into it, all I see is night – limitless, depthless night. One man cannot bring that about, no. But our leniency would send a terrible message. To the lone wolf, the shepherd gives no quarter, lest he return with the pack.'

For a moment no one speaks. Then Topcliffe, who all this while has uttered not a sound, slams his palm down upon the desk, causing all, even Puckering, to jump. 'Why, I am transported!' Topcliffe declares. 'I can practically feel the breath of the hellhound upon my cheek!'

'Master Poley,' Phelippes says, through his teeth, 'this past week you have done everything in your power to stall this investigation – *my* investigation: disrupted interviews, undermined witness testimony—'

'I have done what I have done because this investigation must not fail!' Poley exclaims, passionately.

'It is, I say, *my* investigation, and therefore shall not fail. I suggest you look to your own work, Master Poley, presuming that there is such a thing!'

The Lord Keeper smiles, enjoying the show.

'Why, this *is* my work!' Poley says, nearing the end of his patience. 'This is *God's* work, for which we, all of us, are responsible! After all, that this serpent has slithered his way into the innermost heart of our defences, *we*, the good servants to her Majesty, are to blame, for 'twas *we* who welcomed him in! Seven years ago, this villain, this wretch, sent us a note from Paris, written in blood – in *blood* – and we never thought twice of that, did we, we cared only for the name writ thereupon, never considering the infernal deal we'd struck to obtain it!'

Perhaps he has gone too far, something ugly having made its way into his voice, like the guttering of a flame. Puckering frowns, almost sympathetically. Topcliffe widens his eyes: a warning.

At last, Puckering lets out a soft grunt and reaches for his goblet, taking a restorative sip. He then puts his head back and intones as if from the clouds, '*If*, indeed, Marlowe is not found at the inn in Bishopsgate tomorrow morning, I shall take your concerns before the Archbishop of Canterbury and the Lord Treasurer. But I'll be damned before I unleash such ideas upon the public.' Poley starts to object, but Puckering thunders over him, '*One hundred pounds* to any man in this room, and no others. That is my recommendation, and on that I shall not be moved. One hundred pounds, to be increased by the same after midnight tomorrow, should he remain at large. *Half* for his corpse, and ten pounds to any intelligence that should lead to his capture. So be it!' He misses his old speaker's gavel, it seems, withering ever so slightly in the silence.

Poley looks to Topcliffe, unbreathing. Slowly, Topcliffe's block-shaped head bobs. 'Fair enough. And yet, my Lord Keeper, what price *can* ye put on the Devil's own head?'

The meeting adjourned, Topcliffe leads their group to the cell next door, where John Penry hangs from the ceiling by the wrists, naked and blindfolded, his hands discoloured, long-nailed claws. Each in turn, the spies step up to inspect him like a side of beef while Topcliffe roves the light of a candle up and down Penry's much-abused body, expounding on the physical effects of his favourite method: how the subject's ribs and lungs compress under their own weight, how his bladder and bowels loose, how his arms and hands wither and, if left hanging long enough, eventually die.

'My wife,' Penry mumbles, between gasps for breath. 'My wife, my wife, my wife...'

'Whatever became of Master Kyd?' Poley asks.

'Oh, him?' Topcliffe pshaws. 'Not much use for *him* now, is there?'

Outside, on the courthouse's long, columned portico, Puckering walks the others to their horses while Poley drags his feet at the back, hoping to speak with Topcliffe alone. But before Poley can turn to face him, a hand reaches through the dank night air, grabs Poley by the arm and tugs him backwards into a man's chest. A voice purrs wetly at his ear, 'How daintily you dance, my little bird! I would swear your feet never touch the ground!'

Poley thrashes free and reels about. He might as well be strung up and stripped, Topcliffe smiling at him as if he can see the fleshy whiteness at his core, as if he could drive a fist up inside of him and rip it out all at once.

'You want your ring back?' Topcliffe says.

'I want to see it,' Poley gasps, just above the rain.

Topcliffe replies not to this, musing aloud instead, 'Two hundred pounds... I would be selling it at a pittance.'

'You are not selling it. You are trading it.'

'Ay, I reckon I am. I've never tortured a godless man before. Now you've made me curious. I wonder whether I can make him pray. I've heard that even godless men will pray, if you give them reason enough.'

Poley shivers, his heart throbbing behind his eyes. But footsteps approach from across the colonnade: Puckering. 'Good*night*, Master Poley.' Without stopping, Puckering takes Topcliffe by the elbow and draws him through the doors of the Marshalsea Court, past the rigid guardsmen, who clack their spears as their general passes by. It seems Topcliffe has one eye trained on Poley even after they vanish.

Poley realizes that his hands have gone numb. That his lungs refuse to take air. That his breeches are soaked through with piss.

Perhaps an hour later, Poley stands at the door of Bull's House in the rain. He pounds away for two eternities before Eleanor finally answers, wearing her nightgown and bonnet, her bottle of vinegar in hand. She opens her mouth, utters the beginning of a word, but Poley pushes past her, scanning about the darkness in hope of bringing himself aground. There: the staircase where her children had played. There: the stain where her husband had died.

No threats herein. 'Tis almost a disappointment. He would like to draw his gun on something and fire, to fit his hands around a throat—

'Robin?' Eleanor is saying. 'Robin, my God, what has happened to you?'

He turns and she recoils, her back to the staircase, the candle carving her face out of the shadows. His half-sister, his father's daughter, born to a good house, a good name, in the same year that he was born without either. She looks like herself now, without all the paint and pomp of mourning, but so much older, wizened, spent. How dare she, how dare she wear that half-familiar face? How dare she show him what Time alone can do?

'I need a bed,' Poley says, as if he were any other weary traveller at her door. 'And I need to wash. Three days, I think – three days I have not slept.'

Her eyes dart, an instant of hesitation, of calculation: always looking for the exits. 'You can have the big room. I made it ready, just as you said. Your friend came by, the fat one, Skeres.'

A fuse ignites, and when the sparks clear Poley has his sister pinned against the stair-rail, an elbow to her chest, thinking about spitting into her face, as if they were children; holding her down and drowning her in his spittle, his venom.

'He is *not* my friend,' he snarls.

'Forgive me.'

'He is a bloated parasite for whom I have found a purpose, that is all.'

'Yes, I understand, I understand.' This is typical of her too, playing dead like a hare, so that he in turn shall be cast as the hound. The wolf. All their lives, everything has been his fault, no matter if she'd pinched or slapped him first; all their lives, Eleanor has been made of sugar and silk and Poley has been that vicious little bastard, that issue of a whore.

He steps back. Eleanor slides down from her tiptoes, rubbing her collarbone. 'Do you still have any of Master Bull's old clothes?' Poley says.

'Ay. Why?'

'I need to borrow a suit.'

'It would be big on you.'

'No matter. Something tasteful, I pray. None of that continental foppery.' He starts up the stairs.

'Robin!' Eleanor whispers, mindful, perhaps, of waking the maids. But when he stops and looks down, she says nothing, staring at him with her eyes glazed over, as if she is biting her tongue.

'What?'

Her aspect sours. 'You smell of piss.' She turns and heads for the kitchen, saying the rest over her shoulder. 'I'll bring you a washbasin.'

Upstairs, Poley fumbles his way through the largest bedchamber to the window, throwing open the tall shutters. There on the green lies the *Golden Hind*, her naked masts iced with moonlight. The rain is as thin as gauze upon the air; the moon hangs low, shrieking white behind a muzzle of clouds. Wednesday, he has heard, there will be an eclipse. A good omen, hopefully.

Frizer and Marlowe must be warned. But not even couriers can travel about this late at night. It shall have to wait till first thing tomorrow morning. Hopefully they are no fools, and have left Bishopsgate already. Hopefully they are on their way here even now, gliding down the rain-swollen Thames, their boat hugging the bank, out of the light. But Poley doubts this. Nothing can possibly go so smoothly.

He lies down in the ample bed, restless in his own sticky uncleanliness, his shame. Marlowe must have slept in this bed before, back in the old days on his way to Paris and all that came after it, knowing not that in a few weeks' time he would write a name in blood on a scrap of paper, the first step in a chain of events which would eventually lead to that long, unforgivable hour on St Giles' Field. No one can say it was Marlowe's fault. He was a gear turning within the engine of Evil, a drop of blood pumped through its heart. Poley does not desire Marlowe's suffering. All he desires is the ring. Is it not?

But to restore the ring, there must be a sacrifice, and sacrifices are never of the old and the vicious, are they, but of the young, the innocent, the beguiled. And, having the blood of sacrifice upon it, the ring shall be more than ever it was, and mean more than any mere object could ever mean. Redemption – is that what Poley wants? Never has he had much use for intangible things. When he closes his eyes, he envisions a young man lying beside him, the long, soft desert of his body, the lively ruby of his lips, grey eyes so close that he can make out facets of green in their depths. A body is a tangible thing, like a diamond. Perhaps that is what he wants: a body, unbroken. Whole.

His thoughts slide away into sleep, like flesh from bone: eyes milk white, tongue shrivelled, jaw unhinged in a silent scream, just as Poley had wanted to scream that day, on St Giles' Field.

⋆⁂⋆

Deep into the night, a light rouses Kit from sleep. He squints across the room, through a band of orange light that spills from the open window, into the shadows beyond. A set of crooked eyes gaze back at him from above the desk: the painted Queen, in her skirt of soot.

The light outside is that of human activity, of fire. Kit slips free of Frizer's arms and goes to the window, peering outside with just one eye. Lanterns and braziers blaze all along the Bishopsgate ramparts, raindrops scintillating in their glow. Even now, in darkest night, the gate teems with guards, whose muffled conversations reverberate off the stones as they shift their posts, spear-tips and gun-barrels glinting.

A frame of hellfire gold falls over Frizer's naked body in the bed, cutting him off at the head and limbs. He is just a torso, his scar shining in the light, a seam split from navel to breast. The sight of him reminds Kit of Anthony Babington, makes him aware that he is standing over Frizer's body just as Robin Poley had stood at the back of the scaffold, watching it happen. He feels, suddenly, an urge to scream, as if a clawed animal were clambering up the back of his throat.

Kit covers his mouth with his hand, presses his back to the wall. A minute passes in inhales and exhales. At last, he is able to move again, breaking away to search the clothes strewn about the floor. He returns to the window with Frizer's knife at his side, one eye watching the guards across the square. At any moment, they could march forth, be here before he could so much as get his boots on. It could happen within hours, minutes. Seconds. Soon, he'll hear their footfalls upon the stairs, and they'll break down the door and find him here, stark naked, with a knife in his hands.

Would he fight? It would be futile, of course. Kill one man and there shall be plenty more after him. But if they meant Frizer any harm then yes, without question he would slash and stab, become the mother wolf. The futility of it would not matter, it would be a gesture, a message of sorts, to articulate that which he cannot put into words. He shall write it not with ink but with blood. He shall say it with his dying scream. And for what? What good would it do? Truly, the best he could do for Frizer would be to leave him sleeping and run for the river – yes – the river, and hire a smuggler to take him downstream, avoiding the guard-posts along the way, heading always towards the sea and the vast Beyond, where he shall live – alone, and sick with sorries – but he shall live, not in the world but in some after-world where no one can touch him, as bright and empty as the horizon. He would almost rather die.

With a wince, Kit dips to lay the knife just under the bed, within easy reach. He then crawls in close at Frizer's back, fitting their bodies together at the hips, his fist over Frizer's heart, his face buried between his shoulder-blades.

'I know not what to do,' Kit murmurs, ashamed.

Stillness hangs between them, like a raindrop from the tip of a reed.

Frizer reaches back, gently combs the hair above the nape of Kit's neck with his fingers. A childhood sensation, one Kit has not felt in far too long: that shiver up the back, that soundless sob. Before he can think to do so he is kissing him, he is holding him in both hands like a bowl of something precious, sustenance or drug; and he is cradling his own rib as he climbs over Frizer's hips, cradling his rib as he runs his tongue over Frizer's ribs. He will pour himself into him, like rain into the sea.

Frizer arches back onto his shoulders. He writhes and bucks against Kit's jawbone. He clutches Kit's head like a weapon buried in a wound.

'Do not stop. Oh God, oh God, do not ever stop!'

29 MAY 1593

One day

＊＊＊

Idealism of any sort cannot survive in the Marlovian world.

LISA HOPKINS, *CHRISTOPHER MARLOWE:*
A LITERARY LIFE, 2000

Come live with me, and be my love—

CHRISTOPHER MARLOWE, 'THE PASSIONATE
SHEPHERD TO HIS LOVE', C. 1590

27

J UST AFTER DAWN ON the 29th of May 1593, an army of
some eight hundred men on horseback thunders up the old
Watling Road towards the Marshalsea Prison, leaving a quag-
mire in their wake that stretches all the way back to
Canterbury. At the lead, Archbishop Whitgift rides in his
customary pomp, sheltered from the elements by a velvet
canopy carried by two comely acolytes. Eight hours from
now, the archbishop's old nemesis John Penry will be put to a
lingering death – the same Penry who, in his infamous pamphlets, had amplified certain revolting rumours regarding
the archbishop and his dear, late mentor at university which,
although true, his Holiness is nevertheless obliged to crush
with the utmost prejudice.

Soon, Whitgift and his personal cavalry reach Thomas-
a-Watering, formerly a shrine to Thomas-a-Beckett, now
a desolate crossroads with gallows in the centre. Here, his
Holiness dismounts and trundles alone to the gallows, the
hem of his chimere slapping in the mud. He labours up the
stairs, kneels beneath the gallows-tree and folds his hands in
prayer. 'O heavenly Father, may the condemned be strong of
heart!' For men with weak hearts die quicker.

Across the road, from the second-storey windows of the
old Thomas-a-Beckett Inn, Thomas Walsingham watches
this little spectacle unfold. Deep between his ears, Robin

Poley whispers, over and over: *You do not want to see your friend butchered alive. You do not want to see them pull the heart out of him, still beating.*

Walsingham had left Greenwich hours ago. Not even Nick Skeres knows where he is. For longer than he can estimate he has stood here, on the landing of a staircase, waiting for someone who knows not to expect him.

As the archbishop plods back to his retinue and ascends the saddle by way of a cushioned footstool, footsteps approach on the stairs, from above. Walsingham turns, watching as the man he's awaited all this while finally descends into view: Thomas Phelippes, squinting myopically in the clear light.

They stare at one another for all of three seconds before Phelippes blanches from crown to chin and tries to hurry on his way, muttering, 'Oh, no. No, no, no—'

Walsingham catches him on the landing, his sleeve in his fist. 'Five minutes, I pray!'

Phelippes whispers, 'The *Lord Keeper* is upstairs! If he should see me with *you*—'

'Then talk with me outside.' Walsingham half-draws his short-sword, just for the sound. 'If you do not, Tom, I'll make *certain* he sees you with me.'

The colour in Phelippes's toadish face deepens. Yet he no longer resists, resuming his descent with a grudge in every step. Outside, Walsingham leads him away from the inn and off towards the steep bank of the putrid River Neckinger, sheltered by trees. They are alone here; nothing lies beyond the river but a wasteland of beehive-shaped skips in the mist.

Phelippes's crunching footsteps come to a halt. 'Do you mean to kill me?' he says, a jest, but an anxious one.

'I am afraid I simply do not care enough to kill you, Tom,' Walsingham says. 'Half the intelligencers still active in this country haggled their way out of prison at the expense of my hide. I have not the patience for vengeance of that scale.'

Phelippes lets out a humourless grunt. He says, '*Ille crucem scelaris pretium tulerit, hic diadema*' – for the same crime one man gets the gallows, and another, a crown. There's a twinge of remorse upon his lip, much to Walsingham's surprise. Suppose he might have considered Walsingham a friend once, though the feeling was never mutual. Everyone at Seething Lane used to joke that Phelippes had no friends besides Trimethius and Simonetta, whose weighty, mouldering tomes on cryptology had lain forever splayed upon his desk like drugged concubines.

'You were at the Marshalsea last night,' Walsingham says, 'with the Lord Keeper, and Topcliffe... and Robin Poley.'

Phelippes looks as if a pin were pinching him under the collar. 'You still have your ways, I see.'

'While you and the others took to your horses, Poley spoke privily with Topcliffe for a few moments outside the court-house. I understand they appeared "peculiarly disposed" towards one another. There might have been a quarrel, and some talk of selling and trading...'

Phelippes lets out a jaded grunt as if unsurprised, but then seems to regret having revealed even so little of his own thoughts, looking over his shoulder as if hoping, or fearing, that someone will come. 'If you know the devil's game—' he starts, but stops, saying instead, 'I will not undermine my own work. The case against Marlowe, you see, is my responsibility, and I stand to profit well by it. Better, I think, than you could afford.'

'I only wish to speak of Poley. I have my suspicions, and 'tis plain you have yours. Let us speak simply of what we have observed, and leave one another to our separate conclusions.'

'You cannot help Marlowe, if that is your hope,' Phelippes says.

'I have no hope of that, I warrant you.'

'The Lord Keeper has put out an order for his arrest. Maunder and the others should be arriving at the Inn-in-the-Wall as we speak, if they have not already been and gone.'

Walsingham feels the blood drain from his face. Yet Phelippes seems not to notice; he only goes on, overly familiar: 'My hand to God, old man, I know you to be somewhat unchary with your associates. Even your uncle thought so. But a friend like this, he could be the end of you. I would like to believe that you are but some sheltered, simple fellow, too stupid to know what manner of man he is... but I know you are nothing of the kind.'

Walsingham stays silent, his gaze drawn northwards, as if he might see Bishopsgate from here.

'I suppose that is the trouble with fellows like you,' Phelippes adds, sneeringly. 'You'd rather put both feet in hell then draw one out of it, lest the wine of penitence should wash that other taste out of your mouth.'

Walsingham cannot stop himself from turning a look of both terror and fury upon him. He swallows the yolk of dread in his throat, trying to sound calm as he says, 'Tell me what you saw last night between Poley and Topcliffe, and I'll tell you everything I know of Robin Poley.'

Not everything, of course. What little Walsingham does say, however, is the truth: that Robin Poley is but one of many men upon whose senses he has come to rely these past three years, and that of late he has employed Poley specifically to the end of keeping Kit Marlowe under watch. Phelippes, in turn, can merely confirm that Poley and Topcliffe did seem to have some scheme afloat last night, one requiring an almost grotesquely high price on Kit's head, should the bailiff fail to capture him. 'Two hundred pounds!' Phelippes says, as if he took such extravagance as a personal affront. 'And I daresay they would have tried for a far higher price, had his lordship indulged them any further.'

'What do you make of it?' Walsingham asks, for it must be said that Phelippes is one whose intuition is rarely wrong.

'What do *I* think? Marry, I should think it quite clear that if anything is being sold or traded, 'tis the life of your friend Marlowe – and therefore yours as well!'

Before the hour is out, Walsingham is galloping downriver to Deptford. Along the way, he discovers that the Southwark streets, so deathly serene this morning, are now a garrison for Whitgift's thugs, whose ranks form a necklace of glinting helmets around the village verge – a necklace which, as only the eye of God might see, garrottes the whole throat of the Thames' southern bank, from Thomas-a-Watering to Bankside, from the Neckinger in the east to the Rose estate in the west, where the archbishop's men hover around the Rose Playhouse's boarded-up windows like urchins jostling for a glimpse of the stage.

By the time Walsingham reaches Bull's House, the sun leers high through the *Golden Hind*'s naked masts. He leaves his horse at the fencepost and sprints for the door, hoping that by some chance Kit and Frizer might have set out last night and arrived here in the twilight hours. But as Nick Skeres greets him, looking surprised, such hopes die at once.

'Is *he* here?' Walsingham snarls, panting.

'Who, master?'

'Your "friend", Nick, that the Devil's dam named Robin – is he here?'

Nick stammers, 'He's, he's asleep.'

'Come!' Walsingham tugs Nick outside as if to drag him by the ear, across the lawn and to the edge of the green. 'Who would you say is the dearer of your two friends,' Walsingham asks, 'Master Poley or Master Frizer?'

'What?' Nick looks as muddled as if he's only just been awakened, though Walsingham sent him here hours ago. 'I understand not the question, master.'

'Let me put it in other terms: if I were to hold Master Poley and Master Frizer both at gunpoint, which would you try to save, if either one? Who, to you, matters more?'

Nick has turned a touch pale. He darts his eyes as if hoping to be rescued himself. 'Are you… do you mean to… *do* something, to Ingram?'

'Not I, Master Skeres. But your other friend, Poley, was the last man to see Master Frizer, who is now unaccounted for. I do not mean to suggest that he brought Frizer to any harm, nothing so crude as that, but if I were you, I should wonder at how Poley intends to use him.'

Nick shakes his head, emphatically. 'Master Poley would not hurt Ingram.'

'You trust him, do you?'

Nick's cheeks take on a touch of red. 'Why should I *not* trust him, master, if I may beg your pardon? With all due respect, master, the man's a hero, is he not? It bewilders me, master, the way some fellows talk of him, when they should be *thanking* him, they should, that we're not all praying to the damned Pope and bowing at the feet of some Scottish witch! They resent him, they do, because he's cleverer than they are!'

The oaf has forgotten himself. Walsingham inches closer, his stare a reminder. 'Tell me, then,' he sneers, 'what has the great unsung hero told you of Dick Topcliffe?'

Nick grows still, a dog coming to attention. His eyes dart again, though his answer is, 'Why, nothing, master, nothing!' He takes a step back at last, and with another anxious glance, comes up with the following: ''Tis none of my business anyway, the things that went on in the Marshalsea. I've never asked him. Nor would I ask you, master.'

This last must be intended to stick like a knife, for it succeeds, a stab which Walsingham feels in a place of unspeakable intimacy. He can deny it no longer, there's but one man on earth who may put a stop to all this: Dick Topcliffe, whose foul fingers Walsingham can all but smell beneath his chin, whose voice he can hear less than an inch from his ear: *Strange – I'd thought a fellow like you might enjoy this sort of thing!—*

'Ah, so you received my message!' Poley calls. He leans out of a large window directly above the front door, his elbows on the sill. Even from here, Walsingham notices something odd about his clothes, a bailiff's badge emblazoned upon the doublet. Master Bull was, if memory serves, a bailiff of the Privy Court.

'You are wearing your brother-in-law's clothes,' Walsingham says.

'Yes, my clothes are soaked through, after last night's deluge. Shall we?' He gestures inside, where Walsingham meets him at the foot of the stairs. Down the hall, in the dining room, Widow Bull glances up from setting the table to see Walsingham and Poley approaching, and swiftly orders her maids to the kitchen.

Poley says, 'I sent word to Bishopsgate as early as possible. With any luck, the messenger was not delayed by his Holiness's men, who, I take it, have the whole of Southwark surrounded. Fortunately, the nearest watergate remains unwatched, for now. There's still hope that your man Frizer shall find his way to us.'

'And if not?' Walsingham says, taking a seat at the table.

Poley also sits and barks a fretful laugh. 'I imagine you shall have to pray, in that case! Of course, I am well accustomed to carrying out this sort of work within the confines of a prison, if you should feel it necessary to proceed… although I must admit I was always an inmate myself in such cases. Not a condition I should like to revisit.'

He looks as though he has not slept in days. What is it he hopes to gain from this? Gold? Walsingham has paid him half already, a goodly sum in itself; and belike he'll have the same or double again from Topcliffe, in whatever scheme they are running. But if gold is all Poley needs, 'tis clear he needs it desperately. Perhaps a creditor has come knocking?

'I may recompense you for time spent,' Walsingham says, testing the waters, 'if the loss should pain you overmuch…'

'A generous offer,' Poley says, quite neutrally. He lifts his goblet to drink. 'Let us hope I need not consider it.'

And now, from down the hall: a knock at the door.

Walsingham's stomach grows suddenly heavy, anchoring him to his seat. A moment of stillness falls, as all wait for another knock to come and prove the first. When it sounds, Poley motions to his sister, who sets the pitcher of wine on the sideboard and then sweeps down the hall, skirts rustling. A creak of hinges, followed by a voice. Kit's voice.

As the blood drains from Walsingham's face, a wave of tears rises, forcing him to bow his head, to stiffen his chin, desperately avoiding Poley's gaze. Only seconds later, Kit appears in the doorway, looking such a state: filthy, soaking wet from the waist down, as if he had crawled out of the river, his face mangled with recent wounds. There he stands, the lanky boy who, five years ago, had come to Walsingham for aid, who had sat before his desk with Tom Watson's hand on his shoulder and tortuously, tearfully told of the terrible things that Richard Baines had done to him, and made him do... There is the man who, after the Marshalsea, had waited by Walsingham's side for a month, as patient as an anchorite at his rosary, loving him back to life.

Walsingham bolts to his feet but for a moment remains paralysed. *You do not want to see them pull the heart out of him, still beating.* To his shame, all Walsingham can think of is himself on the scaffold, not Kit, and not even the horrors of death at that, but the humiliation, standing there naked, pelted with shit, as the bailiff reads out his sins for all to hear. To be so hated, so far from mercy! What a horror it is, what a lonely way to die.

Like a child to his mother, Walsingham rushes forth and wraps Kit in both arms, smelling the river's silt upon him, and somewhere beneath it a scent that is inimitably himself, and alive.

Why, Walsingham thinks, *oh, why, Kit!* – why *would you make me do this?*

28

A S DAWN BREAKS ON the 29th of May, a seagull reels, cackling, over the Inn-in-the-Wall's jagged rooftop, as shrill and petulant as a child jumping on the bed. *Wake up! Wake up!* Facedown, Kit traces the gull's noisome progress around the ceiling with one eye, unsure whether he is awake or asleep, on dry land or on a boat. *A boat to where?*

But a moment later a cannon blasts somewhere to the northeast, startling Kit upright – the gun foundry on Houndsditch.

Kit turns to see the man in bed beside him and meets frightened blue eyes. Kit tries to speak, but can only whisper, 'We have to go.'

He scrambles up his underclothes and breeches from the floor, dressing himself halfway in the dim light. He then shakes open his bag and sweeps his arm across the desk, shoving all his effects into its mouth at once. The strongbox, however, is still locked.

'Frizer, the key,' Kit says, from the floor. 'The key, quickly!'

Frizer sits at the edge of the bed, still naked. Painfully slow, he drops his shirt to the floor and picks up his breeches instead, withdrawing the key from a pocket. He hands it over as mournfully as if it were a dead bird.

'Get dressed and then look outside,' Kit says, unlocking the box. 'Try not to be seen.' He packs up his papers, runs his hands through his hair, finishes dressing himself. At last, he turns his attention to the bed and the bedclothes, smoothing over the places where their bodies have been. His search turns up a faint stain on one edge of the bed, another in the centre, and he scrubs away at both with a damp cloth as if it were blood.

Frizer stands with his back to the door, his complexion green.

Kit asks, 'Did you look outside?'

'They are going to torture us,' Frizer gasps.

Kit stops scrubbing. 'Listen… I will not—'

'They are going to kill us!' Frizer lifts his hands as if to claw his own eyes out.

Kit leaves the bed, crosses the room and takes him by the wrists. '*Nothing* will happen to you. I promise.'

'He'll know. He'll take one look at me and he'll know!'

'Who will know?'

'I cannot breathe!' Frizer sucks hard at the air. 'I need to get out!' He turns and barrels outside, stumbling to the gallery's railing as if about to throw himself over. Kit catches him in his arms, glancing down into the yard just as six men emerge from the common room: first the landlord, nervously hunting through his ring of keys, and behind him, moving as patiently as a thunderhead, a man in a bailiff's livery and four helmeted guards, two in the archbishop's livery and two in the Privy Court's, all bound for the opposite staircase. From the centre of the yard, the landlord turns and blithers some excuse for his disarray, shooting a frantic glance upwards, into Kit's eyes.

Kit hauls Frizer backwards into the room and shuts the door, hoping to have done so quietly. For too long, he stares at the latch while his heart kicks away at his ribs, turning at last to find Frizer tearing at his own hair.

'Oh God,' Frizer says. 'Oh God what have I done *what have I done*?'

Kit cups Frizer's face in both hands. 'We need to go. Now. Do you understand?' Frizer's gaze scatters. 'Nod if you understand!'

Frizer's head jerks up and down.

Kit rushes across the room for his bag. Frizer spins in a circle, one hand at the small of his back, his eyes on the floor. 'Wait, my knife! Where's my knife?'

Kit cares nothing for the knife. He takes Frizer's hand, prepared to drag him out, but Frizer twists away and snarls, 'Give it to me!' The eyes are yellow, glistering; the voice as black as pitch. A stranger's voice.

Kit tries to speak, but the words will not come. He can move only his eyes, glancing twice at the space beneath the bed, which is enough for Frizer to deduce the rest. Even as Frizer rises again and slips the knife into its scabbard, Kit remains frozen for a moment too long, as dazed as if he had been slapped.

'We'll have to run,' Kit says, finding his voice at last.

'Can you manage it?'

'I'll have to.' Kit opens the door just enough to peer across the yard with one eye. On the far side of the inn, the guards turn the corner on the fourth landing. The bailiff now leads the rest, the same man, Kit realizes, who had arrested him at Scadbury.

'Keep apace with me,' Kit says. 'Do not charge.' He waits until the whole party of guards have arrived at the fifth gallery, takes a breath and then throws open the door, letting it swing behind him. Shouts come from across the yard, but Kit looks only at the stairs under his feet as he plummets down one flight after another, leaping over the railings, reeling dizzily to the dirt. At the bottom, Frizer nearly crashes into Kit's back and then halts, gawping up at the stairs opposite, where guards tumble down one atop another like ants on a wall. Kit snatches Frizer by the sleeve and pulls him through the gateway, to the street.

The sight of the Black Bull stops Kit in his tracks. There's the Bishopsgate fountain just visible through the smoke, the Wall somewhere behind him, and, just down the street, the toothy row of windows set high up on white Crosby Place. All recedes into a vast, grey distance, like a half-remembered scene. Perhaps out of habit he turns south, swinging Frizer on ahead as if to hurl him with a sling: 'Go, go!' Kit surpasses him in only a few strides. He wonders at his own insensibility to pain. In every doorway light and shadow conspire to imitate the sheen of helmets clustered in wait, around every corner he anticipates their lunge. He thinks of Winding Lane, Leadenhall, Eastcheap, cuts and culverts, parks and piers, anywhere he might conceal himself.

On Winding Lane, the pain in his side hits him like a bullet and he collapses onto all fours. Frizer sprints past, doubles back, clips him about the ribs and hoists him up with a roar, bolting off the moment that Kit is on his feet. Every breath is a knife in the side. By the time Kit staggers to the next crossing he can no longer see Frizer at all, only Leadenhall Market's serried archways stretching left and right into the smoke.

A childish terror of abandonment overtakes him. He limps into the still-quiet market, making full turns about every few paces. Down one row of shuttered stalls or another, men lumber past with rattling carts in tow. No sign of Frizer. There's nowhere to hide here, not for long. Despair rushes in, as sharp as panic. Kit is just beginning to consider lying on the ground and giving up when at last Frizer appears as if out of the ether, grabs him by the arm and drags him into a narrow void behind the empty fish stalls.

Kit doubles over and sucks air into his burning chest. The space is no more than three feet wide and ten feet deep, its other extremity blocked by a midden of reeking oyster shells, sloping towards them like a petrified wave. 'Frizer,' Kit says, his hands on his knees, 'we cannot stop here. We are trapped.'

'We have no choice, do we? Look at you! Would you rather drop dead in the street?' Frizer lets his satchel fall from his shoulder, sidling towards the tunnel's entrance. A second later, he returns shaking his head and says, 'We'll never escape. I saw them yesterday, I saw them on every gate, on every street!'

'Breathe, Frizer.'

'Idiot!' Frizer strikes himself across the cheek. 'Idiot, idiot, idiot! Why did I stay, why did I stay?'

Kit reaches for his hands but Frizer shoves him in the ribs with such force that Kit slams backwards into the wall at a steep angle, taking a crack to the skull and shoulders. Dazed, he slides himself upright, eyes fixed on the shell-strewn ground as Frizer's footsteps crunch past, one way and then the other.

When Kit can breathe again, he blurts out, 'If we are caught, I will say nothing of what happened last night.' He hears the strain in his own voice and immediately feels ashamed, diminished.

Frizer's pacing stops. 'You have ruined my life!'

Again, that black, unfamiliar voice, the deep gnar of a grindstone on naked stone.

'You did all this on purpose,' Frizer says. 'You *knew* what would happen!'

'Why,' Kit stammers, 'why would I do this on purpose?'

'To ruin me, to destroy me. You rapist! You devil!'

Kit almost laughs. 'A *rapist*, am I? Ay, the rapist you begged to suck your cock—'

Frizer silences him with a weak punch to the cheek that nevertheless leaves him stunned blind, his head hanging. Through sobs, Frizer says, 'I trusted you! You knew I was weak, you used me! Why have ye done this to me, you evil bastard, why?'

'Because I love you, and I thought you loved me! It was no ordinary kindness you showed me. It was a benediction, it was love! I am alive because of you; I want to live because of you!' Kit has struck the wall with his fist. He clutches his throbbing hand and sinks onto his haunches, doubly wretched. He can only blame himself. He has been selfish, thoughtless, greedy. He has put his hooks into this man; he can feel himself doing it even now. Always so quick to dig in his nails, to wield the word 'love' like a sling-stone. *But I have nothing else, no one else*, he would like to say. He must not allow himself to say it.

Eventually, Kit looks up from the ground to find Frizer staring at nothing visible, one finger scratching at the scar upon his neck so punishingly that the skin has turned red. Kit imagines the blade of Frizer's knife in place of the fingertip – for that was how it must have happened – but the image touches something raw within himself and he tucks his head behind his knees, fearful he might be sick.

'We should go,' he mumbles.

Frizer says nothing. He offers his hand and helps Kit to his feet, all without looking at him.

They continue south through alleys and backstreets, headed for the river. At a quarter past nine they pass beneath the clock tower at the peak of Fish Street, and descend the steep hill to the wharf. Kit hunches against Frizer's arm, partly in attempt to disguise his height. A few guards mill about the docks, but there are plenty of ways to hide within the crowd; the fish market is like a battlefield this time of morning. Men shout over great silver slabs of meat, ragged children and cutpurses weave about the fishmongers' carts, gulls squabble over piles of viscid guts.

At last, Kit can go no further. At the edge of a pier, he stumbles backwards into a heap of coiled rope taller than himself and collapses, legs sprawled into the path of passers-by. The boards beneath him seem to bob and lurch. Nothing moves but it groans, like cattle overcrowded in a pen.

'You're as white as a sheet, man,' Frizer says. He crouches beside Kit and lays a hand on his shoulder. 'You'll not die, will you?'

Kit has not the breath to reply. He fumbles his half-empty flask free of the hanging on his belt and drinks, restraining himself from downing all at once. Men pass by without looking, step over Kit's legs as they would rubbish. To them, Frizer and he are but drunkards or beggars, the sort of men one deliberately fails to see. 'Tis an unexpected comfort to be so plain-sighted, yet so invisible.

'We must get to Deptford,' Frizer says.

Kit watches his face for some hint of his thoughts, but Frizer avoids his gaze. 'I would need papers to board a ship at Deptford.'

'I'll have to see my master for that, no?'

'So you'll leave me here, at Billingsgate? They'll look for me here.'

'I will leave ye for ten minutes while I find us a boat.' His gaze touches Kit's – a shock, like cold water to a sore tooth – only to drop away at once.

Kit tries not to guess at his mind, so often does he guess wrong. He scans the jungle of masts and rigging past the far end of the pier: St George's crosses receding into the grey-white distance like the wings of the heavenly host. Not a single foreign ship to be seen.

Frizer's hand extends into Kit's periphery, and Kit stares at him blankly before at last understanding. He offers him the flask.

Frizer drinks, wincing at the sting. 'I should not have said those things to you. I should never have hit you.'

At these words, Kit feels a shiver of relief, and more than relief. He cannot say, *I forgive you*, because he would rather imagine there were nothing to forgive. Instead, he finds Frizer's hand at his side and takes it in his own.

Frizer lays his cheek against his knee and is silent for several seconds, his eyes grey against the light reflected off the river. And then, 'It was the morning after Chestnut Sunday,' he murmurs. 'I was twelve or thirteen. My father went out to clean the stables, and he found me curled up in the straw, all naked, feverish, talking nonsense. He put me in my brothers' bed. I thought my skin would burst, as if I were cooking in it. I remember lying there, looking up at them, my father and my brothers, while they argued over whether to call the doctor, what to tell him, how much of me they could let him see. My father said, "What were you thinking? Did ye not think on how this would seem?" My brother, my eldest brother said, "It was a punishment, fit for the crime." My father asked what crime, and he said it was the way I walked. The way I smiled at people. "Like a cunt," he said. "He's got to learn: that's what a cunt gets.'" For a moment Frizer seems unable to go on, his mouth working to form words.

'But what they'd done to me... it left no marks. The doctor looked me over, gave me something for the fever. Told me to pray. A few months later, they did it again. And again. The doctor kept coming. Kept telling me to pray, pray harder. "Malingerer," he said. "There's naught wrong with him. Just likes an audience.'" He laughs silently, bitterly, and takes another drink. 'The next time they did it, I knew it would be the same. No marks. So, I made them myself. The doctor came again, stitched me up... and that was that. They kept doing it, and so did I. The doctor kept coming. Never said a word to me any more, barely looked at me. But I kept trying. I kept trying to, to *show* him.' Frizer touches the centre of his chest with two fingers, looking down upon the hand as if 'tis separate from himself, an enemy who shares his body, his blood.

'I thought, if I could make it terrible enough, someone would... see it. And they would *do* something, they would save me.' His gaze sinks into the sky past the far end of the dock. 'I think he knew. The doctor. That's why he stopped telling me to pray. Because there was no point—'

'Stop, stop.' Kit pulls Frizer into an embrace, thinking nothing of the danger in it. He rubs a tear on his sleeve as if it were a mark of possession, an act of enchantment. Would that they had known one another all their lives! Would that they had been raised together, in neighbouring houses, so that the first time it happened Kit might have stopped it: burst in wielding a knife or a club, bashed the monsters' skulls in or cut their throats, scooped Frizer up in his arms and bore him away from all harm, out into the hills, the forests, sheltering in caves and thickets, feeding on blackberries and songbirds. Wild children, in a kingdom of two.

'I meant what I said before,' Kit says. 'Every word, I meant it.'

Frizer inhales, as if about to speak. He turns Kit's head in both hands, kisses his mouth just briefly before pulling away. Within seconds he is gone.

'There's good money in't if a fellow can take me to Deptford,' Frizer says.

The boatmen double over laughing, leaning against their beached crafts on the shell-and-bone foreshore. 'No man living has the arms to row so far!' A calculated exaggeration, surely. A pair of them begin to argue over who can get him to Wapping Stairs the quickest, but such is not nearly far enough, and the wrong side of the river besides. Frizer walks away, eager to return to Marlowe on the dock above, even if he must return empty-handed, but halfway to the stairs an African with an accent Frizer cannot place stops him and guardedly questions him on his needs, assuring him no fewer than four times that he is a Christian, like his father before him, as if Frizer would not gladly take help from any heathen that offered it. For an exorbitant fee, the African says he will row them to a 'quiet place', just past the mouth of the Neckinger. From there, they'll have to walk the rest of the way. God knows how long it shall take to reach Deptford, or how much; the master's purse is running dry.

Frizer runs to fetch Marlowe, for whom the long stairs down to the bank are a terrible struggle. From the bottom the African watches them descend together, half-embracing, with a twist in his mouth as if he has smelled something sour. When at last they arrive on the shore he treats them as if they are delicate, exotic creatures, easily bruised, easily offended.

'Big fellow in the middle,' he says. 'Try not to move too much.'

They cast off, the bridge's sky-blackening spans sliding away behind them. Frizer spins his knife in an attempt to keep his mind quiet. Marlowe sits facing Frizer, and behind him, the boatman, who mainly keeps his head down, his eyes on the oars. The profile of Marlowe's face catches the light as they pass out of the shadow of a ship and the Tower appears to float by in its ribbon of walls, gleaming like alabaster in the eastern light. Ravens wheel over the parapets only to halt and turn back, as if to bang against a ceiling of glass.

Somewhere inside, men are pouring water over another man's face, a man is hanging from his wrists while pinned to the floor at his ankles and stretched until the hipbones burst their sockets, a man has been folded in half, backwards, until his heels are in his armpits, and they are all screaming, all begging for the pain to stop: *I'll tell you anything! I'll tell you anything!* They will hand over their wives, their children, their souls. A man will strangle his own mother for one moment of peace.

Frizer thinks of himself in the places of those men. How quickly he would break! He thinks of Marlowe in their places and himself forced to hold the bucket, the ropes.

'Will you teach me?' Marlowe says, with his hand out. It takes Frizer a moment to understand – he means knife-spinning. His dark gaze is kindly and solicitous. *I love you* throbs between them, an open wound.

Frizer frowns, as if in doubt of Marlowe's native skills. Truly, he cannot remember another occasion when he has willingly offered his knife to another, not even Nick. How strange it is in Marlowe's hands, a lanky, artless thing, forgetful of all the tricks Frizer ever taught it. He tries to demonstrate a simple twirl using the first and third fingers, his hands bending Marlowe's long hand into shape: 'Nay, *this* finger never moves, ay? *This* one lifts; *this* one presses down…' Marlowe, smouldering with concentration, clumsily endeavours to please him. Perhaps he fumbles on purpose, so that they shall have a reason to keep trying, to laugh and tease one another, forgetting the boatman and the world beyond the river's banks. They are but two men in a boat with all the time in the world, riding the swift spring current to nowhere.

When at last Marlowe manages to complete three slow turns of the blade, Frizer all but bursts with pride, crying, 'Yes! Yes!' and pounding his big shoulder. But then his gaze alights on the boatman's retreating glance and he sees it in his eyes, that fretful look of knowing. *He's a cunt. That's what a cunt gets.*

The tide has risen perilously high by the time they reach the Neckinger's narrow, reedy mouth. Their boat hugs the overgrown bank, at last skirting into an inlet where the remains of a pier jut out over the water by some ten feet. In the dark cavity beneath the boards, Frizer and Marlowe climb out into hip-deep water. Speechlessly, the African indicates a ladder on the far side, pooled in sunlight. Nothing feels right. 'No, no, we cannot stay here,' Frizer says, clinging to the gunwale. 'Take us further.'

'This is as far as I take ye.'

'Listen, I'll give you...' He hunts through the master's purse, coming up with a half-pound in gold, a small fortune really, which the African refuses. 'A sovereign or nothing.' Frizer empties coins into his shaking palm, counting aloud, trying not to drop any, at last pleading, 'I'll give ye the damned purse, ay? I'll give ye whatever you want!'

All the while, Marlowe watches the ladder the way a condemned man looks on the gallows, seeming to hold his breath. 'We should be quiet.' His gaze sweeps the ceiling of loose boards.

Whether out of pity or in haste to be gone, the African orders them aboard again. Frizer grabs Marlowe by both arms and drags him in, tumbling arse-first into the wet hull. 'All's well,' Marlowe murmurs, hugging him, 'all's well.' 'Tis backwards that he should be the one giving comfort, is it not?

As they pull away from the pier, a group of six men become visible on the bank above: men with the archbishop's mitre sewn onto their sleeves. A pair stand by their horses, the rest sit against the belly of an upturned skiff, armed with swords, clubs, pistols. They look as if they are waiting to do violence to someone, anyone.

The boatman lets them drift downriver a while, stretching his arms. '*Más tonto que Abundio!*' he says, or something close to that. 'You fellows are lucky I have a soft heart. *Never* tell a man how much money is in your purse! Innocent as babes, the pair of ye!' All this chastising Frizer gladly endures. He doubles forward and Marlowe does the same, making as if one of them has dropped a coin in the hull and together they search for it among the brown water and dead leaves. They only dare hook two fingers together.

'We will never make it!' Frizer whispers, still shaking, trying not to cry.

'Breathe, breathe. We will make it.'

Somehow, through the still point of their linked fingertips or the slow, steady pump of the oars, Frizer drifts into half-sleep of a kind he'd perfected in childhood: half-death really, for he is not in his body but looking down upon it, watching his jaw slide out of alignment, watching himself turn colour-less and slack. He dreams of a man made of ice, but living, a being through whom light passes like sound through a clarion, amplified, exalted. Frizer thirsts, and so drinks, melting him in his hot mouth, slaking kiss with kiss. His body sings, like a wet finger run around the rim of a glass.

This is a sickness, is it not? He has felt a similar sort of witchcraft before, a vision or a memory capable of wielding terrible power over his body, the way the everyday smell of a stable can send dread coursing through his veins. This is devilry of a different sort, if devilry it is indeed. The Devil puts on a pleasing shape, they say, but they misunderstand

– the Devil is no common seducer, not merely that charming friend who whispers diabolical notions in one's ear. A man does not give his soul to that. A man gives his soul to that which seems to him perfect and pure, that which to him is beloved, even above his own life. Yes: *beloved*. Give me an eternity of this agony.

Why do you love him whom the world hates so?
—Because he loves me, more than all the world!

The sun is hot on Frizer's back when he opens his eyes, wipes spit from his mouth. His toes squelch inside his sodden boots. He knows not where they are, only that the land is wooded and wild on the bank to his left, and to the right the shore is gouged out into a muddy, crescent-shaped slip, strewn with the looming skeletons of half-built ships, smoke-belching storehouses and pyramids of tree trunks, the whole infernal scene crawling with busy, dirty-looking men. On a high point of the embankment, recently hewn masts stand as close together as teeth on a comb, casting a shadow over the water like prison bars.

In Marlowe's fingers, the knife revolves haltingly, like a watermill at low tide. Marlowe grins and bounces his eyebrows when he notices Frizer watching him, as if fearful to glance away from the little act of magic he so tenuously performs. Always so hungry for approval, Marlowe. So desperate to be loved.

'I am so sorry,' Frizer whispers.

'For what?'

'Deptford!' the boatman chimes, the way a bell tolls the hour.

29

FRIZER CRAWLS OUT OF the boat on all fours as it bumps and scrapes against the lowest step of the Deptford water-gate. Above, a steep ramp of scum-furred stairs ascends towards the grey sky. 'Tis too slippery to stand; Frizer can but turn over onto his backside before Marlowe comes scrabbling out almost on top of him.

The African throws their bags out after them. He leans to scan the water in either direction, as if mindful of pirates. Robin had never said anything to Frizer about pirates.

Frizer unfastens the master's purse from his belt and tosses the whole of it to the boatman. 'We are grateful. Truly.'

'Get ye to land,' the boatman says, shooing them. He pushes off with an oar, drifts backwards into the jasper-coloured water. Despite this warning, they sit and watch him float away across the wide, empty bend. Frizer's heart thumps high in his chest. He feels a touch of giddiness. They have made it. They are safe! He turns to Marlowe, smiling, only to find him gazing across the water at the wild shore of the Isle of Dogs, as if contemplating the distance he would have to swim to reach it.

'Perhaps they'll be waiting for us at the house,' Frizer says, to break the silence.

'"They"?'

Frizer groans. 'Hell, Marlowe, "they" are my master and a few unhappy jades like myself who do his bidding.' He loops the strap of his sack over his head and starts to crawl towards land. Above the waterline, he is finally able to stand without slipping, and looks back to find Marlowe seated with one leg dangling carelessly in the Thames, like a seal about to slide in.

'Would you prefer to wait here for better help?' Frizer says.

Marlowe's shoulders rise and fall. Suspicion radiates out of his back. Frizer can hear himself breathing sharp liar's breaths, biting down upon the unspoken, unspeakable name, *Robin*. He has lied so long, by this simple omission, that to confess now would be a bolt to the heart of whatever it is that he and Marlowe share. May it live a little longer, just a little longer, holding the venom of this lie in its mouth.

At last, Marlowe picks up his bag and begins the slippery climb with his head bowed. When he is two steps down Frizer pulls him to his feet. He looks like a drowned man back from the dead, the eyes deep-socketed, his face bloodless save for the purple wound above his eye, whip-stitched in black. 'How is it with you?' Frizer says.

'Well. I'm well.' He seems anxious to move on.

'Wait.'

Frizer pulls him close. On the stairs, he is almost as tall as Marlowe, tall enough to wrap both arms around his neck and look past his head at the swift river, a muscular, serpentine thing, carving the land with its flanks. A thought surfaces and gradually grows louder: *What will come after this?* He has no idea. This may be the last moment they are ever alone. This may be the last moment they are ever, even briefly, safe.

'Do you trust me?' Frizer says.

Marlowe says nothing. He presses his face into the side of Frizer's neck, and there remains a second or two, breathing him in, before pulling away.

At the top of the stairs, they emerge behind a boarded-up victualling house and then onto the green with the ship embedded at its centre, which Robin had showed Frizer two nights ago. 'Tis somehow even more absurd by daylight, but Marlowe seems wholly uninterested in the ship, looking towards the row of grey, keystone-shaped houses on the far side of the grass. He seems to know precisely where they are going: the one on the end, with three horses waiting at the post.

'You've been here before?' Frizer says.

'In another life.' Marlowe is quiet a moment. 'Walsingham told you to bring me here?'

'Ay, of course he did! What's the matter?'

'This is a Privy Council house.'

'So is the house of Walsingham.'

Marlowe grunts. 'Fair enough.'

He takes a breath before starting off across the grass, leaving Frizer skipping to keep up. At the fence, Marlowe recognizes the master's horse even before Frizer does, murmuring, 'Thomas!' as he hurries to the door. A symbol has been branded into the timber lintel, which Frizer had not noticed the other night: a black bull, in full charge.

Marlowe knocks. Twice. At last, a woman answers, dressed head to toe in mourning black, a bottle of some yellowish liquid in hand. She looks like a portrait of the Queen from the neck up, a netted wig, Bess-red, set far back on her head; the eyebrows plucked almost to nothing, so that there seems scant difference between skin and bone. There's something familiar in her high cheekbones, her dimpled, almost masculine chin.

'Master Marlowe,' she says, and curtseys. She makes a brief yet thorough study of his appearance. 'Somewhat taller than I remember you.'

Marlowe bows. 'Madam Bull.'

''Tis Widow Bull now, dear boy.' She lifts the bottle. 'Hold out your hands.'

She rinses both their hands in vinegar. They then follow her into a corridor which stretches unnervingly far into the house's depths, towards a mouth of daylight. Marlowe drags his fingers along the side of a staircase, his own shadow trailing after him as if he had dipped his fingertips in it. A quiet panic seizes Frizer by the chest, throwing into doubt every decision he has made since Sunday night, when Robin had first brought him here. But 'tis too late to turn back, later still with every step.

The corridor ends at a dining room containing an over-large ebony table and little else. Two men bolt to their feet as Marlowe halts at the threshold: the master and Nick. Robin, smiling, keeps to his seat.

The master looks so pale, Frizer wonders if he will faint. But suddenly he darts forward, clipping Marlowe in a force-ful, unreciprocated embrace. Frizer bows low, dodging Robin's steady gaze, though 'tis not for him. Only Marlowe.

'God be praised!' the master says. 'Kit, forgive me, I knew nothing until two hours ago.'

'What is *he* doing here?' Marlowe snarls. He shoulders past the master, exposing Frizer to the room.

The master stammers, 'Kit… There are some things I cannot accomplish on my own. I have not such power as I used to have.'

'Yet you have power enough to engage "the vilest of all two-legged creatures" in my affairs.' Marlowe fills a cup with wine; drinks greedily.

'Now, be not ungrateful. Master Poley is here as a free agent. There is no man whose expertise is more useful to ye—'

''Tis not necessary to defend me, Master Walsingham,' Robin says. 'I take no offence at the epithet, Master Marlowe. I earned it from the man who gave it to me. You, however, I should think might owe me some modicum of gratitude, given the many risks I have taken on your behalf of late. My superi-ors are most exasperated with me.'

'All this time,' Marlowe growls. 'Thomas, why did you never tell me?'

The master and Robin speak at once, but 'tis only Robin's voice that Frizer hears: 'Had he told you, would it have made any difference?'

'Did you know, Thomas, that he has been at the Marshalsea?' Marlowe says. Robin leans forward in his chair, starting to speak again, but Marlowe goes on, 'Did you know he was there, at Topcliffe's side, while Thomas Kyd was being racked!'

'Enough, now!' the master says, pounding the table. 'Enough!'

Marlowe's look of betrayal splits into an eerie grin, a laugh. When he looks up his gaze alights on Frizer, and there is admonition in his stare, perhaps even accusation, at which the fist in Frizer's belly tightens around some buried doubt.

'I would have you come and talk with me outside, Kit,' the master says.

Marlowe is already refilling his cup. 'Only if I may sit.'

'Be not such a child. Come with me.'

No, no, no, Frizer begs them, silently. *Do not leave me here!* But they are already moving towards a corridor at the back of the room wherein Widow Bull has also vanished, one direction leading to a garden door and the other, perhaps, to the kitchens. Through the wide, glazed window, Frizer sees them enter the high-walled garden from the right and, like puppets, pass straight across in tight, earnest conversation, slipping out of view at the other side.

Frizer lets out a breath. He shuffles into the room with his eyes down, conscious of Nick's open-mouthed smile, which seems to hover, with a kind of anguish, upon some suddenly forgotten remark he had planned to make. The moment Frizer sits, he shall fall weeping upon the table. For everything will be known, sooner or later. He cannot conceal that which his entire body betrays. Likely Nick is blind to it, as he's always been, but Robin surely knows. The instant Frizer entered this room, Robin could see Marlowe on his skin, in his mouth, in his walk. It may even be a relief to hear Robin accuse him out loud, for such would set the globe right upon its stand. The world thus restored, he could, perhaps, restore himself too. Yes, he'll say, he knows the enemy, even when the enemy is himself; he agrees with all his heart that its destruction must be total, merciless, and will do his duty as would any loyal subject, any good Christian… And somehow, through enough nodding of his head, make himself so holy that he needs must be pardoned.

The chair gives out a squeak on the floorboards as Frizer sits, but otherwise no one makes a sound, not even Nick, whose look of ready merriment has sunk into the plate of sweating cheese before him.

Across the table, Robin reclines in his chair, arms folded. His gaze is remote as always, yet not disinterested; the gaze of a spectator, looking down from on high. 'Master Skeres,' he says, with an inclination of his chin, 'I would not rob you of the pleasure of delivering Master Frizer the good news.'

'Ingram!' Nick licks his fingers, suddenly rosy. He takes a pause so long that Frizer cannot find his voice when at last he thinks to look for it. Nick sniggers at his distress, and finally proclaims, ''Tis a girl!'

⁂

Kit follows Walsingham to a stone bench on the far side of the garden. It faces in the direction of Greenwich, or where the view would be, were it not obscured by leafy walls that stand a foot taller than Kit himself. Eight years ago, this garden had lain deep in snow, from which oxblood roses bloomed and naked fruit trees shivered. But the roses and trees are gone now. There were children before, too: two boys and a baby girl. While the older boy and Kit threw snowballs, Baines had sat on this bench with the younger one upon his knee, making coins seem to appear from behind the child's ears.

Master Bull had entered the garden from the back door, taken one long, stiff look at the scene, and ordered the children up to bed.

The bones in Kit's side seem to realign as he sits. Still, there's the headache, somehow worse today than it was yesterday, and a sore spot on his cheek where Frizer had struck him.

'What have they done to you?' Walsingham says, standing over him.

Kit finishes the wine, feels momentarily sick. He starts to take off his waterlogged boots. 'Does Frizer know who he is?'

Walsingham kicks idly at the dandelion heads, something petulant in his demeanour. 'I am quite certain he does not, not that it matters.'

'You told him not to tell me?'

'That was Poley's idea. And can you blame him? Marry, I am not fond of the man either, but I know how to manage him, Kit – as my uncle did, with gold.'

Kit briefly considers throwing one of his boots at him. '*Manage* him? You think that's what Sir Francis did? *Manage him?*'

'Yes, in the sense that Poley served his damned purpose, as you and I served ours! I'faith, I never took you for such a holy idiot – is it not hypocrisy of the highest order for the judge, or the bailiff, to hate the executioner?'

This sounds like something Walsingham must have heard somewhere and thought very clever. Kit peels off his wet stockings and stretches out his legs, feeling like a scolded boy, barefoot in the grass. Walsingham has been right before, after all. How many times has Kit misjudged a man and suffered for it?

A terrifying thought arises: what, then, is he to think of Ingram Frizer?

No. No, he will not look behind that door.

'Circumstances being as they are,' Walsingham says, 'Poley has arranged for you to leave tomorrow.'

'And where am I to go?'

'Brittany, I believe.'

'The army?' Kit could laugh, had he the heart.

'It is the best place for you, Kit. Luckily, Sir John Norreys has requested fresh troops, and the Queen capitulated. The first hundred men set sail tomorrow. Poley has assured me that you'll be among them.'

Kit tries to imagine himself boarding a ship, dragging his heavy, sea-drunk legs through the sand on some alien beach, making camp in the mushroom-smelling woods. He can no more imagine it now than he could eight years ago.

'I am no soldier, Thomas,' he says.

'Nay, you are not!' Walsingham agrees. 'But take heart: desertion is so commonplace nowadays that they've ceased to hang men for it. It should be little trouble for you to slip away at the first opportunity...' He trails off, as if considering something anew. 'And, as you know, a deserter's best hope of surviving is to join the enemy. I have no doubt that they would take you in at the seminary in Rheims, if you can find your way there. Strapping fellow like you, with your learning, and your Latin – hell, you ought to have joined the seminarians ages ago!'

Kit feels another urge to laugh, though his throat will not permit it. He would sooner die, is all he can think. *Just let me die.*

'As for myself,' Walsingham goes on, 'I will be at Whitehall tomorrow, for the Council meeting. I know not whether they'll let me in, but I suppose I might stall them a little in any case. Give you time to set sail.' He sits, a posture which it seems the confines of his courtly attire will barely permit, leaving him listing awkwardly to one side, flicking his gloved fingertips. 'So, that's all, then.'

Clearly, he means the opposite. 'Is it?' Kit says.

Walsingham shakes his head, more anxious by the moment. 'God's blood, Kit! I *asked* you – two weeks ago, I asked you whether there was anything you had not told me—'

'Thomas—'

'I asked you what it was, this fearful secret that Baines knew but I did not! Had you told me then... I know not, but I wonder whether we would be here now. Perhaps I might have done something much sooner.'

Kit snorts. 'You would have had me killed!' He expects Walsingham to laugh, but looks over to see his lips quivering, eyes welling with tears.

'I know,' Walsingham rasps, 'I know you are not evil, Kit. I know that.'

'I'm sorry,' Kit says, without knowing what he is sorry for.

'I like ye. I do, God help me. Some days, I think I like ye better than I ever did Tom. I loved him, of course, but you know how unequal those things can be, liking and loving. He had a tyrant's heart, he did. Give him an army and he would have declared himself king!' He laughs, fondly, distantly, and yet looks almost ashamed. 'You have a gentle heart. I knew, even in the beginning, that this was why he chose you: you have a gentle heart, and I do not. Whatever you may have said... all these vicious things, I know you have said them. I believe it. Because you are a boy, and boys can be vicious, it does not make them evil. You are a boy, and you are so lost – I have seen you – I have seen you crawl inside a tiger's mouth for want of warmth, again and again. It breaks my heart.'

It seems right for Kit to take his hand. To comfort him, as he'd used to do, in the months after Walsingham had returned from the Marshalsea. Kit's nervous eyes alight on Tom's ring, glinting between Walsingham's fingers. The running hare. He feels an inexplicable sense of peril, like a gun to the back of the head.

'Well.' Walsingham lets out a long breath, looking up and out at the world as if straining to reacquaint himself with it. 'All will be well. These days will soon be over.'

Something in these words conjures Frizer like a ghost – for Kit and he are strangers who inhabit separate countries, are they not? It has ever been thus, from the moment they'd first met. They are seaborderers, swimming towards doom.

It seems that a string running down the centre of Kit's body comes unwound.

'Master Frizer told me you were hurt,' Walsingham says, looking him over. 'He said that there were two assailants, but by the state of ye I would say more.'

Kit almost laughs, wondering whether he should tell Walsingham what really happened in the attic of the Black Bull; never mind the shame of it, he is plenty humbled already. Not that he would know how to say it. *They did such-and-such to me.* 'Tis an additional humiliation to speak of what was done to oneself, to become a mere instrument, a bowstring that was pulled back, a cup that was smashed, having no say nor power over its own use. Women, things are *done to* them. Frizer was *done to*. But women are weak; Frizer was a child. A man should need some other excuse, should he not? Had he been stabbed or shot, there would be no need. A beaten man is not the same as a raped one.

Kit turns his head a little one way and something heavy, half-liquid, seems to sway inside his skull, like wine settling in a skin. 'Perhaps I am not the fighter I once was.'

Walsingham blows through his lips. 'You never were a fighter. You are a lodestone for violence. That is not the same thing.'

That unstrung feeling has not left. It only worsens. A final thread frayed, snapped.

Walsingham's hand alights on Kit's shoulder and then awkwardly runs up and down his arm, as if to rub the feeling back into it. Still Kit is all but numb to his touch, as small within himself as is a seed to the earth. Is it too soon to be weary? He is suddenly impossibly weary. He could let his chest grow heavier until his lungs have not the strength to lift it; he could lie here on the ground until the grass grows right through him.

'Stop crying, Kit,' Walsingham says. 'When I leave here tonight, I shall not see ye again, and this is not how I wish to remember you.'

⁂

'Ingram, I could not tell ye before,' Nick says. 'The time was not right. But be contented: Betsy is well and so was the babe, when I saw them last. Little chaff-headed poppet, she is. Looks just like you—'

'When you *saw* them?' Frizer sits with his forearms flat against the table, in an effort to steady the world. 'How many days ago? How many!'

Nick looks to Robin, who merely raises his eyebrows.

Nick counts on his fingers. 'A week ago.'

Frizer hides behind his hands. He would like to cry out to God, to beg and plead, as though something dear to him beyond measure had been stolen. But he is a fool, of course; he has fooled himself. He has lived these past few days as if locked inside a room with no windows, a room afloat in time. Within that room, there was no other light but Marlowe.

'How could you not tell me, Nick?' he croaks, shaking his head.

'I wanted to,' Nick says, looking hurt. His gaze darts towards Robin, again and again. 'Had to bite my tongue, I did!'

Frizer's head goes on shaking. All this time he has been a man with a child, a man with a daughter; he has been that man longer than whatever he is now – whatever he became, in the moment he laid his hands on another man's body—

'You knew this day would come,' Robin says. 'Yet you seem astonished!'

Frizer wipes his mind clean. His eyes alight on Robin's hand around the pitcher, the space where the ring finger should be.

Robin empties the last drops of wine into a goblet. Sediment swirls in the bottom. 'I suppose the first is always a shock,' he says. 'But you shall grow accustomed to the idea in time. That is the trick, my son. Children are but an idea until they grow big enough to either knock ye down or take a husband. The future – that is all that matters now.'

He leans back in his chair, glancing through the window. He then passes the goblet to Nick, who, with a reverent nod, delivers it to Frizer.

'Have I done something wrong?' Frizer murmurs.

Robin shrugs. 'You tell me. You are a day early. You are harbouring a fugitive from justice. You aided and abetted a traitor.'

'A *traitor*?' Frizer sputters, breathlessly. 'But, he is not—'

'That is not for you and I to judge, is it?' Robin says. 'Better men than ourselves say he is a traitor. Who are we to question their wisdom?'

Frizer feels something crawl down his cheek, like a flea, and he wipes it away. 'But we are going to help him, are we not?' he says. '*You* are going to help him?'

Robin touches his fingertips together, in an attitude of pity. 'Most traitors are given to the warden of the Marshalsea, for questioning. Have you heard of Dick Topcliffe, the warden of the Marshalsea? Your master certainly has. Perhaps you have heard whispers about his office at least. About the voids in the walls?'

Frizer shakes his head.

'If you stand quietly within Master Topcliffe's office, you will hear voices – voices, sometimes, of men who have been presumed dead for months or years. They are not spirits, of course. They hang from broken arms, stand on broken legs, in spaces so narrow one cannot shift an inch in any direction. Some go their way one day to the gallows, or even, if they are very lucky, to liberty. But some little fellows, you see, whose lives and deaths are of no real consequence to anyone – the accessories, the accomplices – they are not so fortunate. For, once they have shrieked out all the words desired of them, their keeper cuts out their tongues and seals them in until they stop making their unholy clamour altogether. I have overheard them myself, i'faith. Master Topcliffe swears 'tis the only way he can sleep through the night, hearing their speechless song. He calls it "the Hymn of the Blessed Kingdom".'

Frizer swallows sick. Longing fills him, the impossible longing that he shall now awake in bed at the Inn-in-the-Wall, look down and see Marlowe's head upon the pillow beside him, asleep. But a thought, half-image, half-impulse, cleaves through the longing like an axe-head: he sees his own hand press down on Marlowe's face, as if to smear it out of existence. Frizer tries to shake away the thought. Yet it only grows more insistent, more violent, the features erased like chalk, smudged like paint, squeezed through his fingers like wet clay—

A heavy hand falls upon Frizer's left shoulder and he flinches, only to find Nick looking on him with sympathy, shooting Robin a glance of quiet disapproval.

'Master Poley is only trying to say that the situation is...' Nick searches for a word, 'changeable.'

❧❀☙

In time, Poley excuses himself from the table and stands at the garden door, observing Walsingham and Marlowe with no attempt whatsoever at discretion, as if they were personages in a play and he an audience of one. Several times their eyes shoot daggers at him, and he smiles and nods in return.

Eventually they both rise, and each man turns another despising glance on Poley 'ere they appear to say their good-byes. Walsingham bows his head and clasps Marlowe's hand, clinging to him far longer than seems comfortable for either man. At last, he murmurs something, walks away. Marlowe stands barefoot in the grass, as still and straight as a finger-post, as if he'd felt a breath behind his ear.

'You'll not stay for dinner?' Poley says, as Walsingham reaches him. 'My sister's kidney pie is renowned.'

Walsingham sweeps past without a reply. Poley follows. In the dining room, Nick and Frizer bolt to their feet at their master's entrance, the former with his mouth full, the latter dizzily, grasping the back of a chair for balance. Walsingham offers no final words to either of his men, simply charges down the corridor and out the front door, as if fleeing some embarrassing social blunder.

Poley finds him at his horse, yanking the saddle-strap as if he thought the beast's suffering was the whole point. Somehow, Walsingham must have heard Poley coming, or seen him clear through the back of his head, for he mutters without looking, 'It had better not be poison.'

Poley glances towards the house. Thankfully, no one has followed him. 'Certainly not. Things must appear as if he were taken in the act of flight, if we want to avoid an inquiry. A bullet to the head will do, swift and sweet.'

'Where is your pistol?'

'Hidden away, of course. You would not have him get a look of it now, would you?'

Walsingham harrumphs. He fumbles with his gloves, as if unsure whether he had just now been taking them off or putting them on.

'I'll send your man Frizer to Greenwich when the deed is done,' Poley says.

'Send him to Whitehall.'

Poley blinks. 'Whitehall?'

'Ay.'

'There's no need for you to go to Whitehall.'

'Whitehall is where I'll be; to Whitehall you will send him.'

Poley throws a look to the sky, his mind spinning. The whole Council shall meet at Whitehall tomorrow, in the Star Chamber, a place where Walsingham has likely not set foot ever since the day they'd dragged him out of the Marshalsea. What in hell does he intend to do in Whitehall?

Walsingham also squints at the sky, just long enough to find the sun. 'They say there will be an eclipse tomorrow, around midday. I may therefore keep time by the same clock in Whitehall as you do in Deptford. If, by the time the sun and the moon touch, I have not yet received confirmation that our business is finished, I will assume treachery, and shall proceed accordingly.'

'"Accordingly"?'

'I will of course protect myself, Master Poley. You expect that.'

Poley forces a chuckle. Could Walsingham have got hold of Topcliffe somehow? When might it have happened – this morning, or last night even? Perhaps Topcliffe has been playing Poley all this time; perhaps he and Walsingham have struck some sort of deal behind his back; perhaps Topcliffe does not have the ring at all, indeed never had it—

'The Council had an opportunity to hang me once already,' Walsingham says, 'and they did not take it. To hang one such as myself is a complicated thing, you see. But who are *you*, Robin Poley? What are you to anyone, dead or alive?'

Again, Poley laughs, as involuntary as a shiver. What is Walsingham mad enough to try? Would he report Poley for harbouring a fugitive? Have the Council send their men here, where they shall arrest all present, including Marlowe? No, he'd never dare. He is at Poley's mercy, the silly popinjay, and seems too stupid to know it.

'There's no need for hostilities, Master Walsingham,' Poley says. 'I will send your man to Whitehall by midday.' Still, he cannot resist. 'What sort of confirmation shall I send? A finger, or an ear? Or would you prefer some other part of him, one that you could not fail to recognize?'

Predictably, this puts murder in Walsingham's gaze. How fragile they are, these men; how delicious it is to stare down a muzzled dog! Poley could eat the hatred in those eyes.

Walsingham snarls, 'If Marlowe is taken alive, I shall have nothing to lose, will I? You had best take account of all that *you* have to lose, Poley, material and immaterial. You presume I cannot take it from ye, but I can.'

Walsingham rides away towards the village. Poley watches him go, squinting to see which way he turns in the distance: left towards Greenwich, or right towards Southwark, the Marshalsea, Whitehall? But the door of Eleanor's house opens and shuts, causing him to glance away for but a second, long enough for Walsingham to have vanished when he looks again.

He senses Nick Skeres's bearlike bulk lumbering closer, breathing little whistles through the nose. 'Why did you say all that to Ingram?' Nick sounds genuinely perplexed, even sore.

'What things?'

'All that about Topcliffe, and the Marshalsea?'

Poley smirks, but the expression feels strange, as if it comes upon him in the absence of something else. 'You worry too much for your friend, dear boy. He is a grown man, is he not?'

'He is—' Nick stammers, as if about to blurt out a thing that troubles him. 'He's not like you and me. All your stories have got him pissing himself.'

'Master Frizer has never spent a single day of his life unafraid. Why should he start now?'

Nick shakes his head, his doughy face furrowed and severe. An unnatural look with him, it smacks a tad too much of mutiny. *Mutiny*, from the ever-loyal dog? Is it even possible?

'I have something for you,' Poley says, and reaches for his moneybag, emptying the contents into his palm. He picks out enough silver and copper to add up to the somewhat uneven sum of six pounds and sixpence, and hands it over as if his own generosity touched him slightly. 'I must be off to attend John Penry's hanging, I'm afraid. I'll have the rest for you tomorrow.'

Nick looks either disappointed or baffled. Not the response Poley had hoped for. 'Well. It shall be twenty-five altogether, no? Because if the master lands back in the naskin, I'll need me a nest-egg...'

'Oh yes. But I cannot very well carry *twenty-five* pounds on my person, can I?'

Still, Nick looks doubtful, staring at the coins in his palm. 'And twenty for Ingram?'

'Yes, yes, twenty for Master Frizer.'

'And you?'

'Me?'

Nick's eyes narrow. 'Master Walsingham's paid you half already, ay? Twenty-five for me, twenty for Ingram, leaves just five pounds for you. But you'll get something else, no? You'd not... do all this for five pounds!'

Poley puts on a cagey look, strained, perhaps, by the unexpected sensation as if a hand had reached straight through his spine, into his guts. What, indeed, if he has done all this for nothing?

'Will you share the bounty with Topcliffe?' Nick asks, too anxious to let silence hang.

'Yes,' Poley says, 'of course.' And if Nick has espied anything awry in Poley's gaze, there's no knowing, for Nick turns away at once, nodding like a man who is telling himself lies.

Poley walks Nick back to the house. Still, his gaze returns

more than once to the distant domes of Greenwich, as if some perfect resolution shall appear in the eastern sky. At the door, he turns to look again, but this time his eyes alight upon the *Golden Hind*: decks bleaching in the sun, the remnants of tattered sails wagging in the breeze like pallid tongues, the bullet-riddled hull emitting daylight like a sieve.

It occurs to him that all along this ship has been a jest sitting in plain sight, one invisible to Marlowe himself – for it is, and has ever been, the only ship awaiting him in Deptford.

30

WHEREVER YOU GO, LOOK for escapes, Baines had said, on a night long ago. *And if all else fails: find witnesses.*

As soon as Walsingham and Poley vanish into the house, Kit steals across the garden to the wattle-and-daub privy. Beneath the hole in the wooden seat, there's a larger shaft emptying over the bank and into the brown, scummy Thames, which the bony stripling that Kit was eight years ago might have squeezed through, dropped down onto the sand and run as far as the ground would last, or swum out until the current took him off. Not so now. Emerging again, he inspects the privy's woven walls for possible handholds and footholds, tugs at the vines on the garden walls in search of any that might support his weight. He recalls that there had once been a gate leading out to the green, and so fumbles blindly through the ivy until his hand encounters a slab of iron, solid with rust and hope-lessly overgrown. No escape.

When Kit turns to face the other end of the garden, he is startled by an apparition floating several feet above the wall: a child leaning out of a window in a neighbouring house, his head on his arms.

'Hollo?' Kit murmurs.

'Hollo,' says the boy. 'Are you one of the bad men?'

Kit wonders whether his mind might be going.

'Are you one of the bad men?' the boy repeats.

Kit can only think to respond with something he wishes he'd known himself, when he was a lad: 'A bad man will not tell you that. A bad man will always tell you that he is good.'

The boy frowns and starts to speak again, but a woman appears behind him in the window and pulls him inside, closing the shutters.

Kit can see four windows of the next nearest house from here. Two from the house beyond that. It occurs to him that the last time he was here he had failed to notice these neighbours entirely; he'd always remembered Bull's House as being among the most isolated places on earth.

Find witnesses, Baines had said.

Kit halts in the doorway of the dining room, clutching his wet boots and stockings. For another fearful second, Frizer remains slumped facedown at the table as if poisoned, but then at last he lifts his head to reveal a face as pale as an oyster, blue eyes brimming with tears.

'What,' Kit stammers, 'what did they say to you?'

But before Frizer can so much as take in a breath, the fat man and Poley come stomping down the hall, the latter whistling merrily. Kit and Frizer turn away from one another as if slapped.

'There he is!' Poley swoops into a seat at the middle of the table with a flamboyant flip of his open sleeves and a glance from Frizer to Kit that seems to see all. 'Will you join us for some kidney pie, Master Marlowe?' he says, as the other one reaches to cut a slice.

Food seems a ridiculous indulgence under the circumstances, though Kit is so hungry that even the mineral stink of kidney pie is enough to make his stomach growl. He glances towards the head of the table, startled by the sight of his bag lying there, exposed, forgotten. He should have given it to Walsingham; he had not even thought of it!

'You shall find all just as you left it,' Poley says, almost sing-song, as Kit hurries to the end of the table, drops his boots on the floor and makes a half-blind search of the bag's contents, distracted by the heat of Frizer's stare.

'Has Master Walsingham gone?' Kit asks, giving up.

'Oh yes,' Poley answers, wolfing down his pie in haste. 'Back to Greenwich. He's a busy man, you know, as busy as a cock in a henyard.'

Kit keeps his head bowed. For as long as Frizer and he are in the same room together, Poley will take note of their every glance, or glance refused; every catch of the breath or twitch of the lips. 'Tis always plain to see, for those who know how to look.

'Where am I to sleep?' Kit says.

'Why, you have stayed here before. You know the room.'

Again, Kit feels a pinch – not for hunger this time, but because a memory of Baines has stuck him like a needle: his weight beside him on the edge of a bed. His hand burning on the back of his neck.

'Master Frizer will stay with you,' Poley adds, causing Kit and Frizer to meet one another's eyes at last. 'After all this time I would be loath to see you separated.' Poley wipes his mouth as he rises, in a hurry to go. 'Regrettably, I must take my leave of you until tonight – the Council whistles and, cur-like, I must come running! I'll fetch my sister to show you up.'

He heads towards the kitchens. This time, neither Kit nor Frizer has broken their gaze. Doom glides down sound-lessly in the space between them, like a veil dropped from a high window.

'Tis clear now why Frizer had lied about Poley: not out of obedience to his master, and certainly not because he'd been foolish enough to believe that lying was for Kit's own good. He'd lied because Robin Poley terrifies him, simple as that.

Widow Bull leads Kit upstairs, letting him enter the room first. 'It should be as you remember it,' she says, and this he discovers to be perfectly true, though it appears much smaller, like all places from the past. Eight years ago, it had been Master Bull, not his wife, who had showed Kit and Baines up to this room; who had stood at the threshold and watched Baines lurch drunkenly to the bed; who had then turned a look both pitying and solicitous upon the lanky, quiet boy, who'd stood where Kit is standing now.

Shall I leave you?

'I'm sorry about Master Bull,' Kit says, for he should have said so sooner. 'He was very kind to me, when last I was here.'

The widow makes a mute gesture of forgiveness, though her colour wanes slightly. It seems that she must shake herself before speaking again. 'Might I bring you something to eat?'

'No,' Kit lies, 'thank you, I'm not hungry.' The bed is large enough to sleep four men at once, a room within a room. The curtains are drawn only at the foot, giving it the look of a fanged maw.

Eight years ago, as Master Bull had closed the door, Baines sprawled back upon the covers with his arms above his head, crowing:

'"Come live with me and be my love,

And we will all the pleasures prove

That valleys, groves, hills and fields,

Woods, or steepy mountains yields..."'

Kit had written the song for the Parker Scholarship to Cambridge, when he was just fifteen years old. It was his first great success; people were singing it up and down the country that year, and would be for years afterwards. Baines too. Especially whenever there was drink in him.

'"Come live with me and be my love,"' Baines sneered, eyeing him from the bed. 'Who did you write that for, anyway? Some *girl*?'

Widow Bull clears her throat. Just as she turns to go, Kit stops her: 'You... You said you had whisky, ma'am?'

With the widow gone, Kit sits at the edge of the bed and rubs at his headache. Before him, a painted mural of grassy pastures undulates into a crudely foreshortened distance, veined in stone walls and hedgerows like the Kentish downs. Like the way home. How impossibly distant Canterbury had seemed on that December night in 1585, far more distant than the way to Paris! Kit's family had had no idea he was in Deptford, bound for France; they'd believed he was still at Cambridge. If he were to die, Baines had said, they would be told he'd come down with the plague, that his body had been burnt. 'But fear not,' Baines also said. 'I'll keep ye safe.'

His hot hand came to rest, heavily, on the back of Kit's neck. The scent of Scotch whisky on Baines's breath was still exotic to Kit then: smoke, ash, bog. Fire.

'Paris will be dangerous, lad,' Baines said. 'There's no denying that. Times will come when you'll have to fend for yourself. I have much to teach you, marry.'

'Ay,' Kit whispered, mindlessly. Something was different that night. The hand on his neck burnt with an almost impossible heat, pressed down upon him with an unbearable weight.

'Everywhere you go, you must look for escapes,' Baines said. And he went on to tell Kit a number of things that have kept him alive in the years since: what to do when followed, or cornered, what to look for when entering an unfamiliar place, what to look for in an unfamiliar man. 'And if all else fails: find witnesses. Put enough eyes on ye, and whomever means to do ye harm will likely back away. And make sure there are men's eyes – no women or children, no one believes 'em. Never let yourself be alone with another man.'

He fell silent for a while. Hummed a line of song beneath his breath.

'A boy like you needs to know when he's needed. *How* he's needed. You'll live long, if only you can learn that. Living comes at a price. Safety... comes at a price.'

These words were a precipice. There lay the edge, the drop so far, so fatal. The landscape of Kit's life with Richard Baines had changed: always had it been a place of little shelter, little safety, few means of escape. Now, it seemed the only way out was down.

Baines unbuckled his belt, one-handedly, and then struggled with the first button.

'Help me, will you?'

Kit bit his tongue till it bled. He tried to think of the morning to come, of the ship that awaited him, for he had never been on a ship before; and of the sea, which he had never seen before. His mother was from Dover. The first time he ever saw the sea, he decided, he would think of her.

⁂

Three miles to the east, John Penry's sledge makes the short journey from the Marshalsea to Thomas-a-Watering, dragged by a mangy jackass and escorted by Dick Topcliffe, who walks alongside his charge as proudly as if to lead his daughter to the altar. The streets are empty. Southwark's anxious denizens watch the procession from behind cracked casements. There are no nut-sellers or beer-sellers, no throngs chanting for blood. Nothing sounds at all but for the regular bang of a drum and one human voice, railing into the quickening rain: 'Take your spectacles then, and spell your own words, and you shall find that you have affirmed *treason*! Read your own books, hear your own speeches!...'

So, John Penry – naked but for his blindfold and bonds

– rants on, with barely a pause for breath, as the archbishop's mercenaries part ranks to allow the procession into the muddy gallows square. An open-bedded cart, drawn by one piebald horse, waits beneath the noose. To the left of the stage, Puckering and Archbishop Whitgift stand in a row along with the Bishop of London, the Lord Treasurer, and several other privy councillors like crows along a branch. To the right, a small host of spies and officers of the Privy Court struggle not to fidget, Thomas Phelippes and Robin Poley among them.

Guards hustle Penry up the steps, still roaring his invectives. The bailiff steps forward to read the death warrant aloud, but Archbishop Whitgift plucks the paper from his hands and attempts to drown out Penry's rantings himself: '*Elizabethe dei gratia Anglie, Francie et Hibernie Regine—*'

'—therefore *all* the Lord Bishops in England, Ireland and Wales, *all* I say, are petty Popes, and petty usurping Antichrists—'

The two go on trying to shout one another down, one stark naked and the other in full regalia, one declaiming stoically and the other squawking and flapping like a hen. It continues long enough that uncomfortable sniggers and glances begin to flutter through the ranks. At last, Puckering gives a weary nod to one of the guards, who promptly draws his knife and sticks it straight through the prisoner's neck.

A final rebuke sputters from Penry's lips, ruby-red and soundless.

'I congratulate you, by the way,' Phelippes whispers, at Poley's side.

Poley looks away from the spectacle to stare at him, uncomprehending.

'You did not speak with the Lord Keeper?' Phelippes goes on. 'It seems your speech at the Marshalsea made an impression at the Council meeting in Greenwich today. Her

Majesty has given orders that Marlowe should be prosecuted "to the full".'

To think that the Queen – the Queen! – should have any opinion whatsoever on Poley's own words leaves him momentarily stunned, roused only by the executioner's shout. He looks to the stage again, just in time to see the driver's whip crack and the wagon rumble away, leaving Penry swinging like a fish on a line.

'That is most excellent news,' Poley says.

Phelippes adds, 'What's more, on his Holiness's advice, the bounty on Marlowe has been increased. *Three* hundred pounds.'

Poley must suppress a chuckle of astonishment. Three hundred pounds is a tidy fortune – if not a diamond's bounty, then as close as one might dare to hope! 'Surely,' he replies, soberly, 'it will lead to the villain's timely capture.'

But Phelippes has a look in his eye: that of a competent hunter, with the bowstring pulled back. 'Yes, all well and good. Certainly for you. Marlowe is with you, after all, packed away somewhere like winter bacon.'

Poley blinks, tongue-tied, but then rallies himself. 'Master Phelippes, now is hardly the time, nor the place—'

'It suits me well enough. Now, I prefer not to make public accusations which I cannot prove, so I have said nothing to the Lord Keeper, not yet. I can, however, approach Master Topcliffe on this issue.'

Poley's eyes find Topcliffe, who is already watching Poley from his place at the corner of the stage, with a glare as if he were trying to extinguish a candle with his mind.

Phelippes says, 'I care not for Topcliffe's part in this. I begrudge him not his bounty, so long as he brings Marlowe in alive. And you, having made a commitment to the devil, surely you have every intention of honouring it. But it would not be difficult to plant suspicions in the warden's head, would it?'

A winch shrieks as the executioners pull Penry back onto

the stage. Stiff-legged, toes scuffling at the ground. They slacken the rope just until his legs fold at the knees. Two men in long aprons close in upon him at either flank, knives drawn.

'Are you quite finished?' Poley rasps.

'Topcliffe has not *seen* Marlowe since you've had him, has he?' Phelippes needles. 'No, I did not think so. It would take a foolish gamester to play for a pot that exists only in theory. Far be it from me to impugn the royal bloodline, but her Majesty's cousin is not widely lauded for his wits. You, however, are a clever fellow. You've already seen a way to multiply potential gains. Perhaps you've also realized that the bounty could increase exponentially, day by day, as the fugitive remains at large and desperation mounts for his capture.'

Poley seeks a refuge for his eyes. Topcliffe is still watching him, the tip of his tongue worrying the corner of his lips; Penry is still dying, making watery, drowning sounds as his blood pours through the boards in heavy gouts. But above, the skin of rainclouds has opened in one place, exposing a viscera of spotless blue. The sky on the day that Babington had died had been clear, cloudless.

'You have already spoken with Topcliffe,' Poley realizes, smiling, for it is almost a relief to be outflanked.

Curiously, Phelippes does not appear to be revelling in his triumph. He looks as joyless as ever except for the slightest tug at the corner of his mouth, a look of pity, if anything at all. 'Tell me where Marlowe is, and I'll meddle in this rat's nest no further.'

Poley shakes his head. 'Nay, good fellow, for meddling is what you do. Should I play along with your absurd suppositions, who's to say you will not accuse me of harbouring a fugitive or aiding his escape?'

"Tis all in your hands, Poley. But if Marlowe is not in custody by sundown tomorrow, if I were you, I should be looking for a swift way out of London.'

In this same moment, at Greenwich, Thomas Walsingham
sits at a desk in his richly appointed private quarters, gazing
through a window that looks across a narrow courtyard and
into the window of another, identical room. Inside that room,
Robert Cecil stands on a stool so that he may fuck Lady Audrey
Shelton from behind, balls swinging under his blowsy shirt.
Her hands are bound to the bedposts. Through the window,
Cecil watches Walsingham watch him, with a smirk.

On Walsingham's desk lies Poley's most recent message,
which had arrived this morning after Walsingham had already
left for Thomas-a-Watering:

> *Alas my poore syster has took sicke this morninge about*
> *sunrise & I pray you come visit her <u>straight</u> at her house*
> *& bringe with you the physick you promised.*

No signature, but Robin Poley has no need to sign his
letters, his hand being so distinct, so inimitable.

Walsingham takes several fresh sheets of paper from the
writing-box on his desk. Letter by letter, he copies Poley's
message, and then line by line, filling page after page, his
pen moving a little quicker with each repetition. He tucks
his ring finger into his palm. Tries several different quills,
different dilutions of ink. So, this is how the devil cuts his
quill, to a point almost as fine as a needle. So, this is how the
devil scribes 'Alas', the long 's' at the end a rounded slither,
a visual hiss.

Next, Walsingham drafts a new letter, and in the space
below copies it again and again, with slight variations:

> *Alas, my poore syster is sicke & I pray you come <u>not</u> to*
> *visit her...*

*Alas, my poore syster is sicke & I pray you come <u>not</u> to
visit her but come to my house at sunrise…*

*…come straight to <u>my</u> house at sunrise & bringe with you
the physick you promised.*

Once Penry is finally dead, the Council's and the archbishop's
men mill about the square, shaking hands and congratulating
one another on a job well done. Poley's involvement in Penry's
case was small, yet they insist on dragging him into their circle
of back-slapping praise anyway, while, on the stage above, the
executioners butcher the corpse into portions, to distribute
among the city's gates: 'Get the knife behind the joint there.
Use your palm, give it a good push.'

Crunch.

By the time Poley can separate himself from the others,
Topcliffe has gathered up his instruments and made ready to
leave. Poley bounds to meet him at the wayside of Kent Street,
catching him in the act of mounting a truly monstrous horse,
to ride the quarter-mile back to the Marshalsea.

'Master Topcliffe,' Poley says, 'I request a—'

'Oh, you make requests of me now, birdy?' Topcliffe takes
his boot out of the stirrup. 'You think I *want* for two hundred,
or even three hundred pounds? You think my cook grinds up
our stale bread to make more bread withal?'

'I would never dream—'

'Nay, never dream again, little Robin; scrub all wild fancies
from your mind. I catch but one more whiff of imagination
from you and I'll wash my hands of the whole business,
understood?'

'But tomorrow,' Poley sputters, as Topcliffe moves again to
mount his beast. 'Tomorrow, you will—'

'Come at your beck? Bring you your little jewel? I'll come
when I come, and the jewel you'll receive when I am satisfied.'

He looks down from the saddle with bared teeth. 'Tell your sister to kill a bird for my dinner. Tell her to kill her best egg-laying hen, and be sure to leave all the pearly yolks inside her, so I may count them as I sup.'

He canters away, black as a thunderhead, his long-legged instruments loping after his muddy wake.

Walsingham makes three copies of his forgery. One for Poley, one for Topcliffe, one for the Star Chamber. *Come straight to my house.*

By now, the spectacle in the room across the courtyard is well over, the daylight all but gone. Yet even in the darkness beyond the glazed window, Walsingham can make out a strip of white fabric still knotted around Cecil's bedpost, threads dangling from its frayed edges.

The image brings Tom Watson to mind, but also Topcliffe, makes Walsingham's hands numb and his breath short and his cock half-hard. His body is so rife with ghosts that they blend into one another, grotesque chimeras of longing and terror, pleasure and pain. Kit is there too, ticking away at his ear like a clock: *Kit, Kit, Kit, Kit, Kit...*

He will dedicate some portion of his time to the preservation of Kit's memory, that's what he'll do. He'll publish Kit's unpublished works. He'll pay other poets to write epitaphs, to finish anything left unfinished. He'll ensure Kit's legacy lives on for a hundred years.

And over time, this ticking in his ear will grow quieter, and eventually cease.

⁂

Marlowe has been upstairs all afternoon. At some point after supper, Nick ceases pontificating about the joys of fatherhood to regard Frizer with unnerving, unreadable intensity, as if suddenly aware that he has not heeded a word. He then glances out the window and reaches across the dining table, giving a friendly swipe to Frizer's shoulder. 'Come,' Nick says. 'Did ye never fancy yourself a privateer? Did ye never steal into the church at night and pretend the pulpit was a crow's nest?'

From the front door of Bull's House, Nick bounds out onto the damp green, like a dog let out to play. Frizer follows slowly, feeling watched, until Nick doubles back and hurries him along, up the slippery gangway of the *Golden Hind*. Frizer has never been on a ship before. Even unmoving, his footing feels uncertain. The hull groans and murmurs like a massive belly; a breeze snores through the bullet holes in the planks. Above, the weathered mainmast towers towards heaven; the prow plunges into a darkening distance beyond the bend in the Thames, towards the wide unknowable world.

Frizer imagines standing with Marlowe upon the deck of a ship, just like this, exchanging farewells with unbearable discretion, wary of how long to hold one another's gaze, of where and how long to touch. He will bid Marlowe take care, mind his temper, and his tongue. He will thank him for having been so kind. It all seems so fantastical.

'Ingram.' Nick leans over the creaking railing of the upper deck, by the wheel. 'What's the matter with you, man? Were you praying for a miscarriage?'

'Of course not!' Frizer turns his back on him, facing distant Greenwich Hill's ruined tower, the place where Robin had first told him about Deptford.

'Do ye trust this Robin fellow?' Frizer asks.

'Ha!' Nick brays. 'Never mind that. You need not worry about him. Just sit back and collect the money, that's all.' There's a placating tone in his voice, an implicit plea: *Stop asking questions*. 'We'll gain much from this, you and me. Tomorrow we need only follow Master Poley's lead.'

'That is what concerns me, Nick. I know not where he means to lead us.'

Nick screws up his face, scratching the back of his neck. 'Why, nowhere. *We* are not going anywhere.'

'And Marlowe?'

'What does that matter?'

Nick's frustration is showing. Frizer turns a shoulder on him this time, facing the house, the livid sunset behind it. In an upstairs window, a gaunt, white-shirted shape glows against the shadows like a ghost. Having but glimpsed it, Frizer keeps turning, nearly a full circle, praying that Nick will not look where he just did.

'I tried to prepare ye for this,' Nick says. 'Did I not tell ye we would both be coney-catching by June?'

Frizer's heart kicks against his ribs. 'But, I *know* him, Nick. He's my friend!'

Nick scoffs out a sound of pain, bewilderment. He points to his own heart and says, '*I'm* your friend. That lanky bugger in there, what's he to ye? You know him not from Adam!'

Frizer paces to an open hatch, gazing into the dark hull. Danger grows for every second that he spends here, yet his body resists flight, like a hare in the path of a hawk. When he lifts his head Marlowe remains fixed at the window, his gaze likewise fixed upon Frizer, and Frizer glowers back just long enough to scream with his thoughts: *Go away! Please go away!*

Nick's slow footsteps thump across the upper deck. 'Look you now, whatever happens tomorrow, you have to trust me. Let *me* trust Master Poley. As I said before, circumstances are like to shift, and you needs must be ready.' He rethinks his own severity, holding up a mollifying hand. ''Tis nothing you cannot manage. Only be a good servant! Do as you are told. That's all there is to it.'

'Since I have been here, my master has told me nothing!'

'Poor monkey! I am not talking about your master.'

Go away, Frizer thinks, stifling a whimper as he looks again to the house and finds Marlowe unmoved from his place, as still as a portrait. 'Go away!' Frizer whispers, low enough that Nick should not overhear. He could cut Marlowe's eyes out for the way he is looking on him now, like a priest uplifted in song! For a man with no religion, his love is fanaticism, 'tis fatal, existing mainly for the hereafter. Who could ever doubt that a man like him might end his days at some torturer's hands, buried alive between two walls? Perhaps Frizer shall be buried alive too, just a wall apart from him, close enough to overhear one another's tongueless moans – just like the conquered king and queen of Babylon, whom Tamburlaine had locked in dog-cages and left to starve; who had lamented, just before dashing their own brains out:

> *Then is there left no Mahomet, no God,*
> *No fiend, no fortune, nor no hope of end,*
> *To our infamous, monstrous slaveries.*

'Look,' Nick starts to say, and then pauses, silently making a deal with himself. 'I might as well tell ye: Marlowe is not getting on a boat tomorrow, that much is certain.'

Kit lifts the bottle of whisky to his lips. He has drained it halfway since Widow Bull brought it to him, hours ago. Outside, the red of the sunset touches even the clouds in the north, blood upon a ceiling of blue-black muscle. The *Golden Hind* lies too far away to overhear what Frizer and the other one are saying. But perhaps Kit already knows.

A ghost of Richard Baines leans close to his ear and whispers, 'A man like that will betray ye for a slice of cake.'

Kit will not believe it. Must not believe it. This is another kind of precipice. From here, he can look into the distance and see Ingram Frizer as if he were but an anonymous stranger, ageing into a soft, domestic quiescence, living a life marked by church holidays and the baptisms, marriages and burials of his children and grandchildren; a life that draws up the years behind it like a blanket to bed; a life that could fit in the palm of one's hand. A breath could blow it away.

Come live with me, and be my love.

3 1

'WHAT KEPT YOU SO long?' Marlowe pulls Frizer into the room, bolts the door and puts his back against it. Inside it is as dark as a cell, and as close, reeking of whisky and of the piss in the piss-pot. One candle burns upon a little table, Marlowe's bag slumped beside it, packed and ready.

Frizer has no excuse prepared. He can only whisper, 'I'm sorry.'

Marlowe rubs his face in his hands, as if tempering himself. 'Nay, but 'tis well. 'Tis dark now anyway. Better.' He moves past Frizer towards the table, speaking with his back turned. 'I must be gone before Poley comes back. Marry, I know not what he intends for me, but I trust him not. Neither do you. I've seen it in your face. The way you look at me, when he is near...'

Frizer lets out a strangled laugh. He wonders whether Robin knows, somehow, what he will do next, even before he knows it himself. Perhaps Robin has foreseen this very thought, and every thought that follows it. To Robin, Frizer is a simple creature. There's no mystery, is there, in a frightened man?

'Frizer,' Marlowe says, turning to face him. 'I do not care, do you understand? I care not that you lied. Whatever he has asked of you, it does not matter.' He falls silent. Frizer can see him biting his tongue, the light quivering upon his eyes.

'I want you to come with me,' Marlowe says. 'I know, I know it is much to ask of you; I know what you would leave behind. But if we could get as far as Dover, I have family there. And in Dover 'tis easier to steal one's way onto a ship. There are some who do it week after week; every day there are hundreds crossing the Narrow Sea, back and forth. We could stir up a little gold somehow. I'll borrow it or steal it; I'll suck cock for it, I care not. But I will get us on a ship, one way or another. I will get us out of England.' He lifts his long hands into a peak, fingers at his lips. 'I want to see you away from this. I want to see *both* of us away from this!'

'Away from what?' Frizer rasps.

'Everything – I know not – somewhere safe!'

'But where *is* that, Marlowe?' He could break into screams. 'Where *is* that? Where *is* that?'

Frizer drops to his knees. He makes a shield out of his arms, hinges himself at the waist and rocks like a madman. 'I tried to help you. I'm so sorry, I tried!'

Marlowe kneels with him. 'Shh, I know you did. I know.'

'I swear I knew nothing when I brought you here! I thought you would be on a boat tomorrow or the day after. I swear that's what they told me!'

Marlowe grows still, as if feeling the bullet but not yet the wound.

'Some man, some devil is coming for you tomorrow. From the Marshalsea. Robin means to *sell* you to him. If you try to leave, Nick is outside, guarding the door – he will stop you!'

The only response to this is silence. Frizer keeps his head down, blubbering sorries. He reaches out with one hand until it finds Marlowe's knee, only to feel him abruptly shoot to his feet, hear his footsteps clamber away across the room. Frizer sobs aloud, into the floor. He is alone in a way that no other man is alone; there are thousands of miles between himself and the nearest living soul.

Marlowe should kill him. It would be a kindness, all things considered. Even Frizer is sick of himself, having lived all his life as if from a hole in the ground, vile even to his fellow worms. 'Tis an affront to the man he might have been that he lives as the creature he is now. For he is not a man at all. He is a dead boy.

'Enough,' Marlowe whispers, from the window. 'He can hear you.'

Frizer holds his breath to stop crying.

'Who told you all this?'

'Nick.'

'Him, down there?'

Frizer nods.

'And you did not know before? You knew nothing at all?'

Frizer shakes his head.

'Look at me. Say it.'

'I cannot.'

'*Look at me*,' Marlowe growls.

At last, Frizer wipes his face on his sleeve and sits up. Marlowe has blown the candle out, opened the shutters. He seems to glow against the moonless night sky, looking as if he were in another room or another time altogether, long past.

'They told me they would help you,' Frizer says. 'And I believed them! But... the Council has put up a bounty—'

Marlowe laughs. 'A *bounty*?' But his smile fades at once. 'Did they promise you money?'

Frizer cannot speak.

'How much?'

'Twenty pounds.'

'Ha!' Marlowe cries, too loud, stopping his own mouth with a hand. He paces in and out of the light several times and then suddenly halts, the hand now dropped to his heart.

'Is your master a part of this?'

Even before Frizer can answer, Marlowe turns pale.

'I believed it,' Frizer cries. 'I believed it because I trusted him, because I thought he was your *friend*—'

'Stop,' Marlowe says. 'Please, stop.' He turns his back to the wall, doubles forward, slides down to the floor. Seconds pass wherein he only stares, then at last he wraps his arms about his knees, presses his face against them and lets out a muffled cry that shakes his body from head to foot.

Frizer watches, afraid to move. Marlowe could say anything just now and Frizer would believe it; he could order him to do anything and Frizer would do it. Whatever his word, it would be truer than God's own truth, the kind of truth that could burn him alive just to hear it.

Gradually, Marlowe uncurls himself. He sits with his eyes downcast, barely blinking. 'I never asked you, did I, if you would come with me?' he says. 'I never asked you what you wanted.' He seems too calm, as if half-asleep.

Frizer shakes his head. 'Marlowe, 'tis impossible.'

'I know. You need not tell me that. But I had to—I had to say it.' He lets his arms go slack, and then his legs. 'I saw us. Imagined it, I mean. We were ten years older, and far from here. And we were happy. I wonder if that is not mad, to think we would be happy in ten years, you and I.'

Frizer has never considered it. He knows not how two men should live together, happily or unhappily, for years on end. Lodgers, they would be, as they were at the Inn-in-the-Wall, a temporary arrangement made indefinite. Every morning and every night, an agreement to stay on.

'I do not think I can kill myself,' Marlowe says, as if it is the worst of failures.

'I'll do it,' Frizer says. 'If you do it, I'll do it with you.'

'No.'

'Why not?'

'Because you must *live*, Frizer.'

'Why in hell should I live?' He really would like to know. Why should a creature like himself exist, if Marlowe cannot?

Marlowe crawls across the floor, sits at Frizer's side and draws him into an embrace that seems to swallow his body whole, enfolding him with both arms and legs, his eye damp against the crook of Frizer's neck. Yet he gives no answer. No logical reason why Frizer should not simply die when he dies. Perhaps because there is no hope in any case – they are already lashed one to the other, and the further Marlowe sinks the higher the water reaches above Frizer's head. It is no easy thing to surrender. To breathe in, and drown.

Frizer holds Marlowe's head in both hands, pressing a kiss to his lips. But it is not enough. Marlowe's kiss is unbearably patient, lingering, demanding in return that which it gives. A tyranny of tenderness. Frizer wants to bite into his face like an apple. Undo him, mouthful by mouthful. He wants to tear through this body and out the other side, like a trapped rat.

He grips Marlowe's head by the hair, biting into his mouth, pulling his lip with his teeth. Marlowe tugs free and sputters, 'What are you *doing*?' but the world has shrunk to a single pinhole of light, like staring into the sun. Suddenly, Frizer is alone – alone and grappling with a body that seems startlingly smaller and weaker than his own, easy to overpower, to climb atop the hips. The arms begin to flail and Frizer catches them; the mouth is shouting but Frizer cannot hear the noise. With one hand, Frizer tries to hold both wrists above the head, with the other, he fumbles at his own belt, the flap of his breeches. From the ceiling, he watches himself: a child pinned down in the straw. A man pinning another man to the floor.

At last, Marlowe wrestles an arm free. He slams his elbow into the side of Frizer's neck, drives a fist into his stomach. All the world turns white with pain. Frizer doubles over.

Marlowe throws him off and then kicks him with his heels, skidding backwards across the floor. They lie in place, panting, Frizer hugging himself and whimpering like a dog.

Marlowe covers his eyes and shudders violently, as if about to sob. But he seems to shake the impulse away, snarling instead, 'If you ever touch me like that again, I'll kill you. I swear to God, I'll kill you!'

Frizer paws towards him. 'Marlowe,' he murmurs, 'forgive me, I know not what—'

Marlowe sits up out of his reach, holding his rib, his head. He lurches to his feet and limps to the window, looking out. The light passes through his shirt, revealing an outline of the body beneath it: lean, dark. Knife-shaped.

'Is he still there?' Frizer asks softly, afraid of his own voice.

Marlowe takes three steps backwards. He clears his throat and whispers, quieter than ever, 'Ay. Looking straight up at me.'

He is perfectly still. And yet the very air around him seems to hum, like a cloud of flies.

'Your friend,' Marlowe says, 'could he be enticed away from his post? Just for a few minutes?'

Only gradually does Frizer understand. 'No. No, Marlowe, if I do anything that might look to them as if I helped you—'

'Give him drink, then. He'll have to step away at some point, for a piss.'

'For a *piss*, Marlowe? How far do ye think he'll go?'

'I could run. I could try.'

Anger kindles behind Frizer's ribs, as if at the impudence of an underling. 'What then? Leap out the window? Run all the way to the sea? And what of me? What do you think they'll do to me, with you gone? They'll know I told you – they'll kill me!'

To this, Marlowe says nothing. He rubs his skull in both hands, teeth bared. 'My head. Oh God, my *head*…!'

Frizer sits up on his knees. 'Please, Marlowe! You know you cannot run far. They will catch you. You'll not get so far as Deptford Creek—'

'I know!'

These words breathe life into an idea that Frizer has strived to suppress these many hours, one that he cannot put into words but has everything to do with this persistent image in his mind: of pressing down on Marlowe's face until it collapses under his weight. Until it crumbles to dust.

'What will you do?' Frizer says.

Marlowe shakes his head. He seems to change his mind several times as to what he will say. 'Do you love me?'

'Of course,' Frizer says. What else can he say?

'Then help me. Help me one way or another, but do not let them take me!'

They huddle on the floor, Marlowe with his head against the windowsill, Frizer's head resting on his thigh. Outside on the lawn, Nick sits so close beneath the window that he is like a third man in the room with them. When he clears his throat or snaps a twig in his fingers, the sound seems to come from just inches away. But he is quiet tonight. Unusually quiet.

What has he overheard? How much? If Frizer could get to him first, if he could explain, perhaps he could save himself, perhaps it is not too late...

Marlowe says, 'You will look after my papers, no?'

'I will.'

'Your master will try to take them. I know him. But if he comes for them, tell him I said he can go and fuck himself. They belong to you.' He seems to smile, but then falls into even deeper silence than before. Frizer holds his breath, feeling Marlowe holding his.

At last, Marlowe says, 'My mother, and my sisters... they should know what's become of me. But someone must go in person. Not to my father's house, to my sister Mag – Margaret Jorden, she lives nearby – she will tell the others.' His hand slides over Frizer's shoulder, down across his ribs. 'Will you go to Canterbury for me? Will you tell them?'

Robin Poley's face has come to mind. If Frizer is to survive this, then soon he will have to lie. Soon there will come a time when someone will ask him straight-on about Marlowe – about whatever happened between himself and Marlowe, for it must be clear to anyone that something did – and Frizer will have to give an answer that makes sense, that requires little if any elaboration, and closes the matter once and for all.

He realizes that it shall be simplest to say that he detests Marlowe, always has, from the moment he'd laid eyes on him. That the very thought of him invokes a loathing so absolute, so passionate that he would spit, were it not better than the man deserved. No one would raise his eyebrow at that. Hatred is safe.

Frizer hugs him tighter. 'Of course I will,' he says. For there is no sense telling a dying man the truth.

⋙❈⋘

Having drunk countless rounds to her Majesty's health, Poley finally bids farewell to their lordships, his Holiness, and every smiling sycophant in their combined retinues, and stumbles out of the Thomas-a-Beckett Inn in broad, moonless night. A clear sky, littered with stars. A stiff breeze blows through the gallows square, squeaking a winch, scattering the stench of meat left too long in the sun.

Poley rides back to Eleanor's house, grateful that at least his horse is sober. From his post by the front door, Nick pricks up like a watchdog at Poley's approach, skulking up the path to meet him as he secures his horse.

'They were fighting,' Nick whispers, with a glance at the upstairs window.

'Well. Did you look in on them?'

'No.'

'Why not?'

'I...' Nick rubs at the back of his neck. 'I know not what I heard, marry—'

'All the more reason to go up and *look*. What, you were afraid? You dared not go up, for fear of what you might see?'

Nick's face turns as red as a weal. 'Are you drunk, Master Poley?'

'*Celebrating*, Master Nick,' Poley slurs. 'John Penry's hanging went quite according to plan – the Lord Keeper's plan, that is; let us not speak of God's. Rest assured, He looked down on us today.' Poley starts towards the house, labouring to keep the swerve out of his step. 'Be a good lad and water my horse. I'll be at table.'

'Perhaps you should sleep,' Nick calls.

'When I'm dead!' Poley replies, the laziest of banalities, and yet it reminds him of the crunch of the knife through Penry's bones, a sound he can feel in his teeth.

Inside, he fumbles his way down the narrow back corridor and into the hot, reechy kitchen, where Eleanor's maids sleep huddled up in the straw. Quietly, Poley lights a taper from the smouldering hearth, returns to the dining room with his hand cupped around the flame. Having lit the candles, he goes to the cupboard for a bottle of wine, but when he turns again a face has appeared in the doorway, flush as a marigold. His own face, he thinks, for a horrified half-second. No: Ingram Frizer's face.

'You cannot sleep, Master Frizer?' Poley says, pleasantly.

Frizer shakes his head. Those eyes have been crying.

Poley takes a second glass from the cupboard, offers a chair. 'Join me. I am starved for company tonight. Hangings afflict me strangely – my tongue, rather, with such effluence of speech that I could drown a man in dry air talking about nothing at all! You do not mind, do you? I find you a most indulgent listener...'

Poley nattering on thus, Frizer sinks into the room as slowly as a drop of ink into still water, pulls out a chair and sits. He is unbuttoned, dishevelled, like a prisoner in sackcloth.

Poley pours him a drink. 'Nick tells me you have committed some of Master Marlowe's plays to memory. Is that so?'

Frizer fidgets with his fingernails.

'What was the last play you saw, before the playhouses closed?'

Frizer mumbles, 'It was about a Roman general... and a Moor... They cut off the daughter's hands, and they cut out her tongue...'

But Poley takes no interest in this answer. 'The last play I saw was by Master Marlowe,' he says. '*Edward II*. You did not see it, did you?'

Frizer shakes his head.

'Pity. I doubt you shall have another opportunity.'

'I read it.'

Poley blinks, impressed. 'You *did*?'

'He... he let me read it.' He is scratching something at the base of his throat: some sort of reddish mark, like a scrape. Or a scar.

Poley waits, but whatever Frizer has come here to say has evidently grown so large that it stops his mouth, burrowing out of his throat like a rat. 'How is Master Marlowe?' Poley asks, sipping his wine.

'Asleep.'

'He does not know that you are here with me?'

Frizer answers him not, scratching away.

'Master Frizer, have you spoken with Master Skeres about tomorrow?'

Frizer exhales a sound as if he will cry, but instead a deathly blankness comes over his eyes. Damn Nick! Poley should never have trusted him to keep his gob shut around Frizer, his beloved 'little brother'. There's no undoing it now. Anyway, Frizer would not be here had he any intention of resisting what's to come, would he? Suppose he might have come upon Poley now, by dark of night, with some madcap notion of stabbing him to death and putting an end to it all... But that is not in the boy's nature, is it? Ingram Frizer is no killer.

'Have you spoken with Master Marlowe?' Poley asks, sweetly.

'No. But he knows. I did not tell him. But he knows something is, something is wrong.' The Adam's apple bobs in his throat. 'He was going to stay awake, in case Nick should step away, but he fell asleep. He was going to run. He still... wants to run.'

'Ah.' Poley smiles, though his every nerve swells with anger. Of course, the gutless brat is lying; obviously he has told Marlowe everything. Poley never told Babington the truth, but he wonders now what might have happened if he had, in one of those moments when he'd wanted to, desperately. Perhaps he would have eventually found himself in the Spymaster's office, just as Frizer sits here now, insisting, *Nay, I never told him anything, I swear!* Could anything be more wretched, more cowardly? Sir Francis would have had Poley's neck snapped out of sheer disgust!

'Stay here,' Poley says. He finishes his drink, leaves the room perfectly sober. At the door he pauses to look outside, just long enough to stab a furious glance into Nick's worried eyes, and then turns upstairs, down the corridor to the room where Eleanor lies abed. He squats at her bedside – pausing to examine her face, for he knows how women feign sleep – then reaches under the bed, towards a glint of light on metal, muscular and viscid, like a heart: his pistol.

Sunlight beats through Kit's eyelids. 'Tis so bright he cannot peel his eyes open; they are gummed shut with light as if with blood. He has slept upright, his head craned back on the windowsill, his neck stiff. Half-blind, he tries to move but his legs are asleep and he tumbles into the wall, striking a sore spot on the back of his head.

Frizer is no longer beside him.

'Frizer?' Kit murmurs, to the room. No answer comes.

Kit pulls himself up to the window ledge by his elbows. The sun has only just summited distant Greenwich Hill, a grim, carnelian disk floating in a sallow haze of smoke. Gulls roost atop the *Golden Hind*'s masts like pole-sitters. Directly below Kit's window, a stool stands empty by the front door, a horn mug overturned in the grass beside it.

'Frizer!' Kit struggles to his feet. 'He's gone!' But he can see that the room is empty ere he has finished speaking. The bed is unslept-in, the curtains untouched; his bag lies on the table where he'd left it.

Frizer is gone. Gone, and did not wake him.

Kit deserves this. Hypocrite that he is, he deserves this. For he is no sceptic, not as he has always pretended to be – he is a beast of Faith, its willing slave, created out of credulous clay for the sport of ill-intentioned men. Who would pity such an animal?

But no, there's no time for despair. Kit spins around foolishly, as if Frizer shall suddenly appear, having been here from the start, invisible: *Look at me, Marlowe; can you not see me?* Frizer's head upon his thigh, his slow, soft breathing. That shall have to be the end of it. Kit feels buried in time, the seconds heavy upon his chest, moving too slow, far too slow. It should not have ended like this. But the end comes how it will.

He grabs his bag, throws open the door and sprints for the stairs. He can outrun the fat man if necessary, head south into the hills past Blackheath, take cover in the Kentish hedgerows, keep running until the land runs out underfoot, and then swim, and drown when he can swim no more.

Even from atop the stairs, he senses that the front door hangs open below. He can hear birds, see the fan of daylight on the ceiling. But the moment the door comes into view, Kit halts.

Frizer stands upon the threshold, a rigid wooden doll. The world beyond him is calm, bright, callously ordinary: a low tidal thrum, a distant ship's bell, sparrows and gulls.

Fresh tear-trails cut through the faint tarnish of soot on Frizer's face, a bright drop clinging to his jaw.

A hard object touches the back of Kit's skull.

'You may close the door now, Master Frizer,' Poley says.

Kit drops his bag. Darkness shunts across his eyelids, and the latch clicks.

Poley says, '"Hell hath no limits, nor is circumscribed
In one self place, for where we are is Hell,
And where Hell is must we ever be."'

Metal presses harder into the back of Kit's head, urging him to descend. '*Faustus* is my favourite of your works,' Poley goes on. 'But I could speak you a bit of *Tamburlaine* too, if you put drink in me.'

Kit has naught but a scream between his ears, and therefore says nothing.

30 May 1593

Zero

❧❦❧

> Then I perceive
> That heading is one, and hanging the other,
> And death is all.

CHRISTOPHER MARLOWE, *EDWARD II*, C. 1593

32

ROBIN PRESSES MARLOWE INTO a seat at the dining table. Widow Bull, her raw face scrubbed clean of paint, stands in the corner by the garden door, shouting. Several seconds pass before Frizer understands her words: 'Nay, put it away! I'll not have that *thing* drawn in my house!'

She means the pistol. Robin approaches her and stands close, speaking mollifying words, the gun's aim alighting, as if by chance, against her heart. Marlowe sits with his head bowed, his knee jumping under the table. Something nudges Frizer from behind and he turns to see Nick lurching into the room, Marlowe's bag slung over his shoulder. His gaze is brief, yet baleful.

'Master Frizer,' Robin calls.

Widow Bull has fled the room. Robin indicates the chair at the head of the table, the one with the window behind it. The pistol wags in his hand like a switch.

Frizer drifts forward. Beads of sweat run down his scalp, the back of his neck. When he arrives at the head chair, he understands not one word of what is said to him, but Robin takes his wrist and wedges the grip of the pistol into his limp hand, moulds his fist around the dog and slides it back with an icy *click*—

'No no no no no no,' Frizer sputters. 'I cannot, I nay—'

Robin turns him down into the chair like a screw, shushing him.

'No, no, no—I pray you—'

Robin wrenches Frizer's arms up off the table, smacks the underside of his fists, twists his shoulders until the barrel is aimed directly at Marlowe's head.

Robin points. 'You keep that on him.' A slap jolts Frizer in the middle of his back. His arms quiver at the weight of the gun. Its smell is like the taste of sickness, the taste of blood coughed up. Beyond the end of the barrel, Marlowe looks on him in rapid, sidelong glances, vibrating as he breathes, opening and closing his eyes. As if to say to himself, *This is happening now. This is no dream.*

'Now then.' Robin moves to the chair across the table from Marlowe. With one hand, he upends Marlowe's bag, dumping the contents. Sheaves of paper slap onto the floor. He sits. It seems he is about to say one thing, but after a moment of consideration, changes his mind. 'I would like to know something, before we go forward.'

Frizer realizes that Robin is looking directly at him, his close-lipped sneer scornful, betrayed. He knows. He must know.

But he speaks to Marlowe instead. 'What was it that inspired you to run?'

Frizer blurts out, 'I told you he just said it, he just said it out of nowhere—'

'I asked Master Marlowe.' Robin shrugs at him. 'What planted the idea in your head?'

Marlowe's attention hovers on a corner of the ceiling, as if he is gazing down upon this scene from that vantage. His lips move but no words escape, only a high breath of pain, a kind of laugh.

Robin sighs through his nostrils. He sits back in his chair and looks from Marlowe to Frizer and back again, his bloodshot eyes anatomizing, stripping flesh from bone. It seems he will speak venom, but suddenly he throws his head back into a great yawn, at the tail end of which he murmurs, into his fist, 'Complications!'

Frizer flinches as Widow Bull bangs into the room, accompanied by two serving-girls carrying bread and wine and a wedge of white, watery cheese. All business ceases while the women are present, fluttering around the table in their starched skirts, as silent as ghosts. Marlowe turns his cheek on the widow as she leans in to pour out a sputter of dark red wine, only a portion of which finds its way into the goblet. When finished she backs away, nearly scoops her two maids off the floor, and retreats into the rear of the house.

'What happens now?' Marlowe rasps.

Robin seems to deliberate upon this question at length, like a judge upon a plea for clemency. 'We wait.'

'How long?'

'Not long. They shall come before midday, I expect.'

'And then what?'

'What's to come for you, I cannot say. I *can* tell you what is happening upriver at Whitehall, as we speak: the clerk of the Star Chamber is reading Richard Baines's letter aloud before an audience of thirteen sober gentlemen, all seated around their big table like teeth around a tongue. Thirteen noble fellows fuming and sweating and twisting their handkerchiefs, as they silently ponder what sort of fate is deserved by the creature the letter describes. Should they make an example of him? Should they bury him, like a witch-bottle, where he may do no more harm? Do they dare *hang* him – invite him to the stage, for a final turn?'

Robin pauses, as if in hope that Marlowe might pronounce sentence upon himself, but Marlowe is silent, head bowed. Frizer can see the blood leaving his face.

'They say you are the Devil himself,' Robin goes on.

Marlowe grunts. 'They flatter me, then.'

'Is it flattering to you?'

'I prefer it over the alternative.'

'Over being mistaken for *God*?' Robin chuckles.

Marlowe half-smiles, as if at some interior jest. 'Over being taken for a good Christian man,' he says. 'A "godly" man. I would fain rather be the Devil than that.'

Robin seems unsettled. He makes a casual, aimless scan of the papers to his right. 'I assure you, Master Marlowe, you are in no danger of being mistaken. Certainly not by anyone in this room.'

'Is the Word of God so weak that it needs defending from the likes of me?' Marlowe sits forward. 'A *coward*, is your God. A fainting, cringing coward, just like your Queen, that hateful crone. She and your God are the same, so jealous of their reputations that they would rather drown this world in blood than admit to their own weakness—'

Nick murmurs, 'I think you'd better stop him, Master Poley—'

But Marlowe goes on. 'Tyrants they are, and like all tyrants, cowards, just like the Pope and his horde of slathering pederasts, just like the hypocrite Puritans penning their miserable screeds! And what do they fear, these tyrants, what do they all fear, but that some enterprising wight shall tear the mantle off their fraudulence? Why do they kill, *why does any man kill*, except he is afraid, afraid of his own death? Even God, the coward, slaughterer of His own children, He is afraid to die because He knows He *can*, just like His ministers, just like that bloody-minded hag in Greenwich – I spit on her, I shit on your God, I'll see them both in hell!'

'Shut your cursed mouth!' Nick bellows. 'Shut it or I'll shut it for ye!'

Marlowe falls silent. His body is rigid, his head bowed as if to the axe.

Robin clears his throat. Frizer meets his cold eyes, lifts the drooping pistol and obediently aims it at Marlowe's cheek.

'Well,' Robin says, to Marlowe, 'perhaps you *are* the Devil.'

'Perhaps I am,' Marlowe says. 'Had you rather not take a little care with how you use me, in that case?'

'I do not like this, Master Poley,' Nick says.

Robin holds out a hand to shush him. A smirk pulls at Robin's lips, doubtful yet curious, as if pressed into a game he knows to be rigged. 'I suppose we had better establish some proof, then. Convince me you are the Devil. Show me your power.'

In the air between Robin and Marlowe there comes a charge, like the smell that lingers after lightning strikes close. Frizer senses his own lips moving: *Please, please, please, please.* No voice, still the silence echoes with his begging, a soft patter like rain on a windowsill.

He should put the barrel under his own chin, and pull the trigger.

'Master Frizer has spent a full ten days in your company,' Robin says, flinging a gesture in his direction. 'He looks much the worse for wear, does he not, Master Skeres?'

Frizer must squeeze his eyelids to see Nick, leaned into the doorjamb with his hands knotted into the small of his back, his expression grave.

'I never saw Ingram thus,' Nick mumbles.

'Ten days with the Devil!' Robin proclaims with satisfaction, as if he's only just thought of a good title for a play. 'And surely it was Master Marlowe's diabolical influence that brought you to this wretched state? Surely 'twas he that has made you weak?'

'I never said,' Frizer gasps, his mouth almost too dry to speak, 'I never said w-weak—'

'It hardly matters now, does it?' Robin speaks over him. 'Little harm has been done. If I were to ask you to pull that trigger just now, Master Frizer, you would not hesitate, is't not so?'

Frizer's head sweeps back and forth, *no*, though the word will not come to his tongue.

'Is't not so?'

'Ay,' Frizer croaks. ''Tis so!' He sinks towards the table, but Robin snaps his fingers, starting him upright. Marlowe's eyes are clenched shut, as if awaiting the shot. Praying for it, perhaps. Last night, before Frizer had crept downstairs to meet with Robin, he'd had an opportunity to end this.

Marlowe had slept so deeply that only his breath betrayed the life in him. Then and there, Frizer should have killed both Marlowe and himself. He should have cut Marlowe's throat while he was sleeping, he should have stabbed himself through the heart.

Robin rises from his chair. He approaches Frizer with his hand held out, fingers beckoning. 'Give it to me, now.'

Frizer hesitates. He could kill Robin, this very instant – *that* would put an end on it – aim the barrel straight up at his face and watch it disappear... or miss, or fumble, and undo himself utterly.

He surrenders the gun, lays his head on his arms and heaves bruising, vile sobs, choking on his own breath, his own snot. There is naught to do now but preserve himself.

'He is a monster!' Frizer wails. 'Nay but he's the Devil himself! I swear it! On my soul, I swear it!'

⚜

Through the window, ivy leaves glisten, scale-like, along the garden walls, rattled by a sluggish rain. Widow Bull stands in a pool of pecking chickens, scattering corn from her pockets. At some point, she stoops down, gathers the fattest bird into her arms. For a minute or two, she only stands there, stroking seed-pearls of rain from the bird's back; and then, with one motion, takes the hen's neck in her fist and flings its body backwards over her arm, dead.

Inside, Robin reads *Hero & Leander*. Aloud. Frizer lays his head upon the table, his hands over his ears. Robin's mouth, Robin's tongue jawing at the words feels like a violation, 'delicious' gliding off into a forked hiss that slithers coldly down Frizer's spine.

'Exquisitely lewd,' Poley remarks.

'Fit for the privy of a bawdy house!' Nick adds.

Marlowe says nothing at all.

The spatter of raindrops on the glazing gradually fades.

"'It lies not in our power to love or hate,

For will in us is overruled by fate,

When two are stripped, long ere the course begin

We wish that one should lose, the other win;

And one especially do we affect

Of two gold ingots, like in each respect.

The reason no man knows: let it suffice,

What we behold is censured by our eyes.

Where both deliberate, the love is slight;

Whoever loved, that loved not at first—'"

A knock resounds down the corridor. All present hold their breaths and listen. Nick starts upright, his head swivelling to Frizer, Robin, the front door. 'Is that them?' he says, prematurely relieved.

Robin shrugs with his head, looking at Marlowe as he says, 'Let's see.'

He leaves the room. Widow Bull, having just set the leftovers of yesterday's pie upon the table, picks up her skirt and flees into the back of the house. Nick turns and drifts halfway down the corridor, hands at his sides. Marlowe and Frizer are momentarily unobserved: Marlowe with his eyes closed, his face so drained of blood that even his lips are white.

He might have destroyed Frizer today with a word. Instead, he has destroyed himself. It cannot be out of love that he has done this. To love Frizer, Marlowe would have to forgive him, and Frizer has done an unforgivable thing. Perhaps he pities him. A miserable thing, pity, and yet to have even so little from Marlowe would be like manna. One word from his lips, if 'tis the right one, would mean absolution.

'I'm sorry,' Frizer rasps, the sound barely escaping him. 'I'm sorry, I'm sorry, I'm sorry—'

'Shut your God-damned mouth.'

The reddened eyes meet Frizer's just long enough for him to feel their heat, and then drop. Regret? Despair? He knows not what he sees in Marlowe, only that it is at the end, nothing will come after it.

Marlowe draws in a stiff breath, sighs. 'You cannot save yourself this way, you poor fool. They have you forever now.'

Poley hesitates, his hand on the doorlatch. He can see Dick Topcliffe's face even through the door. That doggish, sneering mouth. Wine-stained lips and teeth.

Now, little bird, let us see whether we can find your cunt.

Poley opens the door with his eyes closed. But there is no Topcliffe at all waiting for him, only a boy of twelve or thirteen, strawberry-cheeked, a rim of sweat around his hat. A blue-eyed pony stands snorting in the grass behind him, the reins dangling loose down its neck.

'From Whitehall,' the boy says, and for one moment Poley anticipates a bullet through the forehead. He is handed a letter he has never seen before, though it is sealed with his own customary bolt, written in his very own handwriting:

> *Alas, my poore syster is sicke & I pray you come <u>not</u> to visit her, come straight to <u>my</u> house at sunrise & bringe with you the physick you promised.*

Poley turns the letter over and back like an idiot marvelling at a shard of mirror. On the reverse, a postscript is inscribed in another hand altogether, hidden along a crease:

> *Where is Dicke Topcliffe, Robyn?*

The second hand is Thomas Walsingham's.

Poley startles himself, and the boy too, by laughing aloud, though that reliable armour is of no comfort to him now. 'Tis more like a twinge, a tic, rearing up rampant and bare-arsed whether he would have it or no, his lips pulled back so wide that he imagines his skull will slide out if they open any wider.

'Any reply?' the boy squeaks.

Poley lets the air out of his laughter with a groan, raises his hand and settles it upon the boy's shoulder. A little weed of a thing, where did Walsingham find him? Some minister or secretary's nephew? A sluttish stable-hand? Poley would like to bite off his nose and spit it into the grass.

Instead, he squints up at the sky, and the lad turns to squint with him. From this angle the sun cannot be seen.

'Tell me,' Poley says, 'has the eclipse begun yet?'

The front door slams, making Frizer jump in his seat. After a little pause, Robin re-enters the dining room at a speedy clip, alone, letting out a horsey huff of breath. 'It seems we have a little wait ahead of us.'

Nick baulks. 'Look, I've been up all damned night!'

'Well, it would appear that Master Topcliffe is preoccupied with the session at Whitehall at the moment. Another hour or two, at the most.' Robin had previously arranged Marlowe's papers into several stacks around his place at the table. He now stands fuming over his work, like a cook before a feast that he's only just learned shall go uneaten.

Nick says, 'Marry, I'll need a rest before long, and a piss—'

'He'll be here before suppertime!' Robin snaps, and then follows it with a graceless chuckle, rubbing at his temples. He takes up Marlowe's bag and digs through it, turning up a cut quill and an inkpot; takes a sheet of paper from one of the piles – a page of *Hero & Leander*, perhaps, or *Tamburlaine*, or *Edward II* – and hastily scribbles out a message on the verso without sitting down or giving the ink time to dry.

Again, he leaves, and is gone less than a minute ere he charges back into the room, snapping his inky fingers at Nick.

'Get him up. We'll go outside. There's an eclipse today, you know. A rare sight.'

Nick takes a nervous step or two towards Marlowe but then halts, eyeing him up and down as if he were a snake poised to strike. Marlowe is not even looking at him.

'Pick him up, Nick.'

Nick makes no move. Robin scoffs, jabs the barrel of his gun into Marlowe's cheek and hoists him to his feet by a sleeve, shoving him out the back door.

Frizer rises to follow, weak-kneed. In the henyard, Robin shoves Marlowe so hard he nearly trips, but then catches the back of his doublet, stopping his fall. He spins Marlowe to face the white sky directly above Widow Bull's house, points, and says, 'There,' to be sure he dares look nowhere else. This done, Robin walks half the length of the garden backwards in search of the best view, a hand shielding his eyes. He winces at the light, turns away, attempts another peek. 'Will you look at that?' he says. And to Marlowe: 'Shall we discourse on the movement of the spheres, as Faustus and Mephistopheles did?'

Frizer brims his hand over his eyes. He'd thought that the sun and moon might appear together, overlapping like two coins, gold and silver. But through the thick clouds only the sun shows itself, albeit with a morsel bitten out of its backside, the gloomy day sprawled indifferently around it. Upon looking away, it takes longer than he'd expected for his vision to return, seeing the world through a rondel of molten glass that slowly cools and clears.

Marlowe and Robin stand shoulder-to-shoulder. Both look to the sky through cracks between their fingers, Robin elated, as though the heavens have put on this show for him alone; Marlowe humbled, diffident. Were Frizer and he alone now, Marlowe would have so much to say, with his erring stars and parallaxes. He would point up at the heavens and draw his finger across the sky and explain how it all functions in that perorating way of his, and Frizer would heed nary a word, so consumed with gratitude to be with him, alive with him, anywhere but here.

From across the garden, Poley only feigns to look at the sky, thinking on the message that Walsingham's boy carries, bound for the Marshalsea, scribbled on a page from *Doctor Faustus*:

> *The missyve you receeved this morninge was a fraud, I await you in Dettford & heere is the proof – I have the man.*

Belike the boy will not deliver it to Topcliffe at all. He'll take it, along with the generous gratuity Poley had paid him, back to his master in Whitehall.

Walsingham is a far better forger than Poley would ever have guessed, he'll give him that. Better than necessary to fool an imbecile like Topcliffe. *Come to my house*, the letter had said! Imagine it: Topcliffe swarming Poley's house in St Helen's with all his instruments in tow, banging down the door, threatening God knows what sort of violence upon the servants— Or worse, Topcliffe riding for Poley's other house in Surrey, several hours from London, a place Poley visits barely more than once a year. By afternoon, the wicked cur shall be terrorizing Poley's poor wife and children while his creatures ransack every room, rip up all the floorboards and smash holes in every wall—

But most likely, Topcliffe will have taken but a quick scan of Walsingham's forgery, perceived some knavery afoot, and done just as he'd promised, yesterday afternoon: washed his hands of the whole business.

Now the sun and moon have overlapped, meaning that Walsingham may well have done something foolish already, before the Council. Ingram Frizer – that spineless jade! – were he not so slippery, Poley could have sent him to

Whitehall with false news of Marlowe's death; were Frizer not so treacherous, so craven, Poley could have sent him to the Marshalsea, and had him beg Topcliffe to come back with him. Poley cannot send Nick away; he needs him here. He cannot go himself. He's trapped, waiting for sunset, when Phelippes had said he could expect the Council's full might to fall on Deptford.

In a way this disaster, and all the horrors yet to come, is all Frizer's fault. Look at him now: so miserable, so piteous; eyes dribbling tears the way an old whore dribbles piss! Poley ought to blow his brains out into Marlowe's face.

'A sorry way to end your career,' Poley sneers, 'in farce.'

'I know not what you mean, Poley,' Marlowe replies, smug.

'They said the same thing of Anthony Babington, you remember – that he was the Devil, or possessed by the Devil – but of course he was neither. Neither are you.'

'Your friend does not seem so certain of that.'

'It matters not what that porridge-brained swine thinks of ye. You are here with me until this business is brought to an end, one way or another.'

'One way or another now, is it?'

Poley is silenced. For ay, the ship has veered so far off course there's no telling where it will land. Both Marlowe and himself may be bound for the same fate: to hang by the wrists and ankles behind Topcliffe's walls, naked, blindfolded, till they beg for death.

'I want to know something,' Poley begins, 'about *Edward II*. In watching it, at times, it had seemed almost as though I was but watching ordinary folk – well, mere mortals, anyway – go about their lives. How plainly they spoke. How banal, redundant and futile were their actions...'

Marlowe rubs his eyes and squints, at first in contempt, which then cools into something more like sadness. 'You are not the first to say so.'

Poley is surprised at having been beaten to this punch. He is loath to imagine by whom. 'Well. I've often wondered whether Edward and Gaveston and the rest were, indeed, ordinary men. Perhaps men you have known, intimately, by other names...'

'There's Lightborne, for example,' Marlowe says, with a sidelong glance.

'Oh?'

'He is partly based on *you*.'

Poley's smile spreads. 'Only partly?' he says, but Marlowe does not laugh. He looks sad, even pitying, at which Poley begins to wonder how much of himself he has exposed just now, how far into his heart Marlowe has seen. He regrets his own choice of words: 'intimately'.

'Who told you about the ring?' Poley asks.

'Baines.'

'Ah.' A sourness rises to Poley's mouth. He would have preferred no answer at all over one so mundane. But what had he expected to discover, some supernatural communion between himself, Marlowe, Babington? What a child he is, what a weak, self-deceiving child! The dead do not commune. The dead do not forgive.

'Poley,' Marlowe murmurs, gently, 'you can let me go.'

Poley shakes his head. Marlowe must die, which is all Walsingham had wanted from the first. Phelippes shall not be pleased; still, he'll have little choice but to let the matter lie. The Lord Keeper had promised half for Marlowe's corpse, had he not: one hundred and fifty pounds? Not enough to buy back Topcliffe's favour. Not enough for a diamond. All for nothing, all ruined, and by who else but Ingram Frizer, that snivelling whelp, whose image Marlowe battens upon the way a suicide sucks poison!

Poley should gut the little cretin with his own knife. Show Marlowe how it feels. Rub his face in the cavity and snarl, *Look – look upon his steaming insides, his yellow guts, look upon the last beat of his heart! This is how they made me watch!*

Kit detects a crack in Robin Poley's so carefully polished shell, revealing a hint of soft, jellied insides, into which he would dearly like to stick a knife and twist. But he must be gentle, calm, mannered. He must speak as if to soothe a mad dog, for that is what Robin Poley is becoming.

'Who else knows that I am here?' Kit goes on. 'Walsingham would never speak of it; he is too afraid. Topcliffe shall put this matter behind him for a trifle. If they find me here with you, you'll not fare well by it—'

'Master Frizer lied to me last night,' Poley interrupts. 'I had thought, going into this, that he would walk away no worse than twenty pounds richer when it was over. But now, I know not what trouble he might cause in the future.'

Kit's gaze darts across the yard. Frizer stands near the back door, staring back at him with bands of half-dried tears shining on either cheek. Even now, Kit feels as if there were no distance between them at all, as if his arms were around him, his face buried in Frizer's neck; his hand around Frizer's throat, fighting not to squeeze.

'What matters it to you what becomes of the wretched boy?' Poley goes on, needling. 'He would sooner see you dance the Tyburn jig than risk a hair on his head for you.'

This stings just as intended. Kit looks away. 'You would not give yourself another body to bury,' he says.

'Ha! No one here shall be buried today. Your corpse alone is worth a hundred and fifty pounds! And as for Master Frizer, the river runs deep through Deptford, though not so deep as many suppose, so thick is the bottom with bones.'

'I do not think the other fellow would be pleased with that.'

Poley scoffs. 'Oh, Nick? True, he loves that boy like a favourite dog. But he loves *me* as the dog loves his master.' His hand touches Kit's shoulder, a warm imprint of four fingers, a fatherly smack. He then slips away and poses himself upon the bench as if for a portrait, the pistol hooked over one knee.

Frizer has not moved. If he sees the panic in Kit's face, he shows it not. There's nothing in Frizer's eyes but an echo of the question he'd asked last night: *Why in hell should I live?*

Kit regrets not answering him. How had he let himself be dumbstruck, in that worst of all moments? He would have said, *You must live because I love you – because you must be avenged – because to live is a form of vengeance, when so many have sought to destroy you—* But Kit, also, wants to live. Each and every atomy of his body burns against death like a star against the darkness; not one mote of it wants to die. Death frightens him not, only dying: to have to face, alone, that unravelling of the self, to become a child, an infant, an impulse, nothing.

"'The light of the body is the eye—'"

Kit nearly slaps himself. Suffer what he will, he shall not surrender his anger. 'Tis the only true power, the only true courage he has ever had. He'll run himself upon the knives of his enemies. He'll spit blood in their eyes!

He turns to face the far side of the garden. Above the brick wall, from every visible window in every neighbouring house, pale faces burst forth in clusters like anemones: men, women and children, squinting through their fingers or from beneath their hands, upon the fearful conjunction of sun and moon.

Witnesses.

33

THE MOON'S FINGERNAIL HAS slid out of the sun's eye, unwatched. Frizer looks up from his place on the ground, among the pecking chickens, to find an unexceptional day come upon them, the sky over the garden a dull membrane of eggshell blue, the erring moon now invisible. The world seems diminished in such an ordinary light, as if some singular opportunity has come and gone.

Marlowe has spent the past hour seated in a patch of weedy grass with his back against the garden wall, his eyes darting cease-lessly between Robin and Nick. Only occasionally does he glance to Frizer. Robin remains slumped on the bench like a Roman at a feast, though one with neither appetite nor good humour, jaw tight, eyes hard, tapping his fingers to an ever-slower rhythm. In all this time he has not said a word, and so alien is silence to his demeanour that it reeks, like a candle just blown out.

'Something's gone wrong.'

Nick has squatted down at Frizer's right shoulder, close enough to whisper. Widow Bull's roasted laying-hen hangs on his breath.

Nick nods in Marlowe's direction. 'I think no one's coming for him.'

Frizer dares not look.

Nick knuckles Frizer's arm. 'Will you wake up, man? I need you to help me think! This has gone on too long. The master must have done something, at the Council meeting.' He darts another glance at Marlowe, speaking even lower: 'If you and *him*—I know not what. S'blood, man, I know nothing at all! But if you know something, or *did* something, you can tell me; I'll not be angry, I promise. Hell, that devil's had you bewitched, he has—'

'Do you have grievances, Master Skeres?' Robin says from the bench, wearily.

'I only want to know what in hell's happening!' Nick stands up, flailing his arms. 'Where's Topcliffe? Where's the coin you promised me? How long are we to sit here greasing our pricks? Till my master returns? Till the Lord Keeper gets wind of all this? What do ye suppose this would look like to *him*?'

Robin leans forward with his elbows on his knees, rubs his face in his hands. 'Oh, mutiny!'

'Mutiny? Ay, if you want it that way. I say, let's do as my master asked, put a bullet in him and be done with it!'

''Tis not so simple a matter, my lad.'

'What in God's name is so complicated about it? You've heard him, you've seen what he's done to Ingram! Belike 'tis not safe to be in his company so long, Lord knows what he might do to us!' Nick seems to feel Marlowe's glare, turning to snarl at him, 'Stop *looking* at me!'

Robin springs up from the bench, takes Nick by the arm and draws him into the furthest corner of the garden. There's a touch in his eyes of a man nearing his limit – of patience, of forbearance, of sanity even. They stand close, arguing in hushed voices. In a pocket of silence, Robin slides a meaningful look in Frizer's direction. Nick glances at Frizer twice, first in perplexity, then horror.

He backs away from Robin. 'No! No, no, I'll not hear of it!'

'Come back here, boy.'

'I could never do that,' Nick says. 'I could never let you do that!'

Robin says nothing, though his jaw grinds, his eyes wide, frantic.

'How *dare* you, Master Poley?' Nick starts to turn. 'Ingram, come, we're leaving.'

'Leave and you get not one penny from me, Nick,' Robin snarls, his hand on the butt of his pistol.

'Oh, up your arse with it!' Nick says.

'What will you do now, Nick? Go back to washing Walsingham's dirty linens? With *him*? You trust *him* to keep silent to your master about all this treachery of yours? Even now, knowing exactly what sort of creature he is?'

Nick cries out, on the verge of tears, 'He is my *friend*!'

Frizer feels a rush in his ears like water, or blood. Ten feet away, Robin and Nick go on arguing whether or not to kill him. But this is not fear that he feels, is it? In a way, it could be called relief. Death renders all things alike, so Marlowe and he will be the same again. They will both burn in one fire.

Frizer ventures a step towards Marlowe, and then another, and another. All the while, Marlowe rises also, like Frizer's own shadow on a wall, his eyes fish-hooked to Frizer's eyes.

'Marlowe,' Frizer whispers, 'I—'

Marlowe's arm swings; his fist stops Frizer's mouth, a blow that rattles him from eye-tooth to skull-cap. Frizer stumbles backwards and collapses onto his side, blinded as if by lightning.

'You treacherous coward!' All of Deptford seems to resound with Marlowe's voice. 'Twenty pounds! Twenty pounds for my fucking life!'

Marlowe lurches forward, about to lunge. But from across the garden, Robin rushes in, launching himself at Marlowe's back. Marlowe and he tumble to the ground in a heap.

'Help me!' Robin shouts.

At last, Nick also springs to life. He strides forward, takes hold of Marlowe's head by a fistful of hair and pulls back, levering him onto his knees.

Marlowe spits into Frizer's face. 'You do not deserve this, you poisonous bastard! I have never lied to you, not once! You do not deserve this!' He would say more, it seems, but a sob stops his voice.

Frizer cannot move even to wipe his face. He watches as Nick turns up his lip at the man he holds by the hair, finally flinging Marlowe down in disgust. Marlowe bows into his hands. For a second or two, he only goes on crying, but then he rears his head and lets forth a battery of screams, wordless, and even louder than before.

Nick and Robin exchange a look of panic. For one second, neither moves, but then Nick snatches Robin's pistol from its leather hanging and takes aim at the back of Marlowe's head. Frizer covers his eyes, but the only sound that comes is the dull *thunk* of metal against bone. When he looks again, Marlowe lies prone upon the ground.

A woman shrieks, though she is quickly stifled. Widow Bull stands at the garden door, her hands clasped over the mouth of one of her wide-eyed serving-girls. Frizer, too, presses a hand over his sore mouth. A tooth wiggles loose near the front, leeching warm, coppery blood.

'Stop crying, Ingram!' Nick snarls, though his own face is red and twisted. 'Stop your damned crying!'

Robin harrumphs, waggling his fingers at Nick. Reluctantly, Nick hands over the gun.

Widow Bull grabs her skirt and marches across the yard to Robin. 'You put a stop to this at once! What will the neighbours think of it? What will the *neighbours* think?'

Indeed, the evening has opened upon them suddenly, full of whispers and muffled voices. Figures lean out of nearly every window of the three nearest houses to the west like spectators in a gallery: old men, young men, women, children. Frizer clambers to his feet, taking in what they must see: three men and one woman in the garden. A fourth man facedown in the dirt.

Robin too takes it in, turning in a full circle. He looks as if he might laugh.

'If Topcliffe is not coming then you must be rid of him!' Widow Bull rasps. 'This cannot happen here, Robin. This house is meant to be a refuge! I have a reputation to protect!'

'Shut your God-damned mouth, you witch!' Frizer snarls.

Robin slaps him across the sore side of his face. Shakes a finger at his nose. 'Civility, Master Frizer. I would be a little kinder towards women, had I a cunt where my arsehole should be.'

Marlowe's head lolls, ragdoll-like, as they lift him off the ground, Nick at the shoulders and Frizer at the legs. Hastily, they labour upstairs, while behind them, Widow Bull and Robin snipe at one another like children. As they come upon the door of the room where Frizer and Marlowe had spent the night, a maid darts out like a quail from a bush. She has left the room tidy and dim, the closed shutters admitting only a strip of fading daylight.

Widow Bull scrambles up the fine coverlet in her arms just before Nick and Frizer heave Marlowe's limp body onto the enormous bed. She then turns on Robin as he enters, taking a tone both scolding and deferential, like a steward admonishing his master over some needless expense. 'Now, how much longer do you think it will be before the constables arrive?'

Frizer cradles Marlowe's head, blood seeping, warm, into his breeches. Across the room, Nick and Widow Bull have cornered Robin by the door. Both appear to tower over him, even Widow Bull; he looks small and futile, as if held by the scruff of the neck.

'Take them down to the river,' Widow Bull goes on. 'Do whatever you will, but you must be rid of them!'

'I cannot simply "be rid of" them, Eleanor,' Robin growls, 'now that half the neighbourhood has seen them!'

'Well, you must do something! The constables—'

'The constables are nothing to us. We'll say it was a drunk-ards' quarrel, nothing more, surely not the first to occur under your roof! Now *listen* to me: I have sent word to Topcliffe. He may well have only just received it—'

'To hell with Topcliffe!' Nick shouts. 'I want my share of the master's money, which *you* promised me, and then I want out – my share, and Ingram's too!'

Marlowe turns his face against Frizer's thigh and murmurs something. Frizer hears his own name. Not Frizer. 'Ingram.' Marlowe has never called him this before, and a pained smile pulls at his lips as he says it. They are strangers, feeling one another's names upon their tongues for the first time: 'Ingram'.

'Kit.' Such a little name for such a big man.

Marlowe reaches up, cups the back of Frizer's neck. Gently, he pulls, and Frizer bends down until their foreheads touch. Frizer holds Marlowe's face in both hands. He runs his fingers over the lips, his thumbs over the cheekbones, the eyelids, the way a blind man commits a face to memory, as if it were hewn out of ice and melting fast.

'I'm sorry,' Frizer sputters. 'I'm sorry, I'm sorry, I'm sorry…'

'Witnesses,' Marlowe says. His eyes look straight into Frizer's eyes. 'He cannot hurt you now.'

Frizer draws back slightly, misunderstanding. Marlowe pulls him close again, his lips to Frizer's ear. 'When the constables come, the Council's men will not be long behind them. They shall take you and the others to Deptford jail. I shall go to the Marshalsea.' He tightens his grip on Frizer's neck. 'When they question you, you know nothing. You were here on your master's orders. You do not know me; you have barely spoken with me. Understand? And I—I will never breathe your name.'

Frizer need not ask what will become of Marlowe, in the Marshalsea, and after that. He is thinking of the voids in the walls. The scaffold, and the jeering crowds. The disjointing axes, the butchering knives. That this body should ever be torn apart. That a thing like Marlowe could ever be unmade.

Marlowe's hand moves to the back of Frizer's head, his fingers in his hair, a grip that is somehow fierce and tender, both at once. 'Live,' he whispers, almost too faint to hear. 'Live!'

Frizer shakes his head. But Marlowe's eyes are closed; he sees him not.

Marlowe lets Frizer go, sinking deeper into the bed. Without opening his eyes, he murmurs, "'The light of the body is the eye—'" but breaks off sharply, his face tightening as if with pain. Yet the words seem to force their way out of him, hoarse and fast: "'The light of the body is the eye, therefore when thine eye is single, then thy whole body shall be light, even as when a candle doth light thee...'" It goes on. Headlong, he plummets through the verse, sometimes breaking against a word, sometimes repeating or doubling back: "'... thy whole body shall be light, having no part dark, but then all shall be light, even as when a candle doth light thee...'"

Eye, dark, light, candle. Frizer remembers: *Like blowing out a candle. The quickest way to kill a man—*

Pressure rises inside Frizer's chest until a wail escapes him, ragged and high-pitched, prolonged until his lungs are emptied of breath.

The quickest way to kill a man is to stick him in the eye.

"'... but if thine eye be evil,'" Marlowe says, "'then thy body shall be—'"

Frizer draws his knife and stabs downwards. A muted *crack* of bone, or something like bone. Marlowe's eye-socket swallows the blade like quicksand. His legs kick, his hips jolt upwards and then plunge down again. A hand claws at Frizer's fist, fingernails peel back the skin in strips.

The quickest way, Frizer thinks, almost whispering aloud, *the quickest way—* Nick had said there would not even be a whimper, like blowing out a candle, but Marlowe is thrashing, screaming, mouth open to the back-teeth.

Frizer rips the knife free in an arc of blood, moves to stab again, to end it. But before he can do so, Robin rushes across the room, grabs him by the collar and hurls him against the wall. Frizer slides to the floor, his vision teeming with spots.

Marlowe is no longer screaming. He is drowning. Robin bends over his body like a widow, smoothing the hair back from his brow as blood jumps from his throat.

'Oh God,' Robin says, almost laughing. 'You lucky bastard!'

Frizer sinks to his hands and knees. He hears a clank of metal on the floor and is startled to see the knife still there, fused to his fist in a resin of blood.

'Nick,' Poley says, calmly, with a nod in Frizer's direction. 'Get the knife.'

Nick has been hovering at the foot of the bed with a hand over his mouth, his complexion green. At Robin's command, he barrels towards Frizer, who curls himself up around the blade, wedging it between his ribs and the floor. He will let his body drop, let his weight do the work. It will be a relief, like punching a wall – *my body is the wall; the knife is my fist* – but his limbs are locked in place, his body frozen. Within moments, Nick has hold of him by both arms, and Frizer can do nothing to harm himself save ram his own skull against the pommel-cap.

'*Coward!*' he screams.

A twist of Nick's wrist, and the knife is gone. Frizer collapses, sobbing too hard to pronounce the word: 'Coward, coward, coward, coward!'

Such is all he is. Cowardice has guided his hand, always. He has loved of course, and spited, but above all he has preserved himself, wretched thing that he is. In cowardice he'd cut his own skin, because he could not cut his brothers' throats; in cowardice he'd come into this world, the refuse of a dead woman's womb. Marlowe could not, would not see that in him. Like a moth, he saw only light.

'Shh,' Poley whispers. 'Shh. "Now, body, turn to air... Now, soul, be changed into little waterdrops, and fall into the ocean!"'

It seems fitting that the last words Marlowe ever hears should be his own. The convulsions have ceased; now Death comes to drag him by the ankles, gyring down into the blackness at the centre of his single, staring eye. *Not yet. Not yet.* Every man dies the same – at least, those whom Poley has seen die up close. Terror, struggle, and then, out of nowhere, surrender. Utter surrender, like a lover into the fold of ecstasy.

Without blinking, Poley looks for it, waits for it, that promise, if anything in this life may be promised at all, that every life shall end the same, indiscriminate of sin; that we shall have it, every one of us, no matter what precedes it: a moment of grace.

Kit does not recognize those last words as his own. He does not recognize the face looking down on him, though it rings familiar. Blue eyes. He has a notion of having encountered eyes like these before, though the face is older. He has a sense of being much older, himself, than he had been a moment ago, a dizzying shift in both time and space. His insides give a steep lurch, like when a cart starts off too suddenly, too fast.

You are well now, a voice says. *You are well.*

Kit's thoughts reel, caught between terror like he has never known and the first, tentative stirring of relief – the relief of waking from a too-real nightmare into his own bed, his own life, on a clean, bright morning, in the arms of a man who loves him.

He starts to say, *I think I was dreaming about that day in Deptford—*

But, gently, the other stops him: *Shh. Let it go. 'Tis long over. You are here, with me.*

The wail of gulls. Salt-smell of the sea. A finger is tracing the scar above Kit's right eye, reminding him how much time has passed since it healed. How white it is now. How faint.

Kit smiles. *I have let it go. That was what I wanted to tell you.*

His mind dips below the horizon, and is gone.

28 June 1593

Day twenty-nine

⁂

[Edward II's] cry did move many within the town and castle... to compassion, plainly hearing him utter a wailful noise, as the tormentors were about to murder him...

RAPHAEL HOLINSHED, *THE CHRONICLES OF ENGLAND AND SCOTLAND*, 1577

[Matrevis and Gurney restrain Edward.
Lightborne kills him.]
Matrevis: I fear me that this cry will raise the town,
And therefore let us take horse and away.
Lightborne: Tell me sirs, was it not bravely done?
Gurney: Excellent well: take this for thy reward.
[Gurney kills Lightborne.]

CHRISTOPHER MARLOWE, *EDWARD II*, C. 1593

34

I THINK I WAS DREAMING *about that day. In Deptford—*
A touch comes to Frizer's chin, silencing him.
Think not of that. 'Tis over now. You are here, with me.

The hand passes across Frizer's cheek, then his temple, smoothing back his hair. Still tense with fear, Frizer lays his head against the broad chest and listens, in vain, for the reliable drum of the heart. The body sounds hollow and wide, yet busy with anthill energy, like a great mine or a forge.

He looks up at the face. 'Tis gelid, smooth, the way it had looked at the inquest: head back upon the tidied pillows and pooled in dull hair, not blood; the wound wiped so clean he can make out a watery remnant of the eye in the ruined socket, a diamond nestled in velvet.

A strange impulse overtakes him. His hand alights upon the cheekbone, one finger extended towards the eye's inner, glistering light. Gently, he probes. Penetrates. Beyond, he feels nothing – an utter absence of feeling, surpassing numbness, surpassing sleep – and so withdraws his hand at once, half-expecting to find the finger sheared off to the bone.

Please tell me, Frizer whispers. *Tell me the truth: are you in hell?*

The answer throbs in both his ears at once:

I am with you.

*

Frizer wakes in darkness, hugging his own doublet. The prison sounds come to him: that anthill rummaging, hollow but not empty, and the occasional thud against his ear of a door slamming, somewhere far but near. When he runs his tongue over his teeth, he finds a gap where a fang-tooth used to be. When he moves, his clothes grind against bare planks of wood.

He has been in the Marshalsea nearly a month now. Still, the doublet in his arms reeks of blood.

A rattle at the door, and then with a shove it opens, dragging a quarter-circle into the dust. One of his usual keepers is on the other side, a young man with cabbage ears. He carries a large, soot-black kettle. Even with a cloth tied around the lower half of his face, Frizer can see him smirking.

'Your pardon's come in,' says the jailer.

A shiver starts between Frizer's shoulder-blades, but this he disallows, gripping the edge of the bench till his fingertips turn white. 'Am I—' He has no voice. 'Am I free?'

'Not yet.' The jailer enters, followed by another ragged creature with a mask covering nearly all of his face, a lopsided patch cut out for the eyes. The second one bears a bucket of water, sloshing on the floor. 'Get up, strip yourself.'

This explains the wicked smirk, the bitter smell emanating from the kettle. A lye-bath. Frizer still has scabs from the last one.

'Are we going to have trouble?'

'No,' Frizer whispers.

'Good. Always were a good boy, marry, we'll miss ye when y'are gone. Go to now.'

Frizer stands, undresses himself with his head down. A good boy, yes. No trouble from him. The jailers ruminate aloud upon his obedience, how some men need a dozen beatings ere they learn, if ever they learn at all; but not this one, no:

one beating had done the trick, clearly not the first he's ever earned himself. A dog knows as well as he does, and one like him would surely make an excellent dog for someone, i'faith, quick at the fetch and with a soft mouth to boot.

They laugh, and gaze upon Frizer's nakedness like something they have purchased for little money and hard, short use.

The jailer lifts his kettle over Frizer's head. 'Eyes closed.'

Frizer complies. The liquid is slightly thicker than water and smells like drought, like a tanner's pit, a little like semen. It does not burn immediately. The fire on his skin kindles slow, rising by the second, until eventually he must dive deep for every breath he takes. He must not whine or whimper or flap his arms or writhe or beg or weep, because that is the point of these games they play: to let the wailing woman out of him, so they may tear her to shreds.

He is crouched on the floor, screaming without opening his mouth, when a splash comes straight at his face, turning his seething skin to cool smoke. They leave him with the bucket, a few inches of water at the bottom. That is his reward, for being a good boy.

Frizer bows over the bucket, splashing himself. Even in his frenzy, he remembers that this visit began with a pardon, of all things, and he calls out to the jailers at the door, 'Am I free now?'

The answer is another cruel smirk, a bolted door.

The water provides a little relief, but not enough. Too raw to dress himself, Frizer stands in a narrow shaft of sunlight with his arms out like Faustus summoning devils, imagining that he can see the pain leaving his body as steam. 'Slicing edge,' he whispers, 'slicing edge slicing edge slicing edge,' and when his tongue trips up, 'one thought one grace, one thought one grace.' He cannot speak speeches any more. They all come out in shards.

Perhaps the pardon was all a jest. Perhaps he will never be free, no more so than he is now, eyes closed to the sun, pain crawling through his skin like light through embers. He tries to place himself at a distance to his body, the way he'd used to do, to look down from the ceiling on two scenes at once. He is alone in a cell with his own pain; he is alone with Marlowe at the Inn-in-the-Wall, and he can hear rain tapping the windowsill, and he is held, he is beautiful. To Kit Marlowe – to the man for whom Beauty is a boundless, unknowable thing that hovers in a poet's restless head – he is beautiful.

This is what he must be, from now on, if he is to survive: two men, in two places at once.

'Because he loves me, more than all the world.

Because he loves me, more than all the world.

Because he loves me, more than all the world.'

⋄⟨❈⟩⋄

Today, Ingram Frizer will be released from the Marshalsea. Poley hopes such shall bring an end to his own penance, which has constrained him to remain within London Wall this past month, a witness to the city's slow, miserable death by plague. With the scarlet sun still low above the smoke, he sets out for Seething Lane through lifeless streets. Five thousand dead in June, or so the estimate goes. Poley's house is now among the last in St Helen's parish to be neither boarded up nor marked with a black cross, Death's illiterate signature. Even the markets and churches are shuttered now; sustenance for the body is as scarce as it is for the soul.

The Privy Court's gates unlock at Poley's knocking. The guards on duty – the same fellows he'd used to bribe with tobacco, in better days – abandon their posts to lead him, in unfriendly silence, through empty rooms and corridors that he could easily navigate himself. Upstairs, the long gallery is deserted, the dark curtains stripped away for either cleaning or burning. A bone-white tunnel remains, like the skeleton of a whale.

Poley's destination is the Lord Keeper's office, which is located in a bay just off the gallery: a large room, its crowning glory being its many glazed windows, the most central bearing the same lion-flanked crest that also moulders above the gatehouse. Puckering sits at the desk. Phelippes hovers over his shoulder like a parrot on a stand.

Poley comes to the centre of the room and bows. Puckering releases him with an imperious gesture, grumbling, 'Let's get on with it.' Poley can smell onions on his breath from six feet away.

A film of grey daylight flashes on Phelippes's spectacles as he opens a slipcase. He clears his throat, and, much to Poley's chagrin, begins reading aloud: "*Inquisicio indentata capta apud* Deptford Strand, *super visum corporis Christopheri Morley...*"

Poley sighs inwardly, praying that this shall be the last time he has to hear the blasted thing. Over the past month this document, the inquest report, has been read to him in full at least a dozen times, with all its tedious *praedictus* this and *praefactum* that. The first time had been in the room upstairs in Eleanor's house, two days after it had all happened. Marlowe lay where he'd fallen, his eyes and lips bejewelled in flies. It was no weather for a corpse. Indeed, so obvious was the smell, packed into that stifling room with a jury of no fewer than sixteen of Eleanor's male neighbours, along with the coroner and his attendants, plus Poley, plus Nick, plus Frizer, that as the proceedings had worn on handkerchiefs and nosegays had gone up around the room; sturdy men had begun to look faint. The window was opened, Eleanor's maids came in and sprinkled water and herbs about the bed, all to no avail. Even in death, Marlowe had made his presence known.

Most of the men in attendance that day had not enough Latin to understand the first *ibidem* of the report. But this mattered not: the coroner's verdict was a foregone conclusion.

The respective bodies of killer and victim told a tale that any simpleton could understand, of David and Goliath.

Obviously, Frizer was the true victim. In fact, many of those present at the reading had witnessed the attack in the garden, and vividly recalled the scene: a giant, surely drunk, lunging murderously at poor, puny Frizer while railing about money. Twenty pounds, some remembered him shouting. Others, a mere twenty shillings. All Poley had to say was, yes, yes, 'twas all over money, as most deadly quarrels are, in this case over the reckoning owed to his sister for her food and drink and hospitality, of which Marlowe had enjoyed more than his fill.

And as to what had happened afterwards, in the room upstairs: when Phelippes's reading arrives at this part, Poley interrupts, summarizing, 'Yes: bloodshed narrowly averted, Masters Skeres and Frizer and myself brought Marlowe upstairs and put him to bed, in hope that sleep might prove a balm to his distemper. Alas, such was not to be. With supper served, we three livelier fellows found ourselves seated with our backs to the bed, Master Frizer included. Not a one of us saw Marlowe coming – that is, of course, until Marlowe stole Master Frizer's knife out of its scabbard, and proceeded to attack him with it. A tragedy in the waiting, it was. Any fellow of reasonable intelligence knows that to carry one's knife at the back brings more risk to the wearer than anyone, but Master Frizer is of less than reasonable intelligence, poor lad. More child than man, I have often said.'

Puckering says, 'There is no confusion as to how Marlowe acquired Master Frizer's knife. I remain more puzzled as to you and Master Skeres's failure of alacrity in coming to the defence of your slow-witted friend when Marlowe, apparently, beset upon him with naked blade!'

Poley chuckles, mustering his patience. 'As I have explained, my lord, I was quite hobbled by my position at table, as was

Master Skeres. A small table it was, and with the three of us crammed in elbow-to-elbow, and Frizer in the middle...'

Puckering squints. 'You sat three men, elbow-to-elbow.'

'One bench, my lord.'

'Your sister's rooms are ill-appointed then. Has she fallen so far in fortunes since Master Bull's tragic demise?'

'I cannot account for the furniture, my lord. I assure you, every attempt to come to Master Frizer's aid was made both by myself and Master Skeres. But by the time we'd freed ourselves, it was too late.'

Phelippes reads aloud the relevant section as if he's had his finger at it all this time:

> *Whereupon the aforesaid Ingram, in fear of being slain, in his own defence and to save his life, then and there struggled with the aforesaid Christopher Marlowe to take back from him his aforesaid knife...*
>
> *Thus it befell that in the affray the aforesaid Ingram gave the aforesaid Christopher then and there a mortal wound above his right eye, of the depth of two inches and the breadth of one inch, of which same mortal wound the aforesaid Christopher Marlowe, then and there, instantly died.*

'An accident,' Poley clarifies.

'I thought it was self-defence,' says Puckering.

'Can it not be both?'

With a cough, Phelippes cuts in, 'My lord, if I may: the sort of wound sustained by Marlowe is not uncommon, especially in tavern brawls and the like. The attacker trips, or is pushed, and falls upon his own blade. I agree, there is much to be held in doubt regarding Master Poley's recounting of events, but that Marlowe's death occurred as a matter of chance, I, for one, find perfectly credible.'

'Master Phelippes, you are, as always, a Solomon in judgement,' Poley says, at which Phelippes flushes crimson and directs his gaze at his feet. Oh, the things the cipher could say, if he dared! But it would do him little good to admit he knew of Marlowe's whereabouts on the 30th of May with ample time to have stopped the fatal event, yet chose to hold his tongue.

A pause descends. Puckering looks pensive, even troubled, at last muttering, 'Often, it seems, events occur behind closed doors, when Master Poley is the only man present to witness them.'

Poley clears his throat. 'There were in fact *four* men, my lord, counting the dead, and my sister as well, a woman.'

'Yes: a woman, a dead man, your lackey Nick Skeres, and an apparent idiot.'

'An *innocent* idiot, my lord. The Queen herself has signed Master Frizer's pardon.'

'Your testimony neglects to explain how Marlowe came to be in your company that day, in your sister's house.' Puckering gestures to Phelippes, who turns to another document in his case ere the former has finished speaking. 'At the Star Chamber sessions that same day, you may recall, Thomas Walsingham testified that you had intimated unto him some plan to aid in Marlowe's escape. He also submitted a rather enigmatic letter, written in *your* hand—'

'A slanderous forgery,' Poley growls, before Phelippes can read the damnable thing aloud, 'as I have already sworn, under oath. I found Marlowe's presence at my sister's *public* house entirely surprising, my lord, and most inconvenient. I did make attempts to contact your lordships in Whitehall, but as my missives went unanswered, I did what little I could to keep the fox penned, as 'twere.'

'Explain then: why would Thomas Walsingham go to the trouble to forge this letter, and lie before the Council?'

Poley chuckles bitterly, ire seeping to the surface. 'I'm afraid I cannot explain that which I did not witness. As every man is sole and solitary witness to his own thoughts, Master Walsingham's intentions are not for me to interpret. Well,' he adds, 'a man's thoughts are between himself and God, but God gives no testimony. Such is to my great misfortune, for often I find my testimony discounted, when I have no secondary witness but God. Mind you, the moiety of events in this world have no witness at *all* but God, and yet no one doubts how they occurred. Fish perish in the deep; trees topple in the lonely woods. Master Marlowe's death being every whit as straight-forward as the death of a fish or the toppling of a tree, I do wonder why it needs must be probed so zealously, and by men whose talents are truly wasted upon it.'

When Poley is finished, Puckering blinks as if stupefied, and then lets out a thunderous laugh, mouth agape in his carbuncle face. The laughter goes on for what feels like half a minute – through which Phelippes fiddles anxiously with the nosepiece of his spectacles – before Puckering finally seems to wear himself out, groaning, wiping his eyes.

He says, 'You, Master Poley, are a fork-tongued toad, bur-bling falsehoods and bile. But luckily for you, the dead man was worse.'

Poley feels one half of his face give a twinge. *The dead man was worse* – even after all these years, that is the best anyone can ever say of him.

Afternoon finds him at the Marshalsea. Over the past several weeks, Poley has sent Topcliffe numerous letters, most of which have gone ignored. The handful of replies he has received have been concerned with nothing but the particu-lars of Frizer's keeping, for which Poley has paid himself, out of his own purse. No discussion of Marlowe, nor of Walsingham, nor the ring.

For all that Poley has dreaded coming face-to-face with Topcliffe again, the warden greets him at the Hellmouth with his customary back-slapping embrace, as if all grudges are long forgotten. He then treats Poley to a tour of the prison's innermost courtyard, the site of ever-expanding mass graves, in which the warden evidently takes great pride.

'Go on,' Topcliffe goads him, from the edge of one such pit. 'Look in.'

Had he any choice in the matter, Poley would decline. As things are, he presses his handkerchief tighter to his nose and mouth and dares a half-step forward, intent only on feigning a downward glance. But his eyes defy him, scattering over the tangle of silvery limbs, the black mouths, the sunken, rat-chewed eyes.

Kit Marlowe was buried in a paupers' pit much like this, in a discrete corner of the yard at Deptford Church. The last look Poley had had of him, he was lying naked atop a dead whore and her blue, wrinkled whelp, with half-decayed corpses underneath and bones underneath that, a palimpsest of the dead.

Topcliffe slaps Poley's back. He thoroughly enjoys having startled him. 'What, you think I would push you in, birdy? Ha! The grave could not hold you down, I'd wager, you'd wriggle out like a worm after a good rain. Come now, I'll take you to your boy.'

As Topcliffe turns his back, Poley releases a shudder. On the far side of the pit, a jailer barks a command and a row of emaciated prisoners begin shovelling in heaps of quicklime like snow.

At the door, Topcliffe affixes his mask, a muzzled, wolfish thing that looks as if he's worn it through several plagues already. Calamity has somehow tamed the Marshalsea's usual chaos. Teams of inmates haul bodies down the corridors in efficient ranks, all lorded over by whip-wielding keepers like

HESSE PHILLIPS

foremen on some antipodean plantation. Topcliffe's instruments salute him as they pass; the prisoners hustle out of his way. Poley has never seen the warden so jovial, especially for a king who has lost more than half his subjects to plague. If ruination and despair nourish him in the best of times, then he has grown fat on them now. This is his Blessed Kingdom in its decadence.

Topcliffe leads Poley out of the prison's teeming main hall and into one of the branching corridors, which is eerily unpeopled. Most of the cell doors herein hang open, and for each one they pass, Topcliffe strikes it closed with the head of his club. The same club, Poley realizes, that had once struck the backs of his own knees, at the door to the torture room. *Slam*, and then pause. *Slam*, and then pause…

'I trust Master Frizer is well?' Poley says, in one such pause.

'Oh yes – lives like a king, he does, on your penny!'

As to Frizer, Poley has no other concerns and therefore can think of nothing else to say, the *slam* of Topcliffe's club on every other door wearing away at his nerves.

'Y'are quiet, birdy,' Topcliffe observes.

Say something, Poley chides himself. Silence is nakedness. Silence is penetrable. For every moment that passes, he feels as if he is growing soft, translucent, the way butter melts and runs.

Unthinking, he starts, 'Never could any one of us have imagined that Walsingham would go to such extraordinary measures—'

'That's quite enough of that,' Topcliffe says. He slams a door, then another door which does not shut for him, being propped open by a corpse, the lolling neck distended with black, knotty buboes, some of which had burst before death.

Topcliffe says, 'You still want your ring, I presume?'

Poley has prayed for such an opening. 'As I mentioned in my previous letter, a man has offered me three hundred and fifty pounds for my house in Surrey. That is more than you would have had from Marlowe's bounty...'

Topcliffe chuckles, low in the throat. 'Oh, Bonny Robin! So clever you'll cut yourself, you are, thinking you can seduce anyone with your little songs! I *know* you; you forget that. I have held a mirror up to your frailty, and still, you refuse to see it – because *how* can it be? How can *you* be anything but the cleverest man in the room?' He slams his club on another door, with relish. 'What manner of fool trades his gold tooth for a horse he's never laid eyes on!'

A blade of ice seems to sink into Poley's stomach, yet he keeps walking. He wraps his thumb over the stump of his missing finger and squeezes till the joint pops, mute.

'You were right in one thing,' Topcliffe says. 'I never sold the ring. It made a fine gift, it did, for the lady who owns my heart. I changed the band, for her dainty fingers. She always wears it together with the pearls she got from that treacherous Scottish bitch. 'Tis a reminder, she says, of a time when Death got so big of himself that he thought he could take her – the importunate brute!' His gaze is like teeth at Poley's throat.

'If you want to see your ring again,' he goes on, 'go to Windsor Castle. Go and beg an audience with my cousin. Say you are a poor man, whose only earthly desire is to kiss her sainted hand. It shall be the last time you ever plant your lips upon anything of Babington's, I warrant you. Fitting, that you should take it while on your knees!'

Another turn of a corner, and Poley realizes where Topcliffe is leading him: to his own cell, or what had been his cell, up until the day that Topcliffe had come knocking with his bottle of wine. Beyond a solid oaken door lies a narrow room with a lancet window and bare plaster walls. No feather bed now, no private dining table, only a wooden bench for both sitting and sleeping. There, in that very spot, Poley had used to lie on his back with his hand upheld, waiting for the afternoon sun to make its slow slice through the room, to open the green eye buried in the diamond's heart.

Inside the cell, a man stands with his back to the door, his arms raised to that same shaft of light: stark naked, whispering softly, as if in the midst of some heathen veneration. It takes a second longer than it should for Frizer to fall silent and turn around. Ten years he has aged in twenty-nine days: hair shorn, beard long, fearfully thin. He crosses his arms over his chest.

'Robin.'

Poley cannot answer.

Frizer lowers his arms. 'Am I free? Am I free?' The sound hovers upon the stale air like dust.

Poley fears to enter, lest Topcliffe should shove him in and bolt the door at his back. But even with the light behind Frizer's body, a mark is visible upon his chest, so strange that it draws Poley across the threshold, near enough to reach out and touch it: a vertical scar, running from the navel almost to the throat in a suture-studded slit. As if a surgeon of exceptional skill had cut him open, emptied him and stitched him up again, to stagger hollowly onward.

A flutter of blackness descends. Poley is no longer aware of Topcliffe behind him, nor of the prison around him. Ingram Frizer's body unseams like a stage curtain, through which Poley stumbles onto the scaffold at St Giles' Field: midday under a clear blue sky, a stiff September breeze tugging at his clothes. Around him, a sea of faces swirls into the distance, black mouths barking for blood, blood, blood.

Babington kneels at the foot of the stage. The noose has cut a ring around his neck; he is gasping for breath, held upright on his knees only by the rope. His bloodshot eyes meet Poley's gaze: they seem drained of their colour, greenish-pale, like Dutch glass. But then a man takes Babington's head by the hair, bends his body backwards. Another man stabs a carving knife into his belly, slicing upwards until the blade sticks and skids off the breastbone, nicking his chin.

His scream feels older than the world itself, so loud and long and deep that it carries not by miles, but years.

Do not let them see it, Poley commands himself, gouging the blankest of smiles into his quivering lips. *Do not let them see it, do not dare let them see it. You do not feel it – you see all, hear all, but feel nothing. You are empty, you are hollow. You are nothing, you are nothing, you are nothing...*

And so, what young Kit Marlowe sees from his and Richard Baines's place near the front of the crowd is precisely what Poley intends to be seen: a void in the shape of a man, smiling through Babington's agonies the way a craftsman smiles over his own best work. As if to say, *Yes, yes, 'tis bravely done.*

What sort of man could do that, Kit wonders?

What sort of monster could do that to a man who loved him?

Epilogue

[the witnesses] say upon their oath that [Ingram Frizer, Nicholas Skeres, Robin Poley and Christopher Marlowe] met together in a room of the house of one Eleanor Bull, widow... and after lunch kept company quietly and walked in the garden... and after dinner the aforesaid Ingram and the said Christopher... publicly exchanged diverse malicious words because they could not agree on the payment of the sum of pence, that is to say, *le Reckoninge*...

Christopher Morley then lying on a bed in the room where they dined and moved by ire... suddenly and of malice aforethought... unsheathed the dagger of the aforesaid Ingram which was visible at his back...

... thus because the aforesaid Ingram killed & slew the aforesaid Christopher... in defence and salvation of his life... We therefore, moved by pity, pardon the same Ingram Frizer... for the death above mentioned & grant him our firm peace...

WITNESSED BY THE QUEEN AT KEW [RICHMOND],

28 JUNE 1593

The mystery of Marlowe's death... is now cleared up for good and all on the authority of public records of complete authenticity and gratifying fullness.

G. L. KITTERIDGE, INTRODUCTION TO *THE DEATH OF CHRISTOPHER MARLOWE*, 1925

Most of the grounds for suspicion about Marlowe's death seem baseless on dispassionate examination... The claim that Marlowe and Frizer began quarrelling over the bill is perfectly consistent with what we know about Marlowe, particularly during the last year and a half of his life.

CONSTANCE BROWN KURIYAMA, *CHRISTOPHER MARLOWE: A RENAISSANCE LIFE*, 2002

[However]... there is something queer about the whole episode...

JOHN BAKELESS, *THE TRAGICALL HISTORY OF CHRISTOPHER MARLOWE*, 1942

Arguably, the trouble is that the legal details [of Marlowe's death] tell the whole story about as well as a sieve holds molasses.

PARK HONAN, *CHRISTOPHER MARLOWE: POET & SPY*, 2005

The fact that the official account trivializes the killing should provoke scepticism, not acquiescence.

DAVID RIGGS, *THE WORLD OF CHRISTOPHER MARLOWE*, 2004

Was this, after all, an unplanned brawl, a bar-fight, an accident, of a sort that can happen in a city any week? It can seem so, except that 'accidents' with Poley... were not normally allowed to happen, unless [he] wanted them to.

PARK HONAN, 2005

I believe on present evidence that if Marlowe had not died on the day he did... he could very well have been dead before the month of June was out. Despite the fog of obfuscation, what is undeniably clear is that Marlowe was in grave danger.

ROY KENDALL, CHRISTOPHER MARLOWE AND
RICHARD BAINES, 2003

We will never know for certain exactly what happened in that room in Deptford in 1593. An event like this, which echoes on through the centuries, takes just a few seconds to happen. Once it has happened, it is gone.

CHARLES NICHOLL, THE RECKONING: THE MURDER OF
CHRISTOPHER MARLOWE, 1992

Whether [Marlowe's] soul went to hell, heaven, or oblivion... his plays and poems were safely launched on a career of immortality.

LISA HOPKINS, CHRISTOPHER MARLOWE:
A LITERARY LIFE, 2000

But it is a strange immortality, continually shifting with time and with the perceiver... One suspects that Marlowe would barely recognize many of the images that scholars and admirers have imposed upon him in kaleidoscopic succession.

CONSTANCE BROWN KURIYAMA, 2002

Atheist, intelligencer, heretic, spy, overreacher, tobacco-loving sodomite, intellectual queen, radical tragedian, who held monstrous opinions...

EMILY C. BARTELS & EMMA SMITH,
CHRISTOPHER MARLOWE IN CONTEXT, 2013

His spirit seems to me to have dwelt in the innermost motions of men's hearts... The darkness of Fate overshadowing human life, & the fearful energies of wickedness in men's hearts, strongly possess his imagination...

ALEXANDER BLAIR, PERSONAL LETTER TO JOHN WILSON,
29 APRIL 1819

He was no timorous servile flatterer of the commonwealth... His tongue and his invention were foreborn; what they thought, they would confidently utter. Princes he spared not, that in the least point transgressed... His life he contemned with the liberty of speech.

THOMAS NASHE, *THE UNFORTUNATE TRAVELLER*, 1594

On the whole, Marlowe's inspiration appears to be of a dark kind; he is one of those whom Cicero feared would be made dangerous by eloquence. One may wonder, in fact, if Marlowe is not Plato's first kind of madman, whose genius arises not from divinity, but from alcohol, lechery, or mental disturbance.

CLARK HULSE, *METAMORPHIC VERSE*, 1981

Marlowe was happy in his buskine muse,
Alas unhappy in his life and end,
Pitty it is, that wit so ill should dwell
Wit lent from heaven, but vices sent from hell.

ANONYMOUS, *THE RETURN FROM PARNASSUS*, 1601

Dying in odd circumstances, which we will perhaps never fully understand, he was buried hugger-mugger in a location we can no longer precisely identify. With him died attitudes towards religion, sexuality and society which we are unlikely to ever be able to reconstruct in their original complexity, and he went to the grave leaving his greatest works in a hopeless textual muddle...

LISA HOPKINS, 2000

The intriguing question of who Marlowe was remains to be answered... The facts of his adult life are few, scattered and of doubtful accuracy... All the evidence of his mutinous cast of mind sits at one remove from his own voice… He is an irretrievably textual being.

Where does a biographer go from there?

DAVID RIGGS, 2004

I know not, but of this I am assured:
That death ends all, and I can die but once.

CHRISTOPHER MARLOWE, *EDWARD II*, C. 1593

Author's Note

I was about twelve or thirteen when I first encountered the name Christopher Marlowe, on the spine of my father's mouldering paperback edition of *Doctor Faustus*. Intrigued by the image on the cover – of Ned Alleyn as Faustus, in his circle of black magic symbols – I brought the book to my father, who proceeded to tell me everything he could remember about its author: the mysterious death in Deptford, the charges of treason, heresy, sodomy. The Baines Note. 'All they that love not tobacco & boyes are fooles.' *Edward II*. He never said it in so many words – nor did I have the words to express it myself at the time – but I gradually realized that the person he was describing was someone like me: proof that I was not alone, and that others had existed even centuries before my time. Kit Marlowe was my first queer ancestor.

Later in life, as I entered academia and began to study Marlowe as a subject, I discovered that his queerness, however you define it, was hotly contested. Although in this century Marlowe has been largely accepted as a part of the queer canon, even now some scholars shrink away from the topic of his sexuality altogether, or argue that, in the absence of rock-solid proof requiring nothing short of a time-machine, heterosexuality should always be assumed as the default of our forebearers. And then there are those who apply the circular logic that, although queer *behaviour* has surely occurred since the dawn of humankind, the concept of sexual identity had first to be invented in order for queer *people* to exist, effectively nullifying any sort of queer history that pre-dates the early twentieth century. Oscar Wilde famously said that 'each man kills the thing he loves', and academia, I've found, is where he goes to kill it.

I knew well before I graduated my doctoral programme that I did not belong in academia, much as I truly did enjoy it at times. I wrote the first draft of *Lightborne* and my dissertation simultaneously, often exploiting the resources I used for the latter to write the former. And yet, all the research I collected over the years, the letters, legal documents, pamphlets and registers, told only a fraction of the story, the visible tip of a measurelessly immense iceberg. Queer history is often about chasing the stories for which no material evidence exists: stories never written down, never spoken of, never witnessed outside of those who lived them. It is the study of lost things.

Lightborne is largely a story about silence, suppression, the violence of the 'closet'. It is also about loss: the loss of life, in every sense, when survival requires a betrayal of the self. Even four hundred and thirty years later, LGBTQIA+ people everywhere still face this daily, frightening reality, as evidenced by ever-mounting attacks against gay and trans people across the globe. We are murdered and abused, harassed into silence and suicide, legislated into the shadows even where, so recently, we'd stepped into the light. But we do have one key advantage over our ancestors: we know we are not alone.

A note on the title: there are two spellings of 'Lightborne' found in the earliest printings of Marlowe's *Edward II* (1594, 1598, 1612), either with or without the 'e'. Modern editions of the play often spell 'Lightborn' sans 'e', but I feel this rendering sacrifices some of the name's polysemic qualities.

I have tried to limit references that would be obscure to modern readers, although Marlowe can't help but make a few. On page 67, his papers refer to a 'Jesuit Stephens' who was, in fact, the Jesuit Thomas Stevens, one of the first English missionaries to settle in India, in 1579. Stevens's writings on

Indian culture and Hinduism bolstered growing interest in the subcontinent back home, which eventually culminated in the East India Company's establishment at the beginning of the seventeenth century.

On page 67, the lost Arabic treatise Marlowe mentions is *On the Prophets' Fraudulent Tricks* by the tenth-century physician, philosopher and scientist Abu Bakr al-Razi, or Rhazes as Marlowe would have known him. He is sometimes controversially credited as one of the pioneers of humanistic thought.

On page 175, Marlowe quotes a Latin inscription from his own *Doctor Faustus* which is itself drawn from Ptolemy: 'Through unequal motion with respect to the whole.' He follows with a Latin quote from Tycho Brahe's book on the 1572 supernova, *De nova stella*, in which Brahe rails against fellow astronomers who dismissed the implications of this celestial event: 'Oh gross wits! Oh blind watchers of the sky!'

The English translation of Marlowe's inquest report which appears on page 419 is adapted from a translation by Constance Brown Kuriyama, which can be read in full in her book *Christopher Marlowe: A Renaissance Life*, along with a trove of other documents related to the events in this novel and beyond.

While many of the events in this novel are fictional, all of the main players were real people, most of whom went on with their lives past the last page. Thomas Walsingham did in fact rise to a life of respectability, achieving both his desired seat in Parliament and a knighthood, despite the fact that his marriage to Lady Audrey was plagued by rumours of adultery well into the following century. It was, in fact, Lady Audrey's alleged lover Robert Cecil who may have precipitated Dick Topcliffe's eventual fall from grace, by exposing the torturer's habit of making sexual remarks about the Queen shortly before her death in 1603. Richard Baines's fate is uncertain: a Richard Baines was hanged at Tyburn in 1594 for thievery, but the name was common enough at the time that there's no guaranteeing this was our man. Thomas Kyd died shortly after his release from prison. Nick Skeres eventually became entangled with the Essex Uprising and likely died as a political prisoner in 1601. Ingram Frizer, by then a gentleman of some means, assumed financial care over Nick's orphaned children.

Despite having murdered Thomas Walsingham's friend, Frizer continued in service at Scadbury. Briefly, he acted as a fixer in Nick Skeres's coney-catching schemes, though without any great success. Later in life, he advanced to the lucrative role of property manager for Lady Audrey's extensive, Crown-let farmlands around the village of Eltham. Survived by his daughter Alice, Frizer was buried on 14 August 1627. His exact age remains unknown.

Robin Poley served the Privy Council off and on until July 1602, when a letter from him to Secretary Robert Cecil seems to suggest that he had fallen on desperate times:

you said to me I never made you good intelligence, nor did you service worth reckoning... although I much desire my endeavours might please you, my necessities needing your favour.[1]

He had intelligence to offer: the Jesuits were running a smuggling operation along the Thames, aided by spies embedded within the Privy Council's own men. One of the Jesuits' agents was, of all people, Thomas Phelippes, now working for the enemy.[2]

---

1   Found in *Calendar of the Cecil Papers in Hatfield House*, vol. 12 (18 July 1602): pp. 221–39.
2   Patrick Martin and John Finnis. 'The Secret Sharers: "Anthony Rivers" and the Appellant Controversy, 1601–2', *Huntington Library Quarterly* 69, no. 2 (2006): pp. 195–238. Phelippes's surprising late career as a double agent ended tragically for him. By 1605, he was a prisoner in the Tower of London.

It was the last letter on record that Poley ever sent. He thereafter vanished without a trace.

Edward II remained reviled and obscure until 1903, when a heavily censored production was mounted with Harley Granville-Barker in the titular role. The first known production to make full use of Marlowe's text did not occur until 1969, with Ian McKellen as Edward and James Laurenson as Gaveston. Fittingly enough, during a live-televised rehearsal in Edinburgh, 'all hell broke loose' and police were summoned to the studio following Edward and Gaveston's kiss – only the second gay kiss ever seen on British television.[3] The recorded production's US debut in 1975 featured the first kiss between two men on the American small screen.

I like to think Marlowe would have been pleased.

Hesse Phillips

---

3 Iain Mackintosh, Administrative Director of the Prospect Theatre Company, quoted in James Wallace, 'Marlowe and McKellen on Screen: The Prospect Theatre Company Production of *Edward II* 1969–70', *Shakespeare Bulletin*, 33:4 (Winter 2015), pp. 595–608.

Acknowledgements

You can't spend more than ten years on a book, and nearly twenty years with a subject, without a small army of people to help you along the way. I'm incredibly grateful first of all to the late great Paul Nelsen of Marlboro College, as well as Eric Bass, Tim Little, Geraldine Pittman and Birje Patil, all of whom encouraged me in theatre, writing and my Marlowe obsession. Thanks also to Peter Saccio, who was kind enough to read fifty pages of my first attempt at a novel about Marlowe way back in 2003.

My gratitude also to my advisers in the Drama and Dance Department at Tufts University, whom I can only hope I haven't disappointed too badly: the brilliant Downing Cless, and force-of-nature Laurence Senelick, who often decried the jargon-riddled dullness of much academic writing. 'Just tell a good story, for God's sake!' he said. He could not have known just how deeply I took that to heart.

This book owes a great deal to the hard work of researchers, librarians and archivists, many of whom had no idea I was writing both a dissertation *and* a novel: Chao Chen from Tufts' Tisch Library, Calista Lucy at the Dulwich College Archives, Julian Bowsher, David Saxby, Cath Maloney, Steve Tucker and Karen Thomas at the Museum of London Archaeological Archives and the LAARC, Arnold Hunt at the British Library, and many others who helped me find my way to the right questions. Thanks also to Joanne Hill at the Marlowe Society for being so welcoming, and to Rita Ortolino-Dioguardi at Tufts Drama and Dance for keeping me sane.

I'm fortunate to have found a vibrant and ever-growing community of writers through Grub Street Boston, including my Novel Incubator mentors Michelle Hoover and Lisa Borders, the NI class of 2013 and all the other 'Incubees' before and since. Thanks especially to Emily Ross, Allison Kornet and Tracey Palmer at DeadDarlings.com, and to my patient and insightful beta-readers John McClure, Lise Brody, Deborah Good and Alison Langley, and to my ride-or-die writing buddy these many years, Susan Ray. I'm forever indebted to the Novel Fair team at the Irish Writers Centre, Betty Stenson, Orla Martin, Cassia Gaden Gilmartin and Laura McCormack, and the 2022 judges Neil Hegarty, Cauvery Madhavan and Gavin Corbett. A tip of the hat to my fellow 2022 winners, whose support and friendship have been invaluable.

This novel only exists due to the tireless efforts and unwavering enthusiasm of my agent Brian Langan, and the incredible team at Atlantic Books UK, including Karen Duffy who first took a chance on me, my amazing editor Joanna Lee and copyeditor Tamsin Shelton, Rights Director Alice Latham, plus the marketing and publicity team Laura O'Donnell, Sophie Walker, Kirsty Doole and Aimee Oliver-Powell. A big thank you also to Helen Edwards for always going above and beyond. I am immensely grateful to the supportive and hardworking team at Pegasus Books who brought *Lightborne* to my home country: Publisher Claiborne Hancock, Deputy Publisher Jessica Case, Production Manager Maria Fernandez, and Publicist and Marketing Coordinator Meghan Jusczak.

Personal thanks are due to Paul Richards, the devil on my shoulder, and Jenny Marchand, the devil on my other shoulder, and the many other friends who have kept me going. *Eternamente agradecida a mi familia española, Juan, Ana, Irene y Anita, por su confianza y apoyo; y gracias también a Virginia Blázquez por su talento extraordinario y todas las cervezas compartidas.* Love always to my gracious parents and family, who have always supported me in every journey I've taken. And to my wife Alicia, who has never wavered in her support of this little writing habit of mine: I'd cross the sea with you a hundred times.